# DEALING IN MURDER

**Agatha, Anthony, Barry and Gumshoe nominee**

"Well-crafted . . . [a] wonderful debut."
*Chicago Sun-Times*

"An engaging heroine, a well-rounded cast, and enough plot twists
to keep you guessing into the wee hours . . . Elaine Flinn's stellar
debut is a terrific combination of antiques, murder, and
mystery . . . Find a comfortable chair and a good
cup of coffee and plan to stay up late."
Sheldon Siegal, author of *Final Verdict*

"Mix intriguing characters, a meaty plot, and a murder
or two behind the scenes of the antiques world and
you have Flinn's *Dealing in Murder*. A Keeper!"
Chassie West, author of *Killer Chameleon*

"Delicious . . . a must read."
*Salinas Californian*

# TAGGED FOR MURDER

"Superior storytelling . . . Flinn smoothly combines details of the
antiques business and the varied personalities that the trade
attracts into a solidly plotted amateur-sleuth mystery."
*Ft. Lauderdale Sun-Sentinel*

"Molly's not only the 'real deal' but she's
getting ever better with time."
*Monterey County Herald*

"*Tagged for Murder* mixes a great story, believable characters, and
hints about antiques and the antique business . . . engrossing."
Barbara Fianchi, "Antiques Roadshow" appraiser,
*reviewingtheevidence.com*

**Books by Elaine Flinn**

DEADLY COLLECTION
TAGGED FOR MURDER
DEALING IN MURDER

# ELAINE FLINN

# DEADLY
# COLLECTION

AVON BOOKS

*An Imprint of HarperCollinsPublishers*

AVON BOOKS
*An Imprint of* HarperCollins*Publishers*
10 East 53rd Street
New York, New York 10022-5299

Copyright © 2005 by Elaine Flinn
ISBN-13: 978-0-06-054582-6
ISBN-10: 0-06-054582-8
**www.avonmystery.com**

First Avon Books paperback printing: October 2005

Avon Trademark Reg. U.S. Pat. Off. and in Other Countries, Marca Registrada, Hecho en U.S.A.
HarperCollins® is a registered trademark of HarperCollins Publishers Inc.

Printed in the U.S.A.

10  9  8  7  6  5  4  3  2  1

*Friends in need—are friends in deed. And then some.*
*Chassie, Laura, Ash, Hans, Sam and Paul*
*Thank you all, dear hearts, for being there.*

# Acknowledgments

I've said this before, and I'll say it again—without the love and incredible support of my family, you wouldn't be reading this. So, to Joe, Patrick, Sharon, Kelly, and Karen, my love and my thanks for being the best cheering section any writer could hope to have.

My thanks and gratitude to everyone at Avon for their belief in Molly Doyle, and for their support. And special thanks to my editor, Jennifer Civiletto, and to Merritt Dekle for his gorgeous book covers.

A very, very special thank you to friends who generously agreed to cameo roles: Bridget Bolton, Barbara and Rudy Franchi, Maili Montgomery, and Linda Rutledge, and to Sandra Sechrest for her charity auction bid to be a character. And speaking of cheering sections, who could ask for more support than from two of the best auctioneers around, Scott Bradley and Bert Hem—you guys are the greatest!

My most sincere gratitude to all of you wonderful readers who have embraced Molly Doyle. Your emails, letters, and cards are overwhelming! Thank you for considering Molly a friend—that has to be the highest compliment a writer can receive.

A special note: The artists mentioned in *Deadly Collection*—Joe Tanous, Richard Morgan, Darwin Musselman, and Don Clausen—are the real thing, and if you ever run across their work, grab it!

# DEADLY
# COLLECTION

## 1

*M*olly Doyle marveled at Bitsy Morgan's composure. She hoped when she reached Bitsy's age she could manage her temper as well. Only a half hour ago Bitsy was spitting mad and planning to throttle Frances O'Brien. The ready smile of an antiques dealer, so second nature to Bitsy, was forced this evening, and Molly could not blame her. In her early seventies, Bitsy Morgan's silver chignon—tended twice weekly at the salon—designer clothes, and always perfect makeup were evident this evening as she played the perfect hostess at her Pebble Beach estate. Molly could only imagine the tortures Bitsy was conjuring in her lively mind.

The Sunday evening cocktail party would introduce Frances O'Brien, an exceptionally talented artist, to many of the newer Pebble Beach residents. A Carmel native, Frances had recently returned from a two-year hiatus painting the wine-growing regions of Europe to bury her parents after their auto accident. Bitsy had been a close friend of the O'Briens, and in her generous but busybody way felt obligated to help Frances show off her work, and to ease her grief. Several examples of earlier paintings, many from Bitsy's private collection and the O'Briens's

Carmel inn, were prominently displayed throughout the large living room.

When Molly arrived ahead of the guests, she found Josie, Bitsy's housekeeper, overseeing the catering staff from Daria DeMarco's restaurant, *Daria's*, as they set out a canapé buffet. Josie announced that *Madame* was furiously wearing a path into the library carpet.

Bitsy Morgan's blazing eyes zeroed in on Molly when she entered the library. "Lucky it's you and not Frances! If I was younger, and Frances wasn't still grieving, I'd turn that little princess over my knee and spank the hell out of her."

Molly hadn't seen Bitsy this mad in a while. "What the hell is wrong? Don't tell me Frances isn't coming."

"Oh, she'll be here all right. I made it clear she owed me at least that. Young, willful women today have forgotten the good manners they were taught by a generation who appreciated good breeding. You can be sure I reminded her."

Moving to Bitsy, Molly steered her to a chair. "Sit down, cool off, then tell me what's going on."

"Frances has put the inn up for sale and is planning to return to Europe, that's what's going on. If she'd had the courtesy to tell me, I wouldn't have invited fifty people, or spent a small fortune with Daria on champagne and a buffet to tempt Jacques Pepin."

"When did you find out?"

Bitsy's eyes were smoldering now. "She called me a half hour ago and tried to beg off. Can you imagine the gall? When I asked why, she told me it was a waste of time to meet potential buyers when she wasn't planning on staying."

Leaning against the desk opposite Bitsy, Molly said,

"That is beyond rude. I don't blame you for being furious. Well, there's not much you can do now except put a big smile on your face and let it go. I'm just surprised. I mean, Daria has been saying what a sweet person Frances is, and she seemed awfully nice when we were introduced last week."

"Sweet? Frances?" Bitsy pursed her lips. "Spoiled is more like it. Daria has a soft spot for her. Always did. Frances was very shy as a youngster, and Daria was one of the few who befriended her when her folks moved up here from L.A. Speaking of soft spots, where's my little Emma?"

"She's with Josie in the kitchen."

Yes, Molly thought now as she left the library and moved about the large living room, that smile on Bitsy's face was deadly. She almost pitied Frances when this party was over. Oblivious to Bitsy's dangerous mood, Frances O'Brien flitted from group to group, greeting the many established and newly rich moguls of industry who continued to snap up outrageously priced property in Pebble Beach like lotto tickets.

When Molly's twelve-year-old niece Emma sidled up next to her, Molly suggested she might want to go to the media room and watch a movie until it was time to leave.

"Bitsy bought the new *Shrek* for me. Will I have time to watch it?" Emma asked.

Molly glanced at her watch. "I think so. If I get too bored, I'll join you."

"I'll save some of the cookies Josie made for me just in case. Has Bitsy yelled at Frances yet? Josie told me all about it."

Molly laughed. "No, of course not! She wouldn't do that in front of her guests. Now scoot."

Watching Emma slip out, Molly's eyes caught sight of Frances chatting away with a dot-com tycoon. Though she was nearly as tall as Molly's five-foot-ten frame, Frances O'Brien was as thin as a waif. Battling her weight as she tried to quit smoking, Molly had a good twenty pounds on her. When she first met Frances last week, she was surprised to learn that she was "Mackie," the artist whose paintings at Daria's had so impressed her. Her extraordinary talent, coupled with a ravishing mane of copper hair and blue eyes, was almost too much. Molly had joked to Daria how easy it would be to hate her.

Now, as Molly mingled, her toes felt pinched and she was aching to remove the heels she infrequently wore. Even the dark forest-green silk cocktail suit she'd reluctantly dug out of her closet seemed uncomfortable. Gone were the designer suits and heels of Manhattan. Her new uniform was flat shoes, sweaters, and slacks on weekdays, and jeans, tee shirts, and sneakers on the weekend.

Declining another flute of champagne from the waiter, Molly hoped Randall would show up soon. After Daria left to check on a private celebration at her restaurant, Molly had lost interest in the cocktail chatter. When you didn't play golf, tennis, or show horses, you had little to say to this crowd. It was almost nine, and she was tired and sore from moving furniture in her antiques shop. Emma had been a big help with the chairs and lighter pieces they used to fill the holes made after a few furniture sales. Having her niece living with her was a joy, but the new responsibilities thrust on Molly after her estranged sister literally left Emma on her doorstep were new life lessons. One of which was a sensible bedtime. Tall for her age, with a mop of dark curly hair and round Harry Potter–type glasses, Emma reminded Molly of a young colt filled with energy and a desire to see the world. In this case, at least for the present, it appeared to be the antiques world. She'd nearly inhaled every book Molly had on the subject.

Thanks to Dan Lucero, Monterey County's district attorney and favorite native son, with family ties that went back three generations, Emma would be attending Santa Catalina soon, the private Catholic school in Monterey. Molly wanted her ready for the rigorous schedule she knew was ahead. And thanks to Sister Phil, the retired nun who had been tutoring Emma in the interim, Molly had little doubt her niece would do well. However, there could be no more late nights working in the shop with her, or eating pizza or takeout for dinner.

Molly was aching to go home and fall into bed, but she knew that was out. She still had sales reports to send to her boss and mentor, Max Roman. Nearing seventy-five, Max was finally conceding that his frequent trips to South America to see Pablo, his lover, were taking their toll. Molly hoped he would be staying home long enough to ferret out some spectacular merchandise for *Treasures*, the shop she managed for him. Sales had been terrific the past few months, but now all the star pieces were gone. Her supporting cast of merchandise—known in the trade as "merch"—now lingered in near obscurity. Without stellar pieces to add a touch of glamour to respectable but ho-hum chests, chairs, and small items—or "smalls"—a disastrous slowdown was on the horizon.

Even Max's shop in San Francisco was looking lean. Without his connections to latch onto top-rate pieces, both shops faced a serious drought. Molly's luck at local garage and estate sales lately had been minimal, and with only a small auction house in Monterey, the future looked bleak. And so did her bank account.

She was thankful that Bitsy, who had come to love Emma as if she were her granddaughter, had insisted on paying the expensive school tuition, as well as for her books and uniforms. Adding Emma to her health insurance, and buying her a computer, had been eye-openers for Molly. Living on three hundred dollars a week, less taxes, and ten percent commission on sales was not exactly upmarket. The free rent on the apartment over the shop, and the use of Max's battered El Camino pickup, made a huge difference in her ability to save money for her buys. But stretching that for two, especially with a growing young girl, was beginning to present a shaky picture.

Molly felt Randall come up behind her. It was as if an energy field suddenly erupted when he entered a room. Close to six-foot-five, built like a bear and nearing fifty, the intrepid chief of police of Carmel was, she had to admit, a damn fine-looking man. She was surprised to realize how much she had missed him while he'd been away on a speaking tour. Turning to him, she said, "Good timing. I was thinking about leaving. I wasn't sure if you got my note about the reception."

"I'm not in the mood to meet any of Bitsy's artsy-fartsy cronies, but she's a good old broad and I didn't want to disappoint her."

"You are always such a gentleman. I tell everyone that. How was the conference?"

Randall was used to Molly's backhanded compliments. His crooked grin told her as much. "I hate Las Vegas, if you want the truth. It's an ugly desert, it smells of unwashed bodies, and the food was forgettable. I stepped over bums and backpackers asleep on the lobby floor of the Venetian and the Bellagio. Why they spend billions building palaces and then let bums treat it like a flophouse is beyond me."

Molly laughed. "Couldn't all you cops arrest them for loitering?"

"Not our jurisdiction. That champagne over there?" Steering her to the large buffet table, Randall said, "Two hours in the car with Lucero is enough to make a man drink. But it was nice of him to pick me up at the airport."

"Didn't he come in with you?"

"Naw, he's wiped out. He was in Sacramento all day power planning with his cronies for his reelection campaign next year. So, who's this artist we're here to meet?"

"Frances O'Brien, Daria's friend. She's been in Europe for the past two years and came home to bury her parents after the auto accident."

"Oh, yeah. The people who owned the Ocean Inn. I was in Chicago when they had the funeral."

"And then Denver for a seminar. My, a man in such demand these days. It's a wonder Carmel has survived without you."

"Come on, Molly. Don't give me heat, okay? I can't help it if I'm hot shit on the cop talk circuit. I'm sick of traveling." Reaching for a flute of champagne, he almost froze. "Whoa. Who's the drop-dead redhead over there with that software tycoon who's been bugging me about private guards?"

"The guest of honor. Frances."

Randall's gaze was glued to the striking woman. "That is one beautiful woman."

"Well, I don't think she's all that great," Emma said as she grabbed hold of Randall's hand.

"Hey, squirt. What kind of a welcome home is that? Where's my hug?"

When Randall leaned down, Emma threw her arms around him. "I missed you. I even turned off *Shrek* to come out and see if you were here yet." Darting a look at Molly, she added, "We all missed you. Even Aunt Molly."

"Yeah? Hey, that's heartwarming. So, why don't you think that lady over there isn't so great?"

"Dreamy artist types are boring. They're never *here*, you know?"

Randall looked at Molly and shook his head. "This from a twelve-year-old? What the hell is she reading now?" Not waiting for an answer, Randall said, "See any of her stuff? I mean, is she any good?"

"God, but you're dense sometimes," Molly said. "*Mackie*, remember? Her *stuff* is all over Daria's restaurant."

"That's Mackie? No kidding. How would I know that? Why doesn't she use her real name?"

"Oh, please. Art is still a man's world. Name one celebrated woman artist of today. A lot of women artists use androgynous names when they're starting out."

"That's feminist bullshit," Randall said.

Reaching for Emma's hand, Molly said, "Get real." When she saw that squinty eye thing of his coming on, she was too tired to play their banter game. "I'm beat and going home. We just waited around so Emma could make sure you got back okay."

Randall laughed. "Yeah, sure. Like maybe you were a little worried too?"

"Me? Worry about you? Ha!" Molly hid a grin, and was turning to leave when she saw the guest of honor heading toward them. "Oh, hell. I was hoping to sneak out. Frances is coming this way."

Randall hitched up his slacks and straightened his tie. "Good. You can introduce me."

Emma's loud yawn would have been comical had she not said, "You won't like her."

"Emma!" Molly said. "That's rude."

Before she could say more, Frances was upon them and reaching for Randall's hand. Introducing herself, she said, "Daria has told me so much about you. I'm glad we've had a chance to meet."

"Same here," Randall replied. "I love your work, by the way. I tell Daria that all the time."

Daria hadn't told Molly that despite her looks, Frances was generally quiet and shy. But Molly was skeptical at the way Frances lowered her eyes and barely whispered her thanks. It was almost too coy to believe, and it was a feminine ploy she loathed. Molly wondered if Frances might have changed since she'd been gone, especially after hearing what she'd tried to pull on Bitsy—not telling Bitsy her intention to sell the inn. About to say good-bye, Emma beat her to the punch. "We've got to go home now. It was nice seeing you again, Miss O'Brien."

"Yes," Molly agreed. "It's been a long day, and tomorrow is going to be longer."

"Oh, please wait," Frances begged. "I've been meaning to talk to you about my parents' house. I'm going to sell it, and it's filled to the rafters. I'd like you to handle the estate sale."

Molly held back a shudder. She'd sworn just last week she would never do a house sale again. The last two she'd organized were disasters. The relatives of the deceased at both sales had given her a daily migraine. After hours of pricing box after box of less than mid-range silver, china, linens, and furniture, the family had picked over every item worth a damn and removed them from the sale. By the time Molly had ended each event, her twenty-five percent commission netted her minimum wage for a week's worth of work. "I'd love to, but I'm shorthanded at the shop, and house sales take up a ton of time. I'd be happy to recommend someone for you, though."

"I won't take no for an answer. Daria said you were the best and that I could trust you implicitly. My parents had very eclectic tastes. I haven't a clue about value these days."

"We're awfully busy right now," Emma piped in.

Molly hesitated only because of Daria. She gave Emma a firm look, then said, "How about if I meet you in the morning and see what's involved. I open at ten. Is nine good?"

Frances took both Molly's hands in hers. "I can't thank you enough. I'm returning to Europe and I need to get things settled."

"No promises," Molly said. "Just a look and then we'll go from there."

Molly couldn't miss Frances's hand suddenly moving to Randall's arm when she said, "It's La Casa. It's on Scenic, just past—"

"Oh, I know where it is!" Emma burst out. "Cool house. Aunt Molly and I pass it when we have time to walk on the beach. You can't miss the name on the front wall. How come it's just called 'the House'? I mean, why doesn't it have another Spanish word added like the others do?"

Emma's sudden interest surprised Molly, and she made a mental note to talk to her about her rudeness. "Yes, the lovely Spanish style house. I know right where it is."

"The original owner named it that," Frances told Emma. "Apparently he felt it was grander than anything else around so it didn't need a fancy name too." Turning to Molly, she said, "Nine is perfect. I'll bring some of our famous croissants and Kona coffee from the Inn."

"Oh, don't bother," Emma said. "We stop at Tosca's every morning."

Molly squeezed Emma's hand. "We'd love to have coffee with you. Thank you."

Frances gave Molly a quick smile, then abruptly turned her attention to Randall. Holding onto both his arms now, she said, "I need to talk to you. Could you spare some time for me tomorrow afternoon?"

Randall's eyes darted to Molly, then he said, "Of course. I'll be in all day catching up on paperwork."

"Well, don't take all afternoon," Emma said. "The chief and I need to help Aunt Molly move a big chest of drawers and—"

Before Emma could finish, Molly squeezed her hand again. "We've really got to go. Give my apologies to Bitsy for leaving early, will you, Randall?"

Molly was silent all through the Del Monte Forest in Pebble Beach until they reached the Carmel Gate. "You were unbelievably rude, young lady. I'd like an explanation."

"I don't like her," Emma finally said.

"That's no excuse. Why don't you like her? You hardly know her."

"I've met her twice now, and I'll go with my first impression."

"Which is?" Molly pressed.

"She's too sweet. And did you see the way she was clinging to Randall? Ugh."

It took a great deal of effort for Molly not to laugh. "Oh, come on, Em! And she wasn't clinging to Randall."

"He belongs to us and she can't have him."

Molly almost hit the brakes. "What? Where on earth did you come up with that?"

"Well, you know it's true."

Pulling into the alley behind the shop, Molly parked. "I know nothing of the sort. Randall is a good friend, and that's all. Got it?"

Emma was laughing as she climbed out of the truck. She quickly put on a serious face, and said, "Okay, if you say so."

By the time they finished their hot cocoa, Emma's yawn was genuine. "If business is bad, maybe we ought to think about her house sale. I liked helping you with the other ones."

"What makes you think business is bad?"

"I heard you talking to Bitsy about it. And then with Max on the phone yesterday. Are we in serious trouble?"

Hugging Emma as they sat on the sofa, Molly said, "We're not in trouble. Things are just slow now because all the beauties are sold and we haven't showy merch to jazz up the shop."

"So we look kind of common? Junky maybe?"

"We are definitely not junky! Just not, well, dazzling. People like to see glamour in antiques shops. Gilt, drama, and elegance. Showy to-die-for pieces they might not be able to afford but can dream about owning. Sometimes just walking into an elegant shop makes people feel good."

"Maybe this house job is just what we need," Emma said.

For some reason, Molly didn't think so. There was something about Frances O'Brien that rubbed her the wrong way. "Maybe. And then, maybe not."

## 2

*M*olly eyed the strollers on Carmel beach the next morning as she and Emma drove down Scenic Road to meet Frances. The surf was high, and the whitecaps further out reminded Molly of scattered powdered sugar. Gray clouds were turning dark, and a crisp chill was in the air. With her window open a crack, the cozy scent of wood fires burning in the sprawling homes facing Carmel Bay made Molly wish she and Emma were down on the hard wet sand waving at the regulars they'd come to know. She stole a glance at Emma, and recalled her running on the beach last week flapping her arms like the child she'd hardly had a chance to be. It was a rare act for Emma, and Molly wanted to hold it in her memory. Wise beyond her years, no thanks to Molly's sister, who had spent little time with her, Emma had learned early on to be self-sufficient. Her sharp sense of humor and dry wit were often the brighter parts of Molly's day, and she was determined to give Emma all the love and support she had in her.

Despite her shaky financial situation, Molly wasn't in the mood to tromp through what she assumed would be another rambling home filled with boring furniture. She told herself to remember, though, not to judge a book by its cover. While more than one palatial estate in Pebble Beach had been sparsely furnished with uninspiring merch, she'd found wonderful treasures and buys in more modest homes. Carmel wasn't much different than Pebble Beach in that respect. Downsizing and the turnover of property had been slow lately, and while she couldn't afford not to check out the weekend sales, she nevertheless began to think the great collections that once filled the local homes had all been sold off. Convinced she faced the same situation this morning, she pulled up to La Casa with few expectations.

Set back behind ten-foot-high stone walls, little was visible from the street except a peek of ivy framing the second floor's wrought-iron grilled windows. The steeply pitched tile roof conjured up soaring ceilings. Three chimneys were in evidence, with hints of more.

When they stepped through the iron gates into the front courtyard, Molly felt as if she'd been transported to an ancient villa in Cadiz. A canopy of tree ferns in verdigris copper planters led the way to the entrance. She began to think the morning might not be wasted after all. A dangerous thought, she reminded herself again. An English Tudor down the coast in the Carmel Highlands had been a major disappointment last week. Touted in the paper as one of the most important moving sales of the year by the owners, the furniture had been lackluster; a few vintage La-Z-Boys in a den, and the smalls were deplorable. It was apparent the classical music director's taste did not include his creature comforts, and she'd left within five minutes.

Even now, while she stood before a set of lusciously carved wood doors, she cautioned herself again to remember how many times she'd been fooled lately. The doors were beautifully fashioned in an arabesque style, and the intricate design could only have been made by a master. Judging them to be at least eight feet tall, they were set inside a cavernous entry ablaze with Moorish tiles in deep blues, greens, and yellows. Huge lion heads of cast bronze were centered on each door. It took both of her hands to lift the ring clenched in the lion's mouth. When Emma used the doorbell, Molly gave her a smirk. "You're no fun. These knockers cry to be used."

Before Emma could respond, the door opened and Frances stood before them with a smile. "I'm so glad you didn't change your mind. Come in!"

When Molly entered, her eyes immediately went into scan mode and began bouncing around so fast she had to blink to stop them. It was all she could do not to stammer or babble when she saw the enormous atrium off the foyer. Rising two stories, the wraparound balcony with arched openings and carved pillars on the second floor nearly took her breath away. Stepping closer, hoping her jaw wasn't dropping, Molly said, "Oh, how absolutely lovely, Frances."

"Quite the architectural fantasy, isn't it. Hardly what you think you'd find in sleepy Carmel with its quaint look. It's more suited to Pebble Beach. I've got coffee and pastries set up in the morning room."

Following Frances across the atrium, Molly managed quick peeks through towering banana plants, tree ferns, and palms in huge terra-cotta pots. She could see glimpses of carved friezes on the walls framing leaded double glass doors leading to other interior rooms. Even the moss growing on the stone paved patio was perfect, and the sound of trickling water was soft enough to be romantic. She grabbed Emma's hand and whispered, "Don't comment on anything you see. Just stick to me like glue, okay?"

Emma's eyes were on the move too, and she quickly nodded.

When they stepped into the morning room, Molly faltered. She suddenly imagined herself in Paris or Vienna. A massive marble-topped pastry table on a wonderful wrought-iron base hugged one wall between two arched doors of stained glass. An array of copper and silver serving pieces usually found in an elegant patisserie sparkled with elegance. Two four-tiered brass chandeliers hung from the coffered ceiling. Opposite her, the sun was struggling to break through its shroud of gloom. Filtering through a wall of multipaned glass, it bathed the room in a warm glow. Another patio could be seen, and it too was filled with tree ferns. Several good-sized oil paintings of pastoral scenes in wide gold leaf frames filled two walls, and a stunning limestone fireplace anchored the fourth wall.

Instead of bistro tables with crisp, white linen cloths, a round rosewood breakfast table Molly guessed was William IV and worth at least ten thousand sat in the center upon a faded but still lovely Oriental rug. The highly polished wood floors of hexagon inlay fairly glistened. Molly almost bit her tongue when her eyes rested on the six Burgundy velvet wing armchairs that surrounded the gleaming table and were, she quickly assessed, George I and worth possibly twice the table. When she caught site of a gigantic mahogany and cross-banded satinwood sideboard, her internal calculator valued the likely Regency piece to be between twelve and fifteen thousand. And the exquisite setting of Mason's ironstone china Frances had set out nearly made Molly lick her lips. So very desirable, it was becoming difficult to find and easier to sell than five-figure dining tables or chairs.

Molly's brain was in overdrive, and she was certain just the simple setting for the three of them was worth an easy twenty-five hundred. And her estimates, not even including the exquisite silver and porcelain pieces, or the fabulous gilded wooden dolphin plant stands, were only marginal. Without examining each piece for damages or repairs, this "morning room," as Frances termed it, was worth a small fortune.

"Coffee and nibbles first," Frances said as she pulled out a chair for Emma. "It's a big house and I want to entice you and your aunt Molly with the inn's famous mini-croissants and pure Kona coffee so you'll take on the job."

Looking around the gorgeous room, Emma was about to speak, then remembered Molly's warning. She smiled instead, then added, in a French accent, "I luuve croissants."

Molly hardly noticed Emma's joke. Her knees had begun to spasm and she needed to sit. Delicious merch did that to her. "Uh, well, we still have the rest of the house to see, and to decide if this is something I can squeeze in. Besides, Frances, we have to discuss—"

"Whatever you decide is fine with me." Frances said quickly. "I don't want any of this. I prefer to live simply. I'll be staying at the inn when I'm back and forth in Carmel even if I sell it."

"I can imagine this is awfully big for one person, Frances, but even though—"

"I've made up my mind, Molly. I can't bear to be here even now. It's . . . it's too painful without my parents. Too many memories."

While Frances served and poured coffee, and hot cocoa for Emma, a horrible thought struck Molly. She prayed this room wasn't a ringer. The owners of the last two estate sales had set up their best pieces in the living room when they met to engage her. She crossed her fingers under the table and prayed this would be different. If the rest of the house was only half as good as this room, she had an incredible opportunity to make some serious money.

Not wanting to appear too eager, and wanting to be certain for her own peace of mind that she wasn't being set up for a fall, she decided to hedge her bet. But knowing that Frances was one of Daria's oldest and closest friends, she didn't want to create any bad feelings. "As I said, Frances, before I commit, I naturally need to see the rest of the house."

"I want you to do it. I promise you won't be sorry."

Molly smiled and sipped her coffee. "I've never had pure Kona before. I could easily become addicted. It's wonderful."

On her feet, Frances picked up the silver coffeepot. "I've more in the kitchen. The inn buys direct from a grower on the Big Island. I'll be right back."

Molly waited until Frances left, then whispered to Emma, "I know it's hard not to ooh and ahh, but we've got to keep a straight face, okay?"

Emma rolled her eyes. "Is this stuff fantabulous, or what? Oh, Aunt Molly! We have to do this house! I mean, gosh, George I and Regency? Here? In Carmel?"

"Shhhh," Molly cautioned. "We'll talk after we leave." Emma had been devouring her antiques books, and while her extraordinary talent for nearly instant recall was coming in handy, she was still, after all, only twelve, and had much to learn. Besides, Molly realized, all of it might not be genuine period pieces. "Look, I know you've already recognized the great stuff in this room, but it may be the best of the bunch, okay? Remember what happened before?"

Emma's eyes roamed the room. "Okay, but what about all the artwork in here? The frames alone must be worth zillions."

Molly laughed. "Hardly zillions, but we'll see. Just play it cool and do not—I repeat, do not—react to anything else you see. Deal?"

"Okay. Deal."

When Frances returned, Molly glanced at her watch. "Time for one more cup, then we really should take the tour. I've got to open the shop. But before we go any further, you should know that my fee is twenty-five percent. That's standard, but in a situation like this, I'd make an adjustment for anything that goes to auction."

Pouring for Molly, Frances quickly said, "That sounds fair. I just can't deal with it. I haven't the heart or the time. There's no rush. You can take all the time you need."

Offering Emma another croissant, Frances added, "We can run through most of the first floor before you have to leave, then maybe you could come back this evening. I don't know if Daria mentioned it, but my parents were both set designers for films, and the house is filled with all sorts of movie stuff. I'm telling you all this because some of the rooms are, well, rather dramatic."

Molly's knees began to tingle. Movie memorabilia was going for record prices. Collectors literally frothed at the mouth at auctions. "Really? No, Daria didn't tell me. Movie memorabilia is an area where I am totally clueless. But I have friends in Boston who are experts in the field. I imagine you're talking about posters?"

"Oh, more than posters. Scripts, story boards . . . uh, furniture from movies. Tons of photos from the films, out-takes, and I'd guess dozens and dozens of autographed photos."

Despite the warning bell that clanged in her head when Frances said furniture from movies, the tingles moved to Molly's arms. "Oh? Well, that should be fun." She darted a look at Emma and willed her to be silent.

Each room seemed to follow a separate theme. The grand salon, so very Marie Antoinette, was enormous and filled with furniture and dozens of objets d'art. Molly wondered how long it would take just to dust the room. Artwork and tapestries covered the walls; three chande-liers, which Molly thought could be Limoges, hung from the cathedral ceiling. The huge kitchen, with a large island in the center, reminded her of a Merchant Ivory film and was filled with enough copper pots and pans of all sizes and description to make a Williams-Sonoma devotee drool. The floor-to-ceiling glass shelves in the butler's pantry had Molly salivating when Frances opened them. The dining room was another journey into the O'Briens' movie careers. Errol Flynn would have been comfortable here. The planked walnut table, straddled by rough-hewn benches covered in needlepoint, was long enough to seat Robin Hood and his men. Two sideboards held silver serving pieces, tankards, and crystal wine decanters. Without the camcorder she'd bought for Trudy's sale, what she'd seen so far would take weeks to catalog. Thank God for technology, she thought. The Canon Optura made transferring the video and voice to her computer a dream. The biggest job would be setting the photos up on a Web site for the out of town clients whose names were already creating a gridlock in her head.

When they reached the study, Molly was relieved. It wasn't another jarring theme room, but a sedate pecan-paneled haven befitting a man of taste. At least twenty by thirty, it easily held two overscale pieces of furniture. An enormous French bibliotheque took up most of one wall, and centered almost squarely in the room was a two-sided partners desk. Molly sucked in her breath. The swirling curves on the apron and corners were a seductive dream of the Art Deco period. Surrounding the desk were four leather smoking chairs, each with ebonized smoking stands holding cut crystal ashtrays. Three stained-glass windows, amber and pale green, cast a soft glow in the room, and a lingering scent of pipe tobacco filled the air.

"Oh, I like this room!" Emma blurted. "I could curl up here and read for days. Especially by that fireplace with all those beautiful Art Deco tiles."

"That's exactly what I used to do when I was your age," Frances said. Giving Emma a curious look, Frances added, "How do you know those tiles are Art Deco?"

"Oh, I . . . I saw some in a book Aunt Molly has," Emma said.

"It's absolutely lovely," Molly quickly interrupted. "There's a serenity here—"

"The other rooms don't have?" Frances finished for her. "This house has been a work in progress for as long as I can remember. An occupational hazard for set designers. Just wait until you see the upstairs."

"Your mother did a wonderful job with this," Molly said.

"Dad did this. I was around Emma's age when we moved here. I vaguely remember carpenters coming in and out for days. The former owner, Marius Lerner, was a film producer. My parents designed sets for many of his films. Historical epics were his favorites. In fact, the study and studio used to be a huge playroom that had an Egyptian theme."

Fascinated, Molly said, "With this architecture, such a room would certainly seem out of place."

"Dad must have thought so too. Oh, the bookcase, by the way, is bolted to the wall. There was a strong earthquake just before the room was completed and Dad worried about it toppling over. I can't imagine why, it must weigh a ton. But you know Californians! Always waiting for The Big One."

Molly was as perplexed as Frances. The house was filled with any number of objects that an earthquake might destroy. Certainly not this lumbering bookcase. Standing before it, she shook her head. "That might reduce the value." Running her hands over the carving, she paused for a moment, then opened one of the glass doors and angled it. Satisfied the glass was wavy enough to be authentic, she said, "Then again, maybe not." She next opened a carved door at the end and nearly fainted. On two shelves stood four Art Deco, carved ivory, gilt, and cold-painted bronze figures of women. Could they be genuine chryselephantine statues? The exquisite statutes of lithe women in sensuous roles of dancers and singers were representative of the gaiety and high style of the late 1920s and 1930s.

With both hands Molly carefully ran her fingertips over the bronze casting. Smooth as silk. She knew the figure to be *Cabaret Girl*. She prayed it was a genuine Johann Preiss. If it was, it could easily bring anywhere between eight and twelve thousand. She almost didn't want to believe the one on the bottom shelf was a real Demetre Chiparus. The figure of a woman with two greyhounds was one of the most sought after and an easy six figure sale. While they were limited editions, Molly knew reproductions were also well made, and highly deceptive. Not protected by copyright, they'd flooded the market recently. One of the telltale signs was an inferior base. The originals were mounted on high quality marble and onyx from Brazil. Her lips were bone dry. She fought the urge to moisten them. "These are lovely, Frances. Why are they tucked away like this?"

"Mother hated them. Especially the one on the top shelf. I think it's called *Sun Worshiper.* She used to say they were decadent. I always liked them, but Dad gave in and put them away. They're not copies, by the way. Dad had them authenticated some years ago."

Relieved, Molly nodded. "Hmm, yes, I can see that." Closing the door, she glanced at her watch. "Cripes! I've got to go. I'm already late in opening."

"Wait," Frances said as she moved to the built-in bookcases flanking the windows. The shelves were crammed with books and much of the movie memorabilia she'd mentioned earlier. "Emma, come take a look at these." Two Academy Awards were tucked between a stack of film canisters.

Emma's eyes were huge. "Are they real?"

"As real as can be. My father and mother each won one years ago."

"Please take them with you," Molly said. "If I do the sale, I don't want to be responsible for them."

"Then you've agreed to do this for me?"

"Whoa," Molly said, smiling. "I said *if* I do the sale."

"Oh, come on, Molly! This is Aladdin's trove, and you know it. Don't play hard to get."

Of course she would do the sale, but she didn't like the tone of Frances's voice. "I've got a shop to run, and I'd have to work here at night," she said, keeping her voice even. "I can already see it will take more than a week just to inventory what I've seen. And I haven't been upstairs."

"Of course. I'm sorry. Let's meet back here tonight to see the rest. You pick the time."

Molly hesitated, then said, "Seven is the earliest I can be here."

"You're the boss," Frances said.

Molly smiled, which was hard to do when you were biting your tongue.

## 3

*E*mma nearly flew into the El Camino beside Molly and blurted, "Ohmigosh!"

Still smarting from Frances's taunt, Molly couldn't help but laugh. "Ditto."

"Do you think those Art Deco figures are the real thing?"

"I'm almost afraid to say yes. If the ivory is genuine and the signatures hold up, they could be a mini–gold mine."

"But Frances said they were. Whew! This stuff could really make *Treasures* glamorous."

"Slow down, miss. Frances might just be repeating what her father said. We have to be sure." Molly struggled with the driver's door again, then slammed it hard. "We've got to get this baby into the shop. I can't keep driving around with a door that won't stay shut."

Pulling away from La Casa, Molly eased the truck onto Scenic Road and headed for town. "First of all, none of this is for the shop. We can't buy any of it. I've been asked to establish value. It would be unethical."

"Huh? Why?"

"Because the values I'd set might be in question then. And my reputation for integrity could suffer. I've fought too hard to get my good name back, Emma." With a deep sigh, Molly added, "So even if we were flush, we can't buy a thing."

Emma was silent for a moment and fiddled with her seat belt. Molly could see the disappointment wash across her face. "It's a tricky situation, Em, and one of the reasons many dealers shy away from doing estate sales."

"What about Max, or Bitsy? Couldn't they buy for us?" Emma asked.

"They could, but except for some of the smalls, we can't afford the prices I'm going to have to set. Max could buy for his San Francisco store, though." Giving Emma a wink, she added, "Let's not be greedy, okay? There is that little thing called commission, remember?"

Pretending to twirl a moustache, Emma giggled. "So how much do you think we can make?"

"Ah, life was so dull before you arrived!" Slowing for two cats crossing the street, Molly said, "Give me a few blocks to run my mind over the rooms." She was nearly breathless just thinking about the colossal collection, and didn't know where to begin. She was aching for a cigarette to calm her nerves. The salon alone was filled with what appeared to be Louis XIV! God only knew what the upstairs might be like. When she finally pulled into the alley behind the shop's complex, she said, "If all the furniture we saw is period, and not including the artwork, which I barely got a glimpse of—"

"The frames alone are worth plenty," Emma said.

"Yeah, well, anyway, just a quick off-the-top-of-my-head, we're talking about maybe . . . oh, maybe seventy-five to a hundred grand."

Emma nearly burst through the seat belt. "*Are you serious?* You wouldn't lie to a kid like me, would you?"

"Is the Pope Catholic?"

"Zowie!"

Molly laughed. "Is that all you can say?"

"This is breaking news! We've got to call Randall and tell him. And Bitsy too."

"Hold on. I don't want to discuss this with anyone until we've seen the rest of the house."

"Why?"

"Because."

"That's not an answer. Are you afraid they're going to try to kill the deal?"

"Emma! Where on earth do you come up with those ideas? Why would they care?"

Emma crossed her arms and huffed, "Then why can't we tell them?"

"Because," Molly began as she shoved open the door. "I have to make some plans first. Bitsy will have it all over town, and I haven't even said yes to Frances. So, the moral of the story is . . . don't count your chickens before they hatch. And then there's always Murphy's Law. Suppose we blab it all over and then Frances changes her mind, or asks someone else?"

"But why would she do that? I mean, she's almost begging you to do it."

Molly didn't have an answer, only a gut feeling that maybe something wasn't quite right. With a collection like this, Frances should be contacting Sotheby's or Christie's, not some local antiques dealer.

"Right," Emma finally agreed. "And we don't want Bitsy coming in and getting all bossy like she does. I love it when she orders us all around, I mean, it's kind of funny. But I think I annoyed her the other day when she was showing us the new stuff she bought in Europe."

"Now that you've nearly memorized all those antiques books you've been reading, I think she's afraid you might know more than she does."

Emma's eyes lit up. "Yeah, I really got her when I told her I thought that chair she bought in Rome when she went to see the Pope was Austrian Biedermeier and not Russian."

Molly laughed, but her mind wasn't on Emma's newfound talent. When Frances said her parents were film set designers, an alarm in her head nearly shut down the calculator running at full speed. She was afraid the house could be filled with movie set replicas. Except for the morning room, her quick glances of the other furnishings, while exquisite, only gave her a clue as to style and possible period. She knew firsthand how easy it was to replicate antiques, and some of the finest artisans today worked for films. A small shudder rippled through her. Clutching the small crucifix under her sweater, she prayed everything was genuine. The commission on just what she'd seen would more than replace the safety net she'd lost when she'd had to make good the fake merchandise she'd bought from Trudy Collins, including the jewelry and pair of valuable ivory miniatures her sister had stolen from her.

Until she was able to get on her hands and knees and look under tables, pull out drawers, and examine the back of the chests and sideboards, she wouldn't really know what she was dealing with. On the other hand, the furniture had a fantastic look and wouldn't be at all hard to sell. And, if any of it had in fact been in a film, and there were still photos to verify it, the value would soar.

"So," Molly repeated to Emma, "mum's the word."

"Okay, but I have another question."

"Hold that thought. Let's get the shop open first."

When Molly unlocked the front door to *Treasures*, two women were waiting under the canopy. "I'm sorry I'm late." Molly said. "I . . . ah . . . well, I'm just late." Giving them a smile, she asked, "Can I offer you a cup of coffee while you browse? It's the least I can do to thank you for your patience."

When both women declined, Molly excused herself and set about turning on lamps, plugging in the teapot, and turning on the CD player. When the soft strains of Vivaldi came on, she said, "If I can be of help, just let me know." Scooting Emma away from the computer, she leaned down and whispered, "Would you run up and get my address book? I left it in the kitchen. Oh, and be sure to get Tiger in. It feels like it's going to rain."

"I think Tiger's pregnant. Her belly is getting kind of big."

Molly rolled her eyes. "That's all we need, a knocked-up cat."

"Aunt Molly! Such language. Oh, what about my other question?"

"Address book first, then how about running over to Tosca's for some apple cake? Those tiny croissants didn't do much, did they." When Emma nodded, Molly said, "I thought so. Tell Bennie we'll stop by tomorrow."

Molly flipped open her address book when Emma left

for the small coffee boutique in the courtyard behind *Treasures*. She knew if she was going to take on this job, she had to start lining up experts in many different fields. Cleo Jones, her oldest friend from Sotheby's would be invaluable in offering the latest market values of English furniture and art. Molly wasn't sure about the art in the house either. She hadn't given it more than a passing glance. There was just too much to take in all at once. Bridget Bolton, another London contact, was an expert on china, porcelain, and pottery. Besides the luscious Mason's ware in the morning room, Molly had almost fainted when Frances threw open the cabinets in the butler's pantry. Shelf after shelf of Irish Belleek almost blinded her. And more majolica and Pallisy than she'd seen in shops that specialized in them. The cabinets nearly groaned with Derby, Staffordshire, Spode, Limoges, and Creamware. Molly was up on U.S. prices, but the U.K. was witnessing a renaissance in their famous potters, and it would be her obligation to get Frances the very best prices she could. She hoped the number she had for Linda Rutledge was still good. Linda's expertise on silver would come in handy. Molly had a good grasp on markings, but she knew how quickly prices fluctuated, and she wasn't handling the caliber of silver she'd seen in the dining room and in the pantry.

When the two women said they'd come back another time, Molly was so revved up over what she'd seen this morning, she merely waved and said, "Yes, please do come back again," then gave them little thought. She decided not to call anyone yet. She was jumping too fast. She should wait until she'd seen the rest of the house. There was no point in getting them excited when she didn't even have an accurate list to discuss.

She thumbed through her address book again and began making notes of whom she might want to contact. Her eyes stopped when she saw the first entry under H. Nicholas Hahn. How strange, she thought, that after all these years that name should still make her heart jump. One of the art world's foremost authorities, Nicholas Hahn could spot a missing Picasso under three layers of paint. She'd met him during her first visit to Paris, when she was Cleo's assistant at Sotheby's New York gallery. He was giving a lecture at the Paris branch, and she'd been sent there to attend it. Brilliant, handsome, and sophisticated, he was a fantasy dream come true. As tall as her, Nicholas's eyes met hers evenly, and she'd nearly fainted when he kissed her hand after they'd been introduced. Germanic blond, dressed by Saville Row, Nicholas was the epitome of a suave European heartthrob. When Cleo had whispered she was having an affair with him, Molly nearly wept.

Over the years, she'd had occasion to work with him in New York and London, and they had become good friends. She remembered, with great fondness, his telephone call when her husband and his lover's photo had been front page news. His belief in her innocence had been one of the few times Molly had found a smile on her face during those dark days.

Molly almost didn't see Emma return. She'd been lost in kindness, and her vision had been a bit blurry. After setting the apple cakes on Molly's desk, Emma said, "My question?"

"Right. Your question."

Pulling up a chair next to Molly, Emma said, "How come Frances told Randall at Bitsy's last night she wanted to see him? Do you think she's in some kind of trouble?"

Molly stared at Emma for a moment. Visions of this windfall flittering away, she blurted, "Oh, God. I hope not."

Before Molly could give that nightmare much thought, Daria came in with her arms loaded with flowers. "Help! I've got an overload from my florist. Can you use an armful of Peruvian lilies?"

Rushing to help her, Molly said, "Oh, they're beautiful and I'm fresh out." Taking the huge bouquet from Daria, she asked Emma, "Would you grab two glass vases from the storage room? We'll meet you upstairs."

"I've got time for a quick cup of coffee, and then I've got to run," Daria said as she followed Molly up to the apartment.

Stopping on the stairs, Molly called down to Emma, "Better lock the front door before you come up. We'll open later."

"Are you sure?" Daria asked. "I don't want you to lose a sale just to have coffee."

Molly laughed as she nudged open the door to the apartment. "When have I ever opened on time? Besides, Carmel is like a ghost town this morning. Either the tourists are still sleeping or they went home early."

In the small kitchen, Molly looked up at the crazy cat clock she loved and saw that it was already ten-thirty. Another half hour wouldn't make much difference. Daria DeMarco had proven to be one of the staunchest friends she'd ever had, and missing a sale or two was well worth her company. It was a shame that Daria's stunning looks made women leery of her. If only they could see past those sculptured cheekbones and jet black hair that shimmered like silk, they'd find a rare woman. A woman to call a friend for life.

When Emma arrived with the vases, Molly filled them

with water, then set the lovely flowers inside. Plugging in the teakettle, she joined Daria and Emma in the living room. "Hope instant is okay."

Daria was settled on the sofa and about to light a cigarette when she saw Emma playfully scowling at her. "Hey, come on, Em! Knock it off. I'm trying to quit. I've only had two so far, so give me a break."

"Isn't she just the most perfect little angel?" Molly grinned as she sat next to Emma and tousled her curly hair. "It's funny how I keep losing packs of cigarettes. It's getting so I don't dare lay one down. And considering how much the damn things cost, it's getting expensive."

"I'm just trying to help you two," Emma said. "I need good role models for the next six years and I'd like to keep you around."

Giving Emma a hug, Molly said, "Daria and I are trying. It just isn't easy, Em."

Letting out a dramatic sigh of defeat, Daria returned the cigarette to its pack. "Okay, you win. But just for now. So, Molly, Frances tells me you're going to handle unloading the big house. She really needs guidance. The woman is an exquisite artist, but when it comes to practical matters, she's a little lost."

"She told you I said yes? When?"

"She called me just after you and Emma left."

"But I didn't agree to anything," Molly said. "I told her I needed to see the rest of the house before I made a decision. Damn it, I wish people would listen once in a while."

When Emma heard the teakettle whistle, she said, "I'll make the coffee."

Pulling a cigarette out again, Daria quickly lit it, then said, "Frances and I have been friends since middle school. She's a great gal, but she was an only child, and I have to admit, pretty spoiled. Not in a bad way, just that she's not used to people saying no to her. What I mean is, she just assumes. You know?"

"I don't like people *assuming* for me. It's an incredible opportunity and my knees have been shaking all morning, but I might not be the right person to handle all of it. I can already see areas that are out of my depth. The movie memorabilia is a perfect example."

"But you can call experts, can't you?" Daria asked. "You know all those people, Frances doesn't." Giving Emma a warning smile when she returned with the coffee, Daria tapped her cigarette into the ashtray and added, "The house is a fantasy, isn't it? Did Frances tell you its history and how her parents came to own it?"

Playfully swatting Emma's hands when she tried to snitch her pack of cigarettes, Molly said, "No, there wasn't time. We had coffee and croissants and just a quick tour of most of downstairs. The butler's pantry alone will take hours. What's so unique about another Carmel mansion?"

"It's a story right out of the movies, and so perfect for the O'Briens," Daria said. "I'm not talking out of turn, it's a well-known legend here. The house was built by Marius Lerner, the big movie producer. Name ring a bell?"

Emma had no idea who Daria was talking about, but when she saw Molly's eyes grow huge, she immediately became interested. "I heard her mention the name when we were there. Is he like Steven Spielberg or George Lucas?"

"No. He was before your time. His films are now considered classics. Big costume epics and a few westerns, I think."

Intrigued, Molly asked, "And? Go on . . . I'm riveted. He's a legend!"

"Well, he built it in the late sixties, early seventies.

Lerner was a golf nut and loved coming up every year for the AT&T Tournament. It was the the 'Clambake' when Bing Crosby ran it. All the big-time movie people showed up every year and it was the highlight of the season here. The house—or La Casa, as Lerner named it—was always packed with movie stars, producers, directors . . . you name it. The parties were pretty wild, they say. Frances used to come up for the tournament with her parents when she was around Emma's age. They stayed at the inn they eventually bought."

"So what's the big legend?" Emma asked.

Daria grinned. "I was saving the best for last. Frances's father won La Casa in an all-night poker game with Lerner."

Molly's mouth fell open. "What?"

"The house, the furnishings . . . everything. Even a Bentley. In fact, it's the same one the inn uses to pick up guests from the airport. Frances's mother apparently didn't like the way La Casa was furnished and did it over. It took a few years. I remember when we were going to school the place was always in an uproar with movers and painters. They still worked on movies, but Carmel became their home. They wanted Frances to have a life away from all the glitz."

"So who were the big stars? Anyone I'd know?" Emma asked.

"Unless you like old movies, I doubt it. But the big names of the day all came. Bob Hope was always here with Bing Crosby, and they drew the cream of the crop of the best golfers in the world. It was party time around the clock. A lot of heavy drinking and—" Remembering that Emma was hanging on her every word, Daria added. "Uh, well, you know."

When Emma shrugged, Daria laughed. "I thought so. Anyway, you should have a packed house if you do the sale. Carmelites will come in droves just to get a glimpse of the place." Jumping up from the sofa, Daria said, "Got to run, and you've got to open. See you at seven?"

"Do you have time to come over?" Molly asked.

Giving Emma a hug and a quick kiss on her forehead, Daria said, "Do you think I'd let you two go there at night without me?" When she saw the blank look on Molly's face, she added. "La Casa is supposed to be haunted. Didn't Frances tell you?"

"No way!" Emma blurted.

Daria gave Molly a wink. "Ciao."

## 4

*R*andall steered Frances O'Brien to the small sitting area in his office. Conducting discussions at his desk, or even the large conference table, seemed to inhibit small civic groups when they visited. He'd found the leather sofa, two chairs, and coffee table at a garage sale he'd gone to with Molly and Emma. It had been his first time on the weekend circuit, and, he'd sworn over a late breakfast that morning, the last. He'd likened the hunt to an episode of one of those survivor things on television. Even Emma, as much as he'd come to love her, couldn't convince him to tag along again.

"Are you sure no one else has a key to the house besides the cleaning staff?" Randall asked. He'd noticed Frances had a habit of fluttering her eyelids when she was about to speak. It didn't require a face reading course, which he'd attended some years back, to identify so obvious a sign of anxiety. Coming from her, it was almost charming, he thought.

"I can't imagine who else Mother or Father would have trusted," Frances answered. "Oh, yes, Ed Winslow, our manager at the inn, has one for emergency."

"What do you know about the cleaning staff? Are they new? Any changes in the crew, maybe?"

"No, it's the same family for the past few years. Lovely people from Honduras. A mother and three daughters. Oh, a teenage son too."

"Any chance one of them might have itchy fingers?" When Randall saw the quick frown of denial on Frances's face, he quickly said, "It happens. Especially after a tragedy. And let's face it, you've been away for some time. Maybe one of the kids, or one of their friends, might have taken advantage of your absence to check things out. Pros don't toss, just amateurs."

"I imagine that's possible. I didn't really know them all that well. I lived at the inn mostly when I was home. My studio is on the top floor. The light is more conducive to painting than at La Casa."

"Since you don't know if anything is missing, there's not much use in filing a break-in report."

"How could I know what might be missing? The house is crammed! Heaven only knows what they might have added while I was in Europe. My parents were compulsive buyers. It's just so unnerving to think someone was in the house going through drawers."

"I'll alert the patrol in your area and have them keep an eye open. Tossed beds and closets, doors open that you swear you'd shut, and lights burning in the house are not much for me to go on. I mean, it's obvious someone gained entry and—"

"But there are any number of things to steal if that was the intent. It's almost as if someone was looking for something."

"And you have no idea what that might be?" Randall asked.

"No."

"What about jewelry?"

Frances shook her head. "Mother wore a Timex watch and a plain gold band. Jewelry wasn't her thing."

Randall's tie was beginning to annoy him. He'd quickly eased into Carmel casual, and rarely wore a tie these days. Always a man to look into the mirror and know who faced him, he had to hold back a grin. Frances O'Brien was a beautiful woman, and he'd wanted to look good today. "I don't mean to sound indelicate, but is there a chance there might have been some incriminating letters someone wanted back?"

Frances's laugh was almost musical, reminding Randall of tiny bells. "Oh, my God, but that's funny. You can't be serious. My parents were in their early seventies. I hardly think either of them was having an affair."

He smiled with her. "Past history was what I had in mind."

"I don't think so. But then, who really knows? They were both very attractive in their day."

Randall saw a faint sheen in her eyes, and he was sorry he'd had to ask such a personal question. It was only a short time since she'd come home to bury her parents. He knew her emotions were still raw, but questions, no matter how sensitive, were a daily part of his job.

"My father was very handsome. My mother was . . . vibrant." She shook her head and looked away. "I suppose anything is possible."

"Do you have an alarm on the house?"

"Yes, but it's very complicated. I don't use it. Dad had all sorts of motion sensors installed, but they never worked right. Many of the rooms are semifaux. Walls aren't exactly plumb and doors often stick. Sometimes they won't even close properly. Guests used to think the house was haunted. Daria still believes it!"

"Excuse me? Semi-faux is not a building term I'm familiar with."

The tinkling laughter this time was almost embarrassed. "Movie set rooms. Dad had favorites from some of the films he'd done. When the set was struck, he had one or two reassembled at La Casa. His library was from a remake of one of those English classics. I forget the name of the film now. Anyway, two of the guest rooms upstairs, and mother's room, were from movies. Not my style, though. I prefer simplicity. The house was always a work in progress." When she still saw the puzzled look on his face, she added, "Not everything fit perfectly. Walls on top of walls . . . rooms opened up, rooms within rooms. You know, that kind of thing." Looking away for a moment, Frances said, almost to herself, "Dad had a quirk about that house. It was his fantasy."

"How about if I stop by later and check out the alarm system. We could do a dry run and see what to do about making it easier for you to handle."

"Oh, that would be wonderful. Would this evening be okay? Molly will be coming around seven to see the rest of the house. She should learn how it works too since she'll be spending several evenings doing the inventory for the sale. I'm not into antiques and I'll be happy when it's over. Besides, none of it means much now that my parents are gone."

"Molly's agreed to do the sale?"

"Daria said she was the best and I could trust her. But I did hear a few things. That was another reason I wanted to see you. If you think I'm making a mistake, please tell me.

I mean, we all know a lot of antiques dealers are a bit . . . well, what I mean is—"

"Whatever you heard, forget it. You couldn't ask for anyone better," Randall said.

"It's just that I was told she's from New York and that her husband and his lover were arrested for fraud and—"

The fluttering eyelids suddenly lost their appeal. "She had no part of that, Frances. If anyone can vouch for Molly Doyle, it's me."

"I'll take that as gospel, then." Reaching for her keys in her purse, Frances quickly changed the subject. "I just wish I knew what someone was looking for. It doesn't make sense." She thought for a moment, then said, "Did I just say gospel? Hmm. My father had an early eighteenth century Bible he adored. It wasn't in his bedroom." Before Randall could comment, she added, "They had separate bedrooms. Dad often worked crazy hours on set design, and Mother suffered from migraines. He was known to jump out of bed with an idea and, well—"

"Sure. I understand. The creative type. Let me know if the Bible is missing. That might give us something to start on." When Frances rose, Randall steered her toward the door. "I'm glad you stopped in. You did the right thing bringing this to my attention."

"It's been so hard these past weeks. Losing my parents and now this."

"We'll get that alarm problem solved and then you can stop worrying, okay?"

As they left his office, Randall saw Emma in the hall talking to one of the clerks. "Hey, squirt. Lose your bike or something?"

Emma's eyes were glued to Frances's hand resting on Randall's arm. "I thought I'd come over and see if you were ready to help us move that big chest. You promised, remember?"

"Right. I'll stop by as soon as I'm free."

"Hello, Emma," Frances said. "Will you be coming with your aunt Molly tonight? I could have some cookies sent over from the inn if you are."

"Umm, yes. I'll be there. I'm in training with Aunt Molly."

Frances's laugh was almost mocking "In training? Aren't you a little young to be deciding your future?"

Emma adjusted her glasses, then said, "The Keno twins decided when they were twelve to be antique dealers. I'd say I was right on track." Darting a glance at Randall, she added, "I'm not much of a cookie person, but thank you anyway." Backing down the hall, Emma said to the clerk, "I'll burn a copy of that game for you tomorrow." Turning back to Frances and Randall, she waved and skipped out of the station.

"Interesting child," Frances said. "So grown-up. I can't believe she doesn't like cookies. I imagine she's bookish too. How cute to think she's in training. Who are the Keno twins, by the way?"

Randall knew Emma was a sucker for cookies. He wondered what the hell that was about. "Bookish?" Randall had to laugh. "Yeah, bookish is good. Emma is an authority on Harry Potter. Notice the haircut and the glasses? Got a brain like a sponge. She's been devouring Molly's collection of books on antiques. Been through most of what the library has too. The Keno brothers are hot stuff in the antiques world. High-end kind of guys."

"Really? Well, she should be out roller skating, or

whatever kids do these days, instead of learning about old furniture. I can't imagine a more boring subject. Where's her mother, by the way? Did she die?"

"No. She's in Japan with a new job. Emma's staying with Molly until things get settled." Before Frances could probe further, he asked, "Are you in a gallery here? I'd like to take a look at more of your work."

"No, not yet. I'm not ready."

"From what I've seen at Daria's restaurant, I'd have to disagree."

Reaching up, Frances kissed Randall on the cheek. "Flattery will get you everywhere."

"I hope that Frances won't be breathing down our necks while we're working," Emma said as she peered over Molly's shoulder at the computer. "Did you get in touch with your friends yet? *We have to do that house.* Besides everything else, think of all the movie stuff and how much we'll make on it. Bonham's in Los Angeles gets a ton for that junk. I read an article at the library on the hammer results. Oh, Randall will be here soon. I just, uh, ran into him."

Swinging away from the monitor, Molly reached for the printed sales reports for Max. "Shush, Emma. There are customers in the shop." Jerking her head, she whispered, "In the back looking at those lamps I made from Trudy's fake Meissen vases. That's a cool grand for us, so keep a lid on it, okay?"

"Right. Okay. Uh, I'll go upstairs and fix some lunch. I'm starving. Want me to sneak a sandwich into the storage room for when they leave?"

"Tuna and deviled egg combo? On whole wheat?" Molly smiled.

"Check."

"Oh, Emma? I know you're not crazy about Frances, but I expect you to be polite. She might be a client, and clients are—"

"Our bread and butter."

"Thank you."

After wrapping the pair of lamps and selling a set of six curly maple chairs, Molly was in an expansive mood. Devouring the sandwich Emma made, she kept sneaking a look on the floor in case someone walked in, then gulped down two instant espressos. Relieved the shop was empty, she sneaked a cigarette before Emma returned, then sprayed the room with an air freshener. She faxed the reports to Max, then called the shop in San Francisco to tell him about La Casa. After a moment of silence from Max, an almost impossible feat, Molly finally said, "I haven't seen a collection like this in years. Few of the estates back East could compare to this. Oh, Max! It's incredible, and I've only seen a few rooms."

"Well, I expect to have first viewing!" Max laughed. "I'm already rubbing my hands. When can I see it?"

"I can hear you licking your lips from here. Give me a week. But, Max, don't start drooling yet. You know I have to price it accurately."

"Well, yes, of course you do, you honest little vixen. Just don't get too carried away. I already know where to unload the movie stuff. And if those Art Deco statues are genuine, I'll take them off your hands. Let me do some calculating and I'll call you back."

"Oh, hold up on the movie stuff, will you? I'd like to check with Rudy and Barbara Franchi in Boston first and that might take some time. Frances said there are boxes and boxes filled with movie memorabilia. Speaking of make-believe, I'm not certain what I've seen so far is even real. I haven't had a chance to examine a thing."

"Darling Molly," Max said, "with your eye? If you were impressed and as excited as you sound, I'm not the least bit worried."

Molly winced. "Really? Well, I seemed to have made a huge mistake not too long ago. Remember? Trudy Collins fooled me big-time."

"That was because you trusted a friend. Remember my motto? 'Trust no one'?"

"I'll never forget it. It's etched on my brain." And, Molly thought, it was a favorite motto of Randall's too. It was a pity she'd had to learn it the hard way twice.

"Good girl. I'm glad you called. I scored a major buy yesterday. Huge estate in Atherton. A dot-com genius went belly up. I'll be sending down a truck soon."

"Fantastic! We could use some new blood here. Could you send down a black light? I was going to buy one, but if you've any extra I could use it for the artwork at La Casa."

"Hmm. You *are* worried, aren't you?"

"Just edgy. It's like an abundancy of riches that seems too good to be true. I don't want to get caught with my you-know-whats down again. The O'Briens were movie people, remember? They lived in a world of make-believe. Let's hope they left that in Gollywood."

After she rang off with Max, a new thought struck her. If some of the furniture came from movies, who really owned them? She knew that when sets were struck, not everything found its legal home. Ownership would have to be authenticated or they wouldn't go under the hammer at Sotheby's or Christie's. Max's private buyers might not care, but she did.

*I*t was a few moments past seven when Molly and Emma arrived at La Casa. Every light in the huge home seemed to be on. A brisk wind was whipping in off Carmel Bay. Trees on Scenic Road swayed in protest as each gust grew stronger. By the time Molly parked, it had started to rain. They made a quick dash through the open iron gates and shivered in the cavernous entry. Molly gave Emma a grin and rang the doorbell. When Randall answered, Molly stepped back in surprise. "What are you doing here?" she blurted.

"Nice to see you too." Moving aside, he motioned to Frances just behind him. "Your guests are here."

"I was beginning to think you'd changed your mind. It's five past seven," Frances said.

"Is it?" Molly glanced at her watch, then tapped it. "My watch must be running slow."

Emma looked at her watch. Frances was right. She knew her aunt had a problem being on time, but she wasn't about to let her be scolded. Especially in front of Randall. "Mine too, I guess."

Frances laughed. "Well, it doesn't matter. You're here. That's all that counts. Randall was kind enough to come over and help me with the alarm system. I'm hopelessly dense when it comes to technology. I haven't been able to activate it properly."

"Since you're going to be spending time here, you need to get a grasp of it too, Molly." Randall said.

Molly darted a look at Frances and tried to marshal a semblance of calm. "I'm here tonight to see the rest of the house before I decide. Since you and Frances seem to have some problems to solve, maybe I should come back another time."

"I thought it was a done deal," Randall said.

Molly took hold of Emma's hand. Nodding to Frances, she said, "Call me tomorrow when you have a moment."

"Don't pay any attention to her, Frances," Randall said. "It's an Irish thing. They get huffy easily. Don't like to be told what to do," he added, barely hiding a grin.

Emma pulled on Molly's hand. "Why don't we look around while they're playing with the alarm thing? I mean, we *are* here, and it's kind of silly to come back again."

"Brilliant idea, Emma," Frances said. Moving to Molly, she linked her arm with hers. "I promise not to be so pushy from now on. Will you stay? Please?"

Molly saw the grin on Randall's face grow wider and she wanted to smack him. "Since you put it that way, how can I refuse?"

"Wonderful. I'll take you up while Randall finishes his drink." Turning to him, she said, "I'll only be a few minutes. Molly and Emma can wander while we're down here."

After a quick tour of the upstairs rooms, Frances hurried down the winding marble stairway. When she was out of sight, Emma said, "You didn't really mean all that, did you? I have to be honest, Aunt Molly, you were a little huffy."

"Of course I didn't mean it. I just had to set some parameters. Frances needs to know she does not set my agenda."

"Whew. You had me worried for a minute. And then I thought maybe you believed what Daria said about the house being haunted."

"Haunted? Oh, come on! Daria was only pulling your chain because you've been razzing her about smoking. Besides, do you think I'd let a deal like this get away from us?" Molly shook her head. "Pay attention, squirt. This is how big girls do business."

The tour through the six bedrooms and six baths left Molly silent. Emma too was quiet, and Molly almost forgot she was there. Not ready to join Frances and Randall, Molly needed to stop to gather her thoughts. She sat at the top of the stairs and closed her eyes. When she felt Emma beside her, she said, "I need to think for a few minutes."

"Pretty awesome."

"Way awesome." In fact, Molly thought, *incredibly awesome*. Without Frances in tow, she had taken the opportunity to open the drawers of chests to check the mortise and tenon joints and look for wear on the side rails. It was impossible to examine the bottoms and backs of the drawers without emptying them, but she found enough evidence of authenticity on eight pieces to give her chills. Each bedroom was done in a different style, running the gamut from Gothic to Contemporary to Venetian splendor, with some reproductions of top quality. She'd almost swear the two Barcelona chairs in the contemporary bedroom suite were original Mies van der Rohe. Mrs. O'Brien's bedroom was the epitome of Hollywood glamour in the forties. Every piece of furniture was mirrored *à la* Lana Turner. The tall, silk-padded headboard, in an exquisite soft peach, with bronze rosettes was quietly elegant. Her five-foot-wide dressing table alone was worth a small fortune, never mind the score of Lalique perfume bottles from the twenties.

Molly knew she could only work in the evenings, and she had to face the reality that this job might take a couple of weeks just to videotape, then catalog. Except for Emma, she had no one she could trust. She didn't dare call in the one or two antiques dealers in town she'd become friendly with. Bitsy Morgan was a definite no. Frances O'Brien was no longer at the top of her hit parade.

"Well? When do we start?" Emma asked.

Molly was quiet for a moment, then shook her head. "This might be too big for us."

"Hey, you two get lost?" Randall called from the bottom of the staircase. "Daria's here and so are some friends of Frances's. Come on down and be social."

"We're having a conclave," Emma said.

Climbing the stairs, Randall said, "I don't like the sound of that. You two alone are dangerous. What's up?"

"Aunt Molly doesn't think we can do this job."

Randall paused a few steps from them. "What? Is the great Molly Doyle out of her league?"

That was all Molly needed. She gave Randall a withering look. "This *is* the Great Molly Doyle's league and don't you ever forget it. Of course I'm taking the job."

Emma's mouth fell open. "But you just said—"

"Never mind what I said."

Randall gave Emma his arm. "Shall we join the swells in the drawing room, my dear?"

Emma laughed, and Molly did a slow burn as she followed them into the salon. She didn't need Randall playing mind games with her too.

Frances stood by the walk-in fireplace, sipping cocktails with a man and a woman whose backs were to them as they entered. Daria, she noticed, was alone on one of the flanking sofas.

Frances's eyes seemed unusually bright to Molly when she said, "Molly and Emma, come meet Jason and Steffi Lerner."

"You're twins!" Emma said when the man and woman turned to greet them. "Cool."

Jason Lerner had to look up at Molly when he offered his hand. Slight of build, with dark hair and even darker eyes, he reminded her of an elf. His quick, wide-open smile seemed genuine, and Molly took an immediate liking to him. "Not twins," Jason said. "We're two years apart. But it *was cool* when the four of us used to play hide-and-seek in this big old place when we were kids."

Steffi Lerner laughed as she took Molly's hand. "It nearly drove Daria and Frances nuts. My hair was as short as Jason's back then." Looking around, she laughed again. "And it still is."

Molly noticed that Daria's smile was a bit tight, and she wondered if those childhood memories were not all that great. "It's a wonder any of you could find yourself in this huge place."

"It wasn't easy," Frances said. "What can I offer you to drink, Molly? A soda, for Emma, maybe?"

"Nothing, thanks. Emma and I should be on our way.

It's been a long day and I've got to organize the notes I've made."

"Please stay," Frances said. "Jason and Steffi have been down at Ventana working on a new script and wanted to come up and . . . and offer condolences."

"We only learned about the accident yesterday," Jason said. "We've been holed up for a week. No television, no papers, just our cell phones. We didn't know about the O'Briens."

"Actually," Steffi said, "we'd planned to stop by and see them before we left. Jason and I are putting together a book on our father's long career. He's retired now and in poor health. We'd hoped the O'Briens might want to add some color. Recollections and photos of some of the movies they did together. That sort of thing. Dad lost most of his collection in the fires we had a few years back in Laguna, and he said Jack O'Brien was a photo nut."

Jason smiled fondly. "He said he must have been born with a camera in his hand."

"There are boxes and boxes in the studio," Frances said. "I know Molly will be more than happy to help sort them for you."

Randall saw the pulsing over Molly's eye and braced himself for an explosion.

Molly caught his look and carefully said, "I think you'd be the best person for that, Frances." She hesitated briefly, then added, "I'll call you in the morning. Are you still at the inn?"

Frances didn't see the look of relief on Randall's face, nor the raised eyebrows on Daria's. She answered, "Yes. I'll stop by your little shop around ten." Turning to the Lerners, she said, "Shall we meet tomorrow? Wear your jeans. The studio is probably a dusty dungeon. I haven't been in there since I got home."

Randall set down his drink. "I've got to be running too." Nodding to Daria, he hesitated, then turned to Frances. "Don't forget to call the alarm company tomorrow. They can have that glitch fixed in no time."

Molly offered a halfhearted wave and said, "Nice to meet you both." She blew a kiss to Daria and ignored Frances.

"I'll walk out with you and Em," Randall offered.

Outside, in the courtyard, Randall said, "Well done, Molly Doyle. Didn't think you had it in you."

Brushing past him, she grabbed Emma's hand. "Drop dead."

Molly heard Randall's laughter all the way to the pickup. Slamming the door harder than necessary, she shot a look at Emma. "Don't say one word, okay?"

"Can I laugh?"

"Emma!"

Back at the apartment, Molly's thoughts were running into each other as she tried to organize the scrawls in her small notebook. The cryptic shorthand she'd had to devise as she and Emma toured the upstairs at La Casa was nearly undecipherable. She headed downstairs to check for calls. Max had left a message. If the Art Deco statues are genuine, he said, he'd offer nine thousand each for *Sun Worshiper* and *Cabaret Girl*. For *Bather with a Cap*, he'd go to twenty; and for the *pièce de résistance*, *Friends Forever*, the female figure with the two greyhounds, he was firm at thirty. Molly dropped her pen. Sixty-eight thousand? *Ohmigod!* It didn't take her long to figure twenty-five percent equaled seventeen thousand smackeroos. It was too late to call him, but she decided to play it safe in case he changed his mind. She hurriedly scrawled each figure's name and offered price on a sheet of computer paper, indicated her acceptance, and faxed it to Max's office. She wasn't taking chances. Buyer's remorse afflicted antiques dealers as well as collectors.

All her excitement couldn't stop the fatigue from making her eyes blur. Holding back a yawn, she decided to sort out the rest of her notes in the morning. She did a last minute check of the showroom, then headed upstairs. Popping her head in Emma's room, she saw that her niece was sound asleep with Tiger nestled behind her back. She made a mental note to ask for an extra blessing for Max in her nightly prayers. Climbing into bed, Molly blew a kiss to her father's photo and was about to turn off the lamp when the phone rang. It was almost eleven. Late night calls made her nervous. Her first thought was something happened to Bitsy. When she heard Daria's apology for waking her, she let out a small sigh. "I'm still awake."

"I just wanted you to know what a champ you are," Daria said. "Frances overstepped herself with that boxes in the studio thing."

"I'm hardly a champ. Just nearly broke. It isn't easy trading my ego for what looks to be a huge commission."

"Molly! If you're light on cash, why didn't you tell me?"

"It's not that disastrous. It's just my capital to buy good quality merch is a little anemic."

"If you need an angel, let me know. I'd be happy to front for you. In the meantime, don't get in a snit over Frances. She means well."

"That's reassuring, because I don't take lightly to being treated like a servant."

"I don't either."

"Hey . . . are you okay? You seemed awfully quiet when Emma and I came in."

"I'm fine. Just tired," Daria said.

Molly no sooner hung up when the phone rang again. She had a feeling it was Randall. She picked it up and said, "I'm fine. I'm taking the job. I'm not mad at you, okay?"

She heard his laughter, then a click.

After a quick espresso and apple cake with Emma at Tosca's the next morning, Molly was at her desk preparing the database on the computer. As tired as she'd been, she'd slept little the night before. Thinking about the vast collection, her brain wouldn't shut down. The possibility of a once-in-a-lifetime sale and extraordinary commission was too staggering to allow her to do more than nod off. It had been raining on and off, and tourism had slowed to a trickle. She didn't expect much traffic today. She could work on planning the videos and inventory while the shop was open. First thing she needed to do was categorize each item by type, then style, if a period piece, for approximate date of execution—or the "circa"—and then where it would best sell: local client, local sale, or at auction, and which house would bring the best price. She then decided to ask Sister Phil, who she'd discovered was a closet computer nerd, to create a Web site to showcase the contents of La Casa. Something simple, much like the auction houses had, and then notify clients, dealers, and specialized collectors. There would be no auction, of course, since she wasn't a licensed auctioneer, but she'd set the prices and then consider reasonable offers.

The artwork was the biggest headache. A lovely one,

she had to admit, but much more complex than the furniture, the objets d'art, or the smalls. Research on each and
every artist had to be done and what their current values
were. She'd found several contemporary works in one of
the large modern style bedrooms and wasn't familiar with
the artists. She thought about calling Eve Jensen, a local
gallery owner particularly interested in the California
artists of the early sixties and seventies. The European art
throughout the house, while not household names, Molly
recognized as once obscure artists now enjoying a revival.
The British, Flemish, and Italian regional favorites were
in need of a qualified appraiser, and she immediately
thought of Nicholas Hahn. How funny, she mused, to have
just seen his name in her address book. Putting that
thought aside, she made a list of clients and several dealers who could afford the prices she would have to set, and
to contact them once the Web site was up. Last, but not
least, Max and the auction houses for some of the pricier
items, and then the Franchi's in Boston for the movie
memorabilia.

She had almost finished entering the categories when
Frances rushed into the shop. "I've only got a few minutes
to chat, Molly. I'm meeting Jason and Steffi for lunch.
We've decided to do the boxes another time. It's been
years since I've been down to Ventana, and a change of
scene might do me good." Settling in the chair next to
Molly's desk, she said, "Let's get down to business then,
shall we?"

"Fine. I haven't drawn up a contract, but for the moment we'll do this verbally. I'll do the sale, but there are
some conditions we need to discuss."

Waving her hand in the air, Frances said, "Oh, whatever

you think is fair. Just get started. I want to leave in a few weeks, but you can take all the time you need. I realize it's a huge undertaking, so I'll set up an account for you to deposit funds while I'm gone."

"That's fine, but that's not what I want to discuss. I'd like you to remove anything you don't want sold. If you change your mind about an item after I've valued it and priced it, my commission will stand. Since you won't be present at the sale, I'm not to be held liable for theft or damages. As I mentioned before, my commission will be twenty-five percent on furniture, objets d'art, and smalls. On artwork or anything I have to send to auction, it will be ten percent."

Jumping up from the chair, Frances said, "Great. Type it up and I'll sign it." Checking her watch, she nearly yelped, "I'm going to be late. Look, call me later today and we'll meet at La Casa and get you set up with keys and the alarm system, such as it is."

Before Molly could reply, Frances was already headed out the door. Molly placed her hands on both knees under the desk to stop them from trembling. She took a deep breath and yelled, "Yes!"

Emma poked her head out of the storage room and said, "This calls for a celebration. How's Chinese tonight?" Running to Molly, she threw her arms around her and laughed. "Oh, I can't wait to get started. I've got to see if those bombé chests in the hall are really what I think they are."

Molly grinned. "They're real. I checked them out last night when you were in the Venetian bedroom drooling over the painted furniture."

"We're not going to be lean now, are we?"

Molly hugged Emma. "No. More like fat cats."

*B*y Friday night Molly and Emma had finished the upstairs bedrooms. They'd videotaped every item, checked
for authenticity, condition, and taken measurements. This
time, Molly's handwritten notes were precise and legible.
Emma's gift of instant recall had been a life saver as she
called out style and era sometimes faster than Molly could
form them in her mind. Frances, thankfully, left them
pretty much alone. She flitted in and out to mark an object
she'd decided to keep, and to sometimes drop off more
pastries and a thermos of Kona coffee for Molly. The
Lerners were still down the coast at Ventana, a favored
hideaway resort of celebrities, and had stopped by once
while Molly was there to see the boxes in the studio.
When Jason stopped counting at forty-seven boxes, he
threw up his hands and told Molly they were knee-deep in
the new script and would table the search for later. However, he'd shown an interest in the French bibliotheque in
the study, and when Molly told him she was pricing it at
twenty-five thousand, then warned him about the holes in
the back from the bolts, he hadn't cared. "It's fantastic.
Consider it sold," he'd said, then wrote a check on the
spot. He gave her his home address and asked if she'd

arrange the shipping for him. In the blink of an eye, Molly's merchandise fund gained $6,250. Frances was delighted, and Molly was ecstatic. She and Emma planned to celebrate after the noon mass on Sunday, with lunch at Chevy's Mexican restaurant. They might even invite Randall, she teased Emma.

When Molly pulled into the garage behind the shop on Friday night, Emma was fast asleep. Reaching over to gently wake her, Molly paused and watched her. She thought about the richness Emma had brought to her life. More than a niece, she had quickly become a treasured companion, and, Molly realized, had the makings of one hell of an antiquer. Her astonishing grasp of furniture style and circa, of porcelain and silver makers' marks, was almost spooky. When she said her prayers at night, she thanked God for Emma, then asked forgiveness for hoping her sister Carrie would never return to take her away.

Bitsy, thankfully, had left for a spa in Calistoga, and so wasn't around to bedevil them. And Judith Martin, otherwise known as Sister Phil, Emma's tutor and a retired nun, had decided to join her. Besides, Molly thought, she didn't need the distraction of Bitsy and Emma not seeing eye-to-eye on circa or style.

Virginia, the new salesperson she'd hired to take Bitsy's place on the weekends, was doing a fine job. Sales were still sluggish, and while Max's promised truckload of new merchandise was yet to be seen, Molly felt confident *Treasures* was in good hands.

On Saturday morning, before heading to La Casa, Molly and Emma stopped by Tosca's to see Bennie and have a quick sugar-spiked breakfast. "I checked the garage sale ads last night," Molly told Emma. "Thank God there was nothing to entice us. We need to spend as much time at the big house this weekend as possible. We'll be able to get much more done in the daylight, and the fatigue factor will be less. Eve Jensen is coming by later to check out the contemporary art, and I left a message for Nicholas Hahn about the fine art. Virginia will cover the shop for us, so I'll come back around ten to let her in, then pick up some sandwiches from Bruno's for our lunch."

"Don't forget that pasta salad we like. And some brownies, okay?"

Molly jotted that down on a napkin. "Right, got it."

"Jeeze, Molly!" Bennie Infama, the owner of Tosca's, said as he pulled up a chair. "You gotta write something simple like that down these days? That big hacienda driving you nuts?"

Molly rolled her eyes. "The mind is on overload, Bennie. La Casa has so many different types of merch, it's almost boggling. I've had to set up a database just to keep things straight."

"Sounds like big bucks, huh?"

"Mucho biggo," Emma said.

Filling Molly's cup with the new pot he'd brought, Bennie said, "That's one weird house, huh? I got lost in it at a birthday party when I was a kid. Daria finally found me and saved me from Mr. O'Brien. Man, he was livid."

"Why would he be mad at you for getting lost?" Emma said. "That's kinda dumb if you ask me. People are happy when kids are found."

"Not him! He was red hot, you know? See, they had this big playroom all decked out like an Egyptian tomb or something. I remember because I'd just seen one of those Abbott and Costello movies where they meet the mummy. Anyway, it was being torn out, and stuff was all over the place and another wall was up with a door that hadn't been taken out yet. So I went though the door and found myself in between the rooms. Only the door jammed or something and I couldn't get it back open. I banged and hollered until I was hoarse."

"Good thing Daria heard you," Molly said.

"Good thing Frances's mother was with her too; she saved me from Mr. O'Brien. He was damn near foaming at the mouth." Bennie downed his coffee, then shook his head. "I can still see him now. I thought he was gonna skin me raw. He had a bunch of movie props in between the rooms and said they'd cost a fortune to make and I'd better not have touched them. I swore I hadn't. He shook the hell out of me. I remember telling him that big Egyptian mummy coffin he had in there gave me the creeps. I wanted out of there!"

Emma's eyes seemed to triple in size. "Was there a mummy inside? Did you open it up and see it?"

"Me? No way!"

After Bennie left to care for his customers, Emma said, "Wow! That must have been something to see."

Molly pretended to shudder. "Glad it's not lying around, huh?"

"I wouldn't have been scared. I'd have opened it. Anyway, tell me about this fine art guy. Why do we need him?"

"Nicholas Hahn? Oh, he's . . . ah, he's just an expert I know."

Emma's voice was suddenly flat. "He must be pretty handsome."

Molly looked up from her notes. "Okay, spill it. What's on your mind?"

Emma stabbed at the last bite of her apple cake, then

said, "Your cheeks got all blushy when you mentioned his name."

"Blushy is not a word. And my cheeks are perfectly normal." Reaching for Emma's hand, she brushed it across her face. "See?"

"Well, they *look blushy.*"

"You're being silly, young lady. Nicholas is an old friend and the perfect person to evaluate the art collection."

"Why can't you do it?"

Molly didn't answer for a long moment. She pulled out her cigarettes, gave Emma one of her *don't start* looks, took her time lighting it, then said, "Believe it or not, it's very easy to be fooled by the type of art hanging all over La Casa. We've seen a large number of paintings that depict European landscapes, right?"

"A lot of ships in harbors too. I love the dogs and horse paintings, they're my favorite."

"Yes, they're wonderful. But what I'm worried about is while so many are reminiscent of the nineteenth and twentieth centuries and appear to be genuine, they might not have been painted by the signed artist. And then there are some by artists not that well known except regionally."

When Emma's eyebrows rose, Molly hurriedly said, "Not that they're necessarily fakes, or even reproductions, but they may have been executed by the artist's students. That was very common in those days. Many of the world's most famous artists had students fill in scenery and background colors for their work. If that's the case, then value has to be set differently. I'm not that schooled in detecting the difference. That's why I'm going to contact Nicholas. He's one of the best in the world." But what Molly didn't want to bring up, at least not yet, was the gut-wrenching feeling she'd had when she'd discovered a painting by her cousin Angela's husband, Armand. A branch of the family Molly hadn't mentioned to Emma.

Armand Devereaux was world renowned as one of the finest copyists living. Scores of executive suites all over the world were filled with old masters fresh from Armand's New Orleans studio. All legitimate, all very expensive, and all with Armand's logo deviously entwined in the painting. She had almost fainted last night when examining a painting signed by Hernando Wright, a beloved English artist, she'd noticed something odd about the folds in the gown of a young maid seated under a tree. Taking a closer look with a magnifying glass, she recognized Armand's logo: three small intertwined crosses he incorporated into every copy. When it occurred to her that the film industry was probably a lucrative venue for Armand, and this entire art collection might be phony, visions of thousands of dollar signs floating away in a storm clouded Molly's eyes. She wondered if she should tell Nicholas not to come.

Checking her watch, she said to Emma, "We've got to run."

"Hey, I just got here," Randall said as he came up behind Molly. "Hang on for a few minutes. I haven't seen you two in days."

"We've been working at La Casa every night, and you never did show up to help us move that chest," Emma said.

Setting down his coffee, Randall leaned over and kissed the top of Emma's head. "I got busy. I'll do it today, okay?"

"Too late. Aunt Molly and I managed without you."

Glancing at Molly, Randall said, "Oh, it's like that,

huh? She's already learned the value of laying on guilt? What is it with women?"

Molly laughed. "Leave it to a man to take a simple statement of fact and turn it into a feminine wile. So, Chief, how's tricks? Catch any bad guys lately?"

"Business has been slow. So how're things coming over at Frances's place? You about wrapped up there and ready for the big sale?"

"Are you kidding? We just finished with the upstairs last night. I've still got the studio to go through. Frances tells me there are boxes and boxes of signed celebrity photographs there. Besides, I've still got to get a Web site for the sale."

"Gonna go high-tech on us, huh?"

"It's the best way for my out of town connections to see what's available."

"And then there's the greenhouse," Emma added.

Molly's head almost snapped. "Greenhouse?"

"I saw it yesterday when you were in the atrium having a smoke. I was getting a drink of water in the kitchen and then went out to the herb garden. It's kinda way in back, but it was still light enough to see the sun reflecting on the glass roof, and then you called me and I forgot to tell you about it."

"Well, I'm not about to list a bunch of plants. Frances will have to get a nurseryman or something."

Leaning in toward Molly, Emma said, "Are you going to ask Randall to have Mexican with us tomorrow after mass?"

Before Molly could reply, Randall said, "Hey, I'd love to, but I'm going with Frances up to Phil's Fish House in Moss Landing for lunch. How's about a rain check?"

The disappointment on Emma's face tore at Molly's heart. "Actually," she quickly said to her, "we probably won't have time tomorrow. We might not want to get back to work after a big lunch. I was going to take you to Daria's for an early dinner and then call it quits. She told me she was having gnocchi made for you."

Darting a sly grin at Randall, Emma said, "Cool. I'd rather go to Daria's anyway."

Feeling the chill in the air, Randall finished his coffee. "I'm keeping you two from your work. Maybe I'll stop by later, huh?"

"Great," Molly said as she gave Emma a warning look. "And do give my best to Frances."

Randall eyed Molly. "That sounded bitchy, Molly Doyle."

"Did it, now. Well, gosh. Naughty me."

## ~~~ 7 ~~~

*L*ater that day, Eve Jensen was nearly foaming at the mouth. "I'm so thrilled you asked me to come to La Casa, Molly! There's at least eight paintings in these two bedroom suites that would drive two or three clients of mine nuts! I'll take them all. Write up the consignment papers and we're in business." A good fifteen years older than Molly, Eve was portly, wore chandelier earrings that set off a henna little boy hairstyle, and dressed in colorful jackets over a constant uniform of black skirts and shells. Eve's art gallery in Carmel, *Wood Presents*, specialized in California artists from the early sixties. Now with a new collection of Musselmans, Heckings, Morgans, and three Clausens before her, she was waving her hands in front of her face and laughing. "I never thought I'd welcome these hot flashes, but baby, bring them on!" Holding onto a pair of smaller paintings, she said, "I'll take these two as well. Joe Tanous and Bill Stone are terrific, and both are well-loved local artists. I adore their work. These won't last a day."

Molly liked Eve the moment they'd met. Bitsy had introduced them some months ago in the bar at the La Playa Hotel, where many of the art and antiques dealers congregated to unwind after shops were closed. Down to earth and full of fun, Eve was a rare gallery owner who gave consigning artists a bigger share of the ticket price than most. "I've worked up a preliminary consignment agreement that I'd like you to look over," Molly said, pleased that Eve was thrilled with the artwork. "If you think it's fair, I'll pass it on to Frances for her approval."

Still eyeing a Morgan, Eve sighed. "Damn, but Richard is fantastic. He should be up there with the big guys. National promotion is everything, as usual. Talent doesn't mean a damn if you're not out there in the art world's face. If you're not nuts, or infamous, or a marketing genius like Kincaid, you might as well forget it." Tearing her eyes from the painting, Eve added, "Have Frances look it over, then call me. I'm good to go whenever you're ready."

"I hope to see her today." Pulling a copy of the agreement from her notebook, Molly handed it to Eve. "I have to check on the movers down in the study. Take a look at this and then meet me in the morning room. I've got a thermos full of Bennie's espresso."

As they reached the stairs, Eve paused, then gave Molly a hug. "Thanks so much for calling me first. I'll do good by the boys. And Frances, of course." Glancing around the upper hall, Eve said, "You know, I've always been curious about this house. Mind if I snoop a little? I've been here for charity things, but never got past the salon." Giving Molly a wink, she said, "It's not every day you get to sneak a peek in one of these old mansions. Especially this one."

Molly grinned. "Sure, go ahead. Don't stay too long, though. Frances could pop in at any moment, and well . . ."

"I'll be quick. Just a tiny glance from the doors. Is all this stuff the real thing?"

"Not everything. I think a lot of it came from movie sets. There's a ton of boxes in the studio filled with photos. I'm hoping I'll find stills from sets for verification. A friend of Frances's, Jason Lerner, said he'd run across several, but they're mixed in with celebrity and party photos."

Molly was no sooner back in the study when the doorbell rang.

Emma was on the move before she could blink. "I'll get it," she said.

Using both hands, Emma opened the heavy door and grinned when she saw Randall. He handed her a bag of Pecan Sandies and said, "Got milk?"

"Of course not," Emma replied. "This isn't my house, you know."

Randall pulled his other hand from behind his back and handed her another bag. "I know that. So I brought some."

"Is this supposed to be a peace offering for not helping us the other day?"

"Yeah. You got a problem with that?"

Emma giggled, then reached up and gave Randall a hug. "Accepted. Aunt Molly is in the study with the movers. Let's get her and take a break."

In the study, Molly had stacked dozens of books from the bibliotheque near the fireplace and now stood back with her fingers crossed. She prayed the four men would be able to get the behemoth out to the truck in one piece. Randall and Emma arrived just as the glass doors were taped, and huge, soft mesh belts were strapped around the case. She marveled at how quickly the men had placed a series of furniture dollies under the piece.

As the bookcase was slowly maneuvered away from the wall, Randall said, "You sold that already? Who the hell was the sucker you nicked for that puppy?"

Unfazed, Molly kept her eyes glued to the movers. "Jason Lerner, and he got a good deal." When the bookcase was a few feet away from the wall, Molly began to breathe easier. Eve waved from the hall and said to Randall, "Hey, Mr. Fuzz, how's tricks?"

"Eve! Good to see you too. Come on in," Randall said.

Molly was about to say something to Randall when one of the movers yelled, "It's tipping!"

Randall was at his side like a shot. "Hang on! I've got my shoulder against the back." To the men on the other side, he said, "Easy now . . . take it forward." Two men at the front held on while the third man at the back shoved another dolly under the case. When he shouted all clear, the fourth man, who'd called out that it was tipping, caught his foot on one of the dolly's casters. Falling backward, he crashed through the wall.

Confident the case was stable, Randall reached through the splintered slats and helped the mover to his feet. "You okay?"

"Yeah, sure." Turning to see where he'd fallen, the mover shook his head. "What the hell kind of jerry-built wall is this? It's like cardboard. Three flimsy slats? No wonder I bailed through." Peering into the gap, he pulled a flashlight out of his pocket and sent a beam into the dark space. "Shit! It's another room! Hey, come on over here and take a look."

Randall moved in closer and took the flashlight.

Squeezing in sideways, they could hear him laugh. "He's right. It's another room." Coming back out, he brushed cobwebs from his hair. Looking at the movers, he pointed to the bookcase. "Let's get this thing out of here before Molly here has a stroke. You guys need help, just yell."

Taking Emma's hand, Randall said, "Time for cookies and milk," then gave the movers one of his *no cute remarks looks*.

Eve Jensen wagged her finger. "Watch the carbs, Randall."

"Care to join us?" he asked.

"No thanks. I take my carbs from scotch."

The mover who had fallen returned and said, "I got to go back in that hole. My cell phone must have come off when I fell."

"I'll hold the flashlight while you check it out," Randall said as he moved to the opening in the wall. Ducking in behind the mover, he angled the beam on the floor. "I'll move the light in sweeps, okay? You see something, give me a holler."

Not long afterward, they could hear the mover yell, "To the right . . . yeah, that's it. I got it." And then they heard him shout, "What the hell? Hey, come in closer. You won't believe this!"

Molly moved to the wall. "What's going on?"

The cookie Emma had already snatched from the bag was halfway to her mouth when she heard Randall say, "Well, I'll be damned."

Curious, Eve moved to Molly and poked her in the arm, "Hey, maybe more treasures? Let's take a look."

"I'm not going in there," Molly said. "It's probably full of spiders and dead bugs."

Emma shoved the cookie in her mouth, squeezed between Molly and Eve, and headed to the hole in the wall.
"Scaredy cat! I'm going to see what they found."

Randall was already at the entrance. "Out of the way,
squirt. Go get all those guys outside and tell them we need
a hand here and to bring back those furniture dollies."

"What's in there?" Molly asked.

"Besides dead rats, spiders, and cockroaches." Eve
added.

Randall grinned, thoroughly enjoying the suspense, "A
surprise. You'll probably get big bucks for it too."

"Oh, cool!"

Molly pulled Emma away from the wall. "Maybe I
should call Frances?"

"Save your quarter. She should be here any time. When
I dropped her off, she said she was coming over."

When Emma returned with the movers a few minutes
later, she said Frances had arrived and was on her way in.

The moment Frances stepped into the study, she threw
her hands on her hips and said, "What the hell is going on
here? What happened to that wall?"

"We don't know," Randall answered. "It was like that
when they pulled the bookcase out. Found something interesting, though."

Turning to Molly, Frances said, "I haven't all day, what
did you find?"

Leaning against the desk, Molly kept her arms folded.
A slight pulsing over her eye was about to erupt, and she'd
be damned if she'd let Randall see her tap it. "I have no
idea. You'll have to ask Randall."

"Well, don't just stand there, Molly, go and get it,"
Frances said.

Randall's move between the two women was hardly noticed. Knowing Molly's temper, he decided he'd better head off an eruption. Frances had no idea who she was playing with, and he didn't think this was the time to explain the rules. Randall could see Molly was ready to bite her lip in half. "Okay," he said to the movers, "let's get that puppy out here."

The silence in the room as they waited for the men to come out was almost palpable. Emma, for once, was quiet. Eve Jensen leaned against the bookcase and pretended to examine a book. Molly turned away and said several Hail Marys in rapid succession. When they heard Randall shout, "Coming through," Emma was hovering near the hole in the wall, Eve was standing behind Frances, and Molly continued to keep her back turned.

When Frances said, "Oh, my God!" Molly finally swung around to see what the commotion was.

Her hand flew to her mouth and she said, "Holy moley!"

Rolling out on the furniture dollies was an Egyptian coffin at least six feet long. Emma squealed, "Could that be the one Bennie saw when he was a kid?"

Covered in grime, layers of dirt and cobwebs, the once beautifully painted coffin looked as if it had been buried in a tomb for generations. "It's filthy!" Frances said. "I don't want it in here. Take it back."

"Hold on," Randall said to the movers. His patience at a dangerous level, he looked at Frances and tried to sound upbeat. "Are you sure? Hell, a little cleanup and this could be a big ticket item."

"What do you think, Molly?" Frances finally said. "Is this something you could sell?"

Pretending to brush a stray lock from her forehead,

Molly's fingers moved over her pulsing eye. She darted a look at Randall and said, "I can sell anything. It's your call."

"I can't imagine who would want the thing. Obviously Father didn't. Well, then, I guess it stays. I'm sure you'll make it presentable, Molly."

*You bet your ass I will, and it's gonna cost you, sweetie.* Molly merely nodded, then said, "Maybe we ought to see what's inside? Who knows what we might find?"

One of the movers handed Randall a crowbar. "I figured we might need this for the bolts in the bookcase."

"Let's see if we can get it open," Randall said. Glancing around the room, he nodded to Molly and Eve. "We'll need some room to set the top down once it's off. See what you ladies can move out of the way."

Slowly, and ever so carefully, the lid came free. All four men, including Randall, lifted the carved top and set it on the floor. When they rose, Randall was as surprised as any of them and almost didn't catch Frances when she wilted. Eve's face was frozen in horror, her body so rigid she looked as if her feet were nailed to the floor. Emma's eyes were huge behind her Harry Potter glasses, and both hands were clamped over her mouth. Molly's head, swaying from side to side, looked like a bobbing doll on a dashboard. Her mouth was working oddly and all she could manage was, "*Oh, no . . . not again.*"

The four movers were dumbstruck. Randall steered Frances to one of the leather club chairs, then moved to the open coffin. He understood now why it had been so heavy. Half filled with sand so white it almost sparkled, a human skeleton lay before them. He could even make out remnants of dark hair in the sand, and pieces of what appeared to be a colorful beaded garment covered most of the rib cage.

"Okay," Randall commanded, "everyone move back. Don't touch a thing."

He pulled out his cell phone and called the station, snapping out orders so fast, he barely heard Molly say, *"Goddamn it! I'm not going through this again!"*

## 8

*A* shaken Eve Jensen dropped Molly and Emma off at Daria's. "Fix her a tall one," Eve said to Daria. "She's kind of upset. If I didn't have a client arriving soon, I'd join you. Maybe you can take her to get her car later? I've got to get back to the gallery." When Daria asked what was wrong, Eve just shuddered. "Uh, Molly will fill you in. There was a . . . well, a little problem over at La Casa. I imagine Randall will be by soon enough." Easing out of Daria's private back room at the restaurant, she said again, "I've really got to run."

"I'll tell you," Emma said to Daria. Her face was a tad pale, but she remembered her manners, and thanked Eve for driving them. "Aunt Molly will be fine. She just needs to gather her inner resources."

Eve looked at Emma as if she were from another planet. Daria merely shook her head, then said, "Oh, shit. Now what?"

By the time Molly downed a Gentleman Jack and soda and half smoked two cigarettes, Emma had told Daria what happened, including Frances's rude comments. "Aunt Molly? Did I get all the facts right?" Emma probed.

Staring into space, Molly nodded. "Better than I would have."

"Oh, and then," Emma went on, "Randall sent the movers over to the station to give their prints because they touched the coffin." She paused. "And then Frances came out of her phony girly thing when that movie guy showed up."

"Jason?" Daria asked.

"Right. He was on his way to Monterey to buy some stuff for his computer and decided to stop by and see how the movers made out with that bookcase he bought."

Rapt, Daria said, "And?"

Emma shrugged. "That's all I know. Ms. Wood and I took Aunt Molly out of the house because she was beginning to talk funny, and then we came here."

"I wasn't talking funny, Emma. I was—"

"You were mumbling to yourself," Emma said with concern.

Molly grinned. "I was putting a hex on Frances." Turning to Daria, she said, "Look, I know Frances is a close friend, but I'm about ready to smack her one."

"I know she's kind of bossy, but she gets high-strung when she's nervous."

"High-strung? Baloney! She's arrogant as hell, a spoiled brat and a typical goddamned temperamental artist. It's second nature to her, and I'm not going to let her order me around like a lackey."

"It's a big sale, Aunt Molly."

"Lesson time, Emma. We don't have to grovel. Ever! We'll get by without that damn collection, don't you worry."

"Molly! You're not thinking of quitting, are you?" Daria asked.

"I've had my fill of dead bodies, okay? Carmel was supposed to be a haven . . . a . . . a quiet place to lick my wounds. Since I've been here, I've had a woman die in my arms, her killer stab me; I've opened a closet and found a dead man, and then ducked a bullet from a crazy man. And now . . . a dead body in a mummy coffin? No way! Sorry. I didn't sign up for this."

Before Daria could reply, her busboy captain, Manuel, popped his head in the room and said, "Call for you from *el jefe*." Handing Daria a portable phone, he said to Emma, "You want to come in the kitchen and help me tease *el primo* cooker?"

"Go ahead, Em," Molly said. "Don't worry. I'm fine now, okay?"

Emma shook her head. "Thank you, Manuel, but not this time." Linking her arm with Molly's, she said, "I'll just stay here with you."

Daria waited for Manuel to leave, then took Randall's call. "I'll tell her," she said. "We'll be in the back room." Glancing at her watch, she added, "Yeah, we can have an early dinner. Call Lucero. See if he wants to join us." Daria paused, then said, "Uh, no. I don't think that's wise just now, *capice*?"

"I'm going home," Molly announced when Daria hung up. "And I'm going to call Max and tell him to get that damn truck full of merch he promised down here right away. I am no longer in the estate sale business." Slapping her hand on the table, she added, "Frances will have to find someone else." Reaching down for her tote, she slumped back in the chair. "Damn it! My truck is still at La Casa. Screw it! I'll just walk down there and get it. I need the exercise anyway."

"Aw, come on, Molly," Daria said, "Don't leave now.

Randall is on his way, and he said Officer Wilkins found your keys still in the truck and he's taking it over to the alley behind the shop. You're upset, I know, but you've got to hear what he told me. You'll die laughing."

"Don't talk about death, okay? Randall can keep his black cop humor to himself. Better yet, let him share it with Frances. Let her die laughing. In fact, that's not a bad idea."

"Tsk-tsk, Ms. Doyle. What terrible thoughts from a good Catholic," Randall said as he slid into a chair next to her. "Better go to communion tomorrow."

"How the hell did you get here so fast?" Daria asked.

"I was on my cell outside when I called you. Did you tell Molly the good news?"

"No. I thought I'd let you handle it."

"Frances left town?" Molly shot out.

"Hey, come on. Play nice." Randall said.

"Screw you. I don't play games. Seems to me you ought to know that by now."

"The so-called mummy wasn't real. Jason took one look at that thing and laughed like hell. He recognized it right off from some photos he and Steffi had gone through for their book. He said it was from a movie that had been scrapped back in the seventies. His dad brought it up here for some fancy playroom he'd had built." Patting Molly on the shoulder, he grinned. "So, no dead body and no big mystery." When he heard Emma's sigh of relief, he added, "You weren't scared, were you! You probably figured it out before the rest of us."

"It was kind of movie-ish looking. I mean, they *were* movie people." Glancing at Molly, she said, "Aunt Molly and I weren't scared. Maybe just surprised."

Randall smiled kindly. "That's what I figured."

"Is it still there?" Molly asked. "Never mind. I don't care. I'm done with that place."

Randall stared at her in disbelief. "What the hell is bugging you? Come on! I just told you it was a prop. Get that Irish temper under control. Frances is counting on you."

"You know what? I'm sick of hearing about Frances." Molly picked up her tote and slung it over her shoulder, barely missing Randall's head. "Mind your own business for once. Go arrest a jaywalker. Do something productive instead of catching fainting maidens."

"You two at it again? Jeeze, you'd think they were married," Dan Lucero said as he sauntered in. Giving Daria a kiss on the cheek, the district attorney of Monterey County rubbed his hands. "Thanks for the invite. I was over at Bennie's when Randall called. What's for dinner? No. Don't tell me. I love surprises." Settling across from Randall and Molly, he said to Randall, "What gives, huh? That thing you had the coroner's office pick up? What the hell is going on? I got a call on my cell about it."

"It's nothing. Big mistake on my part. Found out it's an old movie prop. I'd already called it in, so I have to follow the damn procedure through. Phillips will release it tomorrow." Randall caught Lucero's eye and said, "Isn't that right, counselor? That's how things work."

A half beat behind Randall, Lucero answered, "Right. Regulations."

"Well, now that that's settled, who's hungry?" Daria asked.

"I'm famished!" Frances said as she glided in. "Nothing heavy, though, Daria." Fanning her face, she moved up behind Randall, leaned down and hugged him. "My hero!" she said, pulling out the chair next to him. "I don't think I've ever fainted before. How thrilling to have the chief of police catch me. I guess you've all heard about that Egyptian coffin! Thank heavens Jason happened to stop by."

Giving Lucero a big smile, Frances said, "And if it isn't Dan Lucero! It's been ages since we . . . well, since your first election party." Winking at Daria, she said, "That was some party."

Lucero avoided looking at Daria. "Yeah, good to see you too. What a surprise, Frances. I didn't know you'd be here."

Frances's arm trailed along Randall's shoulder. "I was on my way back to the inn when I saw you heading here. I couldn't pass up the chance to say hello. I'm disappointed in you, Dan. You haven't come by to welcome me home."

"I've been meaning to," Lucero said. "Been up to my ears. You know how it is."

Molly was already at the door, motioning to Emma to follow, when Daria said, "Don't leave, Molly. How's osso buco sound? Or maybe lamb shanks and polenta? I'll have it on the table in minutes."

Molly gave Daria a halfhearted wave. "Thanks, but I think I'll head home. We have to check on Tiger anyway. She's pregnant and I want to get her inside."

Not bothering to turn around, Frances called out, "Oh, Molly . . . would you see to it that the mess in the study is cleared up tomorrow? There's dust and dirt all over the place from that ugly coffin."

Daria held her breath and wasn't surprised when she saw Molly stiffen, then leave without answering. She nearly clapped. Lucero shot Randall a questioning look, but Randall purposely avoided eye contact. Frances's high-handed attitude with Molly was bordering on an arrogance he abhorred. While he silently applauded her silence, he kept his face bland and focused on the cut crystal ashtray on the table.

Emma had a hard time keeping up with Molly as they walked home. She had never seen her aunt angry, and knew this wasn't a time to joke about the way her eyebrows were dancing all over her forehead. Sister Phil had told her that prayer was a powerful way to sort out problems. It was much like meditation, and helped clear out cobwebs. Plain talk worked as well as anything. Emma decided she would talk this over with God tonight and try to figure out what to do to help her aunt.

Virginia, the part-time helper for *Treasures*, had already closed the shop when Molly and Emma arrived. Glancing at her watch, Molly didn't realize it was already six. She headed straight for her desk to check the day's sales tags. The tight set of her lips, which had been glued in place since leaving Daria's, softened somewhat when she sat down and added up the receipts. At least Virginia had a good day. Fifteen hundred bucks in smalls was not to be sneezed at.

Peering over Molly's shoulder, Emma said, "Oh, hey, she sold another pair of those Meissen lamps! Yahoo! And the pearl-handled Victorian fruit set too." Picking up the stack of tags, Emma flipped through them. "I'm kinda sorry to see that pond boat go, but we'll find another. At least she didn't take a knock on it."

Molly stared at Emma, then began to laugh. "You're a gem, you know that? What would I do without you?"

Emma threw her arms around Molly. "*Au contraire!*

What would I do without you? We're a good team. We'll be fine. We don't need that uppity *artiste*. I never did like her anyway."

Molly tussled her hair. "Maybe I should have listened to you. Oh, well, it was a nice dream while it lasted. At least we've got a commission on the bibliotheque, the Art Deco statues, and whatever artwork Eve sells. And wait until Frances gets my bill for all the work we've done. I'm not letting her off the hook for that. But first I've got to call Max, and then Nicholas to tell them to ignore my message."

And, Molly thought, she wouldn't have to face Nicholas with Armand's copies. To her disappointment, she'd found more of his works, and much of the French furniture in the salon turned out to be reproductions. Excellent quality, but still not the period pieces her first quick glance had hoped for. The pegs on cabinets and the mortise and tenon joints on the drawers were all there, but under closer examination, she'd seen their perfection; the instant signal of a machine-made piece. So enthralled by the whole of the collection, Molly knew it was easy to become blinded, even for a seasoned dealer. All would not have been lost, however. Furniture from movies would sell like hotcakes. Photo stills of the films showing the pieces would guarantee top price, and were probably in some of those boxes in the studio.

She had planned to give Emma a tour and point out each piece and the telltale signs. Now that wouldn't happen, but Emma was young and there was plenty of time for show and tell.

"I'm in the mood for some of that great meat loaf you made. What about you?" Emma asked.

"How about if we go out and have that Mexican tonight instead of tomorrow after mass?"

Emma sighed. "No, let's just stay home. Maybe we

should get to bed early. We've been up late for two weeks. I can tell you're tired. You've got dark circles under your eyes."

"Really? Do I look that bad?" When Molly saw Emma grin, she said, "Smarty. Go fix anything you want."

"Oh, what about Eve?" Emma asked. "Did anyone let her know the coffin was a fake? She was pretty scared."

"You're right. I forgot all about her. I'll call her."

Molly was surprised Eve didn't answer the phone at the shop. Then she remembered she had an appointment with a client. She left a message. "Hi, Eve. It's Molly. Just wanted to let you know that *thing* was a movie prop. Can you imagine? Anyway, thanks so much for taking Emma and me to Daria's." Molly paused for a second, half ready to tell Eve she was quitting, then decided against it. "Uh, listen, about the artwork . . . evidently there's more somewhere. Frances mentioned it but couldn't remember what or where. Give me a call and we'll set up another time to check it out."

Molly took advantage of Emma's absence and lit a cigarette. Her nerves were still a little shaky, and the more she thought about all the money she was giving up, the more agitated she became. Max was going to have a megahissy fit when she told him. He'd try to talk her out of it, and, she realized, all his arguments would have merit. He would tell her she was being stubborn and letting her pride get in the way of a fantastic opportunity. He would also say that a commission of that probable size was worth putting up with a prima donna. He would tell her he'd done it himself, time and again. If they had to like every customer they ever dealt with, they'd have been out of business years ago. Molly decided to wait on calling

Max. Nicholas was more important. She quickly punched his number before she lost her nerve.

As she'd expected, Nicholas Hahn was utterly charming, warm, and delighted to hear from her. He'd received her message and had planned to call her when he arrived in San Francisco. "Elizabeth? How wonderful that we connected. Oh, forgive me, darling . . . it is Molly now, yes? Max has explained you have reclaimed your name. I was devastated to have missed your call."

She laughed. "Yes, I'm Molly again. And it feels wonderful. I'm glad I was able to catch you before you left. A situation has come up, and while I'd adore seeing you again, I'm giving up the project."

There was a slight pause, then Molly heard his sigh. "Ah, the black light has told you more than you wanted to know, yes?"

"I didn't have to use one. Many of the pictures are Armand's. I was too caught up in the vast treasure trove to spend much time on the artwork at first. The home is huge, and jammed with furniture and smalls. I've spent almost two weeks listing merch. You won't believe the database I had to create. When I finally took a picture down and began to eyeball it, I saw his logo."

"Not to worry, my darling. Armand's works bring good prices. I know several clients who will buy them. As I am in need of a holiday, I will come as planned, yes? It will be wonderful to see you again. I arrive in San Francisco on Monday. Max and I have already spoken, and he will drive me down." There was a pause at Nicholas's end, then he said, "I don't wish to probe, but are you free to tell me why you are not pursuing this? And I assume you have not contacted Max, yes?"

"Not yet. I wanted to reach you first and save you a trip. Shall I be totally blunt?"

Nicholas laughed. "Have we not always been so with each other?"

"Pride, Nicholas. Nothing more than pride. I'm being treated as a servant instead of a professional in my field."

"This client is a woman, yes?"

"Worse. She's an artist. An excellent one too."

"Ah, yes. I see the situation. Do I know of this artist?"

"No." Molly filled Nicholas in on Frances's background, then added, "She will never be a grand master, but her work will endure."

"I am intrigued. As for your frame of mind, I shall not lecture. We must do what we must, yes? In any event, I will see you shortly. It will be a wonderful reunion."

When Molly got off the phone, she was surprised to see Emma sitting at the bottom of the stairs. "Was that Max you were talking to? Did you tell him you quit?" she asked.

"I haven't called Max yet. That was Nicholas. He's still coming. He'll be here in a few days." Coming around from the desk, Molly reached down for Emma's hand. "Let's go up. I'm starving. I'll call Max tomorrow."

## ⚊ 9 ⚊

*E*mma barely touched her food as she and Molly ate at the oversized coffee table in the living room. Molly didn't have much of an appetite either. The movie they were watching on television offered an excuse for little conversation.

"Wow, that was some adventure today, huh? I mean, that phony coffin and mummy?" Emma said during a commercial. "I can't wait to tell Bitsy and Sister Phil when they come home. Bet they'll get a real laugh out of that."

Picking up their dishes, Molly nodded. "Yeah, right out of *Indiana Jones*." She realized how short that sounded and felt awful about it. Emma was doing her best to cheer her up, and here she was sounding like a jerk. "Just goes to show you how clever those movie people are, right? We all fell for it."

The paws on the cat clock on the wall were headed for nine, and Molly held back a yawn. Returning to the living room, she said, "I'm going downstairs to check out the garage sale ads for tomorrow. Looks like we're back on the hunt again. Then I'm calling it a night. Be sure to check Tiger's dishes before you turn in, okay? Mothers-to-be need a lot of food." Leaning over to pet Tiger in Emma's lap, she kissed Emma on the forehead. "Don't stay up too late. We've got to be out of here by seven for the garage sales. Six-thirty if you want fresh hot doughnuts."

When Molly finally climbed into bed, she avoided saying good-night to her father's photo on the night table. She could imagine his face turning dour as he was about to tell her how foolish she was being. Turning away from the photo, she pulled up the blanket and listened to the faint roll of the surf on Carmel Bay. The silence in the village at night was nearly perfect. The loudest sounds, besides the surf and the chatter between the hundreds of pine trees, was an occasional cat announcing that his territory had been breached.

It wasn't too long ago, Molly thought, when her biggest concern when she climbed into bed was what to wear the next day at Porter's. The Manhattan high-end antiques store she ran with her now missing-from-the-law husband catered to the spectrum of society that had buildings named after them. Since moving to Carmel, she'd had more fitful nights than in her entire earlier life. Staring at the ceiling, she said her prayers and fell into her frequent conversations with God. *Go ahead, wag your finger at me. I'm blowing it big time. I should ignore the little diva and just do my job. You did this on purpose just to teach me some humility, right? Hey, I helped solve two murders, remember? Count them . . . two murders. I think that should give me some slack in the big book. Never mind. I can tell you're not impressed.*

Molly closed her eyes, pulled the blanket up over her head, punched her pillow into submission, then sprawled on her stomach. *I don't want to discuss this anymore, if you don't mind. Maybe tomorrow when I stop by to visit. And then, maybe not.*

* * *

In her sweats and sneakers Sunday morning, Molly headed for the kitchen at six and was surprised to find Emma already dressed and pouring hot coffee into the thermos. "What would I do without you?"

'You say that all the time. But don't stop. I like it."

Giving Emma a hug, Molly said, "I'll run down and get the newspaper and checkbook, then we'll head out."

When Molly reached her desk, she almost skidded to a stop. Sitting in the middle were the two Esther Hunt chalk-ware busts of Oriental women Emma had found at a garage sale for the princely sum of twenty dollars. Leaning against the one titled *Lotus Blossom* was an envelope with Molly's name in crisp block letters. She held her breath as she opened it. Inside were the five hundred dollars her sister Carrie had left Emma when she vanished, and a note:

> *My research tells me these two busts will go for a minimum fifteen hundred each.*
>
> *If you don't want to put them in the shop, I know I can sell them on eBay. This should help with the lean days.*
>
> Love, Em

Molly didn't try to stop the tears rushing down her face. After a moment she wiped her eyes on the sleeve of her sweatshirt, then looked up. *Okay, you win. I'm humbled. This is what it's all about, right? Oh, but you're something else.*

Molly put the money back in the envelope, picked up the two busts and ran upstairs. Emma was on the sofa with Tiger in her arms. Molly stood looking at her, then shook her head. "What would I do without you."

Emma cuddled Tiger. "There she goes again."

"Okay, smarty. Put these ladies back in your room. We're off for doughnuts and the wars." She paused, then added, "And we'll go to mass, have that lunch at Chevy's, then get back to work at La Casa."

"Yahoo! She's come to her senses." Emma's yelp spooked Tiger. The plump cat jumped off her lap and ran under a chair.

When Molly saw the concern on Emma's face, she said, "Don't worry. She's fine. And so are we now." Giving Emma a big smile, she jerked her head. "Let's rock and roll."

## ⚑ 10 ⚑

Randall and Lucero were sitting at the far end of the patio at The Village Corner Restaurant in Carmel, having made a date for breakfast to discuss the coffin found at La Casa the day before. They'd just ordered when Randall said, "Lerner's full of shit. That was no movie prop. I know a set of bones when I see them. And they don't use the real thing for movies. Too brittle, not to mention it's probably against some law. Besides which, the design on that beaded fabric wasn't Egyptian-looking. I'm no expert, but I don't think they beaded stuff back then."

Lucero agreed. "Why the big cover-up from Lerner? What's the point?"

"Good question. It's not like it was his house."

"It used to be," Lucero said.

"Come again? What the hell are you talking about?"

Lucero told Randall about the famous poker game. "Everyone around here—well, the old-timers, anyway— know it. Guess you need a Carmel history lesson."

"No shit. A poker game, huh? Anything else I should know?"

"That's all, I think. I was a Monterey kid, but Daria grew up with Frances. She might know more." Draining his coffee, Lucero added, "Let's wait to hear what Phillips has to say."

"I've already heard. It's too early for much, but he said it didn't take a rocket scientist to know the skeleton was a young female, early to mid-twenties, and she'd been in that thing for a good many years. The cause of death appears, at this point, to be a trauma to the temporal bone. He's thinking a bone fracture to the temple went to the brain and most likely made death instant."

"So someone whacked her on the head?"

"He's not sure. Could have been a fall too. It's not the kind of injury a killer would use. It was in front, not from the back."

"Maybe an argument that got out of hand?"

"Maybe. What was interesting, he said, was the use of sand. He said its use dated back to the Egyptians, and he was surprised anyone would know it would absorb the decomposition and odor. He also said that sealing the coffin in the dark, dry room made all that unnecessary. He agreed with me on the fabric thing too. Said the pattern design was more Pop Art than anything ancient. Anyway, he started off on a long-winded monologue about the Egyptian method of burial and I had to cut him short."

Lucero laughed. "Phillips gets off on all that stuff."

"Yeah, well, I'm glad the guy revels in minutiae. Kind of goes with the job. Anyway, Egyptology aside, I've got a huge job ahead of me digging out old files of missing persons. Not that I expect this woman to necessarily be from Carmel, but I've got to start somewhere. Problem is, until Phillips can give me some idea of how old the bones are, I'm hard pressed to figure out how far back to check."

"Try talking to Duff," Lucero offered.

Randall waved for more coffee, then sat back. "Duff?"

"Yeah. He was Carmel's chief before the guy you replaced. He had the desk for years. He lives out in Carmel Valley, in the village." Lucero looked at his watch. "Hey, I got to get to mass. I'm doing St. Joseph's in Spreckles."

"I thought you went there last Sunday."

"No, that was Madonna Del Sasso in Salinas."

"I can't keep up with you. Why don't you just pick one and stick with it?" Randall grinned.

"Hey, it's a great chance to greet my constituents."

"Don't run off so quick. We got a couple of other problems," Randall said.

"I know, Molly. She's in the thick of it again. I was hoping I'd be out of here before you brought that up. What is it about her? I mean, is she some kind of magnet for this shit?"

"Hell if I know, but this ain't gonna happen again, because she's out of it. She's pissed at Frances and said she was going to quit."

"So what's the problem?" Lucero asked.

"I don't believe her. This is one huge piece of change for her. With Emma to take care of now, I can't see her walking away from some pretty heavy dough."

"Well, it's not as if this was a fresh set of bones. I can't see where Molly can get into trouble at La Casa, can you?"

"I'd have to agree with you except for two things," Randall said. "Jason Lerner is lying, and Frances came to see me the day after Bitsy's party for her. She said some of the rooms in the house had been tossed."

"This is getting interesting. So, what are you going to do?"

"I'm not sure yet, but in light of all this, I've got to follow the book and open an investigation. Something this old is tricky. I'll keep it quiet for the present. There's no point in taping the house. Too many years have passed to consider it a viable crime scene. I'm not going to question Frances until I have more to go on. As far as anyone is concerned, we'll ride with Jason's bullshit. Besides, I don't want village gossip running amok and making the place a media attraction."

"Okay, keep me posted." Reaching for his wallet, Lucero said, "Let's hope you don't find any more bodies behind walls."

"Funny you said that. Frances told me there were faux walls all over the house. Before you ask, that's what she called them," Randall explained, then said, "I'm thinking maybe Molly should stay out of that place until we figure out what the hell is going on."

Lucero laid down a twenty, then laughed. "I'd like to see you pull that one off."

"Yeah? Watch me. And put that money away. It's my turn. Oh, by the way, what's with you and Frances? Those eyelashes were fluttering like a butterfly when she saw you at Daria's."

"Some old history you don't want to know about."

"Or Daria either, right?"

Lucero almost winced. "Especially Daria. But, hell, that friendship might not weather the storm after all. Man, I was ready for Molly to pop Frances when she got all high and mighty with her last night. She held it together pretty damn well."

"And then some," Randall said. Paying the bill, he added, "Speaking of Daria, I'd wish you two—"

"Forget it. She won't let the past go." Lucero looked away for a moment, waved to a few people, then hunched in closer to Randall. "She isn't aware that I know about that mess she got into in L.A. with the Lerners years ago and the part you played. When you first came to Carmel, I didn't know you were the cop that helped her out. I've been meaning to thank you. Trouble is, I know she thinks it will hurt me if I take a run for state attorney general. I give a fuck, you know? I can stay here for the rest of my life being the D.A., and no one here will give a shit about her past."

"Why don't you tell her, then? Look, Dan . . . if I can do anything—"

"Go solve this murder first."

Randall watched Lucero leave. The cocky walk was missing, but the politician's smile remained on his face as he was frequently stopped by residents. He'd become a good friend, and so had Daria. It was obvious they were meant for each other. They just had to believe it. But now he had to find Molly Doyle and figure out what to do. He didn't need her underfoot and barging into an investigation again.

He decided to try to catch Molly and Emma at mass at the Mission. She liked to go early sometimes to avoid all the hugging and the "peace be with you" thing you had to do with everyone near you. He knew it wasn't that she was uppity or uncharitable. Molly just wasn't a hugger with strangers. He understood. He was the same way. Big thing he had to do now was agree with her about giving up the house sale. She'd already had two close calls. The third time was supposed to be the charm. It wasn't a situation he wanted to experience.

## ~~~ *11* ~~~

$M$olly swirled the last bite of her pancake in the strawberry syrup, then sighed. Her sweats were already tight. She knew she should show more restraint, but Emma loved going to The Cottage on Lincoln, and after her over-the-top gesture with the Esther Hunt busts, Molly hadn't the heart to say no. The garage sales they'd gone to were total busts. All six sales were filled with children's clothes, toys, exercise equipment, and kitchenware Goodwill might not have accepted. Molly felt a pang of guilt as she watched Emma savor her French toast. She knew she had to expand her cooking repertoire beyond meat loaf, spaghetti casserole, Swiss steak, and twice baked potatoes.

If not for the twice weekly dinners at Daria's in the back room, Molly knew that Emma's diet would be in a rut. She pulled money from her pocket and placed it on the table.

"You're antsy," Emma said. "Maybe you should go out and have a smoke? I mean, you're going to start drumming your fingers pretty soon, and I've still got half my breakfast to finish."

Molly laughed. "I'm not antsy. Just thinking."

"We're still going back to La Casa after mass, right?"

"We're stopping there on the way. There's something I want to check."

It was a good thing Emma had reminded her about the alarm. The neighbors had been out in droves when Randall had a police van pick up the Egyptian coffin. She could just imagine the lecture he would give her if a patrol car had to take a false alarm call. Once inside, Molly found the alarm hadn't been set. Frances must have been there and forgotten again. She told Emma to check out the greenhouse and see if there was anything they might add to the list, then to meet her in the study. Molly remembered seeing a series of books with movie titles on their spines in the bookshelves. She was hoping they might have photos. And, if she were really lucky, some of the furniture in this house might be on them. In any event, she needed to make a list of all the movies the O'Briens had worked on. She would rent them and keep an eye out for anything she might recognize in case she couldn't find other proof.

She found the double doors to the study standing open, the scent of roses filling the air. Gingerly poking her head in, she sighed with relief to see that the carpet had been vacuumed and the grime and grit from the coffin removed. Molly guessed that Frances already had the cleaning staff in to take care of the mess. A vase of yellow roses rested on the partners desk, and the books from the bibliotheque Molly had stacked by the fireplace the day before were now neatly boxed.

She took an armful of the movie books to the desk. After searching through six of them, she realized they were little help. Each book was a chronicle of schedules, memos, a few photos with the actors, some sketches, and general correspondence for a specific movie. At least she had a full list of movie titles to take to a video store, she thought. Jotting them down, she returned the books, then saw a note she'd made to remind herself about a small carriage clock in the salon. With so many smalls in the huge room, she'd somehow neglected to list the hallmark for research. Closing the doors behind her, Molly kept an eye out for Emma in case she was on her way back.

With her notebook ready, Molly stepped into the salon, then stopped so quickly her tennis shoes squeaked on the marble floor. The large oil painting over the walk-in fireplace was off center. Glancing around the room, she saw two more pictures that were slightly askew. Everything else seemed in order until she saw what appeared to be drag marks on the Oriental carpet from the fireplace to just behind one of the sofas. Moving in for a better view, she could see that one of the pair of Bergere chairs was not lined up properly next to the card table behind the sofa. Maybe the housecleaner had used it to dust the painting over the fireplace, as well as the others. She almost laughed at her skittishness. That movie coffin had affected her more than she realized. She found the small clock and copied the hallmark. It was encased in sterling silver, and she knew it would bring an easy one to two thousand.

Molly gave the salon another quick glance. The pillows on the sofas were fully plumped, the two ashtrays on the coffee table were pristine, and the drinks table behind the second sofa looked ready for guests. Satisfied that all was well, she headed back to the study to meet Emma, and found the double doors wide open again. Standing in the hall, she called out, "Hey, we've got to go." When Emma didn't answer and Molly found the room empty, she wondered if Emma was still outside and had found garden ornaments worth adding to the list. She smiled, thinking about the notebook Emma had begun to carry. She'd said making her own observations might come in handy someday.

On her way to the kitchen, Molly found the doors to the morning room and dining room open and all the chandeliers blazing away. She'd hate to have Frances's electric bill. Just past the butler's pantry, she noticed that the door to the studio was ajar. Seeing the lights on, she was almost certain now the cleaners were still somewhere in the house. No doubt they were straightening up the boxes Jason had begun to sort.

During an earlier tour of the house, Molly had been surprised to find the studio fully paneled in lovely planked cypress, and not at all dirty or dusty, as Frances had said. Odds and ends of furniture, possibly decorating rejects, were neatly stacked and covered with plastic drop cloths. About to go in, Molly changed her mind and headed for the greenhouse.

Once outside, she checked her watch and realized if they didn't leave soon, they wouldn't get to mass ahead of the crowd. When she saw the glass roof of the greenhouse peeking over a wall of shrubs, Molly hurried along a flagstone path she hoped was leading her in the right direction. The greenhouse wasn't as big as she'd expected, and was connected to the main house by a breezeway that led to the studio. She had to hold her breath when she entered it. The humidity was overpowering, and the strong scent of wet moss, fertilizers, and damp soil almost made her gag. The maze of ferns and palms, in all sizes and shapes, looked almost threatening as their fronds spilled over into the narrow aisle. That awful movie, *The Little Shop of Horrors*, popped into her head, and she could almost swear the plants seemed to be reaching for her. Visions of spiders and any number of insects swooping down on her made Molly falter.

She pulled her sweatshirt up, held it over her nose, then took a few tentative steps inside. Easing the sweatshirt away, she called out, "Emma? Are you still in here?"

When there was no answer, Molly backed away toward the door. She hesitated in the breezeway, wondering if Emma had gone through the atrium to the study. Heading into the house again, she went back through the kitchen and stopped at the studio door. If Emma wasn't in there, or in the study, Molly figured she had decided to wait for her out by the pickup.

As large as the studio was, it was easy to see Emma wasn't there. The cardboard lids to several storage boxes were on the floor, and file folders, scrapbooks, and books lay next to them as if discarded in a hurry. Molly's first thought was how inconsiderate Jason was to leave such a mess. The least he could have done was put things back the way he'd found them.

Before she could wonder further, she felt a sharp pain in her back and then was flung across the room. Her arms flew out to break her fall, but it was too late to avoid landing on two upended chairs covered in plastic. Unable to hold onto the slick plastic, she crashed to the floor. Her chest felt as if someone had stepped on it. Trying to catch her breath, she jerked her head around to see if her attacker was moving toward her. The room was empty. Only the sound of a door slamming prompted her to breathe a little easier.

Molly managed to get to her knees, then carefully stood up. Grabbing her tote and notebook from the floor, she paused. Whoever had shoved her must have been hiding behind the door. Her first thought was of Emma. The pain in her chest was still sharp, but she had to make sure the attacker hadn't seen Emma. The last thing he would risk is exposure, and she prayed that Emma was out of sight.

She paused again, not sure which way to go, then ran down the hall shouting Emma's name. She reached the atrium out of breath. It was only a few more steps to the front door. She made a dash for them, flung them open and nearly collapsed with relief. Emma was sitting in the entry playing with a lizard.

"Where were you?" Emma asked. "I looked all over. I found this cute little guy in the greenhouse."

Molly blew out her breath. "Oh, I . . . I was, uh, in the studio. I, uh, went out to the greenhouse looking for you. I guess we just missed each other."

"We're late for church. Looks like we won't make it ahead of the crowd."

Molly stepped out of the entry, her eyes darting around the courtyard. "Right. Let's get going. Uh, I'd leave the lizard here, okay?"

As she drove to Carmel Mission, Molly's knees felt like Jell-O and the pulsing over her eyes threatened to explode. Anger was swiftly overriding her fear. For now, Emma didn't need to know about the attack. She didn't want to frighten her. Her big worry was whether to tell Randall what had happened.

It was apparent that something was going on in that house, and she made up her mind to find out what it was. Her Irish was up now. It was bad enough she'd had to endure Frances, but she hadn't signed up for hazard duty. That was definitely adding injury to insult. She knew she had it backward, but it fit. Whoever attacked her wasn't a thief. There was an entire household to ransack if that was the case, not rummaging through boxes in the studio. Someone was looking for something. And she was beginning to wonder about that gruesome coffin. After what Bennie had told them, she found it hard to believe that Frances's father had misplaced it during his remodeling.

Molly and Emma arrived at Carmel Mission in ample time to find an empty pew. Molly quickly knelt, made the sign of the cross and raced through her prayers so she could get to what was on her mind. At first she didn't notice that Emma had decided to kneel and pray too. When she saw Emma next to her on the kneeler, she smiled, and resumed her conversation with God.

*Okay, what's going on? I mean, I got the point. I'll stick with the job for Emma's future. Got that etched in stone. But is it necessary for me to get shoved around? So what do I do now? Buy a flak jacket? I mean, come on! And what about that overbearing teddy bear you've saddled me with? Do I tell him or sit on it? Give it some thought, okay? I'll get back to you later.*

When Randall scooted in next to her, she nearly jumped. She watched him out of the corner of her eye as he made the sign of the cross and bent his head in prayer. She lowered her eyes and continued. *You sure don't waste much time. Okay, you sent him here, right? Is this your answer? Another sign from on high? Don't take this wrong, but I'd like to put a few dots together first, okay? I promise I'll tell him. Really. I promise.*

Molly sensed Randall sitting back in the pew. She kept her eyes closed, stalling for inspiration. After a long moment, she blessed herself, sat back, and whispered, "We're leaving. I've got a ton of things to do."

"I thought you were going to Chevy's for lunch?" he whispered back.

"Oh, uh . . . well, change in plans. I've got to get the inventory finalized for Frances."

Stepping into the aisle, Randall waited to let Molly and Emma out. As soon as they were in the parking lot, he said, 'I owe you an apology. I shouldn't have razzed you about not quitting. I wouldn't take that kind of crap either. That last zinger Frances threw you at Daria's—about cleaning up the mess in the study—would have been the clincher for me too."

Molly was nearly speechless. An apology from Randall? It was a moment to savor. She gave him a big grin and said, "Thank you for understanding."

"Yeah, well, life is too short to mess with jerks. You're too classy to take that shit."

Molly had to bite her tongue. She wished she had a tape recorder to save these historical words for posterity. "Why thank you, sir. How gallant."

"Sure, whatever. Look, I should take off and let you get to work." Ruffling the top of Emma's head, he said, "See you at Daria's tonight, right? Gnocchi con pesto is on the menu. You up for it?"

Emma laughed. "Bet I can eat more than you."

Waving, Randall said, "You're on. See you around seven."

When he was out of earshot, Emma said, "Okay, spill it. What was that all about? Why didn't you tell him you changed your mind?"

Molly smiled dangerously. "I'm playing with his head, that's all."

Emma eyed her suspiciously, then said, "Oh, we're back to that again, huh? Cool."

As they pulled out of the packed parking lot and headed for the shop, Molly thought, Yeah, right . . . cool. It only took her two blocks to figure out what Randall was up to. Reverse psychology? Telling her she was right when he knew she wasn't meant he wanted her out of the way. Okay. But why?

## ≈ 12 ≈

*M*olly left the pickup in the alley, gathered her tote and book, and after slamming the door harder than necessary, said to Emma, "Virginia will be here to open pretty soon. Let's run over to Bennie's first then figure out our next move."

Emma gave her a puzzled look. "Huh? What was the first move?"

"Oh, right. I didn't mention that, did I?"

But before she could make something up, Emma pointed to the courtyard and said, "Hey, there's Bitsy and Sister Phil! They're back!"

Perfect, Molly thought. What timing. Suspicious of Randall's motives, and convinced there was more to that coffin than he'd let on, she wanted to get back to La Casa and get those Art Deco figures Max had bought back to the shop just in case. While she hadn't wanted to risk going back alone, or taking Emma, she figured the attacker had plenty of time to return after she'd left. She'd thought about asking Daria and Eve to meet her there, but seeing Bitsy and Sister Phil was just what she needed. A small smile played at the corner of her mouth as she darted a glance skyward. *Looks like we're on the same page. If we*

*can't be safe with a nun—okay, retired nun, I mean—well,
thanks for your confidence.*

Molly watched Emma run to Bitsy and Sister Phil, give
each a hug and excitedly tell them how much they'd been
missed. Molly waved as she approached their table.
"You're back early. Had enough pampering at the spa, or
just bored?"

Sister Phil laughed. "Oh, Molly! What a hedonistic joy
that spa was! To think I've been missing so much fun!"

Bitsy joined in the laughter. "The food, however, was
not attractive. The presentations were, frankly, a year behind the times. Arugula and chipotle are no longer the darlings of the culinary set."

Taking a seat, Molly said, "Oh, don't be so picky. I'm
just glad to know the spa people didn't send you two
packing."

"They wouldn't dare," Bitsy drawled. "I'm a charter
member. We came home early, because . . . well . . ." She
looked at Sister Phil and grinned. "I'm not going to lie, so
don't give me one of your looks."

"I'll save you the trouble," the retired nun said. "Bitsy
just couldn't stand the thought of you selling some kind of
Irish china before she got home."

"That will be enough, Mother Superior wannabe!"
Bitsy roared. Picking up her cup with utmost elegance,
she said, "I have a collector foaming at the mouth for *all*
that Belleek, and I didn't want you sending it off to auction before I got back."

"They're not all nineteenth century, but there must be a
few dozen pieces," Emma said, jumping in. To Sister Phil,
she explained, "Belleek is a very thin and iridescent par-
ian ware made in Ireland. Vases, candlesticks . . . jugs and

all sorts of display things. They even have a Neptune tea set, and those are worth around six hundred bucks. The lily basket is even more."

"Oh, my," Sister Phil said. "No wonder you had ants in your pants to get home, Bitsy!"

Bitsy's eyes sparkled as she listened to Emma's explanation. Her voice was filled with pride when she asked, "Any meditation figures? Or that triple bird vase that's so hard to find?"

Emma preened from Bitsy's obvious delight. "Yes, and more."

Bitsy gave Molly a broad wink. "She's on top of the game I see. When can I come over and make a shopping list?"

Molly was already one step ahead. She waved at Bennie, strolling toward her with an espresso, and said, "Give me a few minutes for a caffeine fix, and we're on our way."

Before the cup reached her lips, Emma said, "Oh, guess what was found at La Casa!"

Emma rattled off the story so quickly, Molly barely had a chance to get a word in. When she saw a series of frowns cross Bitsy's face, she was certain there was a story behind that damn thing. If a community had a resident historian, Bitsy would qualify. Very little happened in Carmel, past or present, that she didn't know. Molly decided this wasn't the time to probe. She'd have to wait and get her alone.

Her instinct proved to be right when Bitsy said, "On second thought, it was a long drive from Calistoga this morning. Maybe we can meet you at La Casa tomorrow? I'd really like to take it easy today."

"I'll go over with you, Molly," Sister Phil said. "I've always wanted to see the inside of that place."

Breathing a sigh of relief, Molly's fingertips moved to the small crucifix under her sweatshirt. She stole a quick glance at the sky and winked her thanks. With a nun at her side, even a retired one, she knew she was in good hands. "Great. I've got to pick up a few things, and you'd be a big help."

Molly wanted to kick herself when she realized she hadn't set the alarm when she'd left La Casa in such a hurry. Anyone could have come in and robbed the place, and it would have been her fault. Her only excuse would have been that she was scared witless. She could imagine telling that to Randall, then having him ask why she hadn't reported the attack. *Omission is as bad as commission*, he'd likely tell her. The man definitely was personality challenged. But she knew deep down that he was also a fine man, and his tenderness with Emma gave him big marks in her book. But, oh, he could be a pain in the ass.

Sister Phil was speechless as she followed Molly through the atrium toward the study. "Wouldn't this make a marvelous retreat for retired nuns? We rarely have the chance to live in such opulence."

Molly couldn't help but laugh. "A little pricey. I don't think the boys in Rome would spring for it."

Sister Phil's eyes twinkled. "Certainly not for old gals like me. The Jesuits could pull it off, though."

Making a beeline for the study, Molly headed for the mantel where she'd placed the Art Deco statues when she'd emptied the bibliotheque. "We'll have to use these boxes the books are packed in. And I forgot the bubble wrap in the pickup. I'll run out and get it. If you two would empty four of these boxes, I'll be right back."

When Molly returned, she saw a large box on the desk. "Where did that come from?"

"I got it from the studio," Emma said. "All the boxes here were too small for the lady with the greyhounds."

Molly nearly had heart failure. "The studio? Oh, uh . . . good thinking." Handing Emma a long roll of bubble wrap, she said, "Better triple pack that one."

In less than fifteen minutes they were ready to leave, when Emma said, "Hey! I just noticed those Oscars are gone. I guess Frances took them after all."

Molly thought about the alarm not being set but kept her voice calm, "Guess so."

"Oscars?" Sister Phil said. "Oh, my! I had no idea the O'Briens were so celebrated. How exciting."

When Sister Phil asked if she could sneak a few more peeks at the sprawling mansion, Molly hesitated, then quickly agreed. The whirlwind tour she gave her seemed to be satisfactory, and by the time they reached the shop and carried in the boxes, Sister Phil was ready to head home. Giving Emma a hug, she said, "One more week of freedom, and then it's back to our schedule, miss. We've got to get you ready for the new semester at Santa Catalina."

"Uh, I wanted to talk to you about that," Molly said. "I was wondering if you might like to take on a computer job for me. I need a Web site for La Casa's sale. But I insist you charge me for it."

Sister Phil looked at Emma. "Well, looks like you've got a reprieve. I'd love to do it for you, Molly. However, there will be no charge, and I don't want an argument. Emma and I can whip one up in no time. You just let me know what you want, and consider it done." Rubbing her hands together, she added, "We can start any time."

After Sister Phil left, Molly said to Emma, "I think we'll take the rest of the day off. I've got to get a list of Belleek for Bitsy together, and then work up my ideas for the Web site. How about you relaxing for a change? Maybe curl up with Tiger and dig into a good book?"

"Are we still going to Daria's tonight?"

Visions of seeing Randall floated past Molly's eyes like a bad dream. "Uh, sure. Of course."

"Cool."

"Right. Very cool."

Once Emma was upstairs, Molly checked her watch and figured she had time before Virginia showed up to open the shop at noon. She hurried into the small storage room off the showroom floor and dialed Eve Jensen. Eve answered on the second ring.

"Did you get my message?" Molly asked. "About that Egyptian thing?"

"Thanks for letting me know," Eve replied. "It sure fooled me."

Molly laughed. "You're not alone. I almost died when Randall said it was a prop. Listen, I've got the consignment papers ready. I'm going to Daria's for dinner around six. How about if I drop them off then?"

"Oh, that'll be just fine. I'm anxious to get going with them."

"Great. See you."

She was relieved that Eve hadn't been spooked and changed her mind. One never knew how people might react to something like that. It was imperative now to get many sales lined up before something went wrong. Molly wasn't sure exactly what that might be, but she wasn't taking any chances. She dialed Randall's cell number. She knew he'd be with Frances and the Lerners, but didn't care. When he picked up, she was brief. "I need to talk to you before dinner tonight. And not in front of Emma. When can we meet?"

Randall's voice was low. "Inside Bennie's at three work for you?"

"Perfect. Don't be late."

Next, Molly decided to unpack the Art Deco figures and put them in the storage room. She carefully carried each box in, then cleared a shelf and placed them with their faces toward the wall. She didn't want Virginia to think they were stock and tell a customer about them. When she unwrapped the largest, the woman with the greyhounds, she noticed two black books had been added to keep the statue from slipping. How clever of Emma to think of that, she thought. Pulling them out, she realized Emma must have taken them from the studio since they didn't match those in the study. Setting them aside, she placed the figure on the shelf, then gathered up the empty boxes and headed for the garage.

On her way back, the phone was ringing and she rushed to pick it up before the answering machine kicked in. It was Bitsy. "I was just about to get the Belleek list ready for you," Molly said. "Can you give me a half hour?"

"Of course, darling, take your time," Bitsy replied. "By the way, how are you and Frances getting along?"

Molly was surprised by the question. Bitsy hadn't been around when Frances had gotten snippy with her, and she knew there was no way Daria would have told her. After years of avoiding each other, their relationship was slowly finding its way to harmony. "What makes you ask?"

"Just wondering. I hear she's very taken with Randall and, well . . . you know what I mean. Which is actually rather strange since she's planning on returning to Europe in the next few weeks."

"No, I don't know what you mean. And, just to make this crazy conversation a bit more clear, what gives you that impression?"

"I just heard from Sandy Sechrest. She and Freddie were lunching at Phil's up in Moss Landing and saw them. Evidently, Frances was sitting so close to Randall during lunch, you couldn't slide a ruler between them. And feeding him crab, and oh . . . things women do when they want a man's full attention."

Molly was silent for a long moment, then said, "If you just found that out, then what was making your face so dark when Emma was telling you about that movie prop?"

Bitsy's silence was longer than Molly's.

"Well? I'm still here, Bitsy. What's going on?"

"Hmm? Oh, nothing, darling. I was just thinking about that Belleek."

"Baloney."

"Oh, it's nothing, really. Just, well . . . just that La Casa has a checkered past, and memory flashes skittered across my mind, that's all. Really."

"Don't you just hate it when people half tell you things, then brush it off with an *'Oh, it's nothing really'*? It's as bad as being told one of those *they* said, or *someone* said, but no one ever cops to who it really was."

"Darling, I really have to go. Josie's preparing a special dinner and she needs my input. Oh, did I tell you that Sister Phil is moving in with me? Can you imagine me living with a nun? I can just hear the laughs we'll get from that. We had so much fun at the spa and—"

"That's great news," Molly broke in. "Just do me a favor. Don't ever do this to me again. If you've got something to tell me, then do it."

"You *are* upset about Frances, aren't you? Don't give it a thought. Randall is far too—"

"Goddamnit, Bitsy! I don't give a flying . . . flying whatever about who he sees, okay? I'm pissed about you inferring something lurid about La Casa and then brushing it off. What is it with that damn house anyway?"

"Well, darling, it's probably just gossip, but there were rumors years ago about some pretty wild goings-on at that house when Marius Lerner owned it. I understand the cops here kept a few things quiet because he was such a big shot in Los Angeles, and had some pretty heavyweight friends in Pebble Beach."

"And? Come on, Bitsy. What's a wild party? Loud music? Booze flowing from fountains?"

"No, it was more than that. I wasn't living here then, but I often came up for the Clambake. There were rumors of two young local gals being raped. But then I heard there were some big payoffs too. And then there was another young local who wanted to be an actress. She went to a party at La Casa and never returned home. They found her evening bag on the beach two days later. Talk was, she got drunk and told people she was going for a midnight swim."

"Here? In Carmel? She'd freeze the minute she hit the water!"

"Exactly, darling. A local would know that, wouldn't you think? But who knows? She might just have gone down to the beach, changed her mind, dropped her purse and simply run off with some slick talker. It happens all the time. Anyway, the house was filled day and night with celebrities and hangers-on coming up from Los Angeles. I think they used to call the girls 'starlets' then. That's not what I'd call them today, but that's neither here nor there."

"But you remembered all that when Emma told you about the skeleton and the coffin."

"Well, yes. It did pop into my head. But then, at my age, so many things from the past do these days."

"When did all that happen? The missing girl, I mean."

"Oh, Molly! You're exhausting me with all these questions. I'm not really sure. It was during those 'go go days' of drugs, booze, and movie stars."

"A lethal combination," Molly said.

"Amen," Bitsy replied.

## ⚊ 13 ⚊

Shortly after Molly hung up, she heard the bell over the shop door ring and then Virginia calling. "I'm in the storage room," Molly answered. "I'll be out in a minute."

Virginia Harris was in her late sixties, trim and handsome in a typical Carmel matron way. Her hair was expertly cut in a no-nonsense short bob, the blond rinse just highlighting the gray, and she wore cashmere twin sets and tweed skirts with grace and casual style. Her sales persona was low key, and Molly had liked her the minute they'd met.

"Go ahead and fan the air, Molly. I promise not to tell Emma you're sneaking a smoke."

Molly laughed. "I wasn't smoking this time. I was on the phone with Bitsy."

"Oh, she's back? Would you rather I didn't come in today?"

"She's back, but she's still not working. I'd love it if you'd want to keep to the schedule for another month or two."

Dropping her bag in the storage room, Virginia said, "I'll stay as long as you need me. Working here is so much fun. We had a good day yesterday. Did you see the tags?"

"Did I see them? I was dancing around the room. Great job, by the way. Look, I'll be upstairs for the rest of the day. I've got a ton of computer work to do for La Casa. So if you need me, just holler."

"How's the inventory coming along? That place is like a museum. I damn near got lost the first time I was there for a charity event."

"Except for the movie stuff and some books, I'm done. Thank God for modern technology. I've got everything on video, sound and all. And then it converts to some kind of disc so I can put it on the computer. I'm a little sketchy on how it works, but I'll figure it out."

"Terrific. Well, I'll get everything ready for the hordes. There are several tour buses in town and some sunshine is peeking through finally. You go on up and leave everything to me."

Molly spent a few more minutes in the storage room, and was about to leave when she remembered the two books from La Casa. Grabbing them, she tucked them under her arm and headed upstairs. Emma was deep into a new sci-fi book from the library, and Tiger was sound asleep in her maternity box. Molly made a fresh pot of coffee, then went into Emma's room and booted up the computer. She pulled up the file on Belleek, got a grand total, then called Bitsy with the information. A huge smile split her face when she got off the phone. Nine thousand big bucks in just a few moments was the kind of sale to make any dealer jump for joy. Her next call was to Max to confirm her fax. He told her he'd have a check in the mail to Frances the next morning. Molly was so revved up that all thoughts about coffins, skeletons, and attackers seemed like an old dream until she saw the clock on

Emma's nightstand. She was already ten minutes late for her meeting with Randall.

She flew out of Emma's room, paused to tell her she was leaving and found her fast asleep on the sofa. Easing out of the French doors to the balcony overlooking the courtyard, Molly was tempted to slide down the wrought-iron railing. Unfortunately, Randall was sitting at one of the small iron tables near the fountain and glaring at her.

"I thought you told me to be on time. I guess that doesn't hold for you though, huh?"

"I was on the computer. I'm sorry." Seeing the extra cup on the table, she smiled. "For *moi*? How thoughtful. Thank you."

Randall laughed. "Yeah, that's me. Quite the gent."

"So I hear."

"Yeah? What the hell is that supposed to mean?"

"Nothing. Just, ah . . . just kidding back."

His smile was still playful. "I keep hearing what a hard-ass I am, so I'm trying, okay?"

Molly couldn't help but laugh again. "You're not a hard-ass. You're just . . . well, abrasive sometimes. Uh, not that I've ever thought that. I know down deep you're really a sweet guy."

Randall eyed her. "Sweet? Ha! Put a lid on it, okay? I don't want my rep ruined. Okay, Molly Doyle, what's on your mind? All these compliments are making me leery."

Molly examined her cup carefully. She wondered if you could read espresso grounds like tea leaves. She needed something to show her the way. A sign of sorts to ease into what she knew would be an ultimatum from Randall to stay clear of La Casa. She couldn't find a thing. "Someone was at La Casa this morning and shoved me from behind in the studio, then ran out of the room. I scraped my knee, but luckily that's all."

Randall's silent stare was more threatening than the intruder. She could almost see his eyes change from gray to blue and then back again. She didn't know eyes could do that. But then, Randall was like that. And she swore he often read her mind and could tell when she was lying. "Well? What do you think about that? Kind of odd, don't you think? I mean, it couldn't have been a robber. The studio isn't filled with treasures, for God's sake. Just a bunch of photos. Well, celebrity photos are worth a lot of money, but I can't imagine someone breaking into the house and passing up all the other stuff that's much more valuable. And I don't believe in ghosts."

"Stop babbling."

"I'm not babbling. I'm just a little scared, that's all. But I wanted you to know."

"Could you tell if anything was missing from the house?"

Molly rolled her eyes. "Are you serious? How the hell would I know? I ran out of there like a shot looking for Emma. Thank God she was outside playing with a lizard. Besides, I'd have to check every damn thing in the place against the inventory list. There's enough stuff in that house to open three shops."

"Did this happen before or after I saw you at the Mission?"

Molly gulped. Here it comes, she thought. "Before. But I didn't say anything then because I didn't want Emma to know. So don't start yelling at me."

"Was the alarm on when you got there?"

"No, and that scared me even more."

"Who knows you're there getting ready for a sale?"

"I haven't told a soul. Well, except for Bitsy and Max. Oh, and Eve Jensen, who's taking some artwork on consignment, and the Lerners." Molly thought for a moment, then said, "What about those movers?"

Randall didn't answer. He got up from the table and headed for the inside of Tosca's. Molly stared at him, then shook her head.

He was back within moments with a tray of pastries and a pot of espresso. "My treat. It's not every day that Molly Doyle fesses up before it's too late."

"That's not fair. I've always come clean with you. Well, not right away, but this time it's different."

Randall filled her cup, then said, "Oh? And why is this time different?"

"Well, because it is. I mean, I've a job to do, and—"

"I thought you were quitting."

"I changed my mind. Emma and I need these commissions, damn it! I've got to think of her future, you know."

"You've got plenty of time for that. You're outta that place as of now."

Molly played with her pastry, then took a large bite. She spent more time than necessary savoring the apricot glaze and cream filling. "That skeleton isn't a prop, is it? Jason was wrong. Or lying."

"What makes you think that? You a big-time sleuth now?"

"I'd say I've shown some aptitude, wouldn't you?" She knew he'd have a hard time being snarky about that. She took another bite, then told him what Bennie and Bitsy had said, waited for him to run that through the computer he had in his brain, then added, "There could be a connection."

"There might be life on Mars too."

Molly dabbed at her lips with the napkin, then sat back

lazily. "Don't play with me. I think we've been through enough for you to at least be honest." When Randall didn't react, she said, "Oh, are we into the silent treatment now?"

Randall looked away and waved to someone across the courtyard. He sat back in his chair, then reached for his cup. His continued silence was a sure sign he wasn't going to answer.

"Okay then," Molly said, "if you won't give me a good reason to stay out of La Casa, I'm going back to finish the job. Maybe I should go over to the station and report the assault. That's what good citizens are supposed to do, right? And then I should call Frances and tell her what happened."

"Leave it alone," he finally said.

Molly leaned into the table and sputtered, "You know what, Randall? You've got a real authority problem. *Leave it alone?* Oh, wow! That sounds like some B-movie cop dialogue. Why can't you just say you'd appreciate it if I gave you a chance to do some investigating? Or . . . maybe . . . I'm concerned for your safety, Molly, and . . . and until I can—"

"Okay! I apologize. I agree with everything you said. Satisfied? That work?"

"Not really, but I'll take what I can get."

"Good. I take it we're still friends, then."

"Yeah, I guess so." Molly finished her pastry, then said, "It's just all so stupid."

Randall sighed. "Now what? What's so stupid?"

"Kill someone then hide the body in the house. Why not dump it in the ocean? Or bury it somewhere? Seems logical. And then bolting that bibliotheque to the wall? Was it supposed to be a permanent fixture? A piece that valuable?" Molly pushed her dish away and filled her cup with the still steaming espresso. "I should buy one of these pretty thermos things from Bennie. It looks just like a coffeepot. I could have elegant espresso all day long."

"You drink too much of that. It's rotting your brains. Who said anything about murder?"

"See? There you go again! What the hell is this all of a sudden? Some deep, dark secret just because it involves a couple of big Hollywood honchos?"

Seeing Randall's shoulders hunch up and his eyes go squinty, she knew she'd gone too far.

"I'm going to pretend you never said that."

Molly knew she'd hit him below the belt. Randall, she'd learned, had too fine a sense of justice to ever consider sweeping a crime under the carpet. But she was turning the tables on him now, doing her version of reverse psychology. Two could play the same game. She hoped it would work and he'd level with her. "Okay, strike that. Now it's my turn to apologize. So why can't I go back to La Casa and finish my job?"

"You actually want to go back there after what happened this morning? Now I know you're nuts."

"You can come with me. I've only got the movie stuff and some books left."

Randall shoved back his chair, pulled out a cigar and laughed so hard, nearby customers' heads turned. "You're a piece of work, you know? If that isn't the dumbest thing I've ever head come out of your mouth, I don't know what is. I'm not a freakin' bodyguard, okay? I'm the chief of police, remember?"

"If Frances will hire a guard, will you let me go back?"

"No."

"Then something does stink there, or you'd let me do it. You're keeping me out of that house because . . . well, because you think there *was* a murder. Or something. I know it. I can tell by the look on your face."

When Randall didn't answer, she pressed on. "Does Frances know what you think? Or is the arrogant little snip just *too* fragile to know the truth?"

"Your green eyes are sparking, Molly. I wouldn't have expected that from you."

"Screw you."

"Let me think about this, okay? Just cool off and go sell some antiques."

"I just sold a slew of Belleek to Bitsy and I've got to get over there and pack it up for her. And I've also got an art expert arriving on Tuesday with Max. Oh, and I'm waiting to hear from Rudy and Barbara Franchi in Boston for the movie memorabilia. What the hell am I going to tell these people now?"

Randall lit his cigar, then offered his lighter. "Have a smoke, calm down while I think about it."

Molly had a hard time not smiling. She was sure she'd won round one. Now was the time to be politic and slightly complacent. But just slightly. She pulled out her cigarettes, then hesitated. "I'm trying to quit. But, okay. Oh, I almost forgot, could you get hold of Loomis and have him call? I've got some Palissy he might be interested in. And a few pieces of lovely Portuguese majolica. Late nineteenth century, I think."

Randall lit her cigarette. "Those ugly dishes with fishes and sea snakes all over them? Yeah, sure. I'll give him a call. So, how much you stand to make on all this?"

Molly exhaled, then went for the jugular. "Close to a hundred thousand."

Randall almost slipped off the chair. "Pesos or dollars?"

"Very funny."

"No shit?"

"Maybe more."

Randall examined the tip of his cigar, tapped it on the ashtray, then finally said, "I'll give you an answer tonight at Daria's." He put a palm up and added, "That's the best I can do. So don't press me." Shoving the cigar between his lips, he rose. "I got an appointment out in Carmel Valley. See if you can stay out of trouble until tonight."

Molly looked up and gave him a mock salute. "Ten-four, Chief."

Randall had lied to Molly about having an appointment. He needed to get back to the station to think about what she'd told him. He also decided to take Lucero's advice and call Tommy Duff, a former Carmel police chief, to set up a get-together and pick his brains. But first he needed to see the old files. He had a time frame now, thanks to Bitsy, to check out any missing persons and misadventure reports. For as small a force as Carmel was, his predecessors were professionals and had kept meticulous records, and they were all stored in perfectly labeled boxes. He threw off his sport coat the minute he entered his office, asked for a fresh pot of coffee, laid out two cigars, then called one of the clerks. "Get someone over to storage. I want case files between 1965 and 1975. Start stacking them in the hall if you have to."

It was almost six that evening when Randall closed the last file on 1970. His eyes burned and he was hungry. He stretched for a few minutes, then got up and closed the window behind his desk. So far he'd found nothing. The majority of the police calls were minor break-ins, a few domestics, drug busts here and there, and several aids to drunk tourists. Carmel-by-the-Sea lived up to its benign reputation. He made one call before leaving. When Loomis came on the line, Randall jumped right in. They'd kept close contact since he'd left Los Angeles, and they didn't have to start each conversation with catch-up stories. "You packed and ready to go?" Randall asked.

Loomis chuckled. "Are you serious? I've been ready for days."

"Before you leave, how about doing some snooping for me. I got a shopping list for you."

"Fire away."

"I need an updated background on Marius Lerner."

"Shit. Not that bunch again."

"Just wait, okay? Hear me out. This is something else altogether. I need a refresher on the son and daughter too."

"Jason and Steffi Lerner? Don't get me started on those two. That bastard should have fried years ago. No good prick! He's still a craw in my throat. What's up? Why? Oh shit, don't tell me they've moved up there?"

"I'll explain when you get here, okay? Same thing on a Jack O'Brien and his wife, uh, Arlene. Both set designers. Worked with the Lerner group."

"No problem. I've still got juice. How soon do you need it?"

"Yesterday is perfect. Uh, say . . . could you find it in your heart to make a little detour and come up my way? I could use your help for a week or two."

"So, you got something simmering, huh? I'm rubbing my hands in glee as we speak. You know damn well I'd be heading your way first. I wouldn't miss the chance to see Molly Doyle again."

Randall laughed. "Oh, you'll be seeing a lot of her. You're gonna be her shadow."

When Randall hung up, he felt a little easier. He had a few qualms about letting Molly go back to the house, but he'd also had no idea she was looking at that big a commission. He knew with that kind of dough at stake, she'd badger the hell out of him. And he couldn't blame her. With Loomis standing watch, she could finish up. Retired from LAPD Homicide for only a week, Loomis still had juice in the department, as he'd said on the phone, and getting hold of the info he needed would be a piece of cake.

Loomis was an avid collector, and he and Molly had hit it off like gangbusters when he'd played wheel man for them down south. He'd already planned to have Loomis do some digging for him, but asking him to come to Carmel hadn't occurred to him until Molly mentioned those ugly dishes Loomis collected. Perfect. They could talk shop and Loomis could keep her out of Randall's way.

The next call was to Tommy Duff. Randall introduced himself as the current Carmel chief, which Duff knew, and the two men chatted for nearly a half hour before Randall broached the reason for his call. "I've got a situation I'd like to discuss," Randall said. "It may have occurred during your watch. It's not an old case. In fact, I don't even know if it is a case. Just need to pick your brains about what was going on around here then."

"Looking for village history, huh?" Duff asked.

"Yeah. Something like that. Gossip, scandal, maybe a hush-hush affair. You know, the kind of shit that never sees the light of day. There's no one in the station that was around thirty years ago. Hell, I'm lucky you still are!"

"I retired at forty," Duff said. "Broke my hip in a wreck

chasing some kids high on grass down by Carmel Point. Hit a tree. Damn hip never healed right. I've got a little café in Mid-Valley. Come on out anytime. It's called Duff's."

Randall made a date for the following day. He picked up his jacket, threw it over his shoulder, and told the clerk on his way out that he'd be at Daria's for dinner. He stood outside the small station, lit a cigar, then mumbled, "Won the house in a card game, huh? Yeah, right. See you at the movies, pal."

*M*olly and Emma decided to walk to Eve Jensen's gallery on Lincoln, and then to Daria's for dinner. It was a good chance to get their village fix. For the past several days they'd been cooped up in the store, and then at La Casa at night. It would give them a chance to play their favorite building game. Emma had devised it one morning when they'd been on their way to Carmel Beach. As they crossed the planted meridian that divided Ocean Avenue, Emma stopped in front of Harrison Memorial Library. "This is still my favorite building."

"No fair. It's not a shop," Molly said. "It doesn't count."

"I know. But it still is." Looking across the street, she said, "Okay, how about the Pine Inn?"

"Is that your today best?"

"Maybe. What's yours?"

Molly pretended to think as they passed the elegant Pine Inn, with its glossy black planter boxes on the sidewalk. "Hmm, I think I'll go for the Tuck Box."

"Hey! That was my pick last time. Bet you didn't know the Tuck Box was copied after those English Cotswold houses. And the Carmel stone they used almost matches English limestone."

"Where the heck did you learn that? And what's Carmel stone?" Molly pretended not to know.

Emma pushed her glasses up on her nose and preened. "I read all about Carmel's history at the library. Carmel stone is local, and it's kind of a honey color. A lot of the houses around here use it for walks too."

Molly smiled, pleased that Emma was so taken with the town. "How about if I go for Anton and Michel's restaurant? That Court of the Fountains in back is just beautiful."

"Okay. You win. I guess this is kind of a silly game now that I think about it. Everything here is beautiful."

"You really love Carmel, huh?"

Emma reached up and gave Molly a hug. "I don't ever want to leave."

They were only a few doors away from Eve's gallery when Molly saw her outside locking up. Molly hurried and called her, and when Eve turned, she was shocked to see how drawn her face was and how she slumped. "Hey, are you okay?" Molly asked.

"Oh, Molly! I forgot you were coming by. I . . . I'm not feeling well. I decided to close early and head home. Must be a bug or something." Pulling out her keys, she offered a small smile. "I'm so sorry. Let's go back in and I'll sign the papers. A few more minutes won't kill me."

Reaching into her tote, Molly pulled out an envelope and handed it to her. "Don't be silly, you go on home. Take these with you and we'll get together later. Let me know when you want to pick everything up."

Taking the envelope, Eve said, "Great. I'll call you in the morning. I'm sure I'll be fine by then."

"Maybe you caught a germ from that Egyptian thing," Emma said. "You know, like those people in history did when they opened up those pyramids?"

Molly saw Eve's face blanch. For a moment she thought she saw her waver. "Eve? You really ought to get home. Can you drive okay? I can—"

"No, no. I'm fine. Really." Giving Emma a strange look, she said, "That didn't really happen, did it? I mean, did people really get sick from those things?"

"Oh, yes. There were all kinds of bacteria, and . . . well, that was in Egypt, though. Carmel wouldn't have those kinds of uggy bugs. Maybe rat stuff, but—"

Emma didn't get a chance to finish. Eve was already waving and quickly walking to her car. "Well, that sure scared the heck out of her," Emma said. "I just thought she ought to know. We're supposed to learn from history, so maybe she might call the doctor and tell him."

Molly watched Eve pull out of her parking space and speed away. She cringed when she almost hit a tourist crossing at the corner. "I just hope she gets home without killing someone."

They reached Daria's ahead of the others, and Molly was relieved to have a few moments of quiet before Randall and Lucero arrived. Emma was already in the restaurant's kitchen watching the chef make the gnocchi. Daria came in with a drinks tray and nearly fell into a chair. "Whew! What a Sunday! We've been packed since lunch. Emma in the kitchen already?"

"She's determined to learn how to cook something new so she can help me. Poor kid. I should really buy a cookbook and practice."

Daria grinned, then poured them both a drink. "Don't bother. You can always come here. I hear Eve's taking some of the artwork from La Casa. She could use the business."

"Lean times?" Molly asked. "I thought she had a booming gallery."

"She used to. Then the dot-com bust came along and she had to close her Taos and Scottsdale galleries and come back to prop this one up. Talk is, the Southwest art thing is dying, but then, you'd know more about that than me."

Molly sipped her drink. "It's not as popular as it once was, but then, art is trendy." Taking another longish sip, she said, "Something is screwy about La Casa. Is there something I should know? I mean, ancient history? Does Frances have some enemies around? Not that I'd blame anyone, but—"

"Oh, Molly. What now?"

"Well, I might as well tell you what happened this morning."

"Why don't you take out an ad while you're at it?" Randall said as he came in.

"Is it Frances again?" Daria asked.

Molly ignored Randall and told Daria what had happened. "I don't want Emma to know. So mum's the word, okay?"

"You're not going back there, are you?" Daria asked. "I mean if someone is trying to rob the place?" She looked at Randall. "You better talk to her."

Randall poured himself a drink and laughed. "Talk to Molly Doyle? You gotta be kidding. Since when has she ever listened?"

"Does that mean I can finish up there?" Molly asked.

"Not yet."

"Damn it, Randall! You told me today—"

"I told you I'd give you an answer. I just did."

Molly's eye began to pulse. "I think you really enjoy being obstinate."

"Yeah? Well I think you enjoy being ornery. You're not going back there until Loomis arrives."

"Loomis? What the hell has he got to do with this?" Molly blurted.

"You wanted me to tell him about those ugly dishes, right? So I did, and he's coming up to see them. When he gets here in few days, you can take him over and then he'll stick with you until you're done. That's my best and only offer. Take it or leave it."

Molly decided silence was her best defense, then changed her mind. "I guess I have no choice. However, it would be nice if you changed your tone of voice."

"My what? I'm being civil here, considering how hard-headed you are."

"Why is it every time I walk into this back room lately you two are at it?" Lucero said. "I'm going to buy a flak jacket."

Daria was strangely silent, and barely nodded at Lucero. On her feet, she said, "I'll see about dinner."

Randall's eyes followed Daria as she left. He was pensive for a moment, then told Lucero about Molly's encounter. "Looks like someone wanted to do a little lifting. Molly was in the wrong place at the wrong time."

"You okay?" Lucero asked.

"Just a sore chest and a scraped knee. I'll live." Rising from the table, she muttered, "I'll get Emma from the kitchen."

Molly had noticed that Daria's eyes seemed dim when she left, and she began to worry. It finally struck her that Daria had not been herself for the past two weeks. Her big smile wasn't as bright, and her energetic walk had slowed. Molly followed her into the kitchen and found her leaning against a chrome storage rack. "Hey? Are you okay? Maybe we should all leave. Forget dinner if you're not up to it."

Daria's smile was weak. "Don't be silly. I'm okay. Just a little beat." Giving Molly a quick peck on the cheek, she said, "This seven day a week schedule is catching up with me, that's all. Maybe I'll buy a book on how to take a day off without feeling guilty."

Molly hugged her. "Go sit. Emma and I can help Manuel take dinner in."

Daria waved her off. "I'm fine. Honest. You go back in and tease the hell out of those two guys. They love it when you're sassy."

The weekly Sunday night dinner seemed to have lost some of its verve. Between Molly's annoyance with Randall, Lucero's uncharacteristic silence, and Daria's continued stillness, Emma seemed to be the only one oblivious to the tide of disquiet swirling about them. The somewhat somber mood was finally broken when Emma pushed her dish away and said, "Wow, these gnocchi things were delicious! I watched the chef, Antonio, make them, but he was so busy rolling the dough off the fork to make these little balls, I didn't want to bother him. So who can tell me where this kind of pasta comes from?"

Randall and Lucero almost answered at once. Randall waved to Lucero, giving him the floor. "First thing to note is, it's not really pasta and it originated in Sicily. My mother made it a lot, but she used semolina with the potatoes instead of flour and she ladled a ragu sauce over them."

"Wrong," Randall said. "It's from Genoa, my mother's home town. It's a Northern Italian dish. It tastes better with pesto, like the way we have it now. And no semolina. Just flour and potatoes."

"Hey, come on, Randall. They even serve this in Rome. That ain't Northern Italy."

"They stole it from us," Randall said, laughing.

While the good-natured banter about the gnocchi had thankfully lightened the strange mood in the room, Molly wasn't convinced Daria had leveled with her. She was certain something was bothering her. Molly made a point of looking at her watch. "It's already eight. Daria is exhausted and ready to fall asleep on us, and I should get Emma to bed early for once."

"We haven't had coffee or dessert yet," Lucero said.

Molly shot him a dangerous look. "Uh, where were you when I said Daria is exhausted?"

"Oh, right. Sorry. I was just—"

Molly was already on her feet and reaching for her tote. She headed for Daria, gave her a hug, then nodding to Emma, said, "A kiss for Daria and then we're gone."

"You don't have to leave," Daria finally said. "I'll have Manuel bring in—"

"Absolutely not," Molly replied. "You go home and get some rest. I'll call you later."

Waiting for Emma to give Randall and Lucero a hug, Molly continued to keep an eye on Daria, and a thought struck her. Daria had seemed fine until Randall mentioned that Loomis was coming up to Carmel. In fact, she mused as she waved her good-byes, that was exactly when Daria's smile turned off.

As she and Emma passed through the long hallway to the restaurant's entrance, Molly avoided looking at the display of Frances's paintings on the wall. It had always been a joy to stop and admire them each time she walked down the lush carpeted hall. Her feelings for Frances at the moment erased her usual praises. Huge commission aside, Randall had no idea how eager she was to be out of La Casa.

Outside, in the crisp evening air, pretending to be playful, Molly pulled up the collar of her shawl sweater, then tugged at Emma's sweatshirt hood. "Bundle up. A perfect night for a brisk walk, huh? It's getting chilly. Last one to the corner is a scaredy cat."

Emma took off and easily beat Molly. When Molly caught up, Emma said, "No fair. You hardly ran." She looked at Molly, then asked, "Are you worried about Daria? Is she sick? I mean grown-up sick?"

"She's just tired. Running a restaurant is hard work, Em. It's long hours, you're on your feet a lot, and you have to be cheerful all the time."

"Guess having an antiques shop is a lot easier."

Taking hold of Emma's hand as they crossed the street, Molly said, "Some days I'm not so sure. But having you around to help makes it easier."

"Maybe we should call Daria later, like you said. Just to be sure."

"Oh, I plan to. You can bet on that."

When Molly was certain Emma was asleep, she went down to the shop and called Daria at the restaurant. Manuel told her Daria wasn't feeling well and Randall had taken her home. Now Molly was really worried. She was about to call Daria at home when she noticed that the red light on her answering machine was blinking. She was surprised to hear Frances's voice, and wasn't exactly thrilled by her message. The Lerners, Frances had said, met her at La Casa today and had taken tons of the boxes in the studio with them. Frances went on to add that she knew Molly would understand, and considering how long the family had been close, contributing all the photos for the Lerners' book was more important than their monetary value.

Molly couldn't fault Frances's loyalty, but couldn't help feel a twinge of annoyance. The dozens and dozens of autographed celebrity photos would have brought a substantial commission. But since she hadn't had time to value them, Frances didn't owe her a thing. Molly deleted the message and smiled. *How quickly the soul of a dealer beats when a treasure is at hand. And how quickly it turns dark when one is lost.*

Shrugging off thoughts of avarice, an occupational hazard for an antiques dealer, she punched in Daria's home number. After four rings the answering machine kicked in. "Hi, it's me, Molly," she said. "Just wanted to make sure you're okay. Call me if you need anything, okay? Get some rest and I'll talk to you tomorrow. Eve's sick too. Must be a bug going around. I've got chicken soup," she added. "It's in a can, but I can handle that."

Randall sat in the kitchen of Daria's condo at Spanish Bay and listened with Daria to Molly's message. "Want to call her back? Tell her you're okay?" Randall asked.

Daria shook her head.

He sipped the latte she'd made him and waited patiently as she moved about the sleek but hardly used kitchen, wiping counters rarely used and fussing with a vase of flowers. Finally he said, "You've barely said a word since we left Carmel. Mea culpa, okay? I'll apologize on bended knee if that's what you want. I should have given you a heads-up. Loomis is the soul of discretion."

Sitting across from him now, she said, "All it takes is one tiny slip."

"Come on, Daria! The man is a gent. Do you think for one minute he wouldn't realize you'd be worried. Besides, it's ancient history. Just another case. He always asks about you. He admired you very much. Still does."

Daria brushed away tears clouding her eyes. "I don't want Lucero to ever know."

Randall looked away. It wasn't his place to tell her Lucero knew everything.

"His career would be over if I married him. You know my past would kill it. And don't tell me it happened too many years ago for anyone to remember. Those media snakes would find it and link me with that mess."

"We kept your name out of all the records," Randall said. "Loomis, Mario, and I are the only ones who know. And Vince's real name was the one used on the reports, not the one he used in the city. Lucero loves you, Daria. That says it all."

Daria's laugh was bitter. "Oh, sure! Love conquers all, huh? A man without his profession is no man at all. He'd end up hating me."

"I think you're selling him too short. What you did was heroic. You have nothing to be ashamed of."

"You're thinking like a cop, not a voter. I don't want Molly to know either."

"That's up to you. But I gotta tell you, it won't matter to her either. She'd run across hot coals for you. Besides, we'd never have broken the case without you."

"Maybe. Maybe not."

"If you're worried about Jason and Steffi Lerner, forget it," Randall said. "They'd be the last people to talk. Fuckers are lucky they didn't do time."

"I almost fainted when they showed up at Frances's house that night. I had no idea they were up this way. I haven't seen them since . . ." Daria held her head in her hands and sighed. "If only I hadn't introduced them to Vince."

Randall reached across the table and took hold of her hands. "You've got to stop blaming yourself. The Lerners would have found another source. If it hadn't been Vince, it would have been someone else."

"Well, it wasn't someone else. It was Vince. And he's dead because of me."

## ᨈ 15 ᨈ

*M*olly managed to open on time Monday morning. Before her first pot of coffee was ready, the shop was filled with several tourists. Thank God for the tour bus industry. Greeting them warmly, she hurried to her desk, dumped the ashtray she'd used last night and had forgotten to empty, then hurried into the storage room and set it on a shelf. She tried Daria again. The answering machine picked up and she left another message. When she returned, she found Bitsy waiting at her desk.

"I'm on my way to the salon, but since you've got company, I can stay and help." Handing Molly an envelope, she said, "This is the check for the Belleek. I've made it out to Frances, like you wanted. When can I send Robbie over to pack it up?"

Molly didn't want Bitsy to know La Casa was off limits until Loomis arrived, so she said, "I'm okay here. Uh, I'm not going to La Casa tonight, but how's Wednesday?"

"Fine. I'll have Robbie call you. You can't believe the razzing I'm getting now that Sister Phil has moved in. No one can believe I'd end up having a nun live with me!" Bitsy's raspy laugh startled two of the male tourists. When they looked her way, she gave them one of her best winks. "Oh, the talk around town is hilarious. That big old house needs more people in it. I wish you and Emma would move in too." Before Molly could say a word, Bitsy hurried on, "Oh, I know . . . you love living over the shop. It's so close to everything. Sorry I brought it up again."

Molly smiled. "I'm glad you'll have some company. Sister Phil is quite a character. I won't worry about you so much now."

Patting her silver chignon, Bitsy said, "Well, darling, I'm off." Glancing around the shop, she said, "Call me at the salon if you stay busy today." Turning toward the men, she added, "Our little village is filled to the rafters with such lovely guests."

Molly walked Bitsy to the door, then headed to three men examining two glass cases of military miniatures. "If I can be of assistance, please let me know." When they responded only with polite smiles and nods, Molly headed back to her desk. She'd learned a long time ago to let customers make up their minds without too much interference. The hard sell never worked. Particularly with antiques. Many collectors liked to think they knew their own mind, and they didn't need a salesperson hovering.

While she had a moment, she decided to call Max to find out if he and Nicholas would be arriving tomorrow. But first she'd better call Randall and ask when Loomis was arriving. Shit! Of all the time to lose access to La Casa, this was not it. And she'd best call Virginia to see if she could fill in on Tuesday. She couldn't very well ignore Nicholas just because she had a shop to run.

"Excuse me, but may I speak to you about an item?"

Molly looked up to see one of the men who had been eyeing the toy soldiers. "Of course," she replied, and followed him to the display.

"I'm afraid you're sales tag is in error," the man said. Pointing to one of the sets, he went on, "This set of Britain Lancers is not authentic. The officer is wearing a blue jacket instead of a red one."

Molly was careful to keep a smile on her face. Challenges by customers were delicate situations, and composure was everything. The last thing a dealer needed was a reputation for being haughty or adversarial. Not that they couldn't make a mistake, but Molly knew she wasn't wrong. When she bought the set from a customer who'd moved to Hawaii, she'd carefully done her research. By luck, she'd found a set in her copy of *Miller's International Professional Antiques Handbook,* and kept it in the shop to back her up. "Maybe you're thinking of another regiment?" Molly gave him her sweetest smile. "I know how hard it is to keep all the different sets straight. Give me a moment, and I'll check my reference book. There's a similar set illustrated you might like to see. It's so easy to be confused, isn't it? The last thing I'd want to do is mislead anyone."

"Oh, don't bother," he said. "It's a nice enough set as it is. You're a little high, though. Nine hundred seems steep to me."

Molly immediately knew what he was up to. Question the authenticity, and then if the dealer backs down, try to finagle a lower price. One of many variations on the theme. The most popular, with furniture, was trying to pinpoint you on circa. With sets of china, it was usually because the set was too big, or not big enough. However, if a slight price adjustment could be made, the purchase might be considered. Molly knew the toy soldiers were fairly priced. In fact, if she were still in New York, it would be closer to twelve hundred. She pretended to mull his comment over, then said, "I could go eight fifty, but that would be all."

The gentleman played out his role. He paused for a moment, looked at his friend, then shrugged. "That's still more than I feel it's worth. Is that really the best you can do?"

Molly offered a discreet sigh. "I'm afraid so."

Another pause. "Do you take credit cards?"

Molly's smile was brighter now. "Yes, we do. If you'd like to step over to my desk?"

For the next two hours she hardly had a chance to sit. She answered questions, offered suggestions, refused a consignment of lunch pails, and sold three chairs and two lamps.

When the first lull of the afternoon arrived, Molly headed for the telephone. She was about to call Randall when the phone rang. It was Davis Wood, a high-end antiques dealer in Beverly Hills she'd known for years.

"Davis! What a surprise. How nice to hear from you!"

"Well, sweet thing, I've just heard the news about the O'Briens, and while naturally devastated about their demise, I was wondering if there was going to be a mega sale at that fabulous *estancia* of theirs in Pebble Beach."

Molly hadn't felt such glee in days. She knew Davis would have instant heartburn when he found out she was doing the sale.

"As it happens, there will be a sale. Did you know them?"

"Personally? No, lovey, I didn't. But one of my very close friends worked for them, and he's told me the house is a veritable warehouse of treasures. When will it be?"

"Not for a few more weeks. Oh, the house is in Carmel, not Pebble Beach. Your friend is right, though. The merch is to die for."

Molly could swear she heard Davis suck in his breath just before he asked, "You've been there already?"

"I'm doing the sale."

"Ohhh, you gorgeous wench, you! You've been toying with me and just having a marvelous time, haven't you! Well, no matter. I still adore you. You will let me in before the others, won't you?"

"How could I resist?" Naturally, she didn't mention that Max would beat him. "I'll call you as soon as I have a firm date. Bring your checkbook, and plan to spend a few days. You will absolutely die when you see what's here."

"Then the merch is really as fantabulous as Donny has said?"

"Donny? The name doesn't ring a bell. A new dealer?"

"No, no, sweetie. Donny Alquist is—or rather, was— Jack O'Brien's primo set designer. Matter of fact, he did most of the work. He's dying to come up with me. Donny wants to see all the goodies O'Brien bought off his pen. It's a long story, but we can talk later."

"Whoa, Davis. Are you telling me that your friend, er, Donny—"

"You didn't hear this from me, but cross your heart anyway. It's a typical Hollywood fable. O'Brien hasn't lifted a pen in years. Donny did all the creative work, and O'Brien just signed it off. Of course O'Brien got screen credit, but Donny was *very* well paid to keep his sweet little trap shut."

"Were these for Lerner movies?"

"*Naturalamento*. The Lerners and the O'Briens have been joined at the hip for years, darling. But that's all water under the bridge now, wouldn't you say? I'm sure Jason and Steffi will give Donny his due now. I mean, after all, he's been such a grand trouper about the whole thing. Well, listen sweetie, I've kept you long enough. Now get back to that palazzo and get the show on the road. Call me the minute you're ready!"

Molly's thoughts were bouncing all over the room. She barely heard Davis. "You'll be my first call," Molly finally said. She wondered if she should tell Randall. He'd probably think it was just meaningless gossip. But it clearly smacked of those *little things* that he'd told her, over and over, were pieces to a puzzle. What, though, was the puzzle? Was there one? She wasn't sure now. On the other hand, why keep her out of the house if he didn't think something was afoot? Surely not for just some kid that decided to rip the place off. And she was almost convinced it was someone young. Whoever had shoved her couldn't have been all that strong. The blow to her back had been mild. But it had been enough to make her fall. A real thief might have hit her over the head, or at least hard enough to knock her out. She hadn't given that much thought until now, or that the sound of running footsteps hadn't been heavy or clunky. But why the studio?

She sat at her desk and stared out the display window as she tried to make sense of what had happened. Now that the Lerners had taken the boxes, it was too late to dig through them to see what was so important. She hoped whoever the intruder was didn't know Jason and Steffi had them. Randall should know about that too so he could warn them.

*Be careful what you wish for* popped into her mind. She'd been worrying about dwindling finances and a less than exciting array of merch, and now, just when all those problems were on the brink of being solved, this damn thing had to happen. She should have kept her mouth shut, taken Robbie with her for support, and finished the job. She could have told Randall after the fact. He would have yelled at her, but that was nothing new. Randall liked to yell. It seemed to be the only way he knew to show he cared. What a complex man. But what fun it was to trade barbs with him. They'd fallen into the routine so easily, they ought to think about taking it on the road. Maybe they could audition for one of those reality shows.

Molly had to bite back a grin as she punched in his number. Max and Nicholas were due tomorrow and she didn't know what to tell them. Her shoulders slumped when she was told Randall was out. She left a message and said it was important. She no sooner hung up than Max called.

"Now don't hate me," Max began, "but Nicholas and I won't be down tomorrow. I had to interrupt his flight here and ask him to meet me in Jackson Hole. One of my dearest clients is selling out, and he's got half a dozen Georgia O'Keeffe's, and you just *know* Nicholas is the best one to handle them. I mean, love, what perfect timing and all. Not to mention a tidy bit of change for me too."

Molly looked up and said a silent thank-you. "By all means get right on that. I've got plenty of time, so don't worry about rushing here. Take your time. There's been a bit of delay anyway. In fact, I was about to call you, and—"

"The sale isn't off, is it?" Max blurted. "I've already got two collectors frothing at the mouth for those Art Deco darlings."

"No, the sale is still on," Molly quickly assured him.

"I've got them here at the shop waiting for you. It's just some, uh, question on the artwork. I mean, Frances might not sell some of it." She was lying big-time and winging it so fast she hoped she didn't trip over her tongue. "She hasn't, uh, quite made up her mind. I wouldn't want Nicholas to make the trip for nothing. I mean, as much as I'd love to see him, I know how busy he is."

"Oh, love, my stomach almost flip-flopped. You gave me such a scare. Well, then, we won't rush. I have other clients in Jackson Hole that I might drop in on with Nicholas. Shall we figure the end of next week sometime? Will you know by then?"

"I'm sure that will be perfect. By the way, what happened to the truck you were sending down?"

"That's the other reason for my call. It will be there tomorrow. You'll just fall in love with everything. *Soo* many to-die-fors you'll be frothing at the mouth. Honey, I've really got to go. I'm having early drinks with some of the boys and I'm already late. Give Emma a big hug, and I'll call you in a few days."

Molly hung up, relieved. She tapped the small crucifix under her sweater and said, "*Thanks, pal.*"

In the next two hours *Treasures* hosted two couples who'd just bought what sounded like a very plush vacation home at Lake Tahoe and were about to shell out four grand for a mid-eighteenth-century Irish mahogany drop-leaf table until one of the wives nearly screamed, "Why is it called a *wake* table?" Molly held her breath, then tried to make the answer lighthearted. "Oh, it's nothing, really. It's . . . well, it's just a style. The, uh, real tables were built to hold a coffin. Long and narrow, with deep drop leaves. The table was used after the funeral for the, uh, wake feast." Running her hand over the silky smooth surface, she said, "This table is too finely made to have actually been used for that." Turning to the other woman, she added, "You can tell by the patina it's been well looked after. What's so wonderful about this style is that you can use it behind a sofa with lamps, and then open up one leaf to use for dining." She'd hoped changing the subject to a practical use might work.

Finally, the woman who'd been concerned nodded. "Yes, I can see what you mean. There're no scratches or anything. So, it's just a style then, right?"

Molly crossed her fingers behind her back. "Yes. A very popular style. Many of the finer homes back East have at least one." Considering the age of the table, it might very well have held a coffin once or twice. But she wasn't really lying. How could she know anyway?

When they agreed on the table, they then moved to a set of four Eastlake chairs Molly absolutely loathed. Max had sent them down and begged her to take them off his hands. He'd picked them up at an estate sale in Atherton, just south of San Francisco, and they had unfortunately been part and parcel of a larger group of pieces he'd wanted. The woman who'd been reluctant about the table asked if they were genuine Eastlake. Molly immediately said, "I don't know if they're his or not. The design is correct, but Charles Eastlake didn't stamp his pieces, so it's hard to know. His Gothic Revival designs were widely copied." She shuddered to think they might be considering placing them with the wake table. It would be like dressing Audrey Hepburn in urban guerrilla fatigues. "I've priced them as if they were copies. But they're very sturdy, and if you have children, you couldn't ask for a better chair."

By the time she locked the front door and put up the Closed sign, she was feeling the ups and downs of the past few days. She was aching to join Emma upstairs. All in all, it had been a good sales day. She'd sold the wake table and the Eastlake chairs, and along with the miniature soldiers, she'd managed to wrap up another six hundred in a lamp and several smalls.

As she climbed the stairs, she had visions of her shoes off, her sweats on, and a hot cup of Café Francais. Emma was in the kitchen making a salad. "I thought I'd better get started. Do you want avocados?"

Molly kissed the top of her head. "Someday you're going to have to teach me how to cook. Avocado is fine, but easy on the dressing, okay? So, what have you been up to this afternoon?"

Emma moved around the tiny kitchen like a pro. There was no wasted motion as she reached into the fridge, took out the salad dressing, held the door open with her hip, poured the dressing on the salad, then replaced the jar, made a half turn and reached up for two salad dishes, set them on the counter, then pulled open a drawer and took out two forks. "I've got those stuffed chicken breasts we bought the other day in the oven. Should be ready in a half hour. Wanna watch the news while we dine?"

Molly took the dish Emma handed her and smiled. "Remind me to increase your allowance. Cooking wasn't part of the deal, but you've taken over like a champ."

Emma followed Molly into the living room. "Can we afford an increase?"

Molly turned on the evening news, then sat opposite Emma on the floor in front of the oversize coffee table.

"We certainly can. Oh, Max is sending down a truck tomorrow! We've got merch coming!"

Emma raised a fist. "Yeah! Life is good!"

Molly laughed again. "And he and Nicholas won't be here until late next week. So we'll have plenty of time to get the shop in order with all the new stuff." Molly then told Emma about the day's sales, then asked, "So, what were you up to this afternoon?"

"Well, I kept an eye on Tiger a lot. I think she might be having her family any time now. She doesn't want to go out and she's sticking close to her maternity box. Uh, and I studied Toby and Character Jugs too. I highlighted some interesting tips on how to identify the real things."

Molly still couldn't believe how quickly Emma had taken to the trade. She seemed to devour every book she could find on antiques. "Give me a rundown. I'm all ears."

"Well, one of the sure signs is a scalloped top on his hat, and the pipe on his chest should be curled. Umm, the hair should always be brown and with a black fringe. There's a few other things to watch for, but that's a start. Did you know all that?"

"Nope. Never had a clue. Good thing you're on the case, Watson."

"When are we going back to finish up at La Casa?"

Molly hadn't told Emma about Randall's orders, and she didn't plan to. There was no sense in frightening her. "Uh, there's just the books in the study now. Oh, I forgot to tell you that Frances left a message that the Lerners took all the boxes in the studio. So all the movie stuff is gone."

"What? No fair! That stuff is hot!"

"Hey, it's her right. Let's not be greedy, okay? We're still looking at a lot of money."

Emma studied her salad, then sighed. "I saw autographed pictures of someone named Lana something, and that lady that played in that old movie about the South. I looked them up on eBay and they were big ticket items."

"Vivien Leigh?"

"That's the one. Big, big ticket item."

Molly couldn't help but ask. "Okay. How much?"

"Five hundred!"

"That's the way the cookie crumbles."

Emma laughed. "Okay, greed is bad. I'll say a prayer tonight and say I'm sorry."

Molly paused. "Sister Phil teach you a few prayers?"

Emma nodded. "Sort of. She said I could just talk regular too. So that's what I do."

Pleased, Molly smiled. "That's nice. I'll teach you the real ones if you want."

"Okay. It's kind of nice to say them when I get in bed. It's kind of like ending the day on a nice note. I just wish *she* had . . . well, anyway. So, what shall we do tonight? Want to watch a video?"

Molly and Emma had hardly discussed Carrie, and it was apparent Emma still wasn't ready. "Actually, Watson, I thought about running over to La Casa and checking out the books. Then we'll be done and I can concentrate on the merch that's coming in tomorrow while you and Sister Phil get started on the Web site."

"Okay. I'll do the dishes after we're done while you change."

"Uh, why don't you stay here with Tiger. Just in case, okay? It won't take me long. There's only six or eight sets that are worth anything."

\* \* \*

Molly had hurriedly pulled on black sweats, and on her way out of the apartment she said to Emma, "Oh, if Randall calls . . . uh, just tell him I went to the market, okay?"

When Emma raised an eyebrow, Molly said, "It's a long story. Trust me, okay?"

"Are you two mad at each other again?"

"No, silly. It's just . . . well, I'll explain later."

On the way to La Casa, Molly couldn't help but feel nervous. It wasn't as if she expected to run into trouble again. It was crossing Randall that bothered her. She hated going behind his back, but since he wouldn't listen to reason, she felt she had little choice. Granted, she argued with herself, she could wait for Loomis. But that might take days. And now with Max and Nicholas not coming until late next week, her timetable for contacting buyers was woefully behind. She could set things in motion without the artwork. And as soon as she had her inventory database completed, she could begin making calls. All that was left now were the books. She'd be tied up for two or three days as it was with the new merch coming in. Once she had the books listed, Emma could get started on the research, and then the calls could be made. Molly checked her watch. It was a little past seven-thirty. She could be in and out in less than an hour.

When she pulled up in front of La Casa, she didn't give much thought to all the lights on. Frances insisted they be left on so the house looked lived in. Taking out her keys, she checked her notebook for the alarm code, then hurried through the entry courtyard. She was surprised to find the front door unlocked. She wondered if Frances was there, then remembered how careless she was about locking up behind her. Typical artist with her head in the clouds.

Molly headed for the study and found it empty. She thought about calling out, but didn't feel like running into Frances and decided to just do what she came to do and then leave. Frances could be anywhere in the house, and she wasn't going to waste time wandering around looking for her. Heading for the bookcases, Molly quickly began listing the beautifully bound series, noted the number of volumes for each, checked the front page for pertinent information, and then doubled back and counted again just to be sure.

When she stepped out of the study to leave, she thought she heard voices. She paused, then walked down the gallery toward the atrium. The voices grew louder, and an argument seemed to be going on. Moving behind one of the round pillars, she saw Frances waving her hands in the air. Molly stepped back. The last thing she wanted was to walk into a free for all. She flattened her back against the pillar and cocked her ear. The man sounded like Jason Lerner, but she couldn't be certain. She'd only met him a few times, and the conversations had been short. She heard Frances screech, *"You'll regret it!"* Then the man shouted, *"It's over now, understand? This is the end of it!"* It sounded like a lover's quarrel, and she was about to sneak away when she heard another woman yell, *"You bastard! I'll kill you before I let you ruin my life again!"*

Molly's breath caught in her throat when she realized the other woman was Daria. What the hell was going on here? Her hand flew to her mouth. She didn't dare let them see her. She knew Daria had a temper, but maybe if she just pretended she'd just come in and called out, she could defuse them.

Before she could decide what to do, the man was shouting again, *"I didn't come here for you, bitch! So don't threaten me! It's Frances that needs to get her ass straight once and for all. So now she knows the lay of the land. It's been going on too long, and now it's over! All of it!"*

Molly heard one of the French doors slam, and then the man's voice again. *"Come back here! I'm not through with either of you!"* She didn't know who left, but she wasn't going to poke her head around to see.

Very carefully, she tiptoed back down the gallery and let herself out. She didn't even bother to close the front door. Trying to make as little noise as possible, she carefully opened the still battered door to the pickup and started the motor. She hit the gas so hard she nearly spun out on the gravel. After she'd gone a block, her hands began to shake. She hated leaving Daria there, and prayed she was the one who left. How strange. They had all seemed so friendly before. She wondered what the hell caused this sudden anger. Whatever they were arguing about was none of her business, yet she couldn't help but feel like a wuss for not stepping in and maybe forcing them to cool off.

When she was halfway home, it suddenly struck her that she hadn't seen Daria's car at the house. She had no idea what Frances or Jason drove. Their cars could have been any one of those parked on the street. And now that she thought about it again, she was sure it was Jason Lerner's voice she'd heard.

*M*olly was headed for the shower by seven the next morning when the phone rang. She'd not slept well, worrying about Daria. She'd laid awake until eleven trying to make up her mind to call and see if she was okay. Each time she reached for the phone, she changed her mind. She and Daria had shared past history, but Molly knew there were gaps. It was apparent now some were painful.

Emma called out from her room. "Do you want me to get that?"

"I've got it." Molly picked up the phone, and almost had to pull it from her ear. Bitsy was literally screaming. "Turn on the news immediately! I'll hold on!"

"What's wrong?" Molly first thoughts were another terrorist attack. She rushed to the television and switched it on. "Don't tell me it's another bombing!"

"It's La Casa!" she shouted. "Oh, my God! I can't talk! Just listen!"

Molly sank on the sofa as she heard the morning anchor describe the inferno that had nearly destroyed one of Carmel's most famous homes. It was too early to know the cause of the fire, but the reporter on the scene said that two people had been found inside last night, and one was rushed to the burn unit at Community Hospital. A second victim, believed to be dead, had not been identified as yet.

Molly's face turned ashen. Her first thought was of Daria. She picked the phone up from the coffee table and told Bitsy, "I'm on my way to the hospital. I'll call you later." When Emma came out of her room, she said, "There's been a fire at La Casa and someone was taken to the hospital. I'm on my way there. Stay here until I get back."

"Is it Frances? Oh, gosh, I hope she isn't hurt!" Emma gasped.

"I don't know who it is yet." Pulling her pajamas off as she ran to her bedroom, Molly called Daria's house. When the answering machine came on, she almost wilted. *Oh, God! Please don't let it be Daria! Please! I'm sorry if it's Frances, but please not Daria!*

Molly broke every traffic law in the book as she drove through Carmel and up the Holman Highway to Community Hospital. She nearly got lost in the sprawling parking area. Finally finding a parking place, she ran all the way to the information desk in the lobby. Almost out of breath, she managed to ask about the burn victim from the La Casa fire. When little information was forthcoming, Molly was nearly beside herself. One of the volunteers at the desk took pity on her and suggested she sit by the koi pond next to the restaurant while she tried to find someone who could help. Molly took little notice of the huge pond in the middle of the main floor of the hospital. She sat on the ledge and began to cry. When she felt a hand on her shoulder, she looked up and saw Officer Wilkins. "Hey, Molly. Take it easy. The chief's here. Want me to get him?"

Molly brushed the tears from her face, then nodded. Before Wilkins could leave, she grabbed hold of his arm. "Who is it? Who did they find?"

Wilkins hesitated, then said, "It's Frances O'Brien. She's in pretty bad shape. I don't think you can see her today."

"The news said there was a . . . a body. Do you know who—"

"I can't say any more, so don't ask. The chief will kill me."

Molly was ready to go on her knees and beg. "I won't tell him," she pleaded. "I've got to know, Wilkins, damn it!"

"Sorry, Molly. I can't."

When Molly made the sign of the cross and lowered her head, Wilkins said, "Yeah, Frances is gonna need a lot of prayers. So is the other one." He was about to turn away, then said, "Hey, how about I get you some coffee? I'll tell Randall you're here."

"Nothing, thanks. I'll sit here and wait for him." After Wilkins left, Molly said three Hail Marys then wrapped her arms around her chest to stop from shaking. When her body had finally calmed, she fished out her cell phone and called Emma. "Frances is the burn victim, but I don't know how bad it is, and I don't know who died in the fire. Randall is here so I'll ask him. Has Daria called?"

"No. Should I call her and tell her? Oh, gosh, Aunt Molly! I feel so bad for not liking Frances now."

"Don't fret over that, honey. I'm not crazy about her either, but that isn't important now. Uh, don't call Daria, she's probably on her way here. As soon as I see Randall, I'll come back. But if Daria should call, tell her I'm here and to call me, okay? I'll call Bitsy and fill her in."

Molly nervously fiddled with the cell phone as she tried to imagine what happened last night after she'd left. Her anxiety over Daria quickly morphed into an overwhelming sense of remorse for not stepping into the atrium. A simple *Hey, what a surprise! I just stopped in to list some books,* might have cooled everyone off. This tragedy might not have happened if she'd only . . . But before she could complete that thought, she saw Randall coming her way.

He looked like he'd been up all night. He was in jeans and a black polo shirt and his eyes were like slits. His lips were set so tight, Molly wanted to cringe. He stood silently before her for a long moment, then sat next to her on the pond's ledge. "Guess you saw the news."

The smell of smoke clung to him like a second skin. Molly almost gagged. "Bitsy called me. I got up here as quick as I could." She desperately wanted to ask him who the dead person was, but knew he would shut her off. "How's Frances?"

He stared at her, then shrugged. "Wilkins opened his big mouth, huh?" Running his hands over his eyes, he looked at her, then said, "Doesn't matter now. The media already has it by now. She's got first degree burns on her hands and has smoke damage to her lungs. She's lucky to be alive."

Molly was about to speak when Randall said, "Before you bug the hell out of me, the dead body was Jason Lerner."

Molly tried not to let him see the relief on her face. "Oh, God! How horrible! Was . . . was anyone else there? I mean, who called the fire department?"

"A neighbor called it in around eight forty-five. Saw the flames when he was out walking his dog."

Molly gripped the pond ledge so tight her knuckles were white. That was only moments after she'd left. *God, God, God! Oh, Daria! It wasn't you! It couldn't be you!* She took a deep breath, then asked, "Any idea what happened? I mean, how did the fire—"

"Don't know yet." Randall took her hand in his and squeezed it. "Look, this is a tough one for all of us. People we know . . . well, it's hard. Go on home. I'll let you know about Frances when I hear more. Get hold of Daria, would you? Let her know. I've got to send someone down to Ventana to notify Steffi Lerner. I'd go, but I've got to get back to La Casa."

Still holding onto his hand, and surprised at the gesture, Molly asked, "Do you think . . . I mean . . . could any of this have anything to do with—"

Randall turned to face her and grabbed her other hand. He held them both so tight, Molly almost winced. "Stop right there. Please, Molly. This time I'm begging you, okay?"

Molly searched his face and was shocked to realize she hadn't noticed how drawn it was. His eyes, barely visible through the slits, were almost opaque. A light stubble was beginning, and even his eyebrows seemed to droop in anguish. He had the look of a man who was on the verge of losing a loved one. "I'm sorry. I didn't realize how fond of Frances you've become."

Randall abruptly let go of her hands. "Are we on the same page here?"

"I was just . . . I mean, I started to say one thing, and then that came out." Molly closed her eyes. "I guess, well, she is very attractive, and probably charming, and—"

"Stop with the guesses. You're digging a hole on the

wrong property." Randall rose and shrugged. "Go home, will you? I'll let you know when Frances can see visitors." He started to walk away, then turned. "There's a guard at her door, so pass that long. I don't want problems, okay?"

There was no point in pressing him. She watched him leave and was struck by the slump of his shoulders. She had no idea he'd been so taken with Frances O'Brien. The emptiness she felt hit her hard.

Outside, she ignored the No Smoking signs and reached in her tote for a cigarette. As hard as she was trying to quit, today's events stirred up the need for something to calm her nerves. Besides, she thought, it was too early for a drink. Overcoming an addiction, no matter what it was, took a steady dose of discipline and strength she couldn't muster today.

When she dug the Zippo out of her pocket, she noticed a cluster of smokers several yards away and decided to play by the rules. She needed time to think before she went home. When she reached the designated area, she smiled her *Yeah, we're all bad people* smile and lit her cigarette. She was greeted with nods and a few winks from the men. Staying at the edge of the group, she turned away and stared at the pine forest that surrounded the beautiful hospital. She remembered someone calling it the jewel in the crown of health care facilities on the Central Coast. Huge, with immaculate wide corridors, cutting edge equipment, a top staff with, believe it or not, caring and courteous nurses, and an enormous koi pond in the middle of the hospital next to the restaurant. It wasn't a bad place to be if you needed a hospital. How funny, she thought, that her mind should suddenly focus on this sprawling complex. But she knew the reason. She needed something to chase away the guilt consuming her. And, she reluctantly had to admit, the look on Randall's face when he mentioned Frances.

She was about to snuff out her cigarette when she overheard the woman next to her talking on her cell phone about the fire. When Molly recognized her as a local TV reporter, she inched closer, pulled out her cigarettes, and then pretended to search for her lighter. The reporter was asking for a cameraman to join her. Molly froze when she heard her say the dead man had been shot but hadn't been identified yet. Word was, a full-scale homicide investigation was in the works, and that Carmel's police chief had just left. She quickly added that she didn't know the identity of the burn victim, but the scuttlebutt said it was Frances O'Brien, who owned La Casa. It was anyone's guess, she reported, if O'Brien had fired the shot that killed the unknown victim.

Molly's ears began to ring with Daria's threat. Throwing the cigarette in the sand urn, she tried to appear calm as she walked away. Once out of sight, she ran like a demon to the pickup. She yanked the door open and called Emma. Waiting for her to answer, Molly pulled out of the parking lot and headed to the exit on Holman Highway. When Emma answered, she blurted, "Have you heard from Daria?"

"No, not a word."

It was a good thing that she was waiting for the light to turn green, she thought. Her eyes were shut tight in agony. "I'm going over to her condo at Spanish Bay to find her. I, ah . . . she needs to know about Frances. Call Bitsy for me, and tell her Frances has first degree burns on her arms. And that's all I know." When the light turned green, Molly hit the gas, then said, "Oh, shit! I almost forgot. Max is sending a truck down. I don't know when it will arrive. Go down to the shop and be on the lookout, okay? Sorry, Em, but can you handle all that?"

"Sure. If the truck shows up, I'll call you."

"Okay, thanks. Oh, better put the Closed sign up. *Treasures* is not open for business today."

Molly turned right on Holman and tried to remember which road to take to get to the other end of Pebble Beach without turning back and going through the Hill gate. If memory served, it should be the next one on the left. She'd driven these mazelike roads on a number of garage sale weekends and had a fairly good grasp of the lay of the land. Traffic headed for Pacific Grove was heavy, and Molly found herself pounding on the steering wheel in frustration. She yelled a few choice combinations no one would hear, and almost didn't recognize her cell phone's chirp. With one hand free she reached for it on the seat next to her and came up empty. She glanced down at the floorboard and saw the silver case shimmering in the corner. She pulled to the shoulder and put the car in park. Reaching down, she managed to answer before the chirping ended. It was Emma. Every ounce of air flew out of Molly when she heard Emma say Daria was at the apartment and that she looked awful and to hurry home.

"Is she hurt?" she nearly screamed in relief.

"No . . . not that. Just awful! Messy, and her face is all blotchy."

"I'm on my way. Make her some tea and tell her not to leave! That's important, Emma! She's not to leave or talk to anyone until I get there." Molly snapped the cell shut to stop Emma from asking questions she couldn't and wouldn't answer.

Waiting for the traffic to clear so she could make a U-turn and head back to Carmel nearly drove Molly up the wall. The highway was a stretch of twists across the hills that bordered Monterey, and venturing out was almost impossible. The blind curves were deadly enough without asking for trouble. The moment she saw a break, she hit the gas and almost lost control as she skidded onto the opposite shoulder. Back on the road, she ignored the horns honking behind her and prayed a highway patrol vehicle wasn't behind the two SUV drivers she'd angered. She knew she had to slow down, but when she took the Carpenter Street turnoff to Carmel, she was stunned to realize she was doing nearly fifty in the residential area. This was close to Randall's patch, and the last thing she needed was to be hauled into jail for reckless driving.

When she pulled into the alley behind the shop, she jumped out of the pickup, kicked the unruly driver's door shut, and took the courtyard stairs to the apartment two at a time. Bursting through the French doors, Molly skidded to a stop when she saw Daria on the sofa. Her clothes were a mess and her luxuriant silky black hair was a mass of tangles. Mascara had puddled under her lower lids and her face was indeed all blotchy. "Oh, my God! Where have you been?"

Cradling a mug of tea, Daria's head swayed. "Everywhere . . . and nowhere. In my car. On the beach mostly. I . . . I heard about the fire on the car radio. I . . ." But Daria couldn't go on. She set the mug on the coffee table and dropped her head between her hands. The sobs coming from her tore at Molly. She rushed to her and wrapped her arms around her. "Let it out. We'll talk later."

Emma nearly flew into the room from the small kitchen. "What's wrong?"

The tears streaming down Daria's face told Emma all she needed to know. "You told her about Frances?"

She nodded, then said, "She already knew. Maybe you should—"

"I know. I'll go down to the shop. The truck isn't here yet, but Bitsy's on her way."

"Keep her downstairs. Tell her Daria is up here and upset. Call me when she gets here, okay?"

"Right. I'll take care of everything." Moving to Daria, Emma kissed her cheek and said, "Frances will be okay, you'll see. You stay here with Aunt Molly and try to rest. We'll take good care of you. You can have my room too if you want to lie down."

Molly blew Emma a kiss, then said, "That's a good idea."

Emma headed for the door down to the shop, then turned. "Oh, forgot to tell you. Tiger had five babies while you were at the hospital. They're doing fine. Should I put them in your room in case Daria wants to rest?"

"No. Don't move them. I don't think Tiger would like it."

When Emma left, Molly was surprised to hear Daria laugh. "That's all you need! A woman coming apart and a bunch of kittens." Pulling away, Daria sat up and said, "I should go home and take a shower."

"Don't be silly. You stay put. You can shower here. I've got some sweats you can wear."

"Aren't you going to ask why I've been out all night?"

Molly almost told her she'd been at La Casa last night and heard the argument, then for some reason changed her mind. "Not unless you want to tell me."

Daria reached for the mug, took a long sip, then fumbled in the pocket of her slacks. She pulled out a crumpled pack of cigarettes. Trying to find one that wasn't damaged, she took her time lighting it, then stared at the flame of the lighter. "It would take hours and hours." Her smile was rueful. "It's not a pretty story and you might change your opinion of me."

Molly smiled back. "O ye of little faith. Nothing you could ever say would do that."

Daria eyed her warily. "Really? Suppose I told you I had two deaths on my conscience? Suppose I told you some of the wags around here call me the Black Widow behind my back? Suppose I told you Bitsy Morgan still has a problem being in the same room with me?"

Molly kept her face bland. "Then I'd have to tell you that we both have our mea culpas etched on our hearts. As for Bitsy, well—"

Daria waved her off. "Bitsy is the least of my worries." Rising from the sofa, she said, "Maybe another time. I'm going home to crash. How bad is Frances hurt?"

Molly relayed what she'd learned, then said, "I guess you know Jason Lerner is the dead man."

Daria's face was like a death mask, and Molly could have cut out her tongue.

"How would I know?" Daria said.

Molly's recovery was swift. "Oh, I thought they might have said on the news,"

In three quick strides Daria was at the French doors. "No. They didn't say. I'll call you later, okay?" Blowing her a kiss, she added, "Thanks, Molly."

Molly didn't like the faraway look in her eyes. She was afraid for her and worried she might do something stupid. "Daria, wait! Please . . . please let me help. Whatever it is—"

"Not now. I . . . I've got to get home. I need to . . . I need to sleep. One of those deep, deep sleeps."

Daria was out the door and almost to the bottom of the stairs by the time Molly reached the small balcony. She reached for her crucifix and held it so tightly it almost broke away from the gold chain. She leaned over and shouted, "Daria! Please! Don't leave!"

It was too late. She was gone.

## ~~ 17 ~~

*R*andall was a walking zombie by noon. He'd had no sleep, nothing to eat since last night, a dozen cups of coffee, four cigars, a team of fire investigators whose personalities were deader than the ashes they poked through, and now Lucero was on his heels at what once was the magnificent La Casa. "So, what's the prognosis?" Lucero asked.

"They won't say. The regular bullshit line of it's too early to tell. Don't offer an opinion too early and then have egg on your face."

"Hey, come on. These guys know their job. Give them a break. What the hell do you expect?"

"We can get to the moon, right?"

Lucero grinned. "I love that line. But it doesn't mean shit here. However, the fire does smack of a cover-up. It's an old trick that rarely works, especially with today's technology. What's your take on it?"

They stood together in the atrium where the smell of smoke was not so lethal. "My thoughts exactly. I also think you and I need to find a quiet place to talk. Not my office, or yours. Got any ideas?"

"My folks' kitchen? They're up at Tahoe. The house is empty. That work?"

"Perfect. Where's your car?"

"On the street behind here. I sneaked in from the alley between the properties. A lot of the houses down here have what they call beach gates. I figured this one would too. Every news media on the peninsula is camped out front."

"Okay. I'll wait about a half hour, then leave."

"You remember how to get to the house?" Lucero asked.

"After that barbecue a few months ago? I'll never forget it."

"Yeah, that was a party, all right. Best Spaghetti Hill has seen in years."

"A sixtieth wedding anniversary is memorable these days."

Lucero nodded and began jiggling the coins in his pocket. A sure sign, Randall knew, of his agitation. "So, Jason Lerner is shot in the chest, no gun has been found yet, and Frances's hands are too badly burned to find residue. Right?"

"Right. The doc won't let me question her yet." Randall checked his watch. "Better take off. I've got to check with the techs before they leave."

Randall found the senior Lucero residence in Monterey with little trouble. The hillside residential area overlooking Monterey Bay and Fisherman's Wharf, locally referred to as Spaghetti Hill, had long been populated by scores of Italian families going back three and four generations. They were the fishermen and cannery workers before and during the Steinbeck era. Cannery Row had been their second home. Sardines and Doc Ricketts were fond memories, with tales handed down to grandchildren. It was an area of neat, modest homes, always freshly painted, with meticulously maintained front lawns, and the promise of a good-sized vegetable garden in the back. During the late summer months when the morning fog was light, it wasn't a stretch to drive up and down the hills with your window open and suck in the aroma of fresh tomatoes and basil overflowing from a number of home gardens.

The Lucero home sat on the corner of Franklin, the main street going up to the Defense Language Institute. Randall parked and saw Lucero's car in the driveway. He rang the bell, and Lucero opened the door holding a small white porcelain espresso cup. "Come on in. Got one ready for you." As Randall followed him through the simple but well-furnished home to the large kitchen, he was struck once again by how it reminded him of his boyhood home in San Francisco. Tasteful, but nothing fancy. No lace doilies or plastic covers of a former generation. It was immaculate, and Randall noticed a lingering scent of lemon oil.

He heard Lucero laugh. "I bought my mother one of those fancy espresso machines, and guess where it is? In the cabinet in the box. She still makes it the way her mother did on the stove." He shook his head and laughed again. "What the hell. She likes to do it that way. At her age, who's gonna argue, right?"

Randall smiled. They loved talking about their Italian mothers and the way they had clung to many of the old ways and values. It had become the preamble to many of their more serious discussions. After handing Randall a dish of biscotti, Lucero settled across the big kitchen table. "You've got the floor. What's up?"

Randall dunked the biscotti in his espresso, took a quick bite, then said, "I talked to Duff yesterday. The man has a memory that won't quit. He even pulled out old journals he'd kept. Hell of nice guy. Promised to do some fishing with him." Going for another dunk, he added, "Two local women went missing around the time Marius Lerner lost the house in that poker game to Jack O'Brien. The first one, a Susan Hamilton, late twenties, washed up down by Pfiffer State Park three days later. An assumed suicide. Family lived in Seaside, broken home, no siblings. Heavy into the drug scene, so it might even have been an overdose down by the beach. The second was Hillary Thornton. Nineteen, family in Carmel for five or six years, down from Portland. Father was an instructor at Fort Ord. Mother dead, one sister by the name of Ginny, I think Duff called her. Seemed she dogged the hell out of Duff. Anyway, the father filled out a missing persons when she didn't show up for two days. It was Clambake time, heavy parties going on with all the golfers and celebs up from L.A. Hillary wanted to be an actress." Randall looked at Lucero and his grin was just slightly nasty. "Father said she'd gone to a high-class party in Carmel. She never came home. No other missing persons reports for five more years."

"Five years? That's past the time frame Phillips gave you, right? You think Thornton might be the skeleton in the coffin?"

"I'm heading that way. So now we have to wonder, who killed her? Lerner, or O'Brien? Or, was she even killed?

Could be an accident and they panicked. I held off sending Wilkins and Maili Montgomery, my new detective, down to notify Steffi Lerner about her brother until I heard from Phillips. We didn't have a good enough ID last night. Phillips finally confirmed it was Lerner. He found his name and an inscription on his Rolex."

"If it's Thornton, and suppose it was an accident, why stuff her in that stupid thing and then keep it around? Why not dump her in the ocean or bury her somewhere? Hell, they'd probably never find her if they dug up a hole in Pebble Beach."

"Funny, Molly said the same thing the other day."

"Molly? Oh, fuck man! Not again! Can't she mind her own business? What made her come up with that?" Lucero grabbed a biscotti, bit off a hunk and chewed. "Sure. I get it. When she got hit at the house, she started playing Holmes again, right?"

"She's smart, pal. We both know that firsthand. She'd already figured the skeleton was real and was going off on a tangent with me the other day. Said damn near the same thing you did just now."

Lucero opted for dunking this time. "Great minds and all that."

"I'll drink to that. I don't mean to sound crass, considering Jason Lerner is dead and Frances is badly hurt, but Molly just lost one hell of a big job and she might be pissed off enough to butt in. You know what she's like."

Lucero laughed. "Yeah, I do. But this time we're lucky. No antiques involved. Just a simple homicide."

"They're never simple," Randall said as he reached for the last biscotti.

"So where do we go from here?"

"I've got to try to track down the father and sister. Frank Thornton would be in his eighties now. The sister somewhere in her fifties. Phillips thinks there's a chance some DNA could be pulled from the bones. It's iffy, but he's optimistic. If he's right, and we can find the Thornton family, we'll ask for theirs and see if we can get a match."

"But what if the woman isn't from here? She could have come up from L.A., or anywhere for that matter. Hell, you know how many wannabes showed up at those golf tournaments? They still do. In the hundreds. Golf groupies, party girls, high-priced call girls and whores. We get them all every damn year."

"Then I've got one hell of a job ahead of me. Loomis, by the way, is doing some checking for me on the Lerners and O'Briens before he heads up here."

"That your old homicide buddy? The one you thought would make a good investigator for me?"

"Yeah, the same. I asked him to come up for a week or two before he took off to see the world. I wanted him to stick with Molly while she finished up at La Casa. Now that won't work. I was hoping he'd get a good feel for here and decide to stay."

"That's a no-brainer. We just have to wine and dine him a few times at Daria's and he'll be hooked. Speaking of Daria, she hardly spoke the other night at dinner. I had a feeling she was rattled about the Lerners showing up. Now with this mess . . ."

Randall thought it best he not mention the night at La Casa when the Lerners showed up. Daria had handled that well. He'd been surprised Frances hadn't turned them away. And then when she continued to socialize with them, and invited him to have lunch with them at Moss Landing with her, he was intrigued, and agreed. It was beginning to look like two generations of the two families each had tragic ties that kept them together. "She's okay. The Lerners knew enough to stay clear of her. Hey, it's probably just one of those mid-life things. Women get them after forty. They come out of it. On the other hand, she works like a dog. She's at her place at eight and doesn't leave until midnight. Maybe she's just tired and needs some time off."

Lucero was playing with the crumbs on his mother's starched tablecloth. "Yeah, that's probably it. I should talk to her about going to Vegas or something."

Randall was on his feet. He picked up the espresso cup and took it to the sink. "That dump stinks. No place for a lady. Where's the dish soap?"

"Leave it. I'll clean up. Yeah, maybe Tahoe would be better. She's got a small place up there. I'll talk to her."

"Do that. Listen, I got to run. I'll keep you posted every day." Stopping at the kitchen door, he said, "Don't leave any crumbs on the table. Your mother will have a fit."

Lucero laughed. "Will you look at us? The big shot cop from bad-ass L.A., and the D.A. of Monterey County worrying about his mother's tablecloth."

Randall smiled. "We were brought up right."

"Good mothers," Lucero said.

"Yeah. Good mothers."

Randall was at the door when his cell phone rang. Phone calls bearing bad news were part of a cop's job. It didn't take long to develop an impassive manner. With no reaction, Randall listened intently, then said, "I'm on my way." He turned to Lucero. "Wilkins and Montgomery just found Steffi Lerner's body in a ravine off the deck of her suite at Ventana. She was shot in the back. Montgomery thinks she's been dead for maybe ten or twelve hours. Face, jaw, and upper extremities are already in rigor mortis. Just a guess on her part, but she's pretty sure. They've got a call in to the sheriff."

Lucero too had learned that same lesson. He looked at his watch; it was just past ten. "Shit. Sounds like she was killed after her brother. This is getting nasty."

Before Randall could reply, his cell phone rang again. Lucero saw him shake his head. He heard him say, "Fuck," then add, "Well that just rips it all to hell. Jason and Steffi Lerner bought it last night. Yeah, you heard me. Haven't had a chance to call you. Okay. Get it all together and get up here yesterday, *comprende*? I owe you, pal. Big-time."

Lucero began jiggling the coins in his pocket again as he leaned against a wall. When Randall got off, he said, "What?"

"That was Loomis. Marius Lerner died last night in his sleep."

Lucero's eyes popped. "This is a roadblock we don't need. Shit."

"And then some," Randall snorted. "What kind of odds is this, huh? Even a bookie wouldn't touch it."

Lucero pulled away from the wall and patted Randall on the shoulder. "You got your work cut out for you, Chief. Tell me what you need, and I'll do it."

"With Loomis digging down south, and Montgomery on board, I think I'm okay for manpower for now. I might want to take an investigator off your hands now and then. That work for you?"

"You got it. Just let me know. Get back to me as soon as you can."

Randall waved and headed for his car. The Ventana Inn & Spa was about thirty miles south of Carmel, and it would take a good forty-five minutes to get there. In an unmarked station car, Randall opted not to slap a light on the hood or use a siren. While Jason's and Steffi's murders were definitely linked, Ventana was out of his jurisdiction. The Monterey County Sheriff's Department would be the primary on Steffi's murder. It went without saying they would work together, but professional courtesy demanded that Randall remain an interested observer. Barreling down Highway 1 to Big Sur with a red light blinking and siren blaring would have been a breach of etiquette, and a bad display of grandstanding.

His arrival in Carmel, from Internal Affairs in Los Angeles, had set off some low wattage resentment among some of the members of the county law enforcement agencies. Sensing this ahead of time, he'd gone out of his way to make nice. After solving two major homicides since arriving, he'd been reluctantly accepted. The mood slowly changed, and now he got along fine with the other agencies, and he planned to keep it that way.

Lucero was right. Marius Lerner's death just threw a roadblock in his path. The two major principals, Marius Lerner and Jack O'Brien, were dead, and as far as he knew, no one had ever been able to question a corpse. A few psychics might disagree, but he wasn't ready to try that yet. Now, with Jason and Steffi Lerners' homicides, a new can of worms was open. But were their deaths connected to the dead woman in the coffin, he wondered, or something else? He hadn't liked it when the Lerners showed up, but then, was *coincidence* rearing its ugly head again? No way. Never happen. There was a tie-in here. He'd just have to find it. And he would. Burned hands or not, Frances O'Brien had some explaining to do.

## ⚡ *18* ⚡

*B*itsy Morgan was in a big-time snit. "I've just come from the hospital and they wouldn't let me see Frances! Can you imagine? Turning me away? After all the money I've raised for charity in this town?"

Molly steered Bitsy to the storage room and sat her in the tattered easy chair she'd found at a garage sale and had come to love. "Cool off, have some tea, and try to remember that she was badly burned last night and isn't up to visitors. I'd say *that* might be why none of us can see her."

Bitsy couldn't help but give Molly an embarrassed smile. "You're right of course. I'm just not used to being—"

"Is thwarted a good word?" Emma said as she poked her head in.

Bitsy roared. "Come here, you little brat. I want to turn you over my knee."

Bitsy's laughter did little to lighten Molly's mood. Until it was made public, Molly knew she'd better button her lip and not tell her that Jason Lerner was the dead man in the fire. Randall would know it had come from her, and he'd have her head on the block. Her fear for Daria, however, wouldn't let up, and she wondered how the hell she was going to put on a happy face and make it through the day.

While Emma and Bitsy teased each other, Molly filled the teakettle, then went about the shop turning on all the lamps and making a sign for the door that said the shop was closed for restocking. At least Max's truck full of merchandise would keep her mind busy until she was able to talk to Daria. Randall didn't need to know what she'd heard last night. After all, so what if Daria told Jason she could kill him? People say that all the time when they're mad. She knew she'd probably said it herself at least a thousand times.

Molly returned to the storage room and fixed tea for Bitsy. "Is Sister Phil at home? I've got to call her and tell her I won't need a Web site for the La Casa sale."

"Oh, dear. I hadn't thought about that."

"I didn't either until now. I'm still in a state of shock. Poor Frances."

Bitsy rose and said, "I'd better call my customer and tell her to forget the Belleek. I doubt anything survived that fire. Oh, Lord! What a tragedy. God forgive me, but I'm glad the O'Briens didn't live to see their treasure house destroyed. That alone would have killed them."

"Well, the bright side is that Frances at least is alive. We can be thankful for that."

"Of course. I didn't mean to sound so mercenary."

Molly smiled. "I know you didn't mean it that way. It's a loss on so many levels." Oh, if only Bitsy knew how great a loss. Molly didn't want to think about Jason Lerner. "I've got some calls to make too," she said as she walked Bitsy out. "If I hear any more, I'll let you know."

Emma waved good-bye, then said to Molly, "Guess we're back where we started, huh?"

Molly felt guilty thinking about the huge commission that was now only a dream. She tried to make light of it for Emma's sake. "More or less, but we've got the commission check on the bibliotheque, and Max bought the Art Deco statues. We'll have to wait until Frances is well before we can get that commission. And don't forget, sales have been pretty darn good lately."

"And the truck is coming in today too!"

"Right! Maybe we should start making room? Let's see you flex those muscles, kiddo. We've got to get busy."

The brainstorm hit Molly while she and Emma were moving a late nineteenth century four-panel Chinese floor screen. "Be careful, Em. The gilt is flaking." Setting it behind a pair of Hepplewhite-style inlaid mahogany dining chairs, Molly brushed off her hands and said, "How about running over to Bennie's and getting some goodies. The drivers might be ready for a sugar break. I've got a few calls to make before that truck shows up."

As soon as Emma was gone, Molly looked up Davis Wood's number in her address book. A fire in little old Carmel-by-the-Sea would hardly be news in Los Angeles, but the antiques grapevine was quicker than a GPS beam, and she wanted to get to Davis first, to pick his brain before he heard about the fire and no longer felt a need to be so chummy. She wasn't surprised when he picked up on the first ring. The man lived on the telephone. Everyone teased him about having four private lines. "Of course I haven't told anyone else," Molly reassured him. "I was just thinking about adding some spice to my pitch and thought you might be able to help me since you seem to know so much about the O'Briens."

"Honestly, sweetie, I only know what I mentioned the other day."

Molly laughed. "Well, what about the Lerners? Surely you know about the famous card game."

"Oh, that. Old news."

"Okay, then how about Jason and Steffi? Come on, Davis! I need some glitz, some good old Hollywood glamour."

"Does anyone really care about them? They're just producers, for God's sake."

"True. I guess I was just curious since I met them last week. They were up here to work on a new script and stopped by to see Frances O'Brien when they heard about her parents' deaths."

"I never cared for either of them. By far, too too spoiled, if you know what I mean."

Molly laughed. "Normal Hollywood kids?"

"Oh, these two were brats. In and out of private rehab a dozen years back or so. But then, everyone was, and many still are. They were luckier than some of the others, though."

"Well, it's always good news when addictions can be overcome. I'm still trying to quit smoking!"

"I didn't mean thaaat," Davis drawled. "It was their other sideline that nearly got them behind bars."

Molly's ears perked up. "Which was?"

"Dealing, my love."

"Antiques? You're kidding! Why? Did they need some extra play money?"

"You are such a riot. Drugs, sweet thing. Why? Excitement, darling. The rush of walking the wild side was evidently greater than the product. Trouble was, it turned ugly one night and the dealer got shot. I know from a reliable source it was a deal gone bad, and by the time the cops got there, it miraculously morphed into self-defense and Lerner walked away like a victim."

"Oh, my God, Davis. I had no idea."

"Well, don't repeat it. It's only known to a tiny, tiny circle. Donny and a couple of women were there, as it happens, so that's how I know. Donny played witness to the argument and managed to escape the long arm of the law. I have no idea what happened to the women. I think the cops took them in for questioning and that was all. But oh, did the old studio machine do its damage control! Just like the old days when Louis B. Mayer and his cronies ran the town. The cops were outsmarted and a hot scriptwriter wasn't even needed."

"My lips are sealed," Molly lied.

"Well, just don't let them suck you in with their goody-goody bullshit. Those two are piranhas. Are they still up there?"

"Uh, I'm not sure. But if they are, I'll keep my distance."

"Do that. Oh, honey . . . my other line is blinking. Gotta run. Call me day or night when you've got a firm date, and I'll be there so quick it will make your head spin."

Molly was amazed at how easily Davis had told her such a volatile secret. She always knew he was a major gossip; that's why she'd called him. Now she had to decide what was worth telling Randall. That wonder didn't last long. She'd tell him everything. She wasn't going to hold back ever again. The odds working in her favor could only last so long.

Before she could act on this new information, Max's truck pulled up in front of the shop. Emma's arrival with a bag of pastries was just in time. Molly had the door open for Max's delivery men, and as they came in, Molly offered them coffee and a sweet snack. When both men, new to Molly, declined, she realized they were anxious to get back on the road. "Okay, then." She smiled. "I have no idea what you'll be unloading, so if you think we need more room in the center of the floor, let's get at it."

In no time the four of them had a large space ready. The driver made it clear to Molly that they couldn't stay to help her play with arranging the bigger pieces. The traffic between San Francisco and Carmel was a killer, so she'd best figure out where she wanted them unloaded. "Start bringing the big pieces in, and as soon as I see what it is, I'll have a spot ready."

For the rest of the day, except for a hurried lunch break of pastries, Molly and Emma shoved, carried, cajoled, and teased a late Victorian kneehole desk with a raised back holding a half-dozen tiny cubicles, a lady's walnut writing desk, a Renaissance revival fruitwood marquetry center table, a carved gilt wood console table, a George III drum table, and a magnificent Rococo revival rosewood games table.

The larger pieces had been placed in less than ideal spots, but Molly had little time to plot, and trying to imagine the perfect layout with all that was on her mind was multitasking above and beyond the call of duty. The Swedish long case clock looked horrible where it had been positioned. And the bamboo dressing table with an attached mirror was out of its element next to the pair of satinwood commodes. She let out a deep sigh when she stopped to look at a kingwood serpentine vitrine. It was painted a washed-out green, with lovers in a landscape cavorting in a meadow. Besides being gouache and a recent reproduction, it was absolutely ugly. Why Max had included it in the delivery was a mystery. It should have gone straight to auction. The double door French armoire, nearly eight feet tall, was the biggest problem. And then there was the Chippendale-style linen press, which, Molly guessed, was at least seven feet tall. She'd have to call Robbie and see if he could get his brother to come over and help that night.

"What the heck are we going to do with these two music stands?" Emma asked.

Molly's head was beginning to hurt. She threw out her arms, then shook her head. "Find some sheet music and lay them out? Hell if I know."

"We'll think of something," Emma said. "Looks like we're going to be up all night opening these boxes."

Molly stared at the stack of boxes sitting by the front window and piled on the stairs. She stopped counting at thirty-one. "I'll call Robbie, then I think it's time for a dinner run. How's Chinese sound? We can go over to China Gourmet by the post office."

"Okay. I'll go up and check on Tiger and the kitties first. She's being such a good mother. I love watching her groom them." Emma headed for the stairs, then stopped. "I've been meaning to ask if we could keep them all."

Molly had been poking in one of the boxes and almost dropped a Wedgwood blue jasper coffee can. "All of them?"

"Well, Carmel is cat city, so why not?"

Molly sighed. "Later, okay? We'll negotiate." The minute Emma was upstairs, she hurried to the desk and tried Daria again. Her three earlier attempts had been frustrating. Once again the answering machine came on. Her stomach was beginning to do somersaults. She was tempted to call Randall and ask him to check on her. But then she'd have to tell him why she was so worried. She looked at the mess in the shop and suddenly felt a wave of defeat. Slumping into a chair, she closed her eyes and prayed for guidance. *What the hell . . . er, excuse me . . . what the heck should I do?* She didn't wait for inspiration. She knew exactly what she should do. The answer had been nagging her all day.

She ran up the stairs and found Emma with Tiger and her family. "We need to talk."

Emma followed her into the living room and sat on the sofa. "Is this serious stuff?" she asked. "Did I do something wrong?"

Molly tried for an upbeat smile, but she didn't think it worked. "No, you're in the clear. It's . . . well, there's a situation that's going on, and I need to come clean with you about it. I'm only telling you because—"

Emma's eyes grew huge. "Is it about her? She's not coming back for me, is she?"

Molly wasn't surprised that Emma still referred to her mother as *her* or *she.* The child had good reason. "No!" she quickly said. "Nothing like that. It isn't about Carrie. It's . . . well, it's all this horrible mess at La Casa."

"Whew! You had me really scared there for a minute." Emma looked down at her tightly clasped hands. "I don't want to see her again. I want to stay with you. And that's that. End of story."

Molly didn't know whether to laugh or cry. She moved next to Emma on the sofa and hugged her. "You sound like Randall now. Don't you worry about my sister. I won't let her have you. Ever."

"We're a good team," Emma said as she threw her arms around Molly.

Molly hugged her tighter. "The best."

Emma let out a big sigh. "Okay, enough of this girly stuff. What's on your mind?"

Molly wiped her eyes and laughed with her. "Yeah, right. Okay. Remember on the news this morning the reporter said a body was found in La Casa?"

"Oh, my gosh! I was so worried about the fire, and when you said someone was injured, I must have missed that part. What happened? Who was it?"

"Jason Lerner."

Emma's eyes popped open. "Oh, how awful! He seemed like such a nice man. I think that place is jinxed."

"You might be right. But there's more." Molly still wasn't sure how much she should tell her, but considering what she'd already been through with Emma, and how mature and pragmatic her niece was, she felt Emma could handle most of it. Besides, Jason Lerner's murder would be on the news soon, and she would rather Emma heard it from her. Molly explained what she knew and told Emma what she'd learned from Davis Wood.

"He was murdered? Holy cow. Carmel's not so sleepy after all, is it?" Emma cupped her chin in her hand, then said, "I wonder if Frances killed Jason."

"Frances? She was hurt in the fire, remember? If she killed him, she wouldn't have stuck around. Think about it."

"I'm not sure. Maybe it's just because I don't much care for her. What about Randall? You're not going to keep secrets from him again, are you? You're going to tell him everything your antique friend told you, right?"

"Are you kidding? I'm going to call him the minute I know Daria is okay." As soon as she spoke, Molly knew she'd almost blown it. She hadn't told Emma that Daria was at La Casa. "She wasn't feeling well, remember?"

Emma thought that over. "So I guess you want to forget Chinese and leave me here?"

"Nope. I'm going to drop you off at China Gourmet, then make a quick run to Daria's. I'll call you from there, okay?"

"Cool. Maybe she might come back with you and have some won ton soup. It's good when you don't feel well."

"Sure. Great idea. That should do the trick," Molly said.

But she knew that Daria was going to need more than won ton soup.

*I*t was late afternoon when Randall called Lucero on his cell phone as he drove back to Carmel from Ventana. "I'm headed back to the station. We've got a mess on our hands now. The sheriff's new homicide dick's got a chip on his shoulder and I can smell trouble. You might have to set his ass straight. You tell him I want updates as they come in, not when it's convenient. If he thinks he's gonna leave me in the dark, he'd better find out who the fuck he's playing with, *capice*?"

"What's his name? I'll take care of it," Lucero said.

"I'm counting on it. His name is Reynolds. Here's what I know: Steffi Lerner was shot in the back, then either fell or was thrown over the railing of the deck of her suite. It's possible she was trying to get away from the killer. The shot was heard, but that's all so far. The front desk said no one had asked for her. So the killer knew right where to find her, which leads me to believe he or she had either been in the suite before or had been watching her. My new detective had a digital camera with her and took photos, then made sketches and notes before dickhead got there. Smart gal. She had a feeling we might get shoved onto the back burner. I'll get back to you later."

By the time Randall pulled into the station parking lot, his temper had settled to a simmer. He'd gone out of his way to play nice with Reynolds, but he wasn't going to take a backseat to the jerk. He found two messages on his desk from Loomis. Faxes would be coming in later that day. Randall grinned. He'd have to introduce Loomis to Reynolds. That ought to be a few moments to savor. Now that he thought about it, he'd be sure to have Lucero there. "Okay," he mumbled, "it's time to get the show on the road."

Randall spread out the crime scene photos and sketches from La Casa on the conference table. He made a neat pile of the preliminary reports and interviews, then stared at the incident board. MOTIVE? There were no notes yet. He had a few ideas, but decided to see what info Loomis dug up. OPPORTUNITY made him pause. He needed a cigar to help him examine his reluctance to elaborate on the names listed there. He took his time lighting it, then stood by the window and stared blankly at the cars passing on Junipero Street. His eyes moved up, taking in the towering pines that guarded most of the village from the occasional gusts blowing in from Carmel Bay. He usually got a kick out of watching the crows swoop down and snatch up bits of food tourists' children invariably dropped. It wasn't funny today. It was too easy to picture them as carrions picking at a dead body.

He went back to the incident board and shifted his eyes to MEANS. Okay, who among them owned a gun? He added one more column. For lack of a name to put with the skeleton in the coffin, he titled it L.A. NOIR. How many young women, he wondered, lured by the glamour of the movies, had met their end trying to get on that ladder to fame? It was a bigger club than most people knew. It had opened up for membership the day the first movie camera clicked on. It was worse now. The mania for celebrity seemed to be the new national pastime. Every freak in the world was clambering to be on television. He thought those survival shows were the worst. They encouraged greed and dirty tricks. Great examples to the kids sitting in front of the TV.

Randall didn't like where his thoughts were headed. He couldn't change the world. But he could solve homicides, and he knew he'd better get back to what he did best. Philosophizing was for others. He was just a cop. Seated at the conference table, he pushed the photos of Jason Lerner aside and took a look at the crime scene sketches. Lerner had been found in the salon, and Frances in the dining room, apparently overcome by smoke. So far, no weapon had been found. So, did Frances kill Jason and try to run for it? Did someone else pull the trigger and was Frances was fleeing? How did the fire start? An accident, or was it to cover the killer's tracks? Randall thought back to the night he was at La Casa when the Lerners showed up. The huge fireplace was blazing away, and long tapered candles burned in ornate gilt wall sconces. A bit dramatic, he'd thought at the time, for an informal visit. But then, Frances was an artist, and raised in a family with theatrical flair.

The stately mansion was a shambles. A lifetime of memories and treasures were pretty much gone. Why? And more to the point, who did it? By the time the fire department got to the scene, they had managed to contain the fire and keep it from spreading to the upper floors. With one-foot-thick adobe walls, and the floors and staircase primarily marble, the worst of the fire damage was centered on the lower floor. The wood-paneled walls in the study went fast, and the heavy velvet drapes and over-stuffed furniture in the salon were now expensive cinders.

For the next two hours, he studied the photos and sketches. His notes filled three pages. No one heard the shot. Scenic Road was filled with big houses, stone walls, a roaring surf just across the street, and people settled in front of TVs. When he was nearly through reading the resident interviews, he came across one that notched his temper back up to a boil. Two teenage boys who lived near La Casa had been walking home from the nightly gathering at the beach around eight-thirty when they stopped to check out a vintage pickup they thought was retro cool. They'd noticed it before, and when they saw it in front of La Casa again, they'd thought about leaving a note on the windshield to see if the owner might want to sell it. By the time they got close enough, a woman ran out the gate, got in the pickup, and tore off. There was only one battered orange El Camino in town. Randall pushed away from the table and stared at the statements. He wondered how he could have heartburn on an empty stomach.

He kicked his chair back so hard it almost toppled over. The cigar clamped between his teeth was in danger of breaking in half as he made his way to the incident board. He grabbed the marker from the chalk tray. The urge to throw it across the room was overwhelming. He stood before the column headed OPPORTUNITY. Frances O'Brien was already there. The second name was a long shot, but one he had to take. With regret, he'd had to add Daria De-Marco. His hand was nearly shaking with anger now as he added Molly Doyle.

When Molly arrived at Daria's condominium at Spanish Bay, she could feel her heart flutter as she pressed the bell.

*Please be home. Please be okay. Please tell me what's going on!* She waited another moment, then tried again. The Hail Marys were coming fast and furious now. After a third try, she was ready to pound on the door, until she remembered the deck off the living room that faced the golf course. She hurried to the golf cart path between the buildings and pulled her sweater closer. She wasn't sure if the sudden chill she felt was from fear or from the cool marine air over the bay being sucked in by the higher temperatures in the valley. Vaporous wisps of fog began swirling around her, and when the bagpiper on the golf course at the Inn at Spanish Bay began his nightly lament, she almost crumpled. She didn't need that mournful sound right now. Making her way onto the deck, she found the plantation shutters closed. She had no way now to know whether Daria was okay, or pretending not to be home. She knocked on the glass doors and called her.

She was about to try again when a next door neighbor came out and said, "Are you looking for Daria?"

Molly turned and waved. "Yes. I rang the bell, but thought she might be on the deck and didn't hear me."

"She left for the city for a few days to do some shopping. If she calls, shall I tell her you stopped by?"

"Oh, would you? Ask her to call Molly."

Back in the pickup, Molly called Emma on her cell phone. "Daria isn't home. I'm on my way back. Give Ruby my order, okay?"

"We have company," Emma said.

"Don't tell me. It's Randall, right?"

"Uh-huh."

"Is he, uh, in a good mood?"

"Nope."

"Great. That's just great."

"Sweet and sour pork, shrimp fried rice, and what else?" Emma asked.

"Arsenic would go well with the rice."

"I'll tell Ruby."

Molly knew she was in for it. What *it* was, she had no clue. With Randall, one never knew.

Randall was paying close attention to his Cashew Chicken when Molly slid into the chair next to Emma. "Whew! What a day. And what a nice surprise running into you here."

He set his chopsticks down, took a swallow of Kirin beer, then gave her one of his deadliest smiles. "Surprise? You know I eat here at least three times a week."

"Oh, right. I forgot, I guess. Too much going on. Max sent a truck down today with a few dozen boxes and—"

"Loaned out your El Camino lately?"

Ruby appeared with her dinner at that moment. Molly smiled her thanks. Stalling for time, she asked Ruby, "New haircut? Looks cute. I love the way it's cut in the back." When the waitress left, she said, "Sorry? What did you say?"

Emma reached across Molly for the soy sauce. "He wants to know if you loaned anyone the pickup lately."

"Oh, uh, no. Why?" she asked.

"Just wondering. Pass that soy sauce when you're done, Emma, would you please."

Randall's change in gears spelled trouble. A smile was teasing his lips, and he was almost too polite in asking for the soy sauce. Molly suddenly knew what *it* was. Someone must have seen her at La Casa the night of the fire. She was going to have to do something about that truck. It was like a billboard advertising her whereabouts. She knew she had to tell him about being at La Casa, and she'd planned to after she'd talked to Daria. Now she tried to think how *not* to tell him Daria was there.

When Emma excused herself to go to the ladies' room, Molly asked, "How's Frances? I'd like to visit when I can."

"She'll be laid up for a while. The burns aren't too bad, but she's had some lung damage from smoke inhalation. I wouldn't count on sending flowers yet."

"What a horrible tragedy."

Randall drained his beer. "On a lot of levels."

Molly decided to let that go. Seeing Frances so badly hurt must have been hard for him. Or was he hinting at something else? She fought an urge to shift in her chair, or to flick a stray hair from her forehead. She'd frankly like to disappear into thin air. He was playing his cryptic game again. She hated it when he did that. "I hope there isn't any nerve damage to her hands. For an artist that would be—"

"Yeah. Terrible. You lost a big commission too," Randall interrupted. "You must be pretty bummed about that."

Molly gave him a sharp look. Damn him! "That's so insignificant considering what has happened. I can't believe you said that."

Randall inched closer and was nearly eye-to-eye with her. "And I can't believe you failed to tell me you were at La Casa just before the fire broke out. I've got two witnesses who saw the El Camino there, so don't try to weasel your way out of it."

"Is this what you're pissed about?" Molly demanded.

"That and a few other things. I don't suppose you've had your radio on in that junk heap you drive, or watched a little telly today."

Molly threw down her chopsticks. "I don't watch the *telly* during the daytime. I work for a living. And the radio in the pickup doesn't work anymore. What? Did I miss your big news conference or something? Boo-hoo. Bad girl, Molly."

"Steffi Lerner was murdered."

Molly felt like a Mack truck had just hit her. "*What? When?*"

"Last night. Early guess is it was before Jason bought it. Not sure yet."

"Oh, my God!"

"You ready to tell me what you were doing at La Casa now?"

Molly stared at her dish. Her thoughts were like buck-shot splattering all over the place. She lowered her voice. "Okay. I was there. But Jason was alive when I left." Molly saw Emma coming back to the table and quickly said, "I've told Emma about most of this. I . . . I don't want to have to lie to her, or do double-agent stuff again."

"Emma doesn't have to know the rest. She's a kid, for Christ's sake."

"A damned smart one too. And more level-headed than some people I know."

"What the hell is that supposed to mean?" Randall shot back.

"Are you two arguing again?" Emma chided as she took her seat.

"No. We're having a discussion," Randall said.

"Good. Are you talking about, uh, you know what?"

"Yeah. And you're not part of the conversation."

Emma looked at Molly. "Have you told him what you wanted to tell him?"

"Yes, but he's already assuming I wasn't going to."

"No kidding?" Randall snorted. "You were actually planning to tell me you were at La Casa? Gee. Too bad I had to read it in a witness statement first. I might not have ruined a very expensive cigar if you had."

"You should really give those things up," Emma said. "I'm helping Aunt Molly and Daria to quit smoking. If you'd like, I could be your buddy helper too."

Randall's eyes went into slit mode again, but his voice was polite, "Thank you, Emma. I think I can manage on my own." Picking up his chopsticks, he added, "Eat up. We'll have coffee at your place."

After Emma left for bed, and a second pot of coffee was brewing, Molly began telling Randall what she'd seen and heard at La Casa last night. Her stomach was in knots and she felt sick. She didn't want to tell him about Daria, but knew she had to. She'd learned the hard way that holding back only led to disaster. She was near tears when she told him about Daria showing up at the apartment. "She was a wreck. I didn't tell her I'd been there and heard what I had. I . . . I was hoping she would tell me what was going on. I begged her to stay overnight, but she insisted on going home." Molly went on to tell him how she'd called several times today, and that she'd gone looking for her at her condo only to learn from a neighbor that she'd driven to San Francisco for a few days. "Oh, shit, Randall! I hate being a snitch! I wanted to talk to her first. I'm only telling you now because I'm afraid she might do something stupid. If anything happens to her . . . I couldn't live with myself. You've got to find her! She couldn't have killed Jason or Steffi! I don't know what Jason was referring to when he was yelling at her, but I know Daria isn't a murderer."

Randall watched the tears flow down her face and kept silent.

Finally, Molly said, "At least I know you don't think she is either." When Randall didn't answer, Molly's face paled. "Tell me you don't!"

Randall rose, picked his cup up from the table and carried it to the kitchen. Molly held her breath until he returned. She wiped her tears and watched him head for the door, and almost died when he said, "I don't know what to think. I'll put some feelers out in the city and see if we can track her down."

"Wait. There's more you should probably know."

Randall stopped and shook his head. "Are we gonna play this game again? 'Oh, by the way, Randall, I almost forgot to tell you . . .'? Jesus, Molly. Do I have to scream and yell at you all the time before you'll come clean with me? Contrary to popular belief, I'm not a freakin' ogre."

"You *haven't* yelled or screamed. I know you're not an ogre. I tell people that all the time."

Settling near her on the sofa, his grin was weary. "That's one of my lines."

"I know." She reached for a cigarette on the coffee table and then hesitated. Her hand hovered over the pack. When she finally took one, she said, "I keep thinking Emma can see through walls." She changed her mind and threw it on the table, then told him about her conversation with Davis Wood. For once Randall didn't interrupt. Finally she said, "I don't know if any of that helps, but maybe it's tied in somewhere."

"I'll think about it. Good work, Molly. That's twice now your pals have helped. I promise not to badmouth dealers again, okay?"

"I'll hold you to that. I might even buy a recorder in case you compliment me again. I'd like to have it for the next time you're pissed at me, or get snarky." She watched one of his better smiles fill his face, then suddenly felt awkward. "I'm wondering if this is about blackmail and that Jason figured Frances knew about it and he was afraid she was going to continue it. Could that be what he meant by 'It's been going on too long and now it's all over'?"

Randall didn't answer. He had a good idea what Jason Lerner had been yelling about, but he wasn't sure where Frances fit in. He wanted to kick himself now. He should have talked it over with Daria after the Lerners showed up. But according to what Molly had told him, Jason Lerner claimed he wasn't up here for her.

"But I'll bet it's more than Frances's father getting paid for work he didn't do," Molly said. "I think it's tied in to that skeleton, and somehow Jason and Steffi knew about it." She grabbed the cigarette and played with it. "I still don't know where Daria fits in. Maybe if you question Marius Lerner, you'll get some answers." Molly threw the cigarette on the table again and reached for her coffee. "What am I thinking? The poor man will be devastated when he learns about his son and daughter."

Randall was on his feet again. "I don't think so. He died in his sleep last night."

Molly was speechless as he headed for the door.

"Get some sleep," Randall said, "and stop worrying about Daria." He opened the door, then turned back, "Oh, I hired a new homicide detective. Her name is Maili Montgomery. She'll do just fine. So stay the hell out of this one, okay? I'll need you to stop by the station tomorrow and give her a statement."

"No," Molly said.

Randall's neck almost snapped off his shoulders. *"No?"*

Molly shook her head. "That's what I said."

"Excuse me, but it doesn't work that way. You just gave

me vital information about a homicide, and if I were the hotshot cop I'm supposed to be, I'd run you over there right now and make you do it, okay? I'm being a nice guy for a change. So don't press me."

As he moved away from the door and headed toward her, Molly folded her arms and looked him straight in the eye. "I won't do it. If you force me, I'll still refuse. And even if you sic Lucero on me, I'll say I made it up, and that I'm a vindictive bitch who's just trying to make trouble for Frances because she's a condescending snob. I won't do a damn thing until I've had a chance to talk to Daria. I've already said too much, and I won't betray her further, understand? She's been more than a friend." Molly wiped her eyes again. "Daria is the sister I wish I'd had. I owe her."

"I can bring a charge against you for withholding information if I've a mind to."

Molly laughed. "No you can't because I'll deny I told you anything. So how are going to make that stick?" When she saw his jaw tense, she said, "Go ahead. Arrest me."

Randall turned away and headed for the door again. He was furious with Molly. But he had to admire her loyalty. He pulled the door open. "Do me a favor. Put a little less coffee in the filter next time. You could stand a spoon in what you gave me tonight."

Molly held her breath as he left. He'd let her off too easy. That could only mean one thing. She was in big-time trouble with him now.

## ~ 20 ~

*T*he two Excedrin PMs Molly took after Randall left made the alarm going off Wednesday morning sound like far off bells in a foreign land. She found it difficult to open her eyes. Her head felt like it belonged to someone else, and her arms were numb. With a full day ahead of unpacking boxes and setting up the showroom, Molly knew the only way she'd get a full night's sleep was to drug herself. She was so groggy when she got out of bed she swayed all the way to the kitchen. A jolt of instant caffeine might clear the cobwebs and help her stay upright in the shower.

As much as it pained her, Molly knew she needed to put Daria on hold and take care of business. Whether there was anything she could do to help her remained moot. But Daria had been a staunch friend, and Molly was resolved to be no less. And now she and Randall were at odds again. She had mixed feelings about her bravado with him last night. On the one hand, she was proud of the way she'd stood up to him. On the other hand, she knew she was skating on thin ice. He'd totally surprised her. She hated it when he did that.

Routine, Molly decided, was the best way to calm the

anxiety pinching her like a tight girdle. Breakfast at Tosca's would be the first act of the day. It would be soothing to chat with the always good-natured Bennie. She and Emma could have their sugar fix, then roll up their sleeves and get to work. She wasn't looking forward to the calls she had to make now that the sale was off. Eve was the first on her list. Thank God Max and Nicholas were still out of town. A small blessing, but a welcome one.

Bennie made a beeline for Molly and Emma. "Hey, what the hell is going on in this town lately? Did you see the news on TV this morning?"

Before Molly could reply, Bennie was called by a customer who wanted a few tables pushed together. Molly said to Emma, "Uh, before he gets back I need to tell you the latest. Steffi Lerner was killed the same night as her brother."

"Holy cow. Was this some of the stuff I wasn't supposed to hear last night?"

"Yes. Randall didn't want you to be scared."

"I know I'm just a kid, but I'm not scared. But, well, should we be worried? Do we need to keep the doors locked and the alarm on all the time again? And have the cell phone glued to us?"

Molly took Emma's hand in hers. "No, honey. We're okay. I think this is something that goes back a long way. Nothing at all to do with us."

"But you're going to help Randall again, aren't you?"

Molly shook her head. "Not this time."

"But what about Daria?"

Molly's face blanched. "What about her?"

Emma gave her a frown. "Is this something else I'm not

supposed to know? If she's not in trouble of some kind, why are you so worried about her?"

"Oh, well, because she's . . . well, I think she's worn-out and needs a vacation. She's gone to San Francisco for a few days."

"How do you know if she wasn't at home?"

"Her neighbor told me when I went over there last night."

"You didn't tell me that," Emma said. "And I think you're leaving stuff out."

"Well, I forgot. I guess it was because—"

"You thought you were in trouble with Randall again?" Emma laughed now. "I love it when he does that thing with his eyes." She pressed her eyes tight, then opened them slowly, leaving only a hint of her pupils. "Like this."

Molly laughed. "Perfect. Just perfect." As she took the last bite of her pastry, Bennie pulled out a chair and whistled, "A customer just came in and told me there were TV trucks parked all over Scenic Road by La Casa. Even CNN is there! Hell, the village is going to go national again. What a horrible thing to happen. Jason and Steffi, and now the old man too?"

"CNN?" Molly said. "Randall is going to be up the wall now."

"He's gonna go ape shit, is what he's gonna do," Bennie agreed. "What do you hear about Frances? Been able to see her yet? I hear they have a police guard on her door. What's going on, Molly?"

"I haven't a clue," Molly lied. She gave Emma a warning look, then said, "All I know is what I saw on the news."

"Too bad about the house too. Guess there won't be much of a sale now, huh?"

Molly sipped her coffee. "Guess not."

Bennie rose, then patted Molly on the shoulder. "Hey, I'm sorry and all that, but I'm glad you weren't in the house when it happened. Life around here would be pretty dull without you."

Touched, Molly blew him a kiss. "Thanks, Bennie."

Back in the shop, Molly said to Emma, "Okay, here's the plan. We'll get the rest of the new furniture in place, then get cracking on those boxes. We'll just load up every surface with whatever Max sent down, then figure out what we've got and start making decisions."

"Don't you want to go over to La Casa and see what it looks like?"

Molly shuddered. "No way. I'm never going back there again."

"Well, I was thinking last night . . . when you and Randall were talking about the stuff I'm not supposed to hear, that maybe everything didn't burn. So maybe you should take a look?"

Molly was beginning to think Emma was not a twelve-year-old girl, but an alien in disguise. "Why didn't I think of that?"

"Because you've been worried about Daria?"

"That's true, but even if there is stuff to salvage, I don't think there will be a sale for some time. The house is a crime scene now and Randall won't let me in."

"I still think you should go over and see what it looks like."

Molly shook her head. "No way. Not with all those TV people around. I'd never get through anyway."

"You could go around the block and come in from the other street. There's a little alley that goes to the beach and there's a door in the wall. It's kind of hidden, but if you go along the ivy wall and look real close, you'll see an old wood door. It's kind of stuck, but it goes into the back garden of La Casa. I found it when I was chasing the lizard."

Molly stared at her. "So that's why I couldn't find you that day. You were exploring, huh?"

"Yeah. Kids do that, you know."

"Well, this kid is staying put. I'm not going over there and running into Randall. Maybe later. Right now we've got a shop to put together."

Molly hauled several boxes to the center of the show-room and began unpacking. The excitement of discovering what Max had sent was a welcome break from her worries. Emma's eyes lit up when a large pair of Chinese vases were pulled from the first box. "Are they real?" she asked.

"Sure. Just not old enough to be important. But they'll make gorgeous lamps. I'll check that big box of carved stands we found at that garage sale last month. There should be a matching pair we can use for bases." Admiring the vases, Molly said, "These will look stunning in the front window. I might even use them for night-lights. What do you think, most honorable assistant number one?"

Emma giggled. "I like that. It's better than squirt." Pretending to ponder this most important question, she pursed her lips, folded her arms, and said, "Yes. Make it so."

Molly saluted. "Aye aye, Captain."

"I like the way the Chinese made these vases with all the little family figures painted on them. Since these have a pinkish background, I guess they're *famille* rose?" Emma asked as she carefully took them from Molly to set on a nearby table.

Molly smiled, pleased with how quickly she had picked up so many terms. "Right. And they're made with several different background colors. There's *jaune* for yellow, and *noire* for black, which is very rare. Enamel was applied directly to the biscuit porcelain, then a translucent green enamel is added and then it becomes a dense black. I've only seen one since I've been in the biz."

"What about the green one we had last month? Don't they just put green on?"

"Aha, good question, number one. Nope, *verte*, the green one, becomes green when yellow, blue, purple, and an iron red is laid over the biscuit porcelain. Very tricky work and not as simple as you might think. The Chinese were exquisite artisans, and still are."

"Too bad we don't have a sample of all of the colors. That would be a cool display, huh?"

"Very cool. We'll have to work on that."

As they continued to unpack, Molly was surprised at how many Oriental smalls Max had sent. She was particularly pleased, since she was overloaded with English and European style vases and figures. The addition of these exotic and well-made pieces gave the shop a more international appearance. Oriental objets d'art were always present in the finer homes, and it was a look she strived to maintain. As each new piece was unpacked, Molly gave Emma a quick course in Orientalia. When she unpacked a cloisonné censer with a domed cover, she said, "Oh, this is really nice. Look at the elephant head handles. And the colors are beautiful. Bet you don't know how they make cloisonné."

Emma shoved a big pile of bubble wrap into a plastic bag, then sat cross-legged on the floor next to Molly. "Missed that in my studies. Fire away."

"Okay, first thing that's done is copper wire is applied in a pattern to a vase, or a box, or whatever, with vegetable glue, then it's fired in a kiln and polished. The wired fields, or *cloisons*, become tiny lakes ready to hold several layers of enamel."

"Are they rare?"

"Not really. Thousands were exported to the West in the early nineteenth century after they'd been exhibited at international shows. But they're very popular with collectors and interior decorators. We'll get a nice price for this one. It's in great shape."

Like two kids in a candy shop, they continued to unpack, examine, and admire each new piece. When Molly came upon a carved spinach jade brush pot, she got so excited she almost dropped it. "Oh, wow, Em! This is fantastic! I can't believe Max didn't keep this scholars brush pot for his shop!"

Emma inched closer to Molly. "It's beautiful. Funny name, but the colors do kinda look like spinach. Is it worth a lot?"

"You bet! Spinach jade is hard to find. It comes from Siberia. See these black flecks? It's graphite. Oh, this baby is gonna be one of our stars. I've got to find a good spot for this. Somewhere it can't be handled." Giving it to Emma, she said, "Scholars used these pots to store their brushes."

Emma laughed. "Duh?"

"Okay, smarty. Give me a rundown on jade if you know so much."

"Uh, well, I haven't done much reading on it yet. I've been working on European furniture, remember? I just know there's different kinds."

"And colors. But first you have to know the difference

between jade, which here in the States and in Europe is described as nephrite and jadeite."

"Whoa. Why the two names? Aren't they the same?"

"Nope. Nephrite is a silicate of calcium and magnesium, and jadeite is a silicate of aluminum and sodium. Jadeite is harder than nephrite, and it's often a pure green color and used a lot in jewelry. It's heavier too, and it's cold to the touch, besides being very brittle. But you can't scratch it, even with a steel knife, though jadeite can scratch nephrite."

"You've got a good memory. Whew. I'm glad I've got that recall part of my brain working. I wouldn't be able to remember all this stuff."

"Well, it's my job, and I've had a lot of years to learn it." Molly turned the brush pot in her hands and admired the exquisite carving. "And I still don't know half of what I should. Anyway, we'll want to keep our eyes open for this stuff. It's very popular again."

"One more question. If the spinach jade comes from Siberia, does jade—or whatever you wanna call it—come from China?"

"Jade is found all over the world, even down by Big Sur. That's called California jade. But the pure green jade the Chinese used early on came from Burma."

"Uh, it's called Myanmar now."

Molly rolled her eyes. "Okay, I stand corrected. Jeeze, what a pain you are sometimes. Enough with the lessons, let's get a few more boxes unpacked, okay?"

After the sixth box, Molly pulled some money out of her jeans and said to Emma, "How about taking a break and running over to Bruno's for some sandwiches while I start on my calls?"

Her first call was to Eve Jensen. As she waited for Eve to answer, Molly remembered she hadn't been feeling well last Sunday night when she'd given her the consignment papers for the artwork. It took five rings before Eve answered. "Hi, Eve. Hope you're feeling better," Molly quickly offered.

"Oh, I'm in tip-top shape now, Molly. Well, except for hearing about the fire. What a horrible thing! How is Frances doing, have you seen her?"

"Not yet. They won't let her have visitors. About the fire, I guess there's little sense in signing those papers now. I don't know how much of the house was destroyed, but—"

"Oh, I've got the artwork. Didn't Frances tell you? I picked it up from Frances the day before the fire. What lucky timing!"

Surprised Frances hadn't bothered to tell her, Molly said, "Yes, lucky you. I guess Frances forgot to mention it."

"Poor dear. What a shame. Well, I'm sure the house was fully insured. I've got to run, Molly. My buyers are coming to see the new works. I'll call you."

When Molly got off the phone, she let out a tiny yelp. If Eve sold all those paintings, her ten percent commission would be very welcome. Her next call was to Max's cell phone. When his voice mail came on, Molly's message was brief. The trip to Carmel, she'd said, wasn't necessary. She'd love to see Nicholas, and if he was going to be in the city, she'd drive up.

Molly made several more calls to the dealers and collectors she'd contacted about the sale at La Casa. By the time she got off the phone with Kevin Tiernan, a well-known collector of Derby china, she had her apologetic speech down pat. Dealers and collectors were notoriously paranoid, and she worried that those she'd alerted earlier might assume she'd bypassed them for others who would pay more. At least the fire was her proof the sale was off.

Davis Wood was a perfect example of those who suffered from "*merch mania*," and she wanted to be word perfect before she called him. When she saw Emma arriving with their lunch, she considered it a good omen and decided it wasn't time to call Davis. Anything that might stall that call would have been a good omen. Even a fly buzzing around the room. While she was grateful for the information he'd given her, she still didn't trust him. He was a dyed-in-the-wool two-faced bitch who thrived on gossip, and she knew she had to be extra careful with every word. Davis Wood was a master at taking an innocent comment and making it into more. She only hoped that what he'd told her about the Lerners was true. The last thing she needed was to give Randall false information.

## ~ 21 ~

"Yeah, I'm watching the grandstanding prick now," Randall said to Lucero on the phone. The small TV in his office was tuned to CNN. Deputy Sheriff Reynolds was holding court at Ventana. His moustache looked as if he'd had it waxed, and his wide leg stance reminded him of a B-movie actor trying hard to look macho. "It's only day two. I thought we were going to keep this quiet for a few days?"

"Come on, Randall! Get real. You know you can't keep a homicide quiet."

"Yeah? Says who? Now we've got national media dogging us twenty-four/seven. It was front page on *Variety,* for Chrissakes. The phone has been ringing off the hook for interviews, and I was told Larry King's got a panel set for tomorrow night. You shut that Reynolds the fuck up before I let it out that he's got a domestic pending, *capice*? I'm not having Carmel turn into another Modesto!"

"I don't want that either. How did you know about the domestic?"

"You don't need to know."

Randall could hear a deep sigh from Lucero. "Okay, I'll handle it. But the cat's out of the bag now. The Lerners are show biz people. They're always news. The damage is done, so lighten up. I'll give his boss a call and tell them to cool it. I can see I'm going to have to step in and play watchdog. I don't like interfering, but I'll do it. We need to get your two departments together and pool information. What's good for you?"

"I'm reading the faxes Loomis sent. He should be here sometime this afternoon. I'd like to wait until he gets here. And from now on, I want direct feedback from the sheriff. No liaison bullshit."

"Okay. I'll get back to you."

"Hang on for a minute." Randall shifted in his chair, stalling for the right way to say what he'd hoped to avoid. He couldn't find it. "I'm going to have to question Daria. Problem is, she's gone up to the city. Know where I can find her?"

The long pause at the other end made Randall want to throw something. It pained him no end to have had to tell Lucero.

"You still there?"

"Yeah. Why?"

"Just to round out my interviews, and—"

"Don't fucking lie to me, Randall. What's Daria got to do with this?"

"This is killing me, okay? She was at the house when Jason bought it. I don't know when she left, or why, but I've got to talk to her."

"Back up a minute. If you know she was there, why the hell didn't you ask her right away?"

"Because I just found out about it last night and she left yesterday."

"Did Frances tell you this? Because if she did, be careful. The bitch is a first-class liar and a—"

"It wasn't Frances. It was Molly."

"Molly? What the hell is going on here? How does Molly know Daria was there?"

Randall briefed Lucero, then said, "She wasn't going to tell me until she could talk to Daria, but she's worried about her and I think she's afraid Daria might go off the deep end. Now she's denying it and plans to say she made it up. She wants to help, but she's making things worse. If Molly got it right, you and I both know why Daria was on Jason's case."

"Yeah. Shit. After all these years this had to come up now?"

"I made some calls to the city. We'll find her. I'll let you know the minute I hear something. You bring her home, okay?"

"Thanks, Randall. I owe you."

Randall's laugh was kind. "I'll put it on your tab."

Randall spent the next half hour going over the faxes. He shook his head in appreciation. The guy was a national treasure. Loomis had unearthed financial information on the Lerners that he'd bet the IRS didn't even know. The Lerners' production company was losing money hand over fist. Their last three films never landed in the black. According to Loomis's contact, it wasn't a case of creative bookkeeping, it was real. The squeeze was on by investors, and the Lerner's were having a hard time coming up with distributors for two films already completed. Randall's eyebrows rose when he saw the Lerners had been paying the O'Briens a cool million for each of the stinkers now in the red. Loomis's notes on the past twenty years were an eye opener. The previous payoffs had been modest compared to the last three. Nevertheless, the family had been paying through the nose for years. It was beginning to make sense now. Jason Lerner and his sister were up here for one reason, and it wasn't a new script. They'd come to put an end to blackmail. Randall couldn't get to his cigar case fast enough. Thanks to Molly's pal in Beverly Hills, some of the pieces were beginning to fall into place. A surge of excitement filled him.

He was also certain that the blackmail had to do with the coffin they'd found. Now they just had to find Hillary Thornton's sister to make a match. There were plenty of other possibilities, but Randall had a gut feeling this girl was the skeleton in the coffin. He was behind the eight ball when it came to locating Hillary Thornton's sister. So far his inquiries had come up blank. But there were still avenues open, and he was aggressively pursuing them.

When he flipped to the next page, he patted his pockets for his lighter. Coming up empty, he went to the coffee table and grabbed an old French match striker Molly had found for him at a garage sale. Back at the table, he struck the match as his eyes moved across the page. Stunned by what he was reading, he forgot about the match until he felt it sear his fingers. Frances O'Brien was on the Lerners' books as a location scout. A monthly check went out to her for ten grand. He threw down the match and pushed his chair back. The unlit cigar was still in his hand as he stared into space. What the hell? A double header?

When Wilkins and Montgomery popped their heads into the doorway, he waved them in. "Loomis should be here any time now. I want you both to give him an update. He's been digging up info in L.A. for us, and I want him kept in the loop." Pointing to the faxes, he added, "What he's sent so far might just blow this case open." He looked at his watch. "We'll have a meeting later today with him. I want three sets of the Ventana photos ready when I call you back."

Randall spent the next few minutes getting local updates and then glanced at the daily list of local police calls. Two domestic disturbances, loud music at the beach last night, three tipsy tourists driven to their hotels, and a stolen bike. He moved the list aside, nodded then said, "Besides the security people doing their twenty-four/seven, I want the La Casa patrol kept to every half hour. Continue the door and ground checks with the private guards. Anyone found trying to sneak in—print and media press included—haul them in for trespassing."

He waited until they left to sift through the remaining faxes. Once again he nodded at what Loomis had managed to send. He lit his cigar this time and began to read the fifteen-year-old reports. As the familiar names connected to the case appeared before him, he closed his eyes and thought about how rarely the past stays buried.

He'd been at Internal Affairs five years when this case fell on his desk. A homicide detective was being watched after it was discovered he was playing high roller with the movie crowd, sporting expensive Beverly Hills threads from Sy Devore, and driving a Mercedes. A few calls to friends in the industry verified that the detective was spending a lot of time with the Lerners and hitting the craps tables in Vegas. Jason Lerner's Bel Air spread was getting a reputation for hosting some heavy duty drug du jour banquets. The investigation took on a two-prong direction. Randall wanted to nail the dirty cop, and DEA wanted the drug source they suspected the cop was cozy with. Lerner was a minor cog, but could lead them backward through the maze of dealers supplying the movie crowd.

Randall opened his eyes and drew deeply on the cigar as he pondered a word he rarely used. Serendipity, like coincidence, ranked low on his believability scale. But he had to admit that it occasionally had its place in criminal investigations. Two weeks after he'd set up an undercover to penetrate the high flying set, he got a call from an old San Francisco high school buddy who was with DEA. Mario Stefani told him his cousin had come to him with a problem. She'd discovered her husband, a local restaurateur, was dealing. She was torn between family and what was right, and needed his guidance. The hubby was smooth, though. He never shit in his own backyard. His sales area concentrated in smaller venues within the local entertainment and sports fields and was pressing for an entrée into Southern California. After several telephone conferences and two face-to-face meetings with Stefani and his cousin, Randall and his undercover came up with a plan to introduce the restaurateur to the Lerners.

There is no such thing, Randall thought, as a perfect plan. Something or someone would always manage to screw things up. Most often the glitch was minor. That wasn't the case on that sultry, humid night in Beverly Hills. The glitch showed up, but it wasn't minor. Unfortunately, it turned out to be a disaster. When you had a mix of booze, drugs, horny men and willing young women, massive egos, then added a volatile Italian temper, there was bound to be a problem. When the call went out from the undercover, dozens of partygoers whose names got top billing on films all over the world were long gone and all that remained were the host and hostess, two men, two women, the undercover, and a dead man. By the time Loomis, who was the homicide primary on the case, arrived, you couldn't find an aspirin in the house. The undercover was up a creek, and the murder charge conveniently went down as self-defense. Jason Lerner got off, and Steffi Lerner, the other guy, and the two women were questioned, then let go.

Now, Randall's eyes rested on the name of one of the women in the house and he was puzzled by the circle Loomis had made with an arrow to the margin, where it said *See me.* He shrugged, then pushed the report aside. No doubt Loomis had more to say about her. He gathered up the La Casa crime scene photos and sketches and moved to the cork panel alongside the incident board. He was about to tack up the last photo when he heard someone say, "Hey, *Chief,* how's it hangin'?" Besides Molly Doyle, there was only one person in the world who could call him Chief with such pomposity and get away with it. Randall turned, and with a smile that nearly split his face in two, he said, "Took you long enough to get your ass up here, Loomis."

Nearly a foot shorter than Randall, twice as round, and with a graying curly fringe around his bald head, Bevin Loomis threw out his arms. "Can it and give me a hug."

"Don't pull that crap up here! We'll be the talk of the town," Randall said as he gave Loomis a bear hug. Stepping back, he whistled. "Hey, what's with the threads? Where's the bolo tie and the Hawaiian shirt? Shit, you almost look like a real gent in that getup."

Loomis pulled up his alligator belt and grinned. "I've turned a new leaf. I am now a man of leisure and discernment."

"Looks like you cleaned out Brooks Brothers."

Loomis pointed to the small polo player on his golf shirt. "Only a cretin such as you would not recognize Ralph's tasteful line. I'm a Polo man through and through.

Besides, I respect the refined taste of Carmel. My threads are befitting my persona as an avid Bach Festival fan."

"So, you're gonna stick around after all, huh? I won't have to bribe you?"

Loomis moved to Randall's incident board. He quickly ran his eye over the notations and photos. "The festival starts in two weeks, as you well know. Let's try to wrap up this puppy before then." Turning back to Randall, he winked. "I even bought you and Molly a season pass. How is she? I'm dying to see her."

Randall picked up his cigar case from the conference table and offered it to Loomis. "Molly Doyle is fine. A constant pain in the ass, but as lovable as ever."

Loomis gave Randall a quick look over his shoulder, reached for a cigar, then said, "Oh? We've made progress I see."

"I didn't mean it like that."

Loomis grinned, ran the cigar under his nose, then returned to the board. "There are a few things your people don't need to know at this point in the investigation. Best kept between you, me, and your pal the D.A."

Randall pulled out a chair at the conference table. "I'm all ears. Shoot."

Loomis moved closer to the photos, took a moment studying the layout sketches of where Jason's and Frances's bodies had been positioned, then joined Randall at the table. "You saw my note about a Frankie Brown, right?" Randall nodded. "Okay. She was the woman we'd found hiding out in Jason Lerner's screening room the night of the shooting. She was high on something, but lucid enough to question. I was never satisfied with her answers. She claimed she'd been out by the pool when she heard the shot, and when everyone at the party made a run for it, she panicked, ran inside to find a friend, then changed her mind and hid in the first room she came to."

"Okay, so why didn't you buy her story?"

"Gut instinct."

Randall was about to reply when he saw Wilkins and Montgomery in the hall, standing outside his open door. "Give us a few minutes," he said, "We're catching up here." When he saw Loomis shake his head slightly, he added, "Better yet, let's meet around two. I need to take my buddy here for some lunch."

Loomis rose, moved to the two detectives, quickly introduced himself and offered his hand to them. To Montgomery, he said, "You're better looking than Wilkins." With his hand on the doorknob, he said, "Your boss says terrible things about you both, but don't worry, I don't believe him. Looking forward to later." With that he grinned and closed the door.

"Smooth move there," Randall said. "Okay, we left off at gut instinct. Is that why you circled her name and made that note? Come on, spill it, for Christ sakes."

Loomis sat back down, crossed his arms on the table and said, "Frankie Brown wasn't her real name. She was trying to get into the movies and didn't want to trade on her family connections."

"You gonna sit here and play games with me? *Me?*" Randall had a hard time not laughing. "Okay, I'll bite. Who, pray tell, is Frankie Brown?"

Loomis's smile was angelic. "Frances O'Brien."

## ~~ 22 ~~

$\mathcal{M}$olly didn't have a chance to put off contacting Davis. He called just as she took the last bite of her sandwich. "Oh, baby, this news is simply shattering our little circle down here," Davis hurriedly said when she answered the phone.

"Davis?" she asked, hoping against hope she was wrong.

"Who else do you know who is frothing at the mouth to see that pasha's treasure house? What *is* going on up there in sleepy little Carmel? CNN is running it almost daily. Can Larry King and his panel of experts be far behind?"

"Please not that!" Molly said, imagining the look on Randall's face if that happened.

"Don't look a gift horse in the mouth. It might be good for business. Lord Almighty, Molly, it's hardly a secret you upstate people just loathe us down here, but really, did you have to wipe out a dynasty?"

"Isn't it just awful? We're all just reeling with shock. Your friend Donny Alquist must be devastated. I mean, having worked with the Lerners and all."

Davis laughed. "He's actually relieved to come out from under that awful charade. He's already signed up to do a new Miramax film. Donny's contract with the Lerners is . . . well, pardon the pun, dead. You're the one who must be devastated, losing all that dough."

Molly could almost hear the glee in his voice. "Oh, well, yeah. It's a big loss, but I did manage to make a few extraordinary sales before the fire, so all is not lost."

There was a pause before Davis said, "Really? I thought I had first look."

Molly wished he could see her Cheshire grin. "Of course you did. The sales I made were to some of Frances's friends she'd contacted. I couldn't very well tell them no."

"Oh, of course not. Uh, any chance of salvage? The news said the house hadn't been totally destroyed."

"I don't know. The police have sealed the house. And until Frances is out of the hospital, I doubt much will happen. I'll be sure to call you, though."

Davis's chuckle sounded more like a snicker. "Well, Molly Doyle, looks like you're in the thick of things again."

Molly's ears felt like someone had run their nails over a chalkboard. "Not this time, Davis. I'm just a bystander."

When she finally managed to get off the phone, Molly said to Emma, "You know, crime scene or not, I think I will sneak over to La Casa later. Maybe all is not lost after all."

Molly and Emma spent the rest of the afternoon unpacking, taking short lesson breaks as more Orientalia and pieces Emma wasn't familiar with appeared. When Molly unwrapped a lovely Burmese papier-mâché Buddha, she sat back and sighed. "Oh, too bad it's not in better condition. See the red and gold paint flaking? And the tiny holes on the side?"

Emma peered over her shoulder. "Is it ruined? I mean, can't we sell it?"

"Well, it's not going to be worth much as it is, but considering it's almost two feet tall, it will make a stunning a lamp."

"Another lamp?"

"Yep. That's what you do with good merch like this. Well, I mean something that would work, of course. Think about it. Statues, big dramatic vases, candlesticks, oh . . . porcelain figures like those Meissen pieces, and even some musical instruments make unique and stunning lamps. And, they're one of a kind. You won't find these in lamp shops. I'll have the lamp guy put a brass rod behind the Buddha so the figure isn't damaged, then maybe a black silk pagoda style shade. It certainly won't bring the two thousand it would have, but we'll price it at eight hundred."

"Ya think? That's a lot of money just for a lamp."

"Oh, but not for something like this. This baby is at least two hundred years old. This is a good lesson for you. When you run across a small that has value and can still be used in a home, providing it's attractive, try to find a use for it. Remember that foot bath we found at the garage sale in Carmel Woods? The copper one?"

"Oh, right. The bottom was kind of messed up and had some holes."

"Right. We filled it with dried flowers and—"

"Paid five bucks for it and sold it for fifty."

"Now you got it."

"I see there's more to this business than memorizing pictures, styles, and makers' marks. We also have to recognize a good piece and try to keep it alive."

"Exactly. Just like this Buddha. It shouldn't be thrown away just because it's damaged. It took years for the artisan who made this to learn his craft. How awful to think something he labored over with love would eventually be thrown out just because it had a rough life."

On the carpet next to Molly, Emma fiddled with some bubble wrap, then said. "Like my mother? Is that what you're trying to say?"

Molly tousled Emma's dark curls and smiled. "No, that isn't what I was leading to. But it seems to fit. Your mother is—"

"What else is in the box?" Emma asked.

Reaching into the box again, she pulled out several nonmatching brass candlesticks and a small glass vase. Handing the vase to Emma, she said, "See if you can find anything on the bottom."

Emma took the vase, turned it over and squinted. "It's Lalique, right?"

"You're doing good. Find anything?"

"It says René Lalique, and it's signed. I mean etched."

"Good girl. Three hundred for this baby."

By the time they'd emptied all the boxes it was close to five in the evening. They had six garbage bags filled with bubble wrap, the entire shop looked like a mess, and they were worn-out. "Oh, to have such treasures and be so tired I don't give a damn." Molly laughed as Emma gave her a hand as she tried to get up from the floor. "I feel like an old lady. My legs are cramped and my neck feels like it's got a rod holding it up."

"Max outdid himself this time. It's going to take us a while to tag this stuff and place it."

Molly stretched her arms. "I hope he realizes we'll be

closed for a few days." Making a full circle, she eyed the showroom and sighed. Every surface, inch of floor space, even the stairs going up to the apartment, was filled with the new merchandise. "Time for a dinner break and then it's back to the salt mines, kiddo."

"Are you going over to La Casa?" Emma asked as they carefully made their way up the stairs.

Molly stopped at the top stair, thought for a moment, then said, "Yep. But you stay here, okay?"

"Oh shoot. Why can't I come? You'll never find that little gate without me."

"No way. I don't want both of us landing in the pokey. Besides, I want you here in case Daria calls or comes by, okay? And I need you to keep an eye on Tiger and the kittens. Oh, remember those black books you used to pad that box with the Art Deco stature? Well, they're in the storage room downstairs. Take a look at them and see if there's any movie photos that might be worth selling."

"What about that old Bible? Is that worth anything?"

"Huh? What old Bible? There were only two books in the box."

Emma looked a bit sheepish. "I forgot to mention that I found it upstairs. I, uh, well, I kinda borrowed it. I wanted to see what one looked like. Sister Phil was going to get me one, but I guess she forgot."

Molly stood with her hands on hips and slowly shook her head. "Em. You didn't."

"I did. But I was going to return it. I didn't think Frances would mind. I mean, it's really old and it was in that leather fire bucket in her father's bedroom. I think he used it for a waste basket next to his bed. I saw the Bible sticking up between a bunch of crumpled papers. Maybe you should take it back with you."

Molly wasn't angry, but she wanted Emma to under-stand that what she'd done was wrong. "You know I can't go in the house. I'm just going to take a look at it. But as soon as we can go back, I want you to return the Bible. We don't take things, even if they look like they've been thrown away."

Emma's face seemed to crumble. "Are you mad at me?"

Molly moved to her and put her arms around her. "No. Of course not. When Frances is better, you can ask her if you can keep it, okay?"

Relieved, she said, "I was going to take it back next time we went back. I can't read it anyway. It's in Latin, I think."

Molly did a double-take. "Latin? Are you sure?"

"Looks like it to me. It has the same kind of spelling that plants have. So I just guessed. Why? Is that important?"

Molly thought for a moment, then said, "Well, it could be. If it's really old, it might have belonged to a priest or even a bishop. And maybe not. Depends on a lot of things." Anxious to get going, she checked her watch and said, "I'll look at it later."

With daylight savings time still in effect, Molly didn't have to inhale dinner before leaving for La Casa; it would be light until eight. Relishing a few moments alone in the pickup, she greedily lit a cigarette and inhaled deeply like a condemned prisoner. She loved Emma to pieces, but her constant nagging about smoking, even though she kept it humorous, was beginning to drive her up the wall. Head-ing down Ocean Avenue, she turned left on San Antonio, the street behind Scenic Road. With all the million-dollar-plus homes in Carmel, many had only one garage, and parking was at a premium. She finally found an empty spot at the corner of Santa Lucia. She had to backtrack a long half block to the narrow alley that ran to the beach. She remembered Emma said the door in the wall surrounding La Casa was a little stubborn.

It took her several moments to find it. The ivy covering the long wall was a perfect camouflage so she almost didn't see the door. If she didn't know it existed, she would have walked right past it. She leaned her shoulder into the obstinate hinges and eased it open. It didn't open all the way and she barely squeezed through. When she reached the greenhouse, she stopped to catch her breath and get her bearings. Sticking close to the building, she tried not to stand out in case the security guards were making their rounds.

Molly could see the smoke-blackened lower half of the house and it made her want to cry. La Casa was an exquisite structure and she'd loved every moment she'd spent in the splendor of its architecture. It didn't take long to realize there was no way she could get inside, and she decided to go home. She took one last look at the house and was about to head for the wall when she thought she heard something in the greenhouse. Holding held her breath, she cocked her ear and listened. After a moment she figured it was probably a cat wandering around. Or maybe the lizard Emma had found. Then, about to leave again, she froze in her tracks when she saw Daria come out of the greenhouse.

"Oh, my God! Daria!" she whispered. "I've been going crazy worrying about you."

Daria's smile was almost sickly and her eyes looked like dead coals. "I guess this is what's called returning to the scene of the crime."

"Oh, shit, Daria!" Molly moved to her in two steps. She threw her arms around her and hugged her tight. "Damn you! You've scared the hell out of all of us." Stepping back, Molly's eyes filled with tears. "I was afraid you might do something stupid. Will you please tell me what the hell is going on?"

Daria held onto her hands. "There's nothing you can do. This is old stuff. Don't get involved. I'll . . . I'll work it out."

"No way! You mean a lot to me, so that makes me involved." Molly took a deep breath, then said, "I was there. I heard the argument between you, Jason, and Frances."

Daria's face turned white. "You heard? Everything?"

"Only a little. When I got there I saw the door was open and thought Frances was there. I went to the study to check on some books, and when I was ready to leave, I thought I heard voices. I went down the gallery and heard Jason yelling. I hid behind one of the pillars in the atrium."

"And?"

"And nothing. I didn't want to butt in so I left. And then later I was mad at myself for not just barging in and pretending I hadn't heard anything. I thought if I had, maybe you'd all cool off. For once I didn't follow my instincts, and now I'm—"

Daria leaned against the greenhouse. "Don't blame yourself. You couldn't have prevented what happened."

Molly's hand was already clutching the crucifix under her sweater. "What *did* happen? Were you there when Jason was killed?"

When Daria nodded, Molly wanted to melt. But before she could probe further, Daria said, "I was furious with

Jason. I . . . I didn't trust my temper, so I left Frances alone with him. On my way out I heard the shot. I was dumbstruck. I mean, I couldn't move. I didn't know what to think. Who had a gun? Frances? Jason? I ran into the study and hid under the partners desk for maybe five minutes. It seemed like hours. When I got up enough nerve, I ran like hell out the front and toward the beach. I hid behind a huge pine tree to catch my breath. I must have stood there for another ten minutes or so, and that's when I saw the flames shooting out of the first floor."

"You've got to tell Randall all this. You have to let him know you didn't kill Jason."

Daria pulled away from the greenhouse. "No. He doesn't need to know I was there."

Molly reached out, then dropped her hands. Her shame was too great. "He knows. I . . . I had to tell him."

Daria stared at her in shock, then backed away. "You told him? Oh, God, Molly!"

"I didn't say anything until your neighbor said you'd gone to the city. I was afraid for you. I was worried you might . . . Oh, hell, Daria! What else could I do?" Molly lowered her eyes, afraid to see her friend's contempt. "I didn't want to, damn it! But you wouldn't talk to me when you came to the apartment. You ignored my phone calls." Pleading with her now, she said, "Damn it, Daria! I'm trying to help you, for God's sakes!"

Daria's laugh was scathing. "By putting me at a crime scene? That's some help."

"Look, I believe in you and I never once thought you killed Jason. The only way to clear yourself is to be upfront with Randall. He knows you too and—"

Daria stepped away, as if to leave. "Oh, yeah, Randall knows me all right."

Molly threw her hands up and began walking toward the door in the wall. "Okay, fine! Go run away again. I'm sorry I care about you and was just trying to help." She reached the wall and was about to shove the door open when Daria called her back.

"Wait, Molly. I'm sorry. Come back, please. I . . . I need to tell you a few things." She stepped into the greenhouse and waited for Molly to follow.

Molly hesitated. She hated the thought of going into that cloying humid jungle. But if it meant Daria would forgive her, then she'd walk over hot coals. She walked back, stepped in, and instinctively hunched up her shoulders. Her eyes were on the lookout for spiders and Jurassic Park miniatures. "Can't we talk outside? I hate this creepy jungle."

Daria ignored her and pulled out two stools from under a counter filled with clay pots and small garden tools. Molly held her nose and pushed away some bags of nasty smelling plant medicine. She took one of the stools and placed it in the middle of the aisle and as close to the door as possible. When Daria sat and lit a cigarette, Molly followed her example. She knew smoke kept bees away. Maybe it worked on spiders too.

"I guess it's time to fill you in on a few things," Daria said. "Maybe then you'll understand why I ran off to the city. I wasn't running from Randall. I was running from myself. I told you once that people call me the Black Widow behind my back. Now I'll tell you why."

Molly's laugh was a little shaky. "I'm sorry, I know this is serious stuff, but here you are, dressed in black, talking about black widows . . . and I have to tell you my biggest fear in life is spiders. I avoid them like the plague."

Looking around, Daria managed a grin. "It won't take

long. I won't go into every detail, but first you should know why Bitsy and I are not the best of friends. Bitsy was close with my first husband's mother. We'd been married two years before I found out he was bisexual. We had a rip roaring argument when I confronted him. The more we yelled, the more he drank. He stormed out of the house and hit a tree in Pebble Beach. He died instantly. Everyone blamed me . . . said I'd known and married him for his money. Bitsy and his mother were convinced I could have helped him change. Women of that generation still believe those things."

"Daria . . . I don't need to know any of this. All that matters is—"

"No, you have to let me finish. I moved to San Francisco after that. I have cousins there and it was a good place to be for me then. I opened a small café. After a few years, I met Vince Mazzeo, fell hard for him, and we got married. He had a popular restaurant on Union Street, so I sold my place and played hostess at his." Daria leaned against the potting table and held her head in her hand for a moment. She dabbed at her eyes, then looked at Molly. "We tried for a family. I had two miscarriages." She looked away again, then said, "There was some damage after the second one. I . . . I can't carry full term." She took a deep breath. "Anyway, five or six years later I found out he was dealing drugs. I was torn, Molly. I loved Vince, but I couldn't live with what he was doing. He didn't know that I'd found out, and I didn't let on that I had. A chef he'd fired was pissed off and told me. I didn't believe it at first. But he told me it was happening in the kitchen.

All I had to do was check the meat locker on Friday mornings and look for a yellow plastic packing box. Then watch who came in for it. I did, and I saw two guys who I knew were bad news come in and get it from Vince. I was a wreck for almost two weeks. I was still trying to figure out what to do when he started badgering me about taking him to L.A. to meet my Hollywood friends. That's when I went to see my cousin Mario, who was a DEA agent. As it happened, he contacted a cop he knew and they set up a meeting with me."

"Daria . . . please! We both have baggage. I don't care."

Daria angrily threw down her cigarette and stamped it out on the crushed gravel. "Will you please stop interrupting me?"

"Okay . . . okay!"

Daria's hand trembled as she lit another cigarette. She took a deep drag, lifted her chin, then closed her eyes as she exhaled. "Vince and I went to L.A." She opened her eyes and looked directly at Molly. "We stayed with Jason Lerner for a few days. He wanted to throw a big party for us. He invited all his big movie pals. Vince loved it. So did the undercover cop when Jason started laying out Baccarat bowls filled with drugs. Vince and Jason were higher than a kite. They started arguing . . ." Daria shook her head. "I still don't know what started it. I got scared. I didn't know who the undercover was, and I didn't know what to do. Jason was a hothead. Even as a kid he was off the wall. When Jason made a few remarks about Italians and the mob, I went into the kitchen and called a cab to get us out of there. When I went back for Vince, he and Jason were still at it, and then . . . then Jason shot him. The place was a madhouse. People screaming and running . . . it was a nightmare. I . . . I guess I went into shock. Someone pulled me down and hovered over me. I found out later it was the undercover cop. When Randall showed up—"

"*Randall?* Oh, my God! You two knew each other all this time?"

"Randall set it all up. He was with Internal Affairs and was watching a cop that was friends with Jason. Randall suspected him of dealing. He and my cousin, the DEA agent, went to school together in San Francisco."

Molly was almost dizzy. "I can't believe it. I mean, I *do* believe it . . . but what happened to Jason? I mean, did he go to jail?"

"Big money buys big lawyers, Molly. He gave up the drug dealers and got off with self-defense." Daria stared at her dying cigarette, then said, "He never saw the inside of the courtroom."

Molly thought for a moment. "So that's what you two were arguing about at La Casa."

"Yes. I thought he'd come up to put the screws to me. Maybe he'd found out I'd helped set the sting up. Payback maybe. It would have destroyed me. And Lucero."

"After all these years? And how did he know about you and Lucero?"

"Come on, Molly. Everyone knows Dan is in love with me. It would have been easy for Jason to find that out. I get a lot of Hollywood people in my place. Dan knows quite a few of them on his own. He's got a big contingent down south wanting him to run for state attorney general. Besides, you know how that group loves to drop names. Especially when it comes to politicians."

"But why was he yelling at Frances? What did she have to do with any of this?"

"Frances was at the party that night at his house," Daria said. "She saw him kill Vince too."

"Oh, my God!"

"You keep saying that," Daria said.

"Well, I'm sorry, but wouldn't you? Was Frances black-mailing him?"

"That's crazy. We didn't want anything to do with him, or his sister. They were both wired wrong."

Molly didn't buy that. Frances had seemed more than happy to be in their company. No, she thought, there was more to this than Daria even knew. "Then if Randall knows all this, why are you afraid to go see him?"

"Jason told me he'd found out that I'd set up the bust. The cop that was working with him? The one that went to jail? He told Jason. I knew the Lerners were out of money. The last two films they did were losers. Like I said, I get a lot of Hollywood people at the restaurant. They talk. I was afraid he was here to ruin me. No one here would ever trust me again. I turned in my own husband and he got killed. I've worked too hard for my good name to let that bastard ruin me."

"Tell me about that! I'm still suspect in some antiques crowds."

"I know, Molly, but this is different. I've got a motive, don't you get it?"

"Sure I get it. But so does Frances, then." Molly let that sink in, then said, "I didn't tell Randall I heard you threaten Jason. I just said I heard an argument but couldn't make out what was being said."

Daria got off the stool. She brushed a stream of tears from her eyes, then moved to Molly and hugged her. "Thank you. I was furious. I didn't really mean it. I wasn't thinking straight."

"I know that. Go see Randall. Tell him everything. I'll go with you."

"No. I'll go alone."

Molly took her hand and squeezed it. "Okay. I guess you came in through that door in the wall too?"

"How did you know about it?"

Molly laughed. "Emma found it and told me."

"Leave it to Emma. We used it when we were kids. It's a beach gate and it's for the gardeners."

As they left the greenhouse, Molly said, "You go on ahead. But be careful. There's security guards somewhere. I want to take another look around and see how bad the fire damage is. I'm going to try and convince Randall to let me in and see if there's anything to salvage for Frances. She may need all the dough she can lay her hands on for a lawyer."

"Frances couldn't have killed Jason or Steffi. She doesn't have it in her."

Molly wasn't sure she agreed with Daria, but held her tongue for once. "Well, just in case, then."

Daria kissed Molly on the cheek. "Thank you for believing in me."

"Oh, stop it. Go take care of Randall."

Molly waited until she saw Daria go through the gate, then she moved closer to the house. She was tempted to see if she could sneak in through the studio. The blackened stucco hadn't reached that end of the house, and there was a chance the fire hadn't spread that far. She headed toward the breezeway, then stopped and looked around. She figured the security guards were in front to keep the media and nosy gawkers away. Stepping into the breezeway, she headed for the studio door when she heard a voice say, "Hold up there."

Molly nearly jumped. She turned to see a Carmel police officer. "Oh, you scared the hell out of me. Sergeant Jenkins, right? How are you? I was just—"

"You're trespassing, Molly. Orders are to arrest anyone found here without permission."

"What? Oh, come on! You've got to be kidding!"

He shook his head, then reached out for her arm. "Chief's orders. No one is exempt. He made that clear. I'm sorry, but you'll have to come with me."

Molly pulled away. "This is crazy! Don't you dare touch me!"

"Don't make me cuff you, Molly, okay? Give me a break here. It's not personal. I've got a job to do. Now come on. Nice and easy, huh?"

## 23

*"I* want to see a lawyer!" Molly shouted at Randall.

"How's about a shrink too?" Randall shot back. "You need extensive therapy to overcome a few things. You have a serious problem with minding your own business. And it's close to being fatal."

Molly gave him one of her best smirks. "Compliments will get you nowhere with me, copper. Did Daria come in or not? Or did you keep me holed up in the dispatch office just to annoy me?"

"She just left. We're all clear with her. But I'm not through with you."

Molly ignored him and waved to Loomis. "Great to see you! Just get in? I've got some terrific stuff for you to see. My boss sent down a loaded truck. Might even have some—"

"Damn it, Molly! This is serious! Forget Loomis, okay? He's here for a few weeks. You can talk shop later. Right now I've got a few problems to take care of, okay?"

Molly rose from the chair opposite Randall's desk. She winked at Loomis, who was sitting at the conference table. "Fine. I'll leave you to it."

"I just said I'm not through with you," Randall grumbled.

Molly rolled her eyes at Loomis. "Isn't he the biggest pain?" She sat back down. "Emma is going to be worried if I don't get home pretty soon. Can't we talk about this tomorrow?"

Randall picked up the phone and punched in a number. "Emma? It's me, Randall. Your aunt Molly is here at the station. Don't wait up for her. I might have to lock her up if she doesn't behave." He handed Molly the phone. "She wants to talk to you."

Molly winked at Loomis again. "Does this count as one of my two calls?"

Loomis's laugh was close to a roar. Molly smiled at him, then said to Emma, "Randall's only kidding. I'll be leaving in a few minutes. Oh, Mr. Loomis is here. Okay, I'll ask them."

Handing the phone back to Randall, she said, "Emma wants to know if you and Mr. Loomis would like to come over for dessert later. We've already had dinner."

Randall was close to breaking the rubber band he'd been winding through his fingers. It was a good thing Loomis was there. He was in a mood to turn Molly Doyle over his knee. "Yeah, fine. Uh, before you leave, would you like to tell me what the hell you were doing at La Casa? I mean, I realize you noticed the yellow crime scene tape, but since you flaunt authority on a regular basis, inquiring minds would like to know."

"I wanted to see how bad the fire damage was in case there was a chance you'd let me back in—"

"From the back of the house? How did you get in without the security guard seeing you?"

Molly told him about the gate in the wall Emma had found. "Daria said it was for the gardeners and a beach gate or something. You should really station someone back there. Those nosy reporters are sure to find it."

"Yeah, yeah . . . I know all about the gate."

"Well, thank God Emma found it. I might have missed Daria and not had a chance to convince her to see you. You could at least thank me for that."

"Daria would have come in anyway," Randall said.

Molly wasn't going to argue now that she knew their history. But Randall didn't know that, unless Daria had told him. Nor did he know that Daria might not have after she told Daria she'd heard her threaten Jason Lerner. Sneaking a glance at Loomis, Molly wondered just how much he knew about what was going on. "Yes, you're right. Of course she would."

"Tell you what," Randall said. "As soon as I know the house is safe, I'll take you back in myself. You can check around and see if there's anything left that's worth selling for Frances."

Molly eyed him. "What's the catch?"

Loomis laughed again. Randall shot him a look. "No catch. I'm trying to be sensitive, okay?"

Molly knew when it was time to be gracious. "Thank you." She rose from the inquisition chair and offered both hands to Loomis. "Welcome to Carmel. I hope we'll be able to lure you into staying around for a while."

Loomis held onto her hands. "My dear Molly. For you, I would slay dragons."

"You don't have to get smarmy," Randall said.

"I like your smarmy, Loomis. Ignore him."

"He usually does," Randall said. "Okay, enough of this.

Loomis and I need to get some dinner. We'll drop by around eight. That work?"

"Perfect," Molly said as she headed out of the office.

Molly found Emma at her desk in the shop when she returned. "Hey, I forgot to ask, but, uh, do we have any dessert?"

Emma waved her over. "Yes . . . yes. I took care of that. I got stuff from Bennie. But Aunt Molly, come over here quick. I found some other pictures. Take a look at this one." Shoving the book at her, she said, "Look at the dress on that lady!"

Molly took a seat and looked at the photo. Three men and two women, with drinks in hand, appeared to be laughing at something Jack Lemmon, the actor, had said. "Which one?" Molly asked.

"There!" Emma pointed to a woman whose head was thrown back in laughter.

"Okay, nice dress, but that's not an actress I recognize. Except for Jack Lemmon, I don't think the photo has much value."

"Not the lady. The dress!"

Molly looked again. "Okay, what? I'm not with you."

"It's just like the one that was on the skeleton! Remember? That piece of beaded stuff? The pattern is the same. See all the circles and the swirls and the colors?"

Molly pretended to shudder. "I didn't look that close. Just seeing the skeleton freaked me out. Are you sure?"

Emma looked at Molly as if she hadn't heard her right. "I'm positive. That wacky part of my brain never lies."

"Oh, my God! Then I was right about that skeleton! You just proved it."

Pleased, Emma folded her arms and nodded. "I'll bet Randall knew all along too."

"He lied to us."

"He sure did. Do we let on that we know?"

Molly's head snapped up. "Emma! Of course we have to! We're not involved in this, okay? This will help him identify that poor young woman." Molly took the photo out of the plastic cover and set it on the desk.

"Uh-oh, I almost forgot. Eve stopped by and dropped off a check for Frances for those paintings she sold. And then you got here."

"She sold them already?"

Emma reached under the book and handed Molly an envelope. "She said to keep her in mind if you run across any more work by those artists. Oh, and she didn't seal the envelope on purpose so you could see what they went for. She was really happy when she said that. I told her you were on your way back and if she wanted to wait for you I'd make her a cup of tea. She said okay, and when I came back out of the storage room she said she didn't realize how late it was and she had to go."

Molly was anxious to call Randall about the photos, but the tug of her dealer's heart was too much to ignore. Catholic guilt attacked as she held the envelope. She paused for a blink of an eye, then opened it. "Call Randall on his cell." She took one look at Eve's check, and smiled. "Forty-five hundred to us, Em!"

When Randall answered, and Emma handed her the phone, Molly told him what Emma had discovered, then added, "Maybe you ought to order some takeout and have it delivered here."

"Are you positive?" Randall asked.

"You try asking Emma that, okay? She already gave me a wounded look when I did."

"We'll be right over."

Molly spent the next few minutes going through both books, hoping to find another photo of the young woman. She was at the end of the second book when she found one. There were three women in this photo, none of whom she recognized. She picked up the photo she'd removed, and then gathered both books and said to Emma, "Let's take these upstairs. Randall and Loomis are on the way over."

Very carefully sidestepping the new merchandise still on the stairs, they made it up to the apartment without a disaster. "I'll get the coffee up, Em. Will you straighten up the pillows on the sofa and make sure Tiger and the kittens are okay?"

Molly had just enough time to set out a tray when she heard Randall and Loomis coming up the stairs from the courtyard. Rushing to the door, she let them in and said, "I found another photo of her." She handed them to Randall. "Make yourselves comfortable. I've got coffee brewing."

Emma came in and set two large crystal ashtrays on the coffee table. "I think you'll probably need these. I promise not to be a smarty pants." She smiled at Loomis. "You must be Mr. Loomis." She offered him her hand and said, "I'm Emma. I've been waiting to meet you."

Loomis's eyes were already glued to the photos. He looked down at Emma, then took her hand in his. "No female has ever said that to me, young lady. I'm flattered and look forward to many long visits. At the moment, however—"

"Oh, that's okay. We have plenty of time to get to know each other. Right now we have a homicide to solve."

Loomis almost sputtered. He looked at Randall, who ignored him. Molly reached for Emma's hand. "It's okay. Don't be fooled by Emma's age. She knows everything and has already been a big help." Darting a look at Randall, she said, "Even Randall has to admit that."

"No thanks to her aunt here, she's becoming a regular Nancy Drew. So, where did you get these?"

Here it comes, she thought. He's probably going to give me a lecture on removing evidence. "We were packing up the Art Deco statues last week that Max bought and we needed something sturdy to fill a box so one of them wouldn't slide around. Emma got these from the studio. Jason hadn't taken all the boxes."

"Same room you were attacked in, right?" Randall asked.

Molly stared at him. "Do you think it was Jason and this was what he was looking for?"

"Could be."

"Then my theory was right. That poor woman in the coffin is the reason for all this. Jason was trying to find evidence for his father and stop the blackmail. When he didn't find anything in the boxes he took to Ventana, he came back to check out the rest. Only I interrupted him."

"Hard to tell," Randall said.

"Baloney. That's exactly what happened. And then he confronted Frances and—"

Randall put up his hands to stop her. "Whoa. You're going off on me now. Slow down and stop with the Sherlock stuff, okay? Leave the guessing to the pros. Besides, Jason couldn't be sure he'd find anything anyway. It was a long shot at best. I mean, come on . . . who'd leave evidence around like this?"

Molly refused to be dismissed so easily. She didn't care

if Randall didn't want Loomis to think he discussed cases with her. "Obviously an oversight Jason was hoping for. Or maybe his father knew Jack O'Brien would have had some sort of proof to hold over him, and sent Jason and Steffi on a search and destroy mission. But the coffin wasn't it. Finding that was a fluke. It might not have been discovered for years and years. If Jason hadn't bought the bibliotheque, who knows when it might have been found? And by the way, that sale was genuine. I saw his face when he looked at it. It was pure rapture." She looked at Loomis and said, "It was to die for. Just gorgeous and so huge—"

"I don't like that word," Randall said.

"What word?" Emma asked.

"Fluke. It's not in my dictionary. Say, Em, I'll take one of those kittens off your hands when Tiger's ready to let one go."

"Don't change the subject, damn it!" Molly snapped. "And don't worry about Emma. She's not spooked by all this, or having nightmares, if that's what you're thinking."

Randall laughed. "The Doyle women don't get nightmares, is that it? They just give them." He nodded at Loomis. "You ready for some dinner?"

Handing the photo to Randall, Loomis avoided eye contact with Molly and said, "I'm starved."

"You didn't order a delivery for here?" Molly asked. "I thought you were going to stay and have dessert."

"Thanks, Molly," Randall said, cutting her off. "The photo should be a big help."

With tight lips, Molly said, "You're welcome."

Heading for the French doors, Randall turned to Emma. "Hey, sorry about that. I guess I should thank you, huh? Good work."

"How come you're not going to stay?" Emma asked.

Darting a look at Loomis, he said, "We're going to grab a quick bite. Loomis is tired after that long drive from Los Angeles and we've still got to run up to the hospital and see Frances."

Clearly disappointed, Emma said, "Oh. Okay."

"I'll tell her you sent a hug, okay?"

Emma shrugged. "Sure."

"Is Frances able to see visitors now?" Molly asked.

"Not yet."

Molly's curiosity was too great for her to back off. "Has she said anything? I mean, that might be helpful?"

Randall looked at Loomis, then back to Molly. "Let's plan on taking Loomis to Daria's tomorrow night." He leaned over and gave Emma a kiss on the forehead. "You up for that?"

Emma's eyes brightened. "Sounds like a plan. Maybe we can teach him about Italian food."

At the French doors with Randall, Loomis said, "Now, that does sound like a plan."

"Oh, by the way, Ms. Doyle," Randall paused to say, "We are being invaded by media, and I'd appreciate it if you would not talk to anyone about your association with La Casa."

Molly gave him such a cold stare, Loomis moved away from the door. "I'll pretend I didn't hear that."

When they were gone, Emma followed Molly into the kitchen. "We're being shut out, you know."

Molly's laugh was terse. "Ya think? Well, Mr. Chief of Police Randall just made a big goof, didn't he! You didn't give him the extra copies of those pictures, I noticed."

Emma leaned against the sink and giggled. "Surely you jest."

Molly laughed with her. "You almost blew that, Watson."

"Guess we're still on the game, huh?"

Molly almost dropped the cups she'd been putting away. "Where in the world did you pick that up?"

"I heard it on BBC America."

"Uh, Em? I think you mean 'on the case.' That other one means something quite different."

"Oh. Well, whatever. How did you know there were extra copies of the photos?"

"Ah, no fool I. You didn't get them in between the other photos all the way. I saw the bottoms sticking out. So I took a peek. Why did you do that?"

Emma handed her the remaining cups. "I had a feeling he was going to brush us off now that Mr. Loomis is here. But since you gave him that information from your friend in Los Angeles, and I recognized the material in the picture, I thought . . ."

"Uh-uh. What, pray tell?"

"Well, that we're a pretty good team and he should let us help. I'm glad he didn't take the books. He'd know then that I hid the others."

Molly felt a chill run through her. What the hell was she doing, letting Emma think they were going to go behind Randall's back and snoop? It was one thing for her to be hardheaded, but it was not something Emma should emulate. "Forget what I just said. As much as I love a puzzle— and so do you, it seems—we have to butt out. Besides, we've got to get the shop put back together and sell antiques. That's what we do." Molly glanced at the cat clock on the kitchen wall. "It's almost nine. What say we call it a day?"

Holding back a yawn, Emma said, "Guess so. All this excitement sure wears me out."

"Yeah, me too."

* * *

Climbing into bed, Molly thought about what Emma had said. Randall *was* brushing them off, and how astute of Emma to realize it. It rankled her no end, considering how much help she'd been before. But the last thing she wanted was for Emma to think this sleuthing was normal. Besides, Randall had Loomis here, and he couldn't very well discuss an investigation with her in front of him.

Before she turned out the light, she decided to give Daria a call. When Daria picked up on the second ring, Molly said, "I couldn't go to sleep until I knew you were okay."

"I'm fine, Molly. I feel better getting all that off my chest with you and with Randall. I told him what I said to Jason. You don't have to worry about that anymore. Lucero is here. I've told him everything. You won't believe this, but he's known all along."

"Oh, Daria! I'm so glad. Maybe you two can finally—"

"Slow down." Daria chuckled. "I was going to call you, and then, well, we've been talking. You're a rare friend, Molly Doyle, and I love you."

Molly was near tears. "Oh, shush. You'd do the same for me. Listen, I'll let you go. I love you too. I'll see you tomorrow. Oh, Randall warned me about all the media here. I guess he told you the same."

"Yes, and they've already been to the restaurant. Bastards! I don't know who's been yapping, but some of them found out Frances and I are old friends and are trying to get to me to comment. I'm going in tomorrow, and they'd better stay the hell out of my way."

"Good luck," Molly said. "If someone is talking, they'd better stay clear of *Treasures* too."

With a great sense of relief after their conversation, Molly blew a kiss to her father's photo, said her prayers, and added a footnote. *Thanks for keeping Daria safe. And thank you for Dan Lucero. She's going to need both of you to see this through now that Randall knows she threatened Jason. I'll do what I can, but the ball's in your court.*

## ~~ *24* ~~

After visiting Frances at the hospital, and suggesting to Loomis that they eat seafood on Fisherman's Wharf, Randall took the Monterey exit off the freeway. As they drove down Munras Avenue, he pointed out the No Vacancy signs on all the motels. "Well, the media's here in full force already. Shit. I'll bet every stringer in the country is on their way." He picked up his cell phone, called the station and gave orders that no television satellite vans were to be allowed to set up on any street in Carmel proper. Then he punched in the sheriff's unlisted cell number. Randall had established a good relationship with the newly elected sheriff of Monterey County, but wanted to make sure that the sheriff cooperated in his own jurisdiction, which bordered Carmel.

Randall chose a place on the wharf owned by one of Lucero's cousins. He knew he could get a private room if necessary. As it was, it was late and the restaurant had few diners.

"I don't like this mess with Daria," Randall said after they were seated. "My gut tells me she didn't kill Lerner, but she admitted to threatening him, and now I've got no freakin' choice but to consider her a suspect."

Loomis was looking over the menu. He set it down. "Technically, yes, you do. But I'm also not putting much stock in her as the killer. Or what Frances told us tonight either. Now that the murder weapon has been found and the gun was registered to her father, I'm having some serious thoughts about that woman. Very convenient to say she was in the dining room when she heard the shot. So what did she do then? Stay there and wait for the killer to bop her over the head? And how did the killer know where to find her? And how did she get those burns on her hands if she was in the dining room? Her story stinks."

"I don't like it either. Could be she was in the room and didn't see the killer. She likes to stand at the fireplace, so maybe they struggle. In the tussle a log gets kicked, she tries to shove it back. The killer comes in and sees the brawl . . . hides . . . waits until Frances runs out, and then shoots Lerner."

"And leave a witness? I don't buy it."

"I don't either. I think I'll go with the crab cakes."

"Crab cakes? Sounds good, but I've got to try the famous squid. Either she killed Jason or she thinks Daria did and she's trying to protect her. I'm not crazy about the way she flutters her eyelashes when she talks. It's a sure sign of—"

"Yeah, yeah. I know. I don't need a face-reading lesson from you, okay?"

"No, we had an expert teacher."

Randall gave Loomis a broad grin. "She sure was something, remember?"

"Eighty years old and feistier than you or I ever thought about being."

After the waiter took their order, Randall said, "Okay, we've established the means, we think we know the motive, and we've got two women there with opportunity. One admits to threatening the victim, the other is conveniently hit over the head and can't identify the killer. So where the hell does that damn skeleton play in this?"

"Lucky for you Molly and little Emma found that photo."

"I wish to hell we'd found it instead. Last thing I want is them thinking they've got front row seats in another homicide investigation."

"You may want Molly out of this, but her logic is pretty damn sharp. What if she's right about Marius Lerner telling Jason and his daughter? We know they were having money problems. If Jack O'Brien was blackmailing him, like Molly suggested, maybe the old man told them to get up here and find the proof and put an end to it. And what better way to hide the proof than in plain sight, so to speak? Those photos Emma found were not a mistake."

"Possible. But that still doesn't explain why Frances was getting ten grand a month."

"I've been thinking about that," Loomis said. "I dug out my old notes on that case with Jason Lerner and Vince Mazzeo. I'd forgotten that I was suspicious of Frankie aka Frances from the start. I had an idea she'd been in the room when Jason killed Mazzeo. I think that money was her payoff for swearing she hadn't seen what went down. Kind of déjà vu? History repeating itself . . . like now, right?"

"Speaking of the O'Briens," Randall said, "I checked out the highway patrol's accident report when they were killed. They're convinced it's legit. They concluded that O'Brien fell asleep at the wheel and ran off the road. Easy to do driving late at night at his age. Apparently they were on their way back from Reno. Those mountain roads are a bitch."

Randall paused as the waiter brought their salad. He asked for extra grated cheese and more butter for their sourdough bread. Loomis waited patiently until the waiter left, then said, "That ten grand a month is a fortune to you and me, but you know damn well that with movie folks it's chump change. That's a stroll on Rodeo Drive for a few things."

"Yeah, okay. I won't fight you on that." Randall took a sip of wine and thought how great it felt to be hashing out a homicide with Loomis again. He hadn't realized how much he'd missed working with him. "So, you gonna hang around for a spell? I mean, until after the Bach Festival?"

Loomis was into his salad. He speared an artichoke heart and nodded. "I'm thinking about it. The air's clean here. Might be a nice change. How long you willing to put me up?"

"I got plenty of room. Take your time."

"You may regret offering that. Okay, where were we? Right. If Daria can account for her time before and after both killings, I think there's a third party involved," Loomis said. "I can smell it."

Randall had already considered the third party issue, but he wanted to hear Loomis's thoughts. "I'm listening."

"You got the first homicide at Ventana, which is what? A good half hour from Carmel?" Not waiting for Randall to answer, he said, "Okay. Your coroner's report places Steffi Lerner's death roughly around seven or seven-thirty. The hostess in the restaurant at Ventana states Steffi left a little before seven. That gives the killer time to confront Steffi, find out where her brother is, kill her, get up to

Carmel, sneak into La Casa without being seen . . . hear what's going on, kill Jason Lerner, overcome Frances, set the fire and be out of there by eight-thirty, when the fire department shows up. You with me here?"

"Don't get mad, pal, but I've already laid that out on my chart. I'm with you all the way."

Loomis lifted his wineglass. "I figured you would be. The fire, however, is interesting. Why bother? And why leave the gun?"

Randall clinked his glass with Loomis's. "The fire might be a cover-up. The gun? If our killer isn't Frances, then we go with the third party scenario, and it's a plant. Daria, by the way, has an alibi for the coroner's time frame on Steffi Lerner. She and her chef were going over a menu for a private party. Montgomery got his statement."

Loomis almost looked hurt. "You neglected to tell me that."

"I didn't want to blow your theory. But then, her chef could be lying for her too."

"Well, that's been known to happen. By the way, you were pretty cold to Molly tonight. I'm beginning to think she's got a good nose for investigations." Loomis laughed. "She's done pretty damn well for an amateur. You ought to think about hiring her."

"Look, Loomis. If you want to stick around Carmel, you better get one thing straight, okay? Trouble follows that woman, and she's gonna get hurt one of these days if she doesn't mind her own business."

"Seems to me she hasn't had much choice in the matter."

"Don't remind me," Randall said.

"So, nothing going on with you two then?"

Randall ignored that. "The fire still bothers me. If it

wasn't an accident, then why torch just the salon and the study? Why not the whole place?"

"The fire could be a half-assed diversion. If Frances is our killer, what better way to deflect suspicion than by destroying what I assume to be a fortune of antiques in the house?"

"Could be, but that's a lot of dough to leave on the table. Molly's commission alone would have been close to a hundred grand. And that only covered what she'd managed to inventory. She still had artwork and some fancy books, I think."

"Jesus! She must be frothing at the mouth now. Man, that's a big chunk to lose."

"I imagine that hasn't hit her yet. She's too busy trying to butt in where she doesn't belong. At least now that Daria has come in, maybe she'll stop worrying about her and go back to ripping off customers."

Loomis shook his head. "For shame, sir. Molly is on the up and up and you know it."

"I tell her that all the time. She knows I'm kidding." He picked up a fork and seemed to be examining it. After a moment he said, "Come to think of it, Frances told me she wasn't much of an antiques buff. She liked the simple look."

"If she's not our killer, the insurance company will pay up."

When dinner was served, Loomis said, "Okay, Chief. This is your show. What's our next move?"

"We're going out to Carmel Valley tomorrow morning to see Duff—who was chief here a while ago. Let's see if he can ID the woman in the photo."

# ~~~ *25* ~~~

*M*olly and Emma polished off last night's sweets for breakfast as they watched the morning news on CNN. A television reporter was in front of Daria's restaurant. Molly's mouth fell open when she heard the young woman say:

> *"Kenneth Randall, the chief of police of Carmel, has placed a sanction on television satellite trucks in the city limits. However, our remote cams will be tolerated as long as we do not disrupt traffic or create a gridlock on the tourist village streets or sidewalks. I'm standing in front of Daria's, one of Carmel's premier restaurants, which is owned by Daria DeMarco, a close friend of Frances O'Brien, the owner of La Casa, where Jason Lerner was shot and killed. Our sources tell us a full-blown investigation is under way in conjunction with the Monterey County Sheriff's investigation of the murder of Steffi Lerner, who was shot and killed down the Big Sur coast at the exclusive resort and spa, Ventana.*
> *"Surprisingly, residents here in the village are*

*unwilling to offer comments and are actually quite close-mouthed. You may recall that Carmel is the home of Clint Eastwood, who was at one time its mayor, and the village is not a stranger to media attention. However, with many world class events held here and in Pebble Beach throughout the year, one would think the residents would take this attention in stride. That does not seem to be the case now that one of its own might end up being a suspect in a double homicide."*

Molly continued to stare at the television, but tuned out as the reporter went on to relate the back story of the Lerners and O'Briens. She turned off the television and said, "Enough of that. We've got to get to work, Em."

"I wonder who she's talking about? I mean when she said 'one of our own'?"

"Oh that's just hype. Don't worry about that, okay? She has to say something. I mean, we know someone killed Jason and Steffi, but that doesn't mean it's someone from here. But we've got to be careful today and not let anyone in the shop. Even with that Closed sign on the door, some of those TV people might try to lie their way in by saying they want to buy something in the window. No one gets in here unless we know them."

"Gotcha. But how would they know to come here?"

"I don't know, but then, I don't know a lot lately."

"How are we going to go to Daria's tonight for dinner? Won't they be watching?" Emma asked as they headed downstairs.

Molly smiled. "Oh, I know a few alleys and restaurant kitchens we can slip through."

"Okay. Oh, I almost forgot. I'm supposed to call Sister Phil and continue the tutoring now that we're not going back to La Casa."

"I'll call her later. I can't believe it's Thursday already and I haven't heard from Max and Nicholas. And you and I have a full day of deciding what to do with all these smalls. We've got to be ready for the weekend!" Molly looked around the shop. "What a mess."

"Guess we should sort by type, huh?"

"A brilliant idea. Why don't you start with all the teacups and saucers? Put them in the storage room, and I'll tackle all the stuff for the lamp guy."

"I'll run up and get that old Bible. Maybe you could give it to Frances when you can visit her at the hospital."

Molly was trying to weave her way through a minefield of vases. "Put it on my desk. I'll give Randall a call later too and ask when we can see her."

By noon Molly and Emma were ready for a week at a spa. "I think," Molly said, "we're going to splurge and have lunch at one of Carmel's famous restaurants."

"Which one? They're all famous."

"I was thinking about Casanova's."

Emma looked down at her spotted jeans and scuffed tennis shoes. "Are you serious?"

"Nope. Just daydreaming. Besides, we can't afford those fancy prices. We'll walk over to Bruno's, get some sandwiches and have a picnic at Devendorf Park instead."

"Are we still broke?"

"No. But we still have to be careful. The commission money we've made from La Casa has to be for merch. With Frances laid up, that might take some time."

"I'll go get the sandwiches. Let's eat here. It's kind of cold for the park."

Molly moved to the display window and looked at the dull gray overcast still lingering. She was thankful they hadn't been bothered by any of the news people wandering around town with their minicams. She'd peeked through the window on and off, and twice noticed people on the sidewalk shaking their heads or waving a reporter off. Each time she wanted to raise her fist and shout *Yes!* "Good point. Okay, you do the lunch run and I'll keep sorting until you get back." Returning to her desk, she took money out of her wallet and handed it to Emma. "Now remember, don't talk to anyone."

"Duh! Think they're gonna stop a kid?"

"Another good point, Watson. Okay, off with you. I'll give Bitsy a call. I'm going into the storage room to call her and have a smoke."

Emma rolled her eyes. "That's three since this morning."

Molly put her hands on her hips. "Emma!"

Emma laughed and ran out the door before Molly could catch her. Molly watched her leave, then returned to the desk for her cigarettes and saw the Bible that Emma had left there. Curious, she opened it and noted writing inside the front cover. Emma was right, she thought, immediately recognizing the words as Latin. The Bible itself was too damaged to have much value, but it must have been gorgeous at one time. The leather tooling and gold leaf lettering, hardly recognizable now, were of excellent quality. She carefully turned several pages and was impressed by the fine vellum and beautiful illustrations.

She was curious why Jack O'Brien would have a Bible he probably couldn't read by his bed, and wondered if it had been a gift or belonged to someone he'd cared for. A parent perhaps. Or, she thought, he might have gone to Catholic school and it was a childhood treasure. She continued to examine it, and saw that it had been printed in Rome in 1798. Intrigued, she picked up the phone. Sister Phil would probably know some Latin and might help decipher the writing.

Bitsy answered, and by the time Molly finished bringing her up to date, and listened to Bitsy go on and on about the television reporting, she was itching to talk to Sister Phil. "I've found an old book with some Latin writing on the inside cover," she said. "Is Sister Phil around? I was hoping she might be able to translate."

Thankfully, Sister Phil was not as long-winded as Bitsy. Molly slowly spelled each word and then quickly jotted down the translation. By the time they reached the last one, Sister Phil said, "Sounds to me like a lot of old sayings strung together. Whoever wrote them was in great desolation. If you can make any sense from it, please let me know. I'll say a prayer for his or her soul." Molly thanked her and quickly turned on the computer to organize the choppy sentences.

*Jacta alea est*: the die is cast. *Res ipsa loquitur*: the thing speaks for itself. *Horribile dictum*: horrible to relate. *Note bene*: note well. *Ars longa, vita brevis*: art is long, life is short. *Verbum sap*: enough said. *Comes comitis, indigeo*: friend, need.

She sat back and stared at the monitor. Only a person of wealth in those times would have so grand a Bible. She imagined an eighteenth century nobleman or merchant in a huge basilica in Rome praying for forgiveness. What tragedy, she wondered, might have befallen him to inscribe those words? A sharp rapping on the window broke her reverie. Molly almost jumped. She turned to see Randall and Loomis waving.

Lost in ancient Rome, she almost wanted to tell them to

go away. It had been a nice excursion. Unlocking the door, she smiled and waved them in. "You scared the hell out of me knocking like that. I was afraid it was one of those reporters. Welcome to *Treasures*, Mr. Loomis. Please don't think it looks this way all the time. We just got a truckload of new merch, and Emma and I—"

"You're babbling again, Molly," Randall said. "There's no reason for them to bug you. Or is there?"

Molly gave him a nasty look. "You're beginning to sound like a broken record. What the hell is that supposed to mean?"

Randall turned to Loomis and winked. "She babbles when she's nervous. And her eye twitches." He moved farther into the store and looked at the mess. Over his shoulder, he said, "You'll note the various signs soon enough. But I'll give you a heads-up." Turning back, he smiled at Molly. "When the right eye twitches it usually means she's pissed. If it's the left, she's not telling me everything. When she babbles—"

"Ignore him, Molly," Loomis said. "He gets cranky when he misses breakfast."

Molly shot Randall another look. "I frequently do."

"This is a beautiful shop," Loomis said. He looked up at the painted fairy ceiling, then moved to the stairs. He ran his hands over the wrought-iron railing and said, "A master iron man made this." Turning away, his eyes took in the showroom. "Brick walls, a fireplace that works—I presume—and a prime spot on Ocean Avenue. Now that's what I call Antiques Dealer Nirvana."

Molly linked her arm in Loomis's and said, "Except business sucks just now. But as soon as I get all this new merch set out, we'll be back on top."

"Business is *bad* in Carmel?"

"Just for me lately. All my show-stopping pieces were gone until this new delivery. I was left with blah stuff. It wouldn't have enticed any of the crowd coming in for the Bach Festival." She threw her arms out and said, "But now . . . now I've got some beauties."

Eyeing the damaged Buddha that Molly was planning to turn into a lamp, Randall picked it up. "Too bad about the fire. That sure as hell put a crimp in your plans for the sale."

Molly moved two chairs closer to her desk and gestured for them to sit. "I'll live through it. Any chance of salvage? I was wondering about some of the porcelain and china in the butler's pantry and when I could go over and take a look."

"We can't stay. I'll let you know later. I'm going over there now."

"That could be a possibility, Molly," Loomis said. "Porcelain is fired at a higher temperature than that fire would have produced."

"That's what I was thinking," Molly said. "Bitsy had a client for all the Belleek, and if any of it survived, well, it's a big commission for me." Giving Randall a side glance, she said, "There was some interesting Pallisay and majolica too."

Loomis was all ears. "Oh? How many pieces?"

"Several. If you could convince your pal here to let me come over later, I'll show you. If they survived, that is."

"I knew I should have kept you two apart," Randall said, "Come on, Loomis. We've got work to do."

Molly followed them to the door. To Loomis, she said, "Make sure he calls me today."

Loomis gave her a peck on the cheek. "Consider it done."

After lunch, it took Molly and Emma the rest of the afternoon to sort, tag, and place the new smalls. By four they stood back and admired their work. "Looks like a star-studded shop now, Em," Molly said. She gave her a high five. "Without you, I'd still be up to my neck in a mess."

"I just wish I didn't have to start school next month. This is more fun."

"Oh, sure. Tell me that after you've met a bunch of new friends and you want to have sleepovers and go to movies and have pizza."

"Okay, okay. You win. I'll go check on Tiger and the kids."

Molly watched Emma and thought again about the richness she'd brought to her life. She had to remind herself more than once that her niece was a child, and not a contemporary. But it was hard not to think so, and she didn't want to think about how much she was going to miss her when she started school. She didn't have much time to dwell on that when the phone rang.

"Molly, darling," Bitsy said. "With so much going on these past two weeks, I forgot to tell you that three of the paintings Frances brought from the inn for the party were sold. And, I was thinking you might want to have the other three for the shop. I've already talked to Frances, and she'd be delighted if you'd take them."

"You've talked to Frances? When? I thought she was under wraps."

"Well, of course she still is, but she can talk on the phone now. In fact, the other thing I wanted to tell you is that she'll be staying with me as soon as she's released."

"Bitsy! I thought you were furious with her."

"Oh, darling. That's water under the bridge. I mean, really, the poor dear has absolutely no one to look after her, and it's the least I can do."

"But you can't care for her! And Josie is hardly a nurse. Especially with those burns."

"Oh, the burns are actually rather minor. And she's breathing much better now. I'll have a nurse in, naturally, and of course Sister Phil will be here. You know nuns know just about everything. Josie and Charles are just delighted to have a house full again. Oh, one other thing. I spoke to Max. He and Nicholas are still in the boonies and they won't be here until next week."

Molly was tongue-tied and not a little bit put off. Bitsy was doing a complete about-face, Randall was shutting her out of the investigation, and now Max hadn't had the courtesy to call her about the new plans.

"Molly, darling? Are you still there?"

"Uh, yes. I was . . . I was just taking all this in. Well, at least I'm glad to know Frances is doing better. When did Max call?"

"I called him. I know how busy you've been with all the new merch, so I thought I should get the ball rolling. I'm so anxious for Nicholas to see Frances's work. I think he'll be absolutely enthralled."

"I'm sure he will."

"Darling? You sound a bit down. Are you okay? I know you're exhausted, but have you thought about taking a few days off? You've been in such a mad rush."

Molly wasn't about to let Bitsy know she was steaming. "I'm fine. Really. I can't possibly take time off. The shop has been closed long enough. I've got to be ready for the weekend."

"Yes, of course. Can I have Charles drop off some of Frances's work? I'm keeping a few for myself, but with all that's going on around here, you should be able to turn them before Monday. Nothing like a little notoriety, is there?"

Molly knew Bitsy might have sounded a shade too opportunistic to an outsider, but Bitsy Morgan was the consummate dealer. Being three steps ahead in their game was vital for survival. "Sure, that's fine."

"Wonderful. I knew you'd agree. I've priced them for you, darling. Just put them in the front window. Oh, best keep Virginia for a little while longer. I don't know when I'll be able to get back to the shop. With Frances coming tomorrow, and then Max and Nicholas, I'm going to have a house full. I'm even having Ramon come to me for my hair this week. I want to look my best for the cameras, you know."

Bitsy's raspy chuckle usually brought a smile to Molly's face, but at the moment she wanted to throttle her. "What cameras? You're not thinking of doing an interview with those cannibals, are you?"

"Oh, don't get your panty hose in a bind. I'm just being prepared. Charles and I will be using the Rolls to pick up Frances at the hospital tomorrow, and a girl has to look her best, you know."

"Please don't talk to them. If we continue to ignore them they might go away."

"Oh, Molly, darling! Dream on, dear girl. They're here for the duration. We'll have to make the best of it."

*W*hen Loomis called later to tell Molly he'd take her to La Casa the next day, she barely managed a smile. Why hadn't Randall called and why was Loomis taking her? It galled her to think she'd handed him a brilliant motive scenario and now he was ignoring her. While she was convinced Daria was innocent, it was clear to her that Frances was lying about something. Was Randall that besotted with her that he couldn't see it? And to top it off, the idea of Frances staying with Bitsy bothered her no end. She knew Bitsy was quick to take offense and then just as quick to open her arms, but this sudden Fairy Godmother act was annoying. And now Max and Nicholas would be staying with her too. What disturbed her more was that she just didn't like Frances and she knew that was coloring her attitude. But it was the sense of being shut out that maddened her most.

She hadn't heard from Daria either, and wondered if dinner with Loomis was still on. If the fridge wasn't so empty, she'd just as soon stay home. But not going would disappoint Emma and she couldn't do that to her. Molly dialed the restaurant and got Manuel. "La Señora is in the dining room taking care of a rude customer. He is a man with the television people. He is not very simpatico to what La Señora say. She is telling him where to go for the rest of his miserable life."

Molly laughed and wished she could be a fly on the wall. "Do you know if she's expecting us tonight?"

"Oh, yes. It is for the new *policia*, I am correct? *El jefe* has already made the arrangements for six this night. You will be careful of your journey to here, yes?"

"Very careful, Manuel. Thank you. Please tell Daria I'll be there."

Molly checked her watch and saw that it was almost five-thirty. She and Emma had enough time to freshen up and then take a roundabout way to Daria's. She smiled as she climbed the stairs to the apartment. Emma would get a kick out of the crazy walk she was conjuring.

They were both ready to leave when Molly decided to take the photo books and give them to Randall. But first she wanted to take another look at the pictures Emma had hidden. Carefully pulling them out, she set them on the coffee table. It was almost eerie to think the vibrant young woman in the beaded dress was indeed the skeleton in the coffin they'd discovered. As she stared at the photo, Molly's eyes narrowed. Were these two photos somehow different from the others in the book? she wondered. Pulling a photo of Bing Crosby out of the plastic sleeve, she set it next to the one she'd been examining and called to Emma, "Come take a look at these and tell me what you think."

Emma sat next to her and held one in each hand. "Oh, that's Bing Crosby, right? The guy who sang all those Christmas songs?"

"No, I mean yes. But that's not what I meant. Look at the quality of the pictures. And look at the size."

Emma took another look, then nodded. "I see what you

mean. The Bing picture is kinda shinier." Placing one on top of the other, Emma said, "Ohmigosh! They're not the same size!"

"Just a tiny bit off, but enough to make a difference."

"A different camera?"

"Maybe a different photographer," Molly said.

Emma set them back on the table, then crossed her arms and thought for a moment. "All this means what?"

"I'm not sure."

"Hey! No fair! You've got me all excited and you don't have an answer?"

"I'm playing with a few thoughts. Nothing touchable . . . more like tiny whispers in my ear, only they don't make sense."

"Are you going to tell Randall about these pictures?"

Molly gathered the two Emma had hidden, then shook her head. "Nope. Not until I can grab hold of something solid."

"Cool."

Jumping up from the sofa, Molly stashed the two pictures under a cushion, then picked up the books and said, "We've got to go. We're going to be late."

Emma laughed. "We always are."

When they reached the courtyard downstairs, Molly said, "Oh, the hell with the alleys and all that. Let's just go the regular way. No one is going to bother us. They don't even know we exist."

As Molly expected, the walk to Daria's was uneventful. The camera crews and anxious television reporters were either bored or long gone. When they reached the restaurant, Molly hesitated. "Let's keep the evening light. No mention of La Casa, Frances, or anything."

"Like it never happened? Okay. But what if someone else brings it up?"

"Just don't comment. I want Randall to think that—"

"We're minding him?" Emma said.

"Yeah. Something like that."

When they entered, Daria was waiting and gave them both a hug. "You're late as usual. I was afraid you'd changed your mind."

"I'm sorry," Molly said. "I was, uh, on the phone with a customer."

Daria pretended to shiver. "Don't talk about customers! I've had a belly full today. Those damn TV people think they rule the world."

"Manuel told me when I called earlier. Is everything okay now?"

"So far. I'd still like to know who the hell told them Frances and I were old friends."

"Don't stress over it. It's not exactly a secret," Molly said as they made their way down the hall to Daria's private room.

"It's not that. I'm curious to know who's talking, that's all."

When Daria opened the door and they stepped in, Randall abruptly stopped talking. Molly managed to hear him say something, but wasn't sure what it meant. Obviously, he was talking about the murders to Loomis and Lucero and cut it short. Pretending not to notice, she waved, pulled off her jacket, then set her tote and the books on the floor. When she was about to take her usual place at the table, she noted the filled wineglasses and that two baskets of sourdough bread had already been ravaged. "Sorry I'm late. I hope I didn't hold anything up."

When Loomis rose, Molly said, "Thanks, but chivalry is a lost art with this group. We're very informal anyway."

Lucero cleared his throat. "Uh, yeah. Sorry about that. Guess we all feel so much like family we don't think about the social niceties."

Before Randall could do more than wave, Manuel came in with two large platters of antipasti and set them on the table. Loomis's eyes lit up. He bunched three fingers together and blew a kiss to Daria. "Ah, Corcchette di Pollo and Mais con Zucchini Fritte? Am I correct?"

Stunned, Daria said, "*Exactamente!* Good for you, Loomis. I had no idea you were up on Italian food."

"I could have told you that," Molly said as she looked at Randall. "Anyone who appreciates Pallisay and majolica could be no less a raconteur."

Randall's smile seemed pasted on until Emma leaned next to him and said, "They're really chicken fritters and zucchini strips. I saw the chef make them one day. He told me what they were."

"Thank you, Em," Randall stage whispered. "I appreciate your help." Darting a look at Molly, he said, "We're never too old to learn, right?"

Lucero winked at Loomis, sighed loudly, then loosened his tie. Reaching for the wine bottle, he began his Chamber of Commerce routine of extolling the virtues of the Monterey peninsula for Loomis's benefit. By the time the Orecchiette with roasted garlic pesto arrived, he'd moved on to the wine growing regions of the South county. "We're giving the Napa Sonoma area a run for its money. Our vintners are top notch and winning gold medals all over the world."

Loomis raised his wineglass and said, "I can attest to that. This merlot from Bella Lago is superb. I'm looking forward to next year's Masters of Food and Wine at the

Highlands Inn." Glancing at Randall, he asked, "It's the eighteenth year, isn't it?"

Randall made a point of looking at Molly when he replied, "No, that will be the nineteenth year. I imagine they'll have it in honor of Julia Child. She was a big attraction each year."

Molly tried hard to show she wasn't miffed with him. "I'd say she was the main attraction. She'll certainly be missed."

A look of relief crossed Daria's face as she announced the next dish to Loomis. "Manuel will be in with Costolettine d'Agnello alle Olive Verdi and Orzotto con Verdue e Prosciutto."

Randall nudged Emma. "Grilled lamb chops with green olive salsa . . . and uh, Orzotto with artichoke hearts and prosciutto."

Emma laughed the loudest as she clapped her hands. "You're my all-time champ! But wait . . . what's the Orzotto thing?"

"Orzo. It's a tiny rice-shaped pasta. Loomis is pretty good at doing the ID bit, though he only knows a few words of Italian. But we'll get him up to snuff around here."

Molly's ears perked up. She'd been trying to recall what Randall had been talking about when she and Emma entered. ID? Was that it? She fiddled with her napkin, then took the last bite of her pasta. She reached for her wine when his words suddenly took form. *Duff ID'd the photo.* Yes. That was it. *Oh, my God!* They knew who the woman in the coffin was! But who was Duff? Damn him! If it hadn't been for Emma, he'd never have known about the photos! Oh, she wanted to just smack him!

Molly kept a smile on her face and chatted with Daria during the next course. They spoke briefly about the television people, then Molly said, "Bitsy called today. She's picking Frances up tomorrow and taking her home with her." Turning to Randall, she said, "I'm glad to know she's recovering. I thought you were going to let me know when she could have visitors."

Randall glanced at Lucero. "It was a last minute decision. We thought it best to get her out of the hospital. Too many ways for those media vultures to get info. I called Bitsy and suggested she might like to have another house guest. That place of hers is pretty well fortified, and Josie and Charles can be trusted to keep things quiet."

Molly was dumbfounded. She'd gotten the impression Bitsy had invited Frances. "Oh, well, that's certainly a good idea. I know she'll be well cared for."

"Say, Molly," Loomis said, "what's a good time to meet you at La Casa tomorrow?"

Molly pretended to think for a moment. She didn't want to jump too quickly and maybe have Randall change his mind. She never knew what went on in that devious brain of his. "Oh, ah . . . how's ten?"

"Sounds good," Loomis replied. "Be sure to wear jeans and tennis shoes. The place is still a mess."

"Do you think there's anything left that's worth anything?" Daria asked.

Molly shrugged. "Hopefully some of the china survived. I don't know how far the fire spread, but if it didn't reach upstairs, there should be enough for a good local sale. I'll have a better idea tomorrow."

"The fire didn't reach the upstairs," Randall said. "There will be smoke damage, and the artwork on the walls along the staircase will have to go to a restorer for cleaning."

"Great," Molly said. "Maybe all is not lost after all."

"Considering two lives are lost, that sounds a little mercenary, don't you think?" Randall said.

Molly's right eye began to pulse. She had to stop herself from touching it. "I just meant there might be something left to sell for Frances. That's what she hired me for."

"Of course," Loomis quickly interjected. "We know what you meant, Molly."

Randall realized he'd been too sharp. "Sorry, Molly. It's been a bad week, okay? I know you didn't mean it the way it sounded. My apologies."

Molly nodded. "Sure. You must be beat. It's not like you have a huge crew to help you sort this all out. I'm sure Loomis is being a big help."

Daria could see trouble on the horizon. She rose from the table and announced, "Time for dessert. What will it be tonight, Emma?"

Emma's eyes had been darting between Molly and Randall. She hated it when they got snappy with each other, but she knew they always made up. She said to Loomis, "I get to choose dessert whenever we get together. It's great being a kid sometimes. How about tiramisu?"

Lucero groaned. "Oh not again, Em! You pick that every time."

"Well, it's my favorite and it's yummy!"

Molly avoided Randall until after dessert. As coffee was being served, she reached down for the photo books. "You forgot to take these the other night." She handed them to Emma to pass along. "I don't need them. You can give them to Frances tomorrow."

Randall took them and flipped one open. He turned several of the plastic-covered pages then said, "Lot of photos here. Nothing worth selling?"

Molly gave Randall a saucy smile. "I kept two that might be worth something."

## ~ *27* ~

*M*olly decided to wear her garage sale clothes to meet Loomis at La Casa on Friday morning, in case reporters were still hanging around. Daria's encounter yesterday proved someone was blabbing, and she wasn't going to take a chance the media knew she'd been preparing the house for a sale. She threw on a sweatshirt and jeans, grabbed her baseball hat and sunglasses, and told Emma she'd be back soon. Somehow she managed to be on time, and found Loomis in the entry courtyard with a security guard, holding two coffees.

"It's straight espresso," he said as he handed her one. "You're going to need a strong stomach when you get inside. Fires leave a terrible stench. I've got some Vick's in my pocket if you get nauseous."

Molly took the plastic cup and smiled her thanks. "That's very thoughtful. Thanks. Do you always carry Vick's around?"

"Old habits never die. They come in handy on a homicide call. Especially if they're a little old. But you're a cop's daughter, I'd figure you'd know that."

Molly was momentarily stunned. She had no idea

Loomis knew about her father. "There are some things about my dad's job that he never discussed with me."

"Yes, well, that was wise of him. Case talk doesn't belong at home. Let's sit for a minute." Loomis led her to a stone bench and brushed off some soot with his hand. "I want you to know that it was my idea to meet you instead of Randall. Besides, he's a little tied up."

"I know. I guess I've been a bit selfish thinking about the job I'm supposed to be doing, and not what he's facing. It's just that he—"

"I had another reason, Molly," he broke in. "I don't mean to interfere, but you and Randall seem to have a real problem relating." He saw she was about to speak again and held up his hand to stop her. "Hear me out. I've known the guy for twenty-some-odd years. Know him like a book. He tends to be brusque with those he cares for. Now, I read you as one smart cookie, and I'm surprised you haven't figured that out yet."

Molly took a sip of the espresso. "I know he's like that. And we do bitch a lot. But usually it's in fun." She shook her head. "Lately, he . . . oh, hell, I don't know. I know he's attracted to Frances and he's worried about her—"

Loomis eyes bulged. "Where did you get that idea? You're the one he's worried about."

"So that's why he's been such a jerk and won't let me help again."

"Hasn't it occurred to you this isn't your line of work? What do you expect Randall to do? He has no choice."

"He could be a lot less grumpy about it. After all we've been through, I'd think he might welcome my thoughts. It's not as if I expect to be in his hip pocket or anything."

"Ah, but you do," Loomis said. "Come on, be honest. You're pissed because he won't discuss what he knows.

He can't, Molly. It's as simple as that. Cops don't do round table discussions with civilians about homicides."

"It's kind of worked out that way lately."

"So I understand. But it's not routine."

Molly was itching for a cigarette. She knew Loomis meant well, but this conversation was beginning to agitate her big-time. She'd proven to have a good mind when it came to connecting the dots, and she knew she had much to offer again. The photos were a good example. She was certain they were significant. She wasn't sure how, but had given it a lot of thought when she returned from Daria's last night. She was also beginning to think they'd been planted in those photo books on purpose. "How funny you should say that. That's exactly what we did the last two times. But now that you're here, I guess he doesn't need any of us."

Loomis rose. "Let's take a look inside." He rubbed his hands together. "I hope some of that Pallisay and majolica survived."

Loomis said all that he'd planned. Molly didn't press him and stayed close as they entered the house. She didn't know what to expect, but when she saw the mess in the atrium, she thought how difficult it must have been for the firemen to get past all the towering trees in the large planters. She was struck by how wilted and sad the once graceful tree ferns and lush banana trees now stood. It was as if they too were mourning the chaos the fire had created. Puddles of sooty water remained on the flag stones, and the acrid stench of smoke still hung in the air.

It was clear Loomis was familiar with the layout of La Casa when he steered Molly directly to the butler's pantry while avoiding the salon and dining room.

"You know your way around here pretty well," Molly said.

Loomis offered his hand to her as they came upon a pile of water-soaked debris. "I've been here a few times with Randall to look things over."

She stepped over the stack of scorched cabinet doors and examined the open shelves of china. Miraculously, very little had been damaged. She was relieved to see that most of the Belleek Bitsy wanted to buy was intact. She also noted that the Pallisay and majolica pieces she'd planned to show Loomis were unharmed. She folded her arms and looked at him. "You knew all along this was saved."

"Didn't I say you were a pretty smart cookie?"

"So getting me here was just a ruse. Are you playing public relations man for Randall now? Did he put you up to this? Is this his way of saving face?"

Loomis didn't answer. He pulled down a Pallisay plate and examined it. He ran his hand over the surface, feeling for cracks or repairs, then turned it over and scrutinized the back as well. "It's genuine, it's French, and I'd say it's early eighteenth century." He handed the plate to her. "What say you?"

Molly folded her arms and refused it. "Stop playing games with me, okay? You've checked out every piece here already."

"Let's just say it's an illustration of—"

"Of how many steps ahead of me you two are and that I'm out of my element and go away little girl and play with your own toys?" Her words came tumbling out before she could stop. She knew she'd sounded cutting, and wasn't a bit sorry. She began to laugh then. "Fine! I will. So I'm going upstairs to see what can be saved for my client."

She left Loomis staring at her and knew he'd eventually follow. She carefully walked through to the main hall and paused at the marble staircase. There were at least eight or nine marvelous paintings lining the wall to the upper floor that she could see were in need of cleaning. Soot and smoke had settled on many of them. The gilded frames had become depositories for smoke and ash. The shallow carvings were barely recognizable. She climbed slowly and tried to gauge each painting's damage. It was a miracle they'd survived. She could almost imagine errant water hoses snaking through the foyer spouting huge sprays of water as the firemen tried to put the fires out from every possible angle.

Molly began a tour of the bedrooms and found only the lingering smell of smoke. The linens and draperies hadn't been considered for the sale, so she gave them little attention. Her main concern was the furniture. She didn't know how much heat had managed to creep up the stairs and if the patina on the wood furniture had been breached. She ran her hands across many pieces and found only a faint dusting of ash. Mrs. O'Brien's bedroom, with all its mirrored furniture, was only dusty. The remaining bedrooms looked untouched. When she reached Mr. O'Brien's bedroom, she was satisfied that it too had not been affected. She was about to leave when her eyes rested on a painting to the side of the bed. She remembered laughing when she'd first seen it. It was another example of Armand's handiwork. The copy of C. M. Coolidge's famous portrait of dogs playing poker had been reproduced for years. Evidently Mr. O'Brien felt it had personal resonance since he'd won the house in a poker game. In the mad rush to video and catalog, she hadn't given it much thought at the

time. The artwork in the house had been relegated to the
bottom of her list for research.

Molly looked at the painting again. She hadn't noticed
the small brass plaque at the bottom of the frame before.
The title was engraved in script, and so small that she had
to squint to make it out. Moving closer, she saw that the
inscription was in Latin, and it matched the last line writ-
ten in the Bible: *Comes comitis, indigeo.* Friend, need.
C. M. Coolidge had titled the canine poker players, *A
Friend in Need.*

Molly's mind was racing ahead like a train out of control. She had to think fast. Loomis was still downstairs and
might come up at any moment. The painting was on the
wall over the night table where Jack O'Brien had most
likely kept the Bible. How the Bible ended up in the fire
bucket O'Brien used for a waste basket wasn't important.
What *was* important was the proximity of the two. Without thinking, she pulled the painting from the wall, placed
it on the bed and stared at it. She was about to turn it over,
then changed her mind. Hidden wills, maps to treasure
caves, or secret Swiss bank account numbers were only
hidden behind artwork in the movies. People didn't do
that in real life. But then, she thought, Jack O'Brien
worked in the movies, so why not borrow a page from his
profession? It was so obvious, it might make sense. Not
really expecting to discover a thing, Molly turned it over.
Her eyes began to bounce like cherries in a slot machine.
A large manila envelope was taped to the back of the
painting. Her hands shook as she opened the envelope. It
was another photo of the woman in the beaded dress. In
this one she was sprawled on the floor next to a fireplace.
Molly immediately recognized the tiles on the surround
as the same as those in Jack O'Brien's study. But the floor

was different. Instead of the inlaid hardwood, it was tile with a Greek key design.

"Molly? You finished? I've got to leave," Loomis shouted from the hall.

She quickly replaced the photo in the envelope and stuffed it under her sweatshirt. Her hands were still trembling when she replaced the painting on the wall. "Hold your horses, I'm coming!" she yelled back. She made sure the bottom of the envelope was tucked into the waistband of her jeans and smoothed it so it wouldn't bulge, then quickly left to meet Loomis in the hall.

"Everything look okay?" he asked.

Molly didn't trust her voice. She nodded. "Everything reeks of smoke, but that's easily fixed." Waving him on, she said, "After you. The steps are slippery so if I tumble you can break my fall."

She was relieved when Loomis grinned and led the way. She didn't want to take a chance he might hear the envelope rustle under her sweatshirt, so she kept up a chatter as they left. "Would you ask Randall when I might come back and pack up the Belleek? Bitsy has a buyer, and the rest of the china and porcelains should be removed before Frances gets people in to clean up after the fire. Oh, and then there's the Pallisay and majolica. Are you interested in any of the pieces?"

"Depends on the price you decide on."

"Oh, I'll be fair, don't worry. In fact, you'll be surprised. That piece you looked at, by the way, is nineteenth century, not eighteenth."

Loomis stopped at the bottom stair. He turned to her. "I knew that." His eyes rested on her for a moment. "Nice to meet an honest dealer."

"Oh, you knew, did you? Well, guess what? I don't appreciate being tested any more than you or Randall do. So you've made your point. And for your further edification, most dealers are honest. But as you know, there's always a few rotten apples. Even in your business."

"Poor Randall. I'm beginning to feel sorry for him. But give him a break, will you? He's got a lot on his plate."

Molly decided she'd better go along with the program Loomis was obviously orchestrating. She gave him a brief smile. "Sure. Anything to keep the fuzz happy."

As they made their way down the galleria and past the atrium, she had a different view of the damage. It pained her to see that the beautiful stained-glass doors to the salon had been reduced to a pile of jewel like shards and callously swept into a corner. "Do you mind if I take a quick look at the study? There were some wonderful books there and I'd like to see if any survived."

Loomis glanced at his watch. "I doubt it, but sure."

Molly walked ahead of him. When she reached the once lovely room, she had to cover her nose. The smell of smoke was heavier here and hung in the air like a shroud. She knew the room would be a shambles and that none of the books would have survived. A path toward the fireplace had been cleared, and she carefully picked her way there. The bookcases were charred, gaping holes. "I should have guessed it would look like this." She moved to the fireplace and leaned her hand against the tile surround as if to brace herself. She wanted another look at the design. "What a horrible shame," she said as she turned to face Loomis. "Some of the book sets were more than just valuable. They were beautifully bound." Looking down, she noticed that the inlaid hardwood had burned away in places. Anxious to see what lay beneath, she faked a cough as she crouched down. "Oh, look at this.

There was a tiled floor under this hardwood." She pulled a piece away. "This must have been lovely."

"Be careful you don't get a sliver." Down on his haunches, he managed to pry a larger piece away. "Looks like a Greek key design. I don't blame them for covering it up." Standing now, he added, "Doesn't go well with the fireplace tile."

Loomis reached for her arm to guide her out. "Well, Frances will have her hands full getting this place back in shape."

"I don't envy her the job."

At the gate, Molly leaned over and kissed Loomis on the cheek. "Thanks for meeting me and . . . well, for everything."

"It was my pleasure. I just hope I've helped you see things a little clearer."

"Oh, you did. You have no idea."

## ~~ 28 ~~

*M*olly pulled away from La Casa and made a left at Santa Lucia. She drove up to Junipero then turned right on Rio Road and headed for the mouth of the valley. She had no doubt Loomis was going back to the police station, but she wanted to be sure she was far enough away from Carmel proper before she looked at the photograph again. She pulled into the Safeway parking lot, found a space, then removed the envelope from under her sweatshirt and took out the photo. The young woman's eyes were open and her mouth was slack. Molly knew she wasn't drunk or passed out. She was dead. The tiles on the fireplace surround were clearly the same Art Deco, and the Greek key tiles on the floor matched what she had seen just minutes ago.

Almost reverently, Molly returned the photo to the envelope and gently placed it back on the seat. She closed her eyes and said a quick Hail Mary. She could see the links and they were making sense. She had to get back to the shop and pull up the file of the Latin translations she'd saved on the computer, just to be sure her imagination wasn't playing tricks on her.

At the shop, she found a note from Emma saying she was at Tosca's having a late breakfast and she'd wait for

Molly there. Molly's stomach was grumbling, but she was compelled to open the file she'd saved and study it again. She found it quickly and printed it.

*Jacta alea est*: the die is cast.
*Res Ipsa Loquitur*: the thing speaks for itself.
*Horribile dictum*: horrible to relate.
*Note bene*: note well.
*Ars Longa, vita brevis*: art is long, life is short.
*Verbum sap*: enough said.
*Comes comitis, indigeo*: friend, need.

Her hands began to sweat. It was all here. The message couldn't be clearer. Jack O'Brien's blackmail proof had been right out in the open. If Emma hadn't found the Bible and decided to borrow it, it might never have been discovered. Molly leaned back in the chair and crossed her arms. She had to think this out. She was itching for a cigarette. She bit her lip instead. After a dull moment of uninspiring thought waves, she suddenly grinned and looked up at the big smiling painted sun on the ceiling. *Oh, you are so devious! That was very clever using Sister Phil to get to Emma in order to get us to this! Cool, as Emma would say. In fact, way cool. But, uh, what's next? Scratch that. Okay, okay, I'll give it to Randall.*

Molly picked up the printed translation and ran to the stairs. She took them two at a time and had to stop to catch her breath when she hit the top. She looked at the ceiling again and silently said, *But not just yet, okay? I need to check something out first.*

Molly lifted the cushion on the sofa where she'd hidden the two photos she'd saved. She sat down and stared at the one with the three women. She remembered there was something about the woman in the middle that had caught her when she'd first seen the photo. But now nothing registered. The hairstyle, long and parted in the middle, was *the* look of the day when it was taken. Even the heavily made-up eyes with false eyelashes was the Hollywood version of an upscale hippie. Cher did it a bit more dramatically, but it was the same look. Beaded dresses, Molly recalled, were very big in the seventies too. What was it about that particular woman! She continued to stare at her until it finally hit her. *The eyes. Ohmigod! Yes! The eyes!* Add thirty or so years, some weight, and then cut the hair and dye it. What was Eve Jensen doing in this picture?

Molly felt as if her breath had been sucked from her. She didn't care if Emma marched in on her right now, she was going to have a cigarette. She needed something before she blew a gasket. *Eve Jensen? What the hell could this possibly mean?*

Molly lit a cigarette, took one deep drag, then stubbed it out. She picked up both photos she'd saved and set them side by side on the coffee table. She nodded to herself, then began to mumble, "Yes . . . I see it now. It's all in the eyes. Eve and the dead woman were sisters. Look at them, Molly! Look at the mouth now, the chin. See the similarities?"

"I know the fire at La Casa was a big blow, but is this what happens to antiques dealers when they lose a big sale?" Randall asked as he stepped through the French door off the upstairs balcony. "They start talking to themselves?"

Molly stiffened when she heard his voice and closed her eyes. She didn't have to look up this time. *Did you have to do this now? I was going to give it all to him! I said I would!* She opened her eyes and gave Randall a wan smile. "I . . . I was thinking out loud. In fact, I was about to tell myself to call you."

"I just saw Emma down at Bennie's. She told me she thought she heard the truck pull in the alley and you might be upstairs. The French doors were open a crack."

"Oh. Well, come in. Have a seat. You're going to need one," Molly said as she handed Randall the photos. "Take a look at those, and then I've got another surprise for you."

Randall took the photos and gave her a hard stare. "Holding out on me again?" He shook his head. "What the hell am I going to do with you?"

"No lectures, please. And don't be mad. I just . . . well, I just discovered a few things. I was planning on calling you. Honest."

Randall sat on the sofa and spent a moment looking at the photos. He ran a hand over his eyes, then looked at her. "Okay. You're brilliant. Is that what you want me to say? Yeah, it's Eve Jensen in the middle." He set the photo on the coffee table. "She's the dead woman's sister."

Molly sank onto the sofa next to him. "You already know that?"

"Knew it yesterday. Her sister was Hillary Thornton. Eve is Geneive Thornton Jensen."

"But . . . but how did you find all this out?"

"Come on, Molly. It's my job to find these things out, remember? I'm not going to explain how, okay?"

Molly picked up the photo from Jack O'Brien's bedroom and the Latin translation from the coffee table. She handed them to Randall. "You need to see these too. Those Latin words were handwritten in a Bible Emma found in Jack O'Brien's bedroom."

Randall didn't say a word when he took them from her.

It was only a few minutes before he answered, but to Molly it seemed like hours. "Where did you get this picture?"

"It's the proof you need. About the blackmail, I mean."

His voice was very quiet when he said, "I asked you where you got this picture."

Molly explained how, when she'd met with Loomis earlier, she went upstairs to see how much damage there was and stopped to look at the painting of the dogs playing poker. "I guess I was in the mood for a smile. That painting always did that to me. I'd noticed it before when Emma and I were cataloging his room. I figured Mr. O'Brien had hung the print up as humorous reminder of winning this incredible house. I never really got close enough to notice it wasn't a print. It should have registered since it wasn't covered by glass. Anyway, I'd been so focused on the furniture and the smalls, I put the artwork research aside until I could get everything listed."

When he just looked at her and didn't comment, Molly nervously said, "I mean, well, I was impressed by how much was there, but I wasn't sure about some of it and decided to wait until Nicholas arrived."

"And he is?"

"Huh?"

"Nicholas. Who is he? Are you with me?"

"Oh. Uh, well, Nicholas Hahn is a renowned art expert. He does appraisals all over the world."

"A good friend? From your New York days?"

"Yes! A good friend, okay? Who the hell cares?"

"Calm down, okay? I just need to keep all the players straight."

"Well, you'd better add Armand then," Molly said. "It's one of his copies."

"Him again? That jerk gets around."

"Never mind him. Look at that picture, damn it! See the tiles on the fireplace? On the floor? That woman was killed when Marius Lerner owned the house! And the Coolidge? It's perfect, don't you see? The poker game? The title, *A Friend in Need*? That means Marius Lerner killed her and Jack O'Brien was that friend! Losing the house in the poker game was the first payoff to his *friend*. Granted, O'Brien was a blackmailer, but it all fits!"

"So?"

"What?" Molly nearly jumped off the sofa.

"I can't arrest a dead man for murder. Besides, Jack O'Brien might have killed her. And he's dead too."

"No, Marius Lerner was the killer. It doesn't make sense otherwise," Molly said, feeling a sudden sense of defeat. She'd thought she'd found the proof of the old murder, and figured out a major clue linking Eve to the dead woman, only to find that Randall already knew about Eve Jensen, and now it was clear the photo and the writing in the Bible had little meaning. It galled her to think he was right. Both men were dead. Where was the justice in that? "Then what are you going to do?"

"About what?"

Molly grabbed a pillow and squeezed it. "Oh, I could throw this at you! Someone has to pay for killing that young woman."

Randall rose, still holding the photo and paper Molly had given him. "It's too late for her. But someone does have to pay for killing Jason and Steffi Lerner. I'll take these with me, if you don't mind."

"I don't mind at all."

Heading for the door, Randall said, "Anything else you might have lying around that I might be interested in?"

"No."

"Emma would like you to join her when you're free."

"What about Eve? Are you going to tell her? Do you think she recognized that beaded fabric on the skeleton?"

Randall paused at the door. "It's been over thirty years. Who would remember something like that?"

"It's apparent you know little about women. We remember things like expensive evening gowns. Eve Jensen is no different."

"Maybe, but right now she thinks that thing was a movie prop. I don't want you telling her different. Will you promise me that?"

Molly nodded, then said, "She deserves to know."

"She'll have it when the time is right."

"When the time is right? Jesus, Randall! How many years has Eve agonized over not knowing what happened to her sister?"

"Look, we've got a can of worms open here already. I don't want a thirty-year-old homicide to muck things up, okay? A few more days more or less might make a big difference in nailing the killer. Trust me. It's important."

Molly walked out on the balcony with Randall. She saw Emma at a table in the courtyard talking to Bennie and waved. She was about to speak when Randall's cell phone rang. She waited as he answered. When she saw his eyes disappear and his jaw clench, she gripped the wrought-iron railing on the balcony. She almost jumped when he closed the phone with an angry snap.

"Shit!"

Molly held her breath. At least, she thought, it wasn't her fault he was steaming. She was almost afraid to ask, but then, she rarely listened to herself.

"What?"

"Can you keep the shop closed for a few more days and stay out of sight?"

"Huh?"

"I just got a heads-up from a buddy in Atlanta. CNN is doing a special report tonight on the Lerner homicides. The fuckers know about the coffin too. And you. The whole nine yards."

"Me? What the hell have I got—" Molly's hands flew to her mouth. "Ohmigod! If they know about me, what about Daria?"

"What *about* Daria?" Randall snapped.

Molly paused, then touched his arm. "She told me everything. You are a pain in the ass sometimes, but you're a good man, Randall. What you did for her in L.A."

Randall avoided looking at her. "I'd do the same for anyone in her position."

"Can't you ever take a compliment? I mean, how often do I offer you one?"

"Maybe I should carry a recorder around too, huh? For posterity?"

"We could have matching recorders." It was out of her mouth before she realized what she'd said. "I mean—"

"I know what you mean. Okay, now listen up. Somebody's yapping to CNN. They know you were preparing a sale for Frances and about your past, they know about the coffin, and they know about Jason Lerner shooting Daria's husband. I don't know how Daria's identity leaked, but I've got an idea, and I'll take care of that. So now, will you ride this out for me? Keep what you know to yourself?"

"Of course. My lips are sealed."

"I'm sorry you and Daria got dragged into this."

"Yeah, well, that's life. The past is never gone, is it?"

"You'll tough it out. Bitsy will probably think it'll be great for business."

Molly followed Randall down the stairs. "I'll call Daria and warn her. Maybe we should be together when the CNN thing comes on."

Randall paused. "Good idea. I'll get Loomis and Lucero to join us. We need to close ranks and try to figure out who's talking."

## ~ 29 ~

"It worked," Loomis told Randall when he returned to his office. "I think Molly has a better understanding now about what you're up against. Although I've got to say, that is one savvy lady. She didn't fall for my trap on the Pallisay."

Handing Loomis the photo and Latin translation Molly had given him, Randall said, "She also found this photo when you were supposed to be keeping an eye on her." He filled him in on what Molly had discovered, then added, "And we've got some new problems." Randall told him about the telephone call from Atlanta.

Loomis blew out his breath. 'Fuck. Every armchair detective in the country is going to have a field day with this. I can hear it now." Affecting a newscaster's voice, Loomis said, "The crucial forty-eight hours of a homicide investigation is long past. Is former Los Angeles Internal Affairs honcho Kenneth Randall losing his touch? It's been four days since the bodies of—"

"I don't give a shit what they say, okay?" Randall broke in. "And I'd advise you to start wearing a hat or something. Cover up that bald head and cute little fringe around your ears. You're a dead giveaway. You ain't a stranger to the media either. I don't want those assholes to be saying we're both incompetent. Or, worse, I had to pull my old homicide buddy up to help me out."

Loomis laughed. "I love it when you get tough."

"Yeah? Well, speaking of getting tough, Molly isn't going to play nice just because you had a little chat with her. She's too worked up over Daria to stay out of my hair."

Loomis was serious now. "I'm puzzled why Daria is going to be mentioned. Her real name wasn't on any of the reports. I made sure of that. I used a phony."

"I know that. But it may have come from my old office. I need you to get on the phone and find out if Chuck Norton is still with I.A. I don't want the query to come from me."

"Your old right-hand man?"

"Yeah. He's a talk show wonk, and I wouldn't put it past him to be the leak. He used to badmouth those retired cops that did commentary on the O.J. case. He was convinced he'd do a better job. Maybe he still thinks so."

"Okay, let me see what you've got there." Loomis looked at the photo, then read the translation. "I'll be damned. O'Brien had his ace in the hole all along. Good for Molly. Okay, I'll check out Norton." Loomis rose and headed for the door. "I need a soda first. You want one?" When Randall shook his head, he said, "By the way, Alquist? The guy who worked under O'Brien and was at Jason Lerner's shindig the night the shooting went down? He's clean on this. His whereabouts are solid, so cross him off the list." Loomis hesitated for a second, then added, "Don't you think it's time to tell Molly you don't consider Daria a suspect? Come clean with her. You can at least do that."

"Yeah, maybe I will."

"Maybe?" Loomis moved back to the table and sat. "You know, I think you enjoy getting her Irish up. Why the hell don't you just come clean and tell her how you feel?"

Randall's head jerked up and he gave Loomis one of his squints. "How I feel? How the hell do you know how I feel?"

Loomis laughed. "You're an open book, pal. Molly thinks you're interested in Frances." Loomis watched Randall's slow grin, then said, "You're a nasty piece of work sometimes. So that's it, huh?"

"My only interest in Frances is finding out if she's our killer. Molly is a fine woman. And still married. End of story."

Loomis's mouth fell open. "Are you turning into a gent on me?"

"Go get your soda. Then make that friggin' call. I've got some ideas I want to throw at you. I think I know what's going on."

Molly waved Emma upstairs and then called Daria. "Better sit down," she said when Daria came on. "The bad news is that Randall just left and he's found out there'll be a special on CNN tonight about the Lerner murders. The *really* bad news is that you and I are going to be mentioned."

"What? Oh, great!" Daria spat out. "That's just great!"

"Calm down. I'm coming over to watch it with you. We'll cry together. Randall said he was going to call Lucero and have him there too."

"Oh, Molly, I could . . . could just scream."

"Well, don't. Like Randall said, we've got to tough this out. I don't know who's yakking. Have you got any ideas?"

"Do you think it's Bitsy?"

"Bitsy wouldn't do that." Molly could hear Daria's deep sigh. "Look, don't panic. We'll be fine. I promise."

"Speaking of the old bat, she's picking Frances up today. Should we warn them about CNN?"

Molly thought for a moment. "No. That's up to Randall to let them know, and he may not want to. I think we should stay out of it."

"Okay. I'll set up dinner for everyone."

"Oh, that's another thing. Be sure you give Randall a bill for this. It was his idea."

Daria laughed finally. "Not a bad idea."

Emma had been sitting quietly while Molly spoke to Daria. When Molly hung up, she said, "Get comfortable. I've got a history lesson for you. You need to know a few things about your aunt Molly. Things we've never discussed. Things a twelve-year-old wouldn't understand. But then, you're not your average twelve-year-old, so I'm going to level with you, because you may hear it tonight on television."

Molly proceeded to tell Emma about her ill-fated marriage to Derek Porter and the antiques fraud he and his lover had devised.

Emma took it all in as she sat on the floor by the sofa. She never once reacted or interrupted, but sat quite still, her chin cradled in her hands on the coffee table. Finally, when Molly was finished, she said, "Whew. We haven't really talked about why you and your husband aren't together. I was curious, but I didn't want to ask you. But now that you've told me, why don't you get a divorce? Is it because you're Catholic?"

"It's . . . well, it's hard to divorce someone when you can't find them."

"Oh, so you'd do it?"

Molly hesitated. The religious and legal specifics were complicated enough for adults. And while she had few qualms about divorce, the nagging reminder that she'd given her bond in the marriage ceremony did occasionally haunt her. Giving her word or a promise was too deeply ingrained for her to ignore. Her integrity was too important, too much a part of her core to disregard. "Life is like a labyrinth, Emma. Filled with tangled paths, and often a daily diet of choices. Which road is best? Which one is faster, or smoother, or safer? To me, holding to my faith helps me examine those choices and roadblocks. Will my decision to divorce have to do with being Catholic? Hmmm. All I can say, at this very moment, is I don't agree with everything the Church dictates. And divorce, well, even though I gave my word to love, honor, and obey till death us do part, my husband broke that bond when he abandoned me. So, in that sense, I don't feel honor bound to continue mine."

"Then maybe someday you and Randall might—"

"Stop right there. Let's not get into that, young lady."

"Touchy subject, huh?" Before Molly could reply, she quickly said, "What about the other stuff? I mean, do you think they'll mention that on TV tonight?"

"I don't know, but I didn't want you to be shocked. There's no reason for any of this to come out since it has nothing to do with Jason and Steffi Lerner. But since I was doing the sale prep, someone may have decided to check me out."

"But what about Daria? Does she have a racy past too?"

Molly looked at Emma and laughed. "Racy? Where do you get these words?"

"I read, remember?"

Molly wasn't sure how much she should say. She and Daria might be overreacting. "Daria has had some tragedy in her life. She's lost two husbands, and . . . well, they're sad stories."

Emma took Molly's hand in hers and said, "I don't care what they say on TV about you and Daria. I love you both and they better not ask me any questions if they see me on the street. I'll yell child abuse if they stop me."

"Atta girl! Okay, then, come on. We've got to find a piece or two of silver for Daria. We can't keep taking her hospitality without giving back."

Molly didn't believe that Daria would give Randall a bill for dinner. Her generosity was too much a part of her. Even though they'd made a bargain to trade silver pieces Molly found at garage sales for their frequent dinners, she still felt she wanted to do more. Emma found a lovely pair of sterling salt and pepper shakers, and Molly pulled three sterling salt servers from a display. "We've got so much silver out, I think we can manage without these pieces," Molly said. She wrapped them in tissue and put them in one of the stylish new bags Max had ordered for the shop.

When they left for Daria's, Emma said, "I've got my new Sherlock Holmes tape. I can listen to it in case all of you want to talk adult stuff."

"So, you're a mind reader too, huh?"

Emma grabbed her hand as they walked down Ocean Avenue. "I just guessed."

As soon as Molly and Emma entered Daria's private room, Emma saw the grim faces on Randall, Loomis, and Lucero. She whispered to Molly, "I think they're getting ready for an unhappy night."

Molly leaned down and said, "I think so too. Best not to say much, okay?"

Emma nodded, then moved to Randall, gave him a hug, blew Lucero a kiss across the table, and smiled at Loomis. Molly set the gift of silver on the French sideboard, waved hello, then took her usual place at the table. Emma sat between Molly and Randall and folded her hands on her lap. The table had been set, and it was apparent dinner would be served family style. Baskets of sourdough bread, tubs of rosemary butter, platters of pasta and garlic roasted chicken and vegetables were already laid out.

Daria came in, set three bottles of wine on the table, then turned on the television. "We've got a few minutes before the program starts. What you see is what we're having. I thought this would be easier. No busboys coming in and out. The wine should hold us for a while."

"What about grace?" Emma asked. "Do we have time? I think we might need it tonight."

"Amen," Randall said.

Molly darted a look at Daria. It was apparent Randall wasn't trying to be funny. Clearly he wasn't in the mood for lighthearted talk. Emma gave Molly a side glance that told her she got the point. By the time the huge platter of pasta had been devoured, the program they'd been dreading began.

In complete silence, they listened to the anchor introduce the events and watched as a scenic view of Carmel came on the screen and then settled on La Casa, where Jason Lerner had been killed. The next shot was of the Ventana resort and a brief glimpse of Steffi Lerner's suite. The following moments focused on the careers of the two famous Hollywood families, the dynasty that was now ended, and film clips of their celebrated movies. Only the faint sounds of cutlery in motion, wine poured into glasses, and movement in chairs, filtered through the room as the voice-over from the anchor continued.

Just as the first commercial came on there was a knock on the door, and Manuel stuck his head in. "Señora, we got problems in the dining room. You come please."

Lucero rose at the same time as Daria. "What's the problem, Manuel?" he asked.

"It is a man with the fancy camera. He's taking the pictures—"

"Stay here," she said to Lucero. "I can handle it."

"That's what the prick wants. He'll get you on film kicking his ass out," Lucero said.

Randall threw down his napkin. "All of you stay, damn it. I don't need the D.A. on national TV either. Let me handle it."

They all started talking at once the minute Randall left. Finally Lucero said, "Hey, hold up. Let's stay calm. We can't do much about the media now. They're here, and they're going to stay until they get what they want or get bored."

"Or the next big story comes along," Loomis added. "The thing is, not to talk to them, and to keep our tempers under control. If we start playing hardball, they'll only get nastier."

"Hope Randall realizes that," Molly said.

"Don't worry. Randall just has to look at them. It usually works."

Emma tugged at Molly's arm. She did her Randall eye thing. "Like this?"

It was the perfect balm for the jittery mood in the room.

When Randall returned, they were all still laughing. "What's so damn funny?" he asked.

"Later," Lucero said as the string of commercials ended.

The next segment focused on Frances.

". . . the daughter of two Academy Award–winning set designers, recently killed in an auto accident, and now the heir to La Casa and a popular Carmel inn . . ."

The reporter then touched on Frances's long friendship with Jason and Steffi Lerner and her promising career as an artist. Shots of her being wheeled out of the hospital came next.

". . . to the waiting Rolls Royce, owned by Bitsy Morgan, an old family friend of Pebble Beach . . ."

Dressed to the nines, Bitsy, to everyone's relief, ignored the reporters and, along with Charles, helped a silent Frances into the car.

As the anchor droned on about the senior O'Brien's auto accident, Randall quickly assured everyone the cameraman had been swiftly dispatched with a trespassing warning. "I told him to pass the word. I don't think you'll have any more unwanted guests around here."

Before Daria could thank him, her face appeared on the screen. Somehow a shot of her had been taken as she parked her car and entered the restaurant. The anchor identified Daria as a childhood and still close friend of Frances O'Brien, and the owner of one of Carmel's premier restaurants.

"It has also been discovered that Ms. DeMarco was the widow of a reputed drug dealer from San Francisco who Jason Lerner had shot and killed in self-defense at a party in his Beverley Hills home some years before."

Lucero wrapped his arms around Daria and held her

close. When she buried her face in her hands, no one said a word. Molly was devastated for her. Her hands were clenched into tight balls and she could feel her heart hammering against her rib cage. Randall's and Loomis's eyes were glued to the screen, but Molly saw the flush of anger on Randall's face. Emma was riveted, and her fork seemed to hover in the air.

As everyone continued to hold their breath, a shot of the Egyptian coffin appeared on the screen.

*"In a bizarre twist to this double homicide, and the intertwining relationships, a coffin reputed to be a movie prop from a Lerner film had been discovered by workmen removing a large bookcase Jason Lerner had purchased from Jack O'Brien's palatial seaside home. The antique French bookcase had been bolted to a wall in O'Brien's study. When it was removed, a hastily covered wall had concealed a small room where the coffin was found.*

*"Kenneth Randall, Carmel's chief of police, who had been present at the discovery, ordered it opened and a skeleton was found inside. Jason Lerner, we've been told, claimed he'd recognized it as a prop from an old film and there was no need for further investigation. The coffin, however, was sent to the county coroner's office. The coroner refused to comment if the skeleton was indeed genuine. Randall, who also refused to elaborate when questioned, took over the helm of Carmel's small force last year. A former homicide captain in Los Angeles, and later a high ranking official in Internal Affairs, he is reputed to have ties to the Lerner family as a*

*police procedural consultant. Formerly married to
a Pasadena socialite, there were rumors circulating
in this popular tourist village that he and Frances
O'Brien were romantically involved."*

The next bombshell hit so fast there wasn't time to blink.
Molly's face was suddenly staring back at them on the
screen. Only this wasn't a recent photo. It was her police
mug shot when she'd been arrested along with her runaway
husband and his lover in New York over the antiques fraud.

The shock in the room rolled over them like a California tremor. No one spoke.

Molly's ears began to throb. She barely heard the anchor lay out the back story of the antiques scandal, her arrest, subsequent release after the determination of her
innocence, her flight to Carmel, and then a brief mention
of her role in a series of homicides that took place shortly
after her arrival in the famous seaside village Clint Eastwood called home. The anchor then went on to note that
she had been hired by Frances O'Brien to catalog the
multi-million-dollar contents at La Casa where Jason
Lerner had been shot to death shortly after his sister's
murder. "Unnamed sources close to the investigation have
hinted that the tempestuous Molly Doyle, whose relationship with Frances O'Brien had been strained, was being
looked at as a possible suspect in the double homicide. It
is also hinted that she had a falling out with Jason Lerner
over the purchase of the bookcase he made from her at the
La Casa estate."

The *pièce de résistance*, the report concluded, was the
close-knit ties of the principals, which included Dan
Lucero, the district attorney of Monterey County. Stay

tuned, the anchor winked, then added, "Like Alice in Wonderland said, things are becoming curious*er* and curi-ous*er.*"

The commercial break that immediately followed left gaping jaws, raised eyebrows, and general shock. All were frozen in place except Molly.

She slammed her hands on the table. Both eyes were twitching so hard, she had to squeeze them shut. *"I don't believe this!"* She whirled on Randall and yelled, "You'd better straighten this out, buster! And you'd better find out who the unnamed source is before my so-called temper really takes off! *Me? A suspect? Me?* Oh, this is just too much!"

Randall's voice was very calm when he said, "Looks like you got your wish. As of now, you're part of the in-vestigation."

Molly was trying to stop her eyebrows from dancing when she shot back, "You bet I am! Just try and keep me out now, pal!"

Loomis cleared his throat. "Hold up, you two. This could be a break for us."

Lucero was right behind him. "The killer's probably laughing his ass off now and might make a mistake." He looked at Randall. "Think about it."

Randall nodded. "I am. And I'm three steps ahead al-ready."

Molly, still fuming, was about to say more when an angry Emma punched Randall in the arm. "My aunt Molly didn't do it! And you better get to work and find out who did."

Before Randall could react, Daria said, "Welcome to the club, Molly. Looks like we'll both have to leave town now."

The practiced logical mind of a prosecutor was in overdrive, and it rewarded the group when Lucero said, "Neither one of you are going anywhere. If you both can stand the heat for a little while, I promise I'll make it up to you."

"How?" Molly nearly screamed. "What? We get a key to the city?"

"I'll have a press conference to clear you both, and I'll make sure it hits every network and cable news outlet on the air."

"Oh, big deal! What the hell are we supposed to do in the meantime? Hide out? We've got businesses to run, damn it!"

"Look, Molly, it's the best I can do. I'll make sure both you and Daria, including what happened in L.A., are presented as key elements in solving both cases."

Molly stared at him for a moment, then laughed. "In the meantime neither one of us can show our face in town after tonight!" She looked at Daria, who remained silent. "Well? Am I right or not, Daria?"

Before Daria could answer, Manuel burst into the room. "Señora! This place is the madhouse! You come, yes? The telephone is ringing, the waiters are in the kitchen doing the gossip with the chef in front of the television. No persons are doing their jobs, and the peoples in the dining room are—"

Daria's sudden composure was a testament to the deep strength she'd had to gather over the years. She rose and said, "Calm down, Manuel. I'll take care of it." She looked at everyone, then turned to Molly. "Like you said this afternoon, we'll live through it. When I come back, we've got a lot to discuss." On her way out she stopped at Randall's side and said, "You did the best you could for me a long time ago, and I've never forgotten it. Try again, will you? Like, real soon?"

Molly reached for the wine bottle and filled her glass. She then dug into her tote and pulled out her cigarettes and her father's Zippo. She slammed them on the table as if to dare anyone to say a word to her. She took a deep swallow of wine, lit a cigarette, and stared across the table at Daria's empty chair.

Randall broke the silence in the room when he said to Emma, "I know your aunt Molly isn't the killer. You should know me better than that by now. So we're going to play a little game, okay? We're going to pretend. Can you play along with us?"

Emma sneaked at look at Molly, then nodded. "Of course I can. Just tell me the game plan and the rules."

"Ah, well, we're going to have to work on that. But I'll let you know, okay?"

"Cool."

During the several moments that Daria was absent, the large platter of garlic roasted chicken and vegetables, barely warm now, became the focus of attention. Randall fixed a plate for Emma, then said, "Molly? Can I—"

"I'm not hungry," she said.

Randall looked at Emma and put a finger to his lips. "Maybe later."

Emma and the men ate in silence, until Manuel entered again with a platter of roasted duck. "The Señora says to eat this because the chicken went cold. She's coming soon." He gave them a nervous smile, then said, "Enjoy, yes?" He backed away, then added, "I shall bring more wine?"

Lucero said, "Great, Manuel. Anything is fine. Thank you."

Daria returned a moment later. When she took her

place at the table, she noticed Molly's dish was empty. "Have some duck. It's delicious."

"I'm not hungry. I'm drinking, I'm smoking, and I'm thinking."

Loomis had helped himself to the duck, and after taking a bite, said, "Do I detect a hint of anise in the sauce, Daria?"

A small flicker of light returned to Daria's eyes. When she'd first met Loomis, years ago, he was a hard-talking, cigar-chomping cop who looked like he slept in his clothes. Surprised by this well-spoken man with an educated palate, she gave him a tiny smile. "Excellent deduction. No wonder you were such a good cop."

"I thank you. And yes, deduction, as we all know, is the primary key to solving any puzzle. When one is lacking in evidence, forensics, credible witnesses, smoking gun clues, and confessions, deduction is our strongest attribute. Take this situation we presently face. A homicide is frequently the result of greed, love, hate, sex or money, and—"

"Revenge!" Molly blurted. "Damn if we're not all stupid!"

Randall set his fork down and began a slow clap. Loomis grinned and joined him. Lucero looked at both men and said, "Okay, hotshots. Is there a new development you two neglected to tell me?"

Randall gave Molly one of his widest smiles. "Molly? You want the floor?"

Molly was about to burst. "You bastards. You've known all along." Her anger, however, was quickly replaced by the joy of her keen detection and accuracy. She looked at Daria and said, "Who else but Eve Jensen would want revenge?"

Daria's eyes were huge. "Eve? What's Eve got to do with this?"

Since Randall had offered her the floor, Molly no longer felt bound by her promise to keep what she knew quiet. "That skeleton in the coffin is not a movie prop. It's Eve's sister, Hillary Thornton." Molly didn't wait for Daria to absorb this, she went right on, "Eve was at La Casa when the coffin was discovered, remember? She drove Emma and me here?"

"But . . . but how do you know all this?" Daria asked. She looked at Lucero, then to Randall. "Will someone please fill in the blanks?"

Buoyed by her reasoning Molly rubbed her hands together, picked up her plate and said, "Randall will explain the rest. But first, may I have some of that glorious duck?"

While Randall gave them a full briefing, Molly tore into the duck. Molly nudged Emma and whispered, "Could you pass the bread basket and butter?"

By the time Molly'd polished off a second helping and another glass of wine, Randall was winding down. "So," he continued, "we'll let the CNN report do its job for us. Let Eve think she's in the clear. I've got a tail on her, and so far she seems to be keeping to a normal schedule."

"But how are you going to catch her?" Emma asked Randall.

Molly dabbed at her lips with her napkin and said, "He's not going to. Daria and I are."

Randall set his wineglass down so hard it nearly toppled. "Whoa. Let's not get carried away with success, okay? I'm still running this investigation, if you don't mind."

"Of course you are," Molly said sweetly. "But we have

a much better chance of getting her to come clean. She'll never open up to you."

"Oh? What makes you think you and Daria can work this miracle, huh? This woman is a coldhearted killer. You think you're going to get a confession at some coffee klatch?"

"Why not?" Molly shot back.

"Oh, sure, load her up with latte and persimmon bars or some designer cookie and she'll tumble, right? She's killed two people. What makes you think she won't try it again?"

Calmer now, Molly answered, "Because we didn't have anything to do with her sister's death. Don't you see? For years, nothing was done to solve her sister's disappearance, and then, out of the blue, the proof hits her in the face when that coffin is discovered at La Casa. So, knowing the story about how the O'Briens ended up with the house, she puts it all together. I think, when Jason Lerner began laughing that day and insisted the skeleton was a movie prop, she went over the edge."

"But why kill the Lerners and not the father?" Daria asked. "That doesn't make sense."

"I agree," Molly said. "I think they were just handier. Maybe she wanted Marius Lerner to know how it feels to lose loved ones." Molly reached for her wineglass, took a sip, then added, "Hell, I don't know. But what else could it be?"

Randall was pensive. He took out his cigar case and stared at it. "People have done stranger things," he said. "But Molly might be right. Emotions rule. Jason Lerner's cavalier attitude may actually have set her off."

"Like the straw that broke the camel's back?" Emma asked.

"Good shot, Em!" Lucero said.

Loomis scanned the table. "This is the wackiest bunch of people I've ever had the good fortune to know." Glancing at Emma, he added, "I've run across a lot of kids your age in my job. The troubled ones, and the grounded ones. Your generation is more clued in to what's happening in the world than mine was. And you, Miss Emma, are something else." He raised his wineglass. "I think I'm going to love living here. Salud."

Randall picked up his glass and toasted each of them, "Chin chin."

Not to be outdone, Lucero rose, glass in hand. "To the ladies. And our junior sleuth in the making, Ms. Emma."

Molly, Daria, and even Emma held their glasses high and smiled.

Then Lucero added, "Before we get too happy-go-lucky here, we'd better wait and see what else Larry King and his armchair experts have to say. They're coming on next. You know, it ain't over until it's over?"

And it wasn't over, they soon found out.

But luckily, Larry King's program was filled with many of the same film shots taken in Carmel, and the cinematic history of Marius Lerner, his son and daughter, and the O'Briens. The local players, Molly, Randall, Daria, and Lucero were scheduled for later in the week.

After ten minutes Randall said, "Turn it off, Daria. I think we know the story."

## ~~ *30* ~~

*B*y the time coffee and desert arrived, Daria had been called to the kitchen two more times to break up gossiping waiters neglecting the diners. Daria's private room was beginning to look like a bookie joint, with cell phones chirping one after the other. Molly was jostling calls from Bitsy, Max, and Bennie, calming each and reassuring them she wasn't a suspect. Lucero fielded calls from his mother, his secretary, and his aide. Randall had soothed Carmel's mayor and two city council members who'd called him, and Loomis sat away from the table on the daybed speaking quietly to contacts in Los Angeles.

In the first moment of calm, Molly examined the assortment of tortes, cheesecakes, slivers of pie, mousse cakes, and puff pastries filled with fresh fruits and whipped cream on a double-handled Sheffield silver tray. Selecting a lemon cheesecake, she said, "I'm going to ask Eve to take over what remains of the La Casa house sale for me. I'll tell her I can't continue under the circumstances and that she's the only friend I can trust. If she asks about Bitsy, I'll say Bitsy isn't well enough to handle the strain."

The silence that followed Molly's announcement was only momentary. Randall was the first to speak. "I don't like it, but go on."

Molly took a bite of the cheesecake and examined her fork briefly. "I don't know. I've just got started, okay? Give me a minute. Genius is not on demand, you know?"

Daria gave her a wink. "You're doing fine. I think I'm seeing where this might go."

"Maybe I'll break down in front of her? Maybe I'll commiserate with her . . . play on her sympathy or . . . no, that won't work. I'm not supposed to know it was her sister in the coffin. Shit."

"We can leak that anytime," Loomis said.

"We can do this," Lucero agreed.

Randall played with his cigar. He lit it, lifted his chin, then watched the aromatic smoke drift upward. "It's risky. We need to set up a timeline first. Key elements have to be put in place before you can meet with her. The leak has to be made, verified by Phillips, then Dan has to have a press conference. After that, we wait for a day, then Molly can hit Eve with the sob story."

"Molly and me," Daria added. "She's not doing this alone."

"But won't she see the trap if I call her after the announcement is made? Shouldn't I ask her to take over first? Then offer condolences and sympathize after?"

"Wait," Emma said. "How can you tell her you're sorry about her sister being the dead person thing when the name is different than Eve's?" Emma looked around and added, "How will you know?"

"Emma's right," Lucero said.

"How about this," Daria began. "We'll get Eve over to

Molly's apartment just before Dan goes on TV with the announcement. Molly will ask her to take over the sale, the TV will be on, and Dan comes on with his thing and identifies the dead woman, gives her background, you know . . . Carmel resident, blah blah blah . . . daughter of Mr. Whoever and sister of Carmel art gallery owner, Eve Jensen."

"Won't work," Randall said. "Next of kin are always notified before a public announcement is made."

"So bend the rules, for Chrissakes!" Daria snapped.

"We can do this," Lucero said again.

"Why the hell not? Who's going to notice anyway?"

"I'll make it work," Molly said. "In fact, Daria, that's brilliant. That just might set her off and make her lose it. But I just realized it might not be that easy. I mean, what if Eve doesn't want to take over for me? What if I can't get her to my apartment at the right time? I mean, suppose she has customers in the shop? She doesn't close until seven. Or maybe has an appointment?"

"Trapping a killer," Randall said, "is never easy. Let me think for a minute."

Anxious to set Molly's plan in motion, they all knew it wouldn't happen if Randall didn't agree. They gave him time to respond.

"Let's see how this plays," Randall said. "Molly, you call Eve tonight when you get home. Tell her you need to find someone to take over what's left of the La Casa sale until this mess is cleared up. Ask her if she'd do it. You say you won't be able to leave the apartment because you're being hounded by the media, and would she stop by tomorrow morning before she opens the gallery. You can tell her I've released the house and there was no damage upstairs so there's still much to sell."

"And I've got the inventory records she'll need to see what's available?" Molly quickly asked.

"Hold up!" Lucero said. "How the hell am I going to set up a press conference that quick?"

Randall gave him a look. "Don't give me that baloney. One call from you and the local news people will be on your doorstep before you hang up. We don't need to go national on this. They'll pick it up later anyway. Besides, giving the local people the exclusive is good PR for you."

"Timing is everything," Loomis said.

Randall rose, hitched up his slacks, and asked Molly, "What time does Eve open?"

"Oh, ah . . . ten, I think."

"Okay. Ask her to come over at nine. Tell her you've got someone coming at ten to pick you and Daria up to drive you both to the city. Tell her you're taking off for a few days." He turned to Lucero. "Set up the news conference for nine-fifteen. That will give us some leeway in case Eve's a few minutes late, and it gives Molly time to cry on Eve's shoulder."

"I don't want Emma home when Eve shows up," Molly said.

"She won't be. I'll take her home with Loomis and me." Randall looked at Emma. "That okay with you?"

"No. I should be with Aunt Molly in case she needs help."

Molly reached for Emma's hand. "Randall is right. Besides, Daria is going to be with me and we'll be fine."

"Loomis and I will be there too, okay? You don't think I'd leave two of my favorite women alone, do you?"

Emma giggled, then looked at Molly. "See? I told you."

Molly could feel a blush creeping up her neck. "This is

serious, Em. Randall is right. I'd feel better knowing you weren't there."

"Okay, I'll go, but you and Mr. Loomis should hide in my room. It's closer to the living room than Aunt Molly's room." As an afterthought, Emma raised her finger. "Oh, no cigar smoking in my room, please."

Randall smiled. "Cross my heart."

"A thought," Daria said. "In case there's any press still hanging around tonight, I've got extra sets of chef pants and tunics here. And caps. We can both change before we leave."

"Good idea. In fact, maybe you should stay at Molly's tonight too," Randall added. He picked up his cell phone from the table and said, "I'll call the station and make sure the back entrance here and Molly's alley is clear when you leave."

"What about Frances?" Molly asked. "Do you think she's okay? I mean, what if Eve—"

"Already taken care of," Randall answered. "I have Montgomery there. She's been warned if Eve shows up to stick to Frances like glue."

"Okay, then," Loomis said. "Maybe we should call it a night and get the show on the road."

While Randall called the station, Molly and Emma helped Daria clear the table for Manuel. After setting everything on the bus tray, Daria said, "Wait here. I'll get our kitchen clothes. We can change in here after they leave."

"Hold up here," Lucero said. "I've got second thoughts. We're jumping too fast. I'm not convinced this will work. What if Eve doesn't want to take over the sale? And I'm still not persuaded Frances is off the hook."

Daria sat back down. She looked at Lucero and shook her head. "I was with Frances at La Casa when Steffi was killed." She turned to Randall, who was still seated. "Didn't you tell him?" she asked.

"Randall told me. But I don't mean Steffi," Lucero answered. "I'm talking about Jason."

"Frances didn't kill Jason Lerner," Randall replied.

Molly sat back down. Lucero was right, she thought. The shock of the newscast had caught them off guard and maybe they *were* jumping too fast. Eve certainly had a viable motive, but then so did Frances. But Randall's utter belief in Frances's innocence infuriated her to no end, and she was hard put to hold her temper in check. She knew she had to stay clear of the antagonism she felt for Frances and to keep her voice even, but she'd forgotten to edit her words. "Oh? Pray tell how you know that so clearly." She shot a glance at Lucero, crossed her arms and said, "Good question, counselor! We've been so revved up over Eve, seems we've forgotten the dear little princess."

"You're being bitchy," Randall said.

"Really? Oh, gosh. Naughty me. Well, since I'm the one on the hot seat, I think I'm allowed. I've taken enough from her, I'll be damned if I'll—"

"I guess I'm not off the hook either," Daria said, staring at Randall.

"Ladies, please," Loomis broke in. "Randall has every reason not to—"

"I can speak for myself, Loomis," Randall said. "You *are* off the hook, Daria. Because I know you didn't kill Jason Lerner, and because I say so." He shot a glance at Lucero and added, "While that wouldn't hold up in court, as chief of police, and with no evidence to charge Daria, it's my prerogative to decide that." Looking squarely at

Molly, he said, "As for Frances, she's technically still a suspect."

"Oh, goody. I'm glad to at least hear that. And, since we're speaking of Frances, what the hell was Jason Lerner screaming at her about anyway? I thought they were close friends." When Molly saw Randall's eyes shut down, she wagged a finger at him. "Don't you dare pull that it's-none-of-your-business look again. If I'm willing to take some heat and confront Eve, I damn well ought to be able to know what caused that blow-up."

Randall looked at Loomis. "Okay. I'll tell you." He glanced next at Emma and said, "Maybe you should see if there's any tiramisu in the kitchen? I'd hate to have you miss that since it wasn't on the dessert tray."

Emma pulled out her head phones. "I brought this along just in case."

"Oh, for Christ's sakes, Randall," Lucero said, "after all we've already said? Emma can handle the rest. Besides, when it's all over, it'll be on the news anyway. She might as well hear the truth and not some sound bite version."

"Okay, okay. Here's the story. After the fiasco in L.A., Jason Lerner was convinced Frances had seen him shoot Vince Mazzeo in anger, and not in self-defense as they later claimed. Frances, by the way, denies this. Anyway, he set up a monthly payment to Frances to shut her up and swear she was in another room. She was on the studio books as a location scout, and the checks, while made out to Frances, went directly to her father. She claims she never looked at the checks he'd have her endorse. He handled all her finances, and she thought they were from a trust fund he'd set up years before. A very creative excuse, I might add, and one I don't believe. So, when the Lerners' finances began to take a nosedive, Jason and Steffi came up to stop the money flow. At least that's what Frances told me, and Daria has corroborated the conversation."

"So he didn't know about Eve's sister and the coffin? He wasn't here because of that?" Molly asked.

"Frances said it wasn't mentioned until just after Daria left. He'd gone on a new tirade about how the O'Brien family had been bleeding them to death. He told Frances about the skeleton, and said his father claimed the woman's death was an accident but that Jack O'Brien said he didn't believe him and that he'd keep quiet for a price. He wanted La Casa, and suggested the phony poker game to make it look legit. Frances said she didn't believe him, they got into a tussle in front of the fireplace—which we figure might have happened—and Jason's foot somehow kicked a log and it rolled onto the carpet. Frances said she tried to shove it back in and that's how she burned her hands. Then she said she thought she saw Jason coming after her again. She was backing away from him when she heard the shot. She claims it came from behind her."

"Oh, right. Good excuse. I mean, what? The killer was in the room all the time and hiding behind the draperies?"

"Look, I don't have evidence to clear her, or to charge her, okay? Since you people are harboring some cocka-mamy idea you're charter members of Carmel Crime-busters and this room of Daria's is our boardroom, I'm going along with this experiment because while I don't think it will work, it will at least get all you busybodies off my back. If Eve doesn't show, or doesn't tumble if she does, I'll take it from there. And at that point you will all mind your freakin' business and let me do my job. You will go about your lives during this unusual time, as best as you can, and stay the hell out of my hair."

With that speech under his belt, Randall rose, nodded at

Loomis, then said, "Let's go." He turned to Emma and offered her his hand. "Come on, squirt. Loomis makes a mean hot cocoa."

By the time Molly and Daria arrived at Molly's apartment, it was close to nine P.M. In their kitchen garb, Molly made coffee, then joined Daria in the living room. "I'm not going downstairs to check the answering machine until tomorrow morning. I don't want to know how many calls might be there." She set a crystal ashtray on the table and gave Daria a wry smile. "I think Emma will forgive us if we indulge in our bad habits tonight. I need a few drags before I call Eve."

"My machine at home is probably loaded too. They can all wait. By the way, Randall gets a little testy when you bring up Frances, I've noticed," Daria said.

Plopping down on the sofa, Molly said, "He's . . . well, maybe he's attracted to her."

"No. I don't think she's his type. But I have to admit, she brings that protective bullshit out in men like a pro. I've never understood how she did it."

"They've never caught on to women's wiles, have they? Funny, though, Bitsy said that about you. With Frances, I mean. That you've got a soft spot or something like that and are always protecting her."

"Soft spot? Baloney. Self-preservation is more like it. Ever since the night Jason shot Vince, I've been leery of her." Lighting a cigarette, she said, "You know that old saying . . . keep your friends close, and your enemies closer? Well, that should tell you all you need to know."

"As Randall would say, in spades." Snuffing out her cigarette, Molly picked up the phone. "Well, here goes."

Eve answered on the second ring. Molly took a deep breath and said, "Eve? It's Molly."

Before Molly could say another word, Eve quickly said, "Oh, Lord, Molly! I saw the news and I . . . well, I didn't know if I should call, but I want you to know I don't believe a word of it! Why, Molly, I was there, remember? Jason Lerner wasn't angry with you."

"Oh, Eve! I'm so relived you believe in me. I'm just beside myself. I mean, who came up with this nonsense? Jason was thrilled with the bookcase. But Eve, about my past, I wanted you to know that—"

"Molly, please! I know you were cleared, so don't say another word, dear."

"Thank you. I really mean that. Uh, Eve, the other reason I called is about the La Casa sale. I . . . I can't carry on with it until this mess is cleared up, and I was hoping you—"

"La Casa? But what about the fire? Wasn't everything destroyed?"

"No. The upstairs wasn't harmed at all. There's still a ton of stuff to sell. Would you consider taking over for me? I can't think of anyone I'd trust more. I know Frances would be fine with it."

"I really don't know, Molly. If it's just artwork, I could handle that. What about Bitsy?"

Molly eyed Daria and crossed her fingers. "Bitsy isn't really up to it right now. She's, uh, planning a trip to Europe. But I have the inventory. You could go off that, and I've got a list of clients waiting. Oh, with all that's been going on, I almost forgot to tell you I ran across two more Morgans. They're in a storage room upstairs."

There was a long pause on Eve's end that made Molly nervous. She wanted to say more but didn't want to sound pushy. Finally, Eve said, "Well, I guess I couldn't muck it up too much. You've been so kind to think of me with the contemporary art, it's the least I can do."

"Oh, bless you, Eve. Could you come by tomorrow morning? I'll have everything ready for you." Before Eve could change her mind, Molly quickly added, "Nine would be perfect if that works for you. I've got a friend coming by to pick me up and drive me to the city. I need to get away from here for a few days. The press—"

"You're leaving Carmel? But what about Randall? I mean, is he going to let you go?"

Molly hadn't expected Eve to ask that. She paused, then said, "Of course. I haven't been charged with anything. In fact, I'm going up to see an attorney just in case."

"Good thinking," Eve said. "That's what I'd do too. Okay, I'll be there at nine, give or take a few minutes."

"Great. I can't thank you enough, Eve. Oh, listen, come up the back stairs from the courtyard. I'm going to be down in the shop at eight-thirty in case any of the media have decided to attack. They'll be able to see me from the front window. That ought to keep them occupied. I'll run upstairs at nine to let you in."

Molly heard Eve's chuckle, and it almost gave her shivers. "Clever girl! I'd never think of that. I'll see you then."

When Molly hung up, she gave Daria two thumbs up, then collapsed against the sofa's cushions. "Forget the coffee. I need a tall drink."

Daria wiped her brow. "Whew! That was one hell of great acting job, Ms. Doyle. You sit, I'll get us both one."

"I'll call Randall and tell him we're set." When he answered, Molly gave him a full report of her conversation with Eve and told him she would be downstairs between eight-thirty and just before nine to lure the media, if any, to the front of the shop. "Make sure the courtyard is clear, okay? I don't want her to get stressed if anyone is there and tries to hound her."

"I've already taken care of it. Bennie has his cousins showing up at six A.M. to stand by and try to keep everyone out. Uh, what exactly do you plan to do for a half hour? Don't tease them, Molly, okay? They don't take kindly to smart-asses," Randall said.

"I wasn't planning on sticking my tongue out at them. I'll pretend to ignore them. I'll probably be on the phone, answering calls from my fan clubs."

"I'm not kidding. They'll rip you to shreds if you don't behave."

"I think I already know that."

When Molly got off the phone, Daria handed her a drink and sat down next to her. She touched Molly's glass and said, "Here's to tomorrow."

Molly nodded. "Tomorrow."

## ~~~ *31* ~~~

$A$s the paws on the cat clock in Molly's tiny kitchen hit eight-thirty on Saturday morning, Randall and Loomis, dressed in jeans and sweatshirts, were inside her apartment. Daria's laugh, when she saw the bags of doughnuts, was shaky. "I don't think we'll need the sugar. My body is already jangling with anxiety."

"Think of it as comfort food," Loomis said. "Haven't you heard that cops always start the day with doughnuts?"

Daria took the bags and headed for the kitchen. "I thought that was just in the movies."

"Molly downstairs?" Randall asked.

"Yes. And there's five or six reporters in front of the shop already."

"We saw them," Randall said. "I hope she's—"

"Don't worry," Daria replied. "She's got her back to the window while she's on the phone. She'll come up about ten to nine just in case Eve is early."

Randall headed to the stairs leading down to the shop. "Keep this door open in case we have to call her." Standing on the top stair, he called to Molly, "We're here. Emma is fine. She's at the station playing on my computer."

Molly was on the phone with her cousin Jack, an FBI

agent at Quantico, and waved to Randall to let him know she'd heard him. Her knees were wiggling under the desk and she was yearning for a cigarette. Her unease was at an all-time high, and the last thing she wanted to do was return the several messages on her answering machine. But it was a perfect way to stall for time, and to keep the news people in front of the shop and out of the courtyard. She ignored the knocking on the front door from the media and said to Jack, "Honest, it's okay, you don't need to get involved. I didn't have a problem with Jason Lerner, and Randall knows I'm clear. I'm not talking to the press to deny anything. We're going along with it for now."

"You need to get out of there when this is over," Jack said. "How about coming out my way? It's been a few years, Molly."

"Tell you what. I'll meet you in New Orleans. We can have a family reunion of sorts with Angela and Armand. Besides, I want you to meet Emma, Carrie's daughter. I'd like her to know there are some sane people in this family."

"Yeah, right. Tell Armand to make himself scarce, then," Jack said.

Molly checked her watch. "I've got to go, Jack. I've got to . . . uh, well, see an art dealer."

The minute she rose from the desk, a new round of knocks on the door and front window began in earnest. Molly kept her back to the front of the shop and headed for the stairs. She ignored that perverse sense of humor, always hovering and bedeviling her, to turn around and stick out her tongue. She had to focus on the possible ways to force Eve to lose her temper. When she got halfway up the stairs, she saw Randall waiting for her. "You were ready to tease them, weren't you?" he said.

"I thought about it. A few minutes of hell for them is hardly payback for what they do to people."

"Yeah, well, you'll have your day to thumb your nose at them. Right now we've got more pressing matters to get through." Randall placed both hands on her shoulders. "You still okay with this? I can call it off right now."

She hoped he didn't feel the slight tremors racing through her. Smiling, she said, "Naw, I'm cool. I'll pretend I'm auditioning for a play or something."

Randall looked at her, then smiled too. He leaned down and kissed her forehead. "Just be sure that cranky, pain in the neck Molly Doyle steps back in, okay?"

Surprised by this display of affection, Molly was tongue-tied. She finally managed to say, "I promise."

Stepping back so she could pass, Randall said, "You've got five minutes until she gets here. Grab a doughnut, look natural. Loomis and I will be in Emma's room. The door will be ajar so we can hear what's going on."

As Molly brushed past him, he added, "And this is the last time, okay? Never again. You hear me Molly Doyle?"

Her throat was beginning to tighten. All she could manage was a nod. She watched him enter Emma's room, then she gave Daria a weak smile and stepped into the kitchen. Seeing a huge apple fritter sitting on a dish next to a cup of coffee on the chipped tile counter, she smiled. Randall knew she loved them, and she was positive he'd set it out for her. He'd even folded a napkin and placed it alongside the dish. A macabre thought struck her: Was this her final meal before the switch was turned on? She reached for the sugary fritter and bit off a large piece. Her eyes moved up to the cat clock. It was two minutes before nine. She took a large gulp of coffee, wiped her hands on the napkin, then joined Daria in the living room.

Neither spoke. The suspense they felt was too palatable. The moment of silence between them was quickly interrupted by a sharp rap on the French door. To Molly, it sounded like a cannon burst. She brushed her sweating palms on her jeans, gave the silent Daria a thumbs-up, then opened the door.

She almost didn't recognize Eve, who was dressed in a black running suit with a floppy golf hat and wore sunglasses that wrapped around her face. Molly nearly pulled her into the living room. "Thanks for coming. You can't believe how much I appreciate this."

Eve gave her a tiny smile, pulled off her sunglasses, then started when she saw Daria. Her recovery was quick. "I'm so glad you're here with Molly, Daria. I can't get past all this garbage about you on television! Of course no one in town believes any of it, but really, the jungle drums are beating up a storm." When she reached up and gave Molly a quick kiss on the cheek, Molly wanted to faint. "Don't you worry about it, though, sweetie. We'll all be back to normal soon."

Moving to Daria, Eve said, "And you! How brave you were to see justice done." Reaching for Daria's hands, she said, "And to think it was your own husband! Oh, I'm so proud of you."

Daria managed to look appreciative. "Thank you, Eve. I'm glad it's finally out in the open. It was hell wondering when it would come out."

Taking a seat on the sofa, Eve agreed. "It's always good to tie up the loose ends in one's life. I'm a firm believer in that."

Molly handed Eve the inventory folder and said,

"Speaking of loose ends, here's the list for La Casa. There's also a page of the dealers, collectors, and clients who are interested in being contacted."

Eve spent the next few moments thumbing through the inventory. Molly and Daria avoided looking at each other. The television was on, and tuned to the local morning news show. The sound was off, and Daria clutched the remote in her hand, ready to click it on the minute Lucero appeared.

Closing the folder, that Eve said, "What an incredible job you've done, Molly. Just looking over the different categories of antiques convinces me I'm not the right person for this. This is way over my head."

Molly hadn't anticipated that Eve would back out. After all their planning, she couldn't let her leave. "Oh, no, don't be silly. Those buyers listed have already indicated their wants. All you'll have to do is go by the low to high prices I've set. You'll be fine."

Eve rose and shook her head. "No, I don't think I'm the best choice."

Molly darted a look at Daria, then got up. "Oh, damn. I was counting on you. But sure, I understand. No problem. But don't go yet. I mean, I've forgotten my manners. How about some coffee?

"I should really be getting back. I've got to change before I open," Eve replied.

"Oh, come on. One cup with us, okay?"

Eve glanced at Daria and shrugged. "Well, I do have time for one."

Molly hurried into the kitchen and looked at the clock. It was nine-twelve. Three more minutes! "Sugar? Cream?" Molly yelled.

"Just sugar," Eve responded.

She took her time pouring the coffee, then placing it and the sugar bowl on a tray, counted the seconds as she returned to the living room. Just as she set the tray on the table, Daria hit the volume on the remote and Lucero's face filled the screen.

"Oh, no!" Daria said. "Lucero is having a press conference. Now what the hell is going on?"

Dan Lucero stood in front of the courthouse in Salinas. Both his hands were in his pockets, and Molly could swear she heard change jiggling. She was so nervous, she had to force herself to hear what Lucero was saying.

". . . discovered just last week at the home of Jack O'Brien. The remains of a young woman, apparently murdered, have been identified as a former Carmel resident who went missing in the early 1970s after last being seen at a party at La Casa, which at that time was owned by the movie producer, Marius Lerner. A full investigation is under way to determine the identity of the killer. A longtime resident, and former law enforcement officer in Carmel during that period, was instrumental in aiding us in identifying the victim as Hillary Thornton. He recalls Marius Lerner had made a complaint to the police that Ms. Thornton, an aspiring actress, had been stalking him. Efforts to reach the family . . ."

Eve's cup clattered in the saucer. She jumped up from the sofa and shouted, "What? Oh, my God! Did you hear that?"

Molly winced. It was now or never. "Can you believe that? That wasn't a movie prop after all. Poor girl, how awful. But then what can you expect? I'm not surprised. Aspiring actress, my foot! Probably some call girl. Most of those so-called actresses running around half naked are nothing but cleaned-up whores."

"Shut up!" Eve screamed. "Don't you dare say that! You don't know what the hell you're talking about!"

"Hey, hold on, okay?" Molly shot back. "You know I'm right. Just open up *People* magazine and look at them!"

When Eve whirled toward her, Molly put her hands out, ready to fend her off. Eve's face was flushed and her eyes were bulging. Molly wasn't ready for her next words. "That was no whore in that coffin! Hillary was my sister!"

"What? Are you sure?"

Eve's clenched hands flew to her heart and pounded her breasts. "Yes! Goddamnit! My sister!" Her fury spent, she lowered her head, then sank back onto the sofa next to Daria and began to sob.

Unable to stop herself, Daria wrapped an arm around her and said, "Oh, Eve. Oh, I'm so sorry."

Her arms across her chest, Eve's fingers plucked at her jacket. "I knew the minute they opened that coffin it was my Hillary. It was the beaded fabric, you see. It . . . it was one of my gowns. I let Hillary wear it that night. I left the party early. I never saw her again."

Molly sat on the other side of Eve. She knew she was facing a killer, but still felt compelled to comfort her. And somehow, deep inside, she knew Eve Jensen would not harm either her or Daria. "But why did you kill Jason and Steffi Lerner? They were only kids then. They were innocent of your sister's death."

Eve wiped her eyes, looked at Daria and then to Molly. She smiled suddenly. "So, you know, do you? You're a clever lady, Molly Doyle. I knew I could count on you."

Molly's mouth fell open. "It was you? You were the leak to the press?"

Eve nodded. "I figured if I put you on the hot seat, you'd tear heaven and hell apart to clear your name."

Molly was stunned. In fact, she was almost speechless. It didn't last long, however. "Well, it worked. Here I am."

"Yes," Eve said. "Here you are. And so am I. This is a setup, isn't it?" Before Molly could answer, Eve began to laugh. "Oh, don't bother answering. I had an inkling that was why you wanted me to take over the house sale. By the way, was Dan Lucero's press conference on the level?"

"Yes, it was," Molly lied.

Eve looked at Daria and shook her head. "Molly's not a good liar. The timing was too perfect. But that's okay, I understand."

"Then help us to understand why you killed the Lerners," Molly said.

"I had to. It was the only way, don't you see? I had to get Randall back on the case. He believed Jason Lerner when he said the coffin was a movie prop. Finally there was proof of what happened to Hilly! I . . . I couldn't let that fall through the cracks. I wanted justice for my sister. When I met Frances at La Casa to pick up the artwork I was taking on consignment, I snooped around Jack O'Brien's bedroom when Frances was downstairs on the phone. I wanted to see what kind of man would do such a horrible thing. I wanted to sit on his bed and curse him to hell."

"But why did you think he killed your sister?" Molly asked.

"Oh, I knew he didn't do it. I was sure it was Marius Lerner. He'd promised Hilly he'd give her a screen test. But he lied. He only wanted to fuck her. But O'Brien kept her in his house, didn't he? What kind of sick person would do that?" Brushing a hand over her eyes, Eve said,

"I went through all his drawers and looked in his closet. I found his gun in a sweater drawer. I took that as a sign for what I had to do. So I killed those Lerner brats.

"And then, when a week went by and nothing was happening, I called CNN. I pretended to be an informed source close to the investigation. I researched your background and knew Randall would get pissed then and get off his ass and do something. I was frankly surprised CNN believed me, but it doesn't matter now."

The insanity of it made Molly want to scream. "But Eve . . . murder? Why didn't you just go to Randall and tell him?"

"Oh, don't be so naive! What proof did I have? And why would he take my word against those Hollywood big shots?"

"Didn't you have the pictures of you and your sister taken at the party?"

Eve looked at Molly with surprise. "What pictures? What are you talking about?"

Molly's hand flew to her mouth. "Then it wasn't you? You didn't put them in the photo album? You didn't attack me in Frances's studio?"

Eve grabbed hold of Molly's arm. "Don't be stupid. I wouldn't hurt you. You have a picture of Hillary and me? Where? Oh, Molly, could I have it?"

The pleading in Eve's voice was pathetic, and Molly had to fight the empathy she felt for her. "I, ah . . . well, no. I don't have it here. I mean, well, maybe I was wrong."

"You're lying again, Molly. I can tell," Eve said.

Molly knew there was no point in trying to get out of it. She'd been mistaken thinking Eve had hidden the photos for someone to find. The size difference apparently wasn't the smoking gun she'd imagined. "Okay, I found two pictures. I think Jack O'Brien must not have known they remained. I'm sure now it was Jason Lerner who attacked me. No wonder he was so intent on those boxes. There were hundreds of photos. He must have thought it was possible there might be something there."

"Well," Eve said as she leaned forward and took a sip of her coffee, "it doesn't matter now, does it?"

Out of Eve's view, Daria put a finger to her head and circled it as if to say the woman was off her rocker.

Molly replied by blinking and tilting her head toward Emma's bedroom door. "Eve?" she said gently. "Didn't you realize you'd be found out?"

Eve set down her cup and gave Molly a stubborn grin. "Of course I did. I don't care either. Jason and his sister were rotten apples from the same tree. I heard him screaming at Daria and Frances. I saw what a no good prick he was."

"But what about Steffi?" Daria asked. "She might not have known."

Eve's eyes turned hard. "Oh, you're so blind! She was the stronger of the two. I rented the suite next to theirs at Ventana the minute I knew they were here so I could keep an eye on them. I'd go down in the evening and sit on the deck. I was able to reach their deck from mine, and then I heard them arguing about the blackmail money. It was what I'd been waiting for. Jason was ready to call it quits, but oh no, she wouldn't let him."

Eve paused, then reached for her cup to take another sip. Molly and Daria hardly dared to breathe. It was as if both feared she'd stop if so much as a muscle twitched.

"He reminded her," Eve continued as she set the cup back on the table, "that he hadn't found the proof Jack

O'Brien held over the family, and assured her it would never be found. Jason told her that he'd torn La Casa apart and all the boxes they'd taken back to Ventana were worthless. Finally, Steffi demanded Jason confront Frances and get it over with. I knew it was time for me to make my move. I didn't care about any damn proof. That coffin was all I needed. So when he left, I killed Steffi. I drove back to Carmel and parked on San Antonio then sneaked in from the beach gate. The door to the studio was unlocked and I went into the house from there." She looked at Daria. "When I got to the dining room, I heard voices in the salon. I was surprised to see you there. You were giving him hell, honey. I have to give you that. I wasn't expecting to see you there, and I was relieved when you left."

Eve's composure was unnerving Molly. She wasn't sure if it was going to last, and she needed her to say more. "But why did you start the fire?" she asked.

"Oh, I didn't. Well, not the one in the salon. After Daria left, Frances and Jason got into it again and Frances went after Jason. They began to struggle in front of the fireplace. Jason's foot hit a burning log and it rolled out onto the rug. Frances tried to roll it back onto the hearth, when Jason went after her. That's when I shot him and then knocked Frances out. She didn't see me, thank heavens. By then the log was still on that gorgeous rug, and it was too late. I dragged Frances to the dining room and left her. I figured someone would call the fire department and she'd be okay. But the fire gave me an idea. I wanted to destroy that room where we'd found the coffin. So I set the fire in the study. I watched it for a minute, then left."

Eve turned to Daria and patted her arm. "I'm glad I

waited until you left. You weren't a part of it. But leave it to dear little Frances to call you. The spoiled little bitch. She was always running to you when she needed help. Anyway, honey, you've been through enough. You didn't need to be involved."

Daria hid her astonishment well. She smiled and said, "Thank you, Eve. I appreciate that more than you know. It must have been awfully difficult for you all these years."

Eve fanned her face. "Oh, you have no idea. I can't tell you how many nights I couldn't sleep, wondering what had happened to Hilly. My father was never the same. It killed him." Reaching for her cup again, she asked, "Is there more coffee? I'm suddenly so thirsty."

Molly was on her feet. "I've got a full pot. You just relax, I'll be right back. Daria? More for you?"

Daria's eyes were darting toward Emma's room again. "I'd love some. Do you need help?"

Molly caught Daria's signal and said, "No. Stay here with Eve, I'm fine." Molly's legs were shaking as she got up from the sofa. She kept her back stiff as she headed for the kitchen. From there, she could see Randall standing in the open doorway to Emma's room. She gave him a quick nod, and when he stepped into the living room, with Loomis behind him, she had to hold onto the doorjamb to steady herself.

"Eve?" Randall said. "I think you'd better come with me now, okay?"

Eve set down her cup. "Hello, Randall. You saved me a trip. I was just telling Molly and Daria about—"

Randall nodded kindly. "Yeah, I know, Eve. I heard. I was in the other room."

"Well then, I guess it's all over now." Giving him a smile, she said, "Mission accomplished. My father was an instructor at Fort Ord, over in Seaside, and he always taught Hilly and me that when you start out to do something, finish it. I promised him before he died I'd find out what happened to Hilly." Giving Daria a pat on the arm again, she said, "Well, I did. I saw it through."

"Yes, Eve. You did," Daria said.

Eve stood up, looked at Loomis and said, "Oh, hello. I don't believe we've met. Are you new in town?"

Loomis introduced himself, then calmly said, "Yes, I'm here for the Bach Festival next week."

"Oh, that's nice. I'm afraid I'll be missing it this year." She reached for her bag on the sofa. The instant she opened it, Randall pulled a gun from under his sweatshirt. "Stop right there!" he commanded.

Eve blinked, looked at Randall and said, "I was looking for a business card in case your friend is interested in contemporary art."

Randall put his gun back under his sweatshirt. "I'll do that for you, Eve. Why don't you give me your bag." He took it from her, then tossed it to Molly, who was behind him. "Hang onto that." He pulled a pair of handcuffs from his pocket, then said, "I'm going to read you your rights, Eve, and then we've got to put these on."

"Oh, must you? I'm not going to try to run." She looked at each of them intently. "I know you all think I'm a nutcase. Well, I'm not. Just because I'm being so civilized about all this doesn't mean I'm crazy. I'm well aware of what I've done, and I know I have to pay for it. I'm also going to get one hell of a smart lawyer." She thrust her wrists out and said to Randall, "Would you mind not cuffing my hands behind me? The arthritis in my shoulder is killing me."

"Sure, Eve. No problem," Randall said. "Call Montgomery downstairs, Loomis. Make sure we've got a clear path to the car. I don't want reporters seeing this."

On his cell phone, Loomis relayed the message. His face turned sour as he listened. "Ocean Avenue is in gridlock," he said. "The sidewalk in front of the shop is three deep with news cameras. Somebody named Bitsy is giving interviews claiming Molly is innocent and not a suspect. Apparently she's giving them an earful."

"What the hell is she thinking?" Molly exclaimed. "Damn, but I wish she'd mind her own business for once!"

"Don't be to hard on her, Molly," Eve said. "We women have to stick together. She's only trying to help. There are still some Carmelites with style left." She smiled at Loomis. "Stick around. You might meet a few more."

Randall was strangely silent. Finally, he said, "Okay, Loomis, let's go. The minute we hit the sidewalk, we'll keep Eve between us."

Molly and Daria followed behind as they went down. When they stepped outside, pandemonium erupted as reporters shouted over each other and tried to break through the flank of officers holding them back. Montgomery was at the patrol car holding the door open when a cameraman broke through and rushed Eve. As deft as a ballet dancer, Eve whirled away from Randall, lowered her head and tried to get away. She lost her balance, and as she reached for Randall's sweatshirt to keep herself from falling, the gun tucked in the waistband of his jeans became visible. When Montgomery saw Eve's hands only inches from the gun, she acted on instinct and fired.

The world had suddenly morphed into slow motion for Molly. Her arms felt like lead weights as she reached for Randall when he went down.

## ~ 32 ~

$M$olly's knees ached from kneeling. She had to sit to complete the final decade of her rosary. The last time she'd said two rosaries in a row had been when her father died in prison. The quiet of Carmel Mission did little to blot out the lingering sounds of yesterday's screams and shouts. She squeezed her eyes shut, willing away the horrible images that would not leave.

Emma sat quietly beside her. Molly leaned down and whispered, "Thank you for being so patient."

Randall was still kneeling, his head bent low in prayer. Molly saw the sadness on his face as his rosary dangled from his hands. Her eyes fixed on the crucifix as it swayed gently when his fingers moved over the last bead. She wondered how many rosaries she would offer before the guilt of luring poor Eve to confess had lessened. If only there had been another way, she would still be alive. Randall had tried to convince her last night that she wasn't to blame. The best laid plans, he'd said, were always open to failure. The only predictable thing about human reactions was that they were unpredictable. If the photographer had been a half minute later, Eve would have been safely in the patrol car.

Randall sat back and turned to Molly. "We're gonna be late."

She gave him a cheerless smile. "I really don't care. Besides, since when have I ever been on time?"

He stepped into the aisle, genuflected, then stood aside to let Molly and Emma out. After Molly kneeled and crossed herself, she and Emma moved into the aisle with Randall. Emma reached for his hand and said softly, "We should do this together every Sunday. I mean, the three of us. What do you think about that?"

Randall glanced at Molly, then said, "We'll work on it."

When they reached Randall's car, Molly said, "As much as I'm dying to see Nicholas and Max, I'm not in the mood for this. I really don't want to go to Bitsy's for late lunch, or whatever she's planning. And I have to admit I'm furious with her. If she hadn't been grandstanding yesterday with those reporters, maybe—"

"We can't fault Bitsy for trying to help, or blame her for what happened after. It was just one of those things you can't plan on. I should have been wearing a shoulder holster and not had my gun tucked in my jeans. Life goes on, okay? It'll do you good to see your old friend. Take your mind off things for a couple of hours."

"I'm glad Daria and Lucero went away for a few days. Maybe they can have a meeting of the minds finally."

"I'd like to see that happen too."

"Rotten time for the El Camino to die on me. I could call a cab, or have Charles pick us up if you have to get back."

"I promised Bitsy I'd drop by. But I can't stay too long. Loomis is holding down the fort, so to speak. I had to deputize him yesterday."

"Are you sure?"

"Yeah. I could use a break too."

"How's Montgomery doing? Is she okay?"

Randall pulled the back door open for Emma. "She's a good cop. She reacted properly under the circumstances. I'll stand by her."

"I'm beginning to wonder if I'm in the wrong business after all. So far, this antiques biz is a killer."

Randall grinned. "And then some."

The drive to Bitsy's villa in Pebble Beach was a Chamber of Commerce dream. Azure sky, a slight tang of salt in the air, Monterey pine trees giving off an alpine scent, and a doe and her fawn lazing under the shade of a storm-shaped cypress. The sounds of the surf grew stronger as they pulled passed the open iron gates into Bitsy's drive. The sprawling Spanish villa, built in the twenties, sat like a jewel perched at the edge of the world.

When Josie let them in, she threw her arms around Molly. "I'm so glad you're okay." She looked at Randall and shook her head, "Close call there. We saw it on TV and our hearts were in our throats!" Giving him a pat on the arm, she sighed. "It took a few shots of scotch to settle Charles and me down. I thought Ms. *Artiste* was going to faint again. That woman swoons if a bee lands on the flowers in her room. Bitsy and Max are in the library. You-know-who is resting in her room and is refusing to come down. She claims she's not up to visitors. The doctor said her lungs were fine now, and her hands weren't burned that bad. Madame's ass is in a sling again, so be warned."

Molly said, "Oh, no. Not again."

Josie nodded. "Déjà vu, huh?" Then she told Randall

what had happened two weeks ago when Bitsy was having the cocktail party for Frances. "By the way, Molly. That friend of yours? Nicholas Hahn? He's on the terrace. Ohhh, what a hunk! Watch your step, Chief. The man's a real charmer."

"Is that right? Think he's my type?"

Emma giggled, then playfully punched Randall in the arm. "You're so funny."

Molly glanced at Randall. "Yeah. A real comedian." She sucked in her stomach, tucked a stray hair behind her ear, and headed for the terrace.

Randall and Emma followed, then paused as Molly headed to the man leaning against the sculpted balustrade. A glass of wine was on the railing, and he was staring at the ocean. When Molly called out his name, Nicholas Hahn turned and gave her a lingering smile. Randall watched as Nicholas's measured, elegant stride reached Molly. He saw a stylish and graceful man reach for both her hands, then raise them to his lips.

When Molly embraced him, then pulled back and said, "Oh, Nicholas! How I've missed you," Randall looked away and said to Emma, "We should say hello to our hostess, don't you think?"

Emma shook her head. "No way am I leaving her out there with him."

"Hey, it's her life, okay?"

When Molly and Nicholas joined the others in the living room, Bitsy wiped tears from her eyes as she sat down next to Emma on the sofa. She apologized to Randall for her meddling. Randall stood near Max by the drinks tray.

Max Roman, nattily dressed as ever in his navy cash-mere sport coat and tan slacks, patted his close-cropped silver hair and was about to freshen his drink. "Ah, Molly!" he said. He set down his glass, moved to her and placed a kiss on her forehead. "I'm beginning to wonder if Bitsy and my conspiring to get you to Carmel was such a good idea. You've been in and out of the frying pan ever since you arrived."

"We were just discussing that very subject," Nicholas said. Moving to Emma, he bowed. "And you are, I presume, Miss Emma?" When she nodded, he took her hand and lightly brushed it with his lips. "*Enchanté*, mademoiselle."

Emma's lips were tight, and when Nicholas moved away, she wiped her hand on her skirt.

Only Randall saw her.

Nicholas strode to Randall and offered his hand. "I am so pleased to meet you. Elizabeth—oh . . . excuse me, Molly has told me much about you."

Randall eyed Molly. "Has she now. I'd be less than honest to say it's all probably true."

Nicholas laughed. "Then she is correct. You are not a modest man. Her words were complimentary."

The surprise on Randall's face was clear. He gave Molly a look. "She's also an accomplished liar. But in my profession, I'm used to that."

"Ah, yes. Your profession. I am glad to hear you were not injured yesterday. That was a terrible tragedy. In fact, I have just been telling Molly she is in need of a holiday. There is an extraordinary estate auction coming up in New Orleans I wish Molly to see. Max and I have been discussing the possibility. The merchandise is exquisite. French Renaissance, Louis XIII and Louis IV, several Regence pieces! This is Molly's milieu. She has an eye that is formidable."

Randall took a sip of his drink. "I'm sure Molly would

have a wonderful time. New Orleans is a fascinating city. I've made some great purchases at auction there."

Nicholas's eyes glinted with respect. "Aha, a collector I see. And what, may I ask, is your pleasure?"

"Randall has some gorgeous Directoire and Louis Phillipe pieces you'd love Nicholas," Molly said.

"Wonderful periods," Nicholas said. "My compliments."

Glancing at Bitsy, Molly asked, "Have you shown Nicholas Mackie's work yet?"

Bitsy's hand flew to her lips. "Oh, Lord! I completely forgot! With all that's been going on, it slipped my mind. I'll have Charles bring them in."

Nicholas said to Molly, "Mackie? Is this the artist you mentioned on the telephone?"

"Yes. The very same. In fact, while you're drooling over her work, I'll get her."

Randall's and Emma's eyes met at the same time. Emma rolled hers and then made a thumbs-down sign. Randall had to look away to keep from laughing.

Molly took the marble stairs two at a time to the second floor. She figured Frances was in the largest guest room, and headed that way. She knocked once, then opened the door. Frances was lying on the canopy bed, fully dressed, reading a magazine. "Up and at it, Frances. Nicholas Hahn is here and I want you to meet him."

"How dare you barge into my room!" Frances screeched.

After weeks of ignoring Frances's high-handed attitude, it was an effort for Molly to keep her voice calm. "Let's not get huffy, okay? Besides, this isn't *your* room."

Frances swung her legs off the bed and stared at her. "Huffy? I've been the soul of patience with you, and I'm sick of hearing about the fabulous Molly Doyle. Why don't you just go downstairs and bask in your newfound glory. I've had enough to contend with lately."

That was it. Molly threw all semblance of calm to the wind. "Three people are dead and *you've* had enough to contend with?" She moved to within inches of Frances. "Lives have been destroyed because of your father, yet you show no remorse or sympathy. I endured your arrogance because I needed the job, but listening to you now is more than I can handle. For two cents I'd slap you silly, you spoiled little brat. For a nickel, I'd wring your freakin' neck!" With that, Molly grabbed Frances by the arm and literally dragged her from the room. Stunned, Frances was speechless.

When they reached the hall, Molly said, "Why I'm even bothering to take you downstairs to meet a man who will make you a star in the art world is beyond me. As a person, you are despicable. My passion for art and hating to see your talent go unrealized is blurring my good sense. So learn to play nice once in a while, okay?"

Frances bit her lip, then fluttered her eyelashes. "Okay."

Just as they were about to reach the living room, Molly jerked her to a halt. "Fix your hair. It's all over your face. And stand up straight. Try pretending you're likable."

When they entered, Nicholas's back was to them as he examined one of Frances's paintings. Max stood at his side. Molly gave Frances a warning glance to keep quiet. No one said a word when they saw Molly and Frances.

"Magnificent!" Nicholas said to Max. "The brushwork is like an angel wing. The colors are tender, blended with grace. I see embryonic greatness. With the proper guidance, this Mackie will be—"

Shaking free of Molly's grip, Frances glided across the room. "That is one of my earlier works," she said as she quickly moved to Nicholas. "I think you will change your opinion when you see my recent pieces." Holding out her hand, fully expecting adoration, she said, "I'm Mackie." Her eyelids fluttered when she added, "But please call me Frances."

Molly saw Randall shake his head, set down his drink, and head out. She followed him to the door. "Can't take much more, huh? Coward."

"Remember that movie with Cornel Wilde and Gene Tierney? *Leave Her to Heaven*?"

Molly grinned. "I think Vincent Price was in it too."

"Yeah, well, whatever. The story here is different, but I always loved that title. Figured it fit somehow."

"How about 'Leave Her to Nicholas'?"

Randall laughed. "Yeah. That works." He stepped out on the broad tile stairs. "So, you going to New Orleans?"

Molly took a moment, then said, "I was thinking about it anyway. I could use some time off. I'd like Emma to meet Angela and Armand. My cousin Jack suggested a family reunion of sorts."

"Great idea. Families should stay in touch. I wouldn't spend too much time with Armand, though. A New Orleans jail ain't no place for a lady."

"I'll call you if I run into trouble."

Randall looked at her for a long moment, then said, "Yeah. Do that."